Dep g
Footprints

MICHAEL PATTERSON

Copyright © 2018 Michael Patterson

First printed 2018

Copies can be ordered from Amazon or via the internet
at:

www.detectivestevemurray.co.uk

Cover design and layout by
JAG Designs

Printed and bound in Great Britain
ISBN: 9781980455660

This second book in the Detective Inspector Murray series was a challenge. The information was gathered, noted and written in a vastly different way from the first. In essence, it was the polar opposite. I sincerely hope the characters, plot and storyline are better for it.

However, with that said, each of us are *'a work in progress,'* and what a wonderful opportunity we have each day to develop, to increase our knowledge and learn new skills. To be the role model, friend and example that someone is desperately looking out for.

To ultimately leave a legacy in the sand.

Thank you to all those who continue to inspire me on a daily basis.

And Remember:

Good things come to those who wait

But

The best things come to those who

DO!

Departing Footprints:

Prologue

Fighting intensely, akin to the busy bellows of a hearty overworked accordion. One heaving, gasping and straining painfully for every last precious ounce of air. Frantic breaths had become shorter and sharper. Lashing out had proved pointless. Futile shouts and screams had ceased as delicate, fragile airwaves filled rapidly. Hands that were set to auto pilot continued to fiercely block and stretch. Desperately they'd attempt but to no avail, to provide a barrier or barricade to keep it back.

The ferocious 'it' in question, being the loose, fast moving, lightweight east coast sand. Sand, that naturally occurring granular material composed of finely divided rock and mineral particles. It continued at speed to cascade endlessly over her slender, virtuous body, like 'Pennies from Heaven.' As if at that very moment, a lucky long-term Las Vegas gambler had successfully hit the jackpot on a crooked slot machine and was now being ceremoniously rewarded with endless streams of shining, shimmering gold!

Her ribs, head and internal organs were being relentlessly crushed and compressed from within. The precious gift of life itself, gradually and agonisingly withdrawn. Her personalised hourglass had been deliberately overturned and drained. Literally, grain by grain, the sands of time were running out. She would be dead in the next twenty seconds.

Chapter One

"There's a dying voice within me reaching out somewhere, toiling in the danger and the morals of despair. In the fury of the moment I can see the master's hand, in every leaf that trembles, in every grain of sand."

- Bob Dylan

As the light early morning haze settled across the rugged skyline on the outskirts of Edinburgh. Detective Inspector Steven Murray lay in his sumptuous king-size bed, wide awake and alert. It was 7am. By all accounts it was breakfast time. That is, for those who regularly ate such a meal. Unfortunately his humble west coast upbringing, with loving parents in a 1960's built council housing scheme, had never introduced him to that particular habit.

This sunrise, workmen had begun to go about their daily business on the rooftops opposite. He had listened intently all week as random construction noise and general hubbub began at the same time each day. Old tiles and weathered surfaces seemed to be making way for brand new modern technology. Would it include those unsightly, yet cost effective solar panels Murray asked himself. The distorted hammering and muffled sounds continued to ring out as backing vocals. This allowed nostalgic thoughts of his pubescent days at High School in Renfrewshire to make a swift appearance for no apparent connected reason. Memories of the tedious early morning registration class resurfaced, then random recollections and named individuals popped into his mind. They were interspersed occasionally by the fine stifled arrangements of the nearby tradesmen!

Camphill's roll of honour included Ann Young, Iain Lindsay, Douglas Campbell and Lynn Beech. Kenny Allison, Gary Waters and Isobel Fleming were a host of other names from a bygone era. Teenagers with a myriad of roads yet to travel. Each eager to experience the so called 'Big Bad World,' and all it had to offer. Murray's deliberations soon drifted to the words of a Joni Mitchell song. A tune he first heard in the early nineties as part of the soundtrack to an obscure movie entitled, 'Married to It.' The story concerned a group of couples, their ever complex relationships and how they had evolved and changed over the years. It questioned their choices and the direction in which they now found themselves heading. The chorus sang to your heart:

"And the seasons they go round and round and the painted ponies go up and down, we're captive on the carousel of time. We can't return, we can only look behind from where we came - And go round and round and round in the circle game."

It was a beautiful song. One which had grown to be a real favourite of Steven Murray's over the intervening years. As he began to gently hum the tune, he suitably adjusted one of the two foam pillows at his back and sat bolt upright in his bed. He continued with his range of sentimental, nostalgic thoughts and a varied selection of memories from that period of time spent in secondary school came flooding back.

Like turning on a running tap, they gushed freely. His mind swimming in the torrent of historic recall. For five years, every day, Monday to Friday with the same people. Seven hours of assorted timetables. Subjects such as Art, P.E, English, Maths and a variety of other classes that he never attended! Flared, high waisted trousers, platform shoes and pilot shirts. The Arthur Fonzarelli black leather jacket completed the look. The Bay City Rollers bubble had burst, punk had arrived and it was a decade that fashion forgot!

He remembered THE RULE though - to walk on the left hand side of the corridor (as running was not allowed). Then, when the bell rang to signify break times there would be a mad rush to play football non-stop (with a tennis ball). Cigarettes would also be revealed and that 'rebellious' element would congregate at 'smoker's corner.' At lunch times - mickey-taking, storytelling, continuous laughter and the occasional bullying could be found regular as clockwork in the school dinner queue. After the two-course delight and tuck shop offerings, many of the boys would play 'liney.' A game that involved each of you throwing a similar value coin toward a wall and whoever got closest, won a small fortune! For Murray it was a seemingly innocent, yet addictive playground pastime.

Academia back then consisted of favourite teachers, school bullies and dreaded hated subjects. That initial first crush and trying desperately to get close to the young lady that had won your affections. Aiming always to impress her, win her heart and then pay the price later. No doubt your insolence and cheek would be rewarded in the classroom by those cruel, heavy-handed and obviously extremely poor educators. Those guardians of power who carried with them the regulation one inch thick, brown leather strap - the tawse, to give it its proper name. However, Steven Murray didn't give a 'tawse' what its proper name was. Because throughout the whole of Scotland, it was better known by all his fellow classmates or so-called inmates, ... as the BELT!

It was intended as corporal punishment for young tender teenage hands. Hands that may never go on to do an honest day's work in their life. In the late seventies Murray reckoned there definitely seemed to be a growing breed of teacher. An individual with a character that was completely incapable of having the ability to create within the majority of his or her students - a passion and fervour for their particular area of expertise. Those uninspiring N.U.T members failed miserably to engage with young teenage minds, to stimulate or pique their interest in certain subjects. Misbehaving, talking, looking out of the window, whatever the distraction, it all ended the same in Murray's academic experience.

He could still recall the words verbatim: "Murray! Get out here boy. Hands up."

The accompanying sound painfully echoed around the room. Classmates winced and instantly made fists. No sympathy was offered. They were just delighted it was you standing there with burning red, scorched palms and blistered fingertips and not them. 'Thwack, thwack,' with anything up to a further four times, depending on who the specific 'sadist of the day' was that delivered the normally merited, although often at times fully unjustified retribution! You could certainly make time stand still Murray reckoned, even if just for that briefest of moments.

That morning, as he lay still and motionless on his bed, he found himself asking the question - Where are they now? All those classroom pals from school were frozen in his mind as thirteen or fourteen years of age. Their youthful faces remembered as was. Their innocent lives yet to go down many wondrous and diverse paths. He instantly recalled yet another of his favourite all time movies. 'Stand By Me,' with its final line: *"I never had any friends later on, like the ones I had when I was 12. Does anyone?"*

On screen it was delivered by Richard Dreyfuss as he typed it up on his computer. It perfectly encapsulated the film's entire message. Murray believed it was a quote that probably defined coming of age and truly captured the essence of childhood friendships, as well as the way children are naive to their significance during their teenage years. Now, over four decades later, Steven Murray Esquire understood that there was a reality behind that statement. That it didn't just relate to the theme of the film. But to the very theme of life itself. The friendships and associations we make as children, are never quite the same as the ones we form as adults.

In the movie it talked about a time in your life that felt incredibly complicated, but as you got older you realized it was actually incredibly simple. And we then get the tremendous gift of not knowing that it is never going to be like that again for the rest of our lives. We are reminded that schooldays were just pure and uncomplicated. And it was a time in our lives that would stay with us, even as we grew into adulthood, with all its complexities and challenges.

Murray was acutely aware that several of his classmates, like River Phoenix in the movie and in real life, had died relatively young. Several others had gone to prison, a small percentage had never worked, and a select few had become financially wealthy and successful in their chosen careers and business ventures. During those brief moments reflecting, another home truth had sunk in. And that was how there was always something bittersweet about reminiscing upon one's childhood. Rediscovering that those really were exceptionally special times. However, often it's not until we become older and wiser and more aware of ourselves, that we can fully comprehend and appreciate the uncomplicated beauty of innocence. As for the busy inconsiderate workmen. They continued their noisy, early morning roof installation unabated!

Murray, two minutes beforehand made his way into the shower and his phone went unanswered. He'd carefully washed and cleansed the tender area around his neck. The burn marks and abrasions were beginning to clear. It was early March 2015, and over two months had passed since the downfall of gangster Kenny Dixon's sleazy empire. Twice now, DC Joseph Hanlon had gone uncredited in saving his Inspector's life. As Murray dried, dressed and hastily, yet carefully, pulled on a soft woollen polo neck jersey over his head, his mobile phone rang once again.

"Hello, DI Murray here," he answered. Oblivious to having missed an earlier call. "What? At Gullane you say. Female? Okay, yep I've got that. See you there 'Sandy,' thanks."

'Sandy,' was his beloved friend Sandra Kerr. She had returned into the fold. Back fresh from maternity leave, after giving birth to twins just a few months previously. She would no longer be Steven Murray's sidekick, confidante and guardian angel though. That role had been filled more than adequately by the young widower Joseph Hanlon. Joe was now known affectionately to Murray and others around the station as 'Sherlock.' In the main, because of his fine unearthing and exploring in the Taunton/Dixon case. It was outstanding work. No longer was he Acting Detective Constable Hanlon, but a fully fledged DC, complete with commendation.

As for Kerr, she was now Detective Sergeant Sandra Kerr. Due to the sudden, yet understandable 6 month leave of absence granted to DS 'Ally' Coulter on health grounds. It had taken the Inspector all his power, charm and influence to convince his dear friend 'Ally' not to retire. To rip up the resignation letter that he had drafted and instead accept the temporary leave granted to him. Eventually Coulter relented. Probably to stop the daily phone calls and continual pestering from his buddy. But possibly deep down, because he knew he needed time to get over the tragic events of the previous few months.

DI Murray meanwhile, knew that 'Sandy' was always destined for bigger and better things and was genuinely happy for her. As well as that, he was excited to have her onboard for her knowledge, experience and crucial input as a valued member of his new team. A team that included the intrepid Western partnership of Hayes and Curry. The all star formation was completed fully with the installation of Kerr's new partner. He was a six foot four Glaswegian named Machur Rasul. Quickly nicknamed 'Big Mac' by his new colleagues. Absolutely in part due to his height, but coupled with when asked, "how he liked his new station?" He would always answer, "I'm lovin' it!"

Chapter Two

"If I die young bury me in satin. Lay me down on a bed of roses. Sink me in the river at dawn. And send me away with the words of a love song."

- The Band Perry

It was a chilly, yet bright Spring morning as Steven Murray closed the front door of his home. He had decided there was no room in the car today for the 'black dog.' Indoors would be best suited for him. These past few weeks he'd had plenty of exercise, especially when William Taunton had died just two weeks before his historic sexual abuse trial. Having been badly beaten by gangland boss Kenny Dixon before his own sudden demise, Taunton had been expected to make a full recovery, even given that he was well into his eighties.

Doctors reckoned however, that he had merely given up the fight to live. That the thought of going through a well publicised trial - one that would inevitably see him branded a paedophile and long term child molester - his good name gone - his Knighthood rescinded - his celebrity star shot down in flames - the successful business that he'd built up over the past forty years imploding - That the whole combination of either one or all of those events happening had simply been too much to face up to!

Driving the twenty plus miles from his home in the west side of Edinburgh to East Lothian on the east coast, the Inspector soon found himself singing a raft of The Beach Boys classics. Travelling the coastal route on the A198 that Saturday morning, locals would hear the delicate strains of *"I'm pickin' up good vibrations, she's giving me excitations, I'm pickin' up good vibrations."* That would then seamlessly segue straight into *"A bushy bushy blonde hairdo - Surfin' U. S. A."*

Murray remembering the scene of crime he was about to visit, ceased the vocals when he heard himself sing: *"Wouldn't it be nice if we were older…"*
Silence was then welcomed for the remainder of the journey.

As he travelled, DI Murray reflected on his knowledge of Gullane. Instantly he recalled many years ago being corrected by natives of the area. They informed him about how the town name was always incorrectly pronounced by outsiders. "There is NO LANE in this town laddie, AN that will be the end of it," the old timer had reminded him. So from that day to this, it was stamped clearly in his mind as 'Gullan.'

The town itself lay on the southern shore of the Firth of Forth. The Inspector had been lucky enough during 2013 to attend The Open Golf Championship held there. It had been played at Muirfield, one of several courses in the area. It was whilst over the course (no pun intended) of that weekend that Steven Murray had first been made aware of internationally acclaimed artist Frank W. Wood. Back in 1933, Wood had painted the most magnificent view of Gullane, and ever since, whenever Muirfield played host to the Championship - there it was! There was no hiding place - Newspapers, magazines, every gift shop in town and numerous online articles all offered up a wide variety of angles of this legendary painting.

Now, turning up what Murray was certain was a 'lane.' Although here, dare he question, surely not? He had arrived at Gullane Bents, the award winning East Lothian beach. It was backed by large sand dunes, that in more recent years had become rather overgrown with invasive shrubs. The DI suddenly felt an unnerving sense of foreboding as he carefully made to park his latest Volvo. His previous aged model having battled with one wall too many last December. From street level he could plainly observe that the forensics tent had been put in situ at the top of one of the numerous sandy mounds. This will be interesting, he thought quietly to himself.

"Morning Steven," a voice cried out. "T'ats an interesting fashion statement you've been makin' t'ese last few months."

Murray turned to see the 'T'inker,' Doc Patterson, his favourite Irish pathologist smiling brightly at his side.

"It's still a bit chilly Tom," he replied. Tugging at the top of his dark polo neck jersey with both of his hands.

Changing the topic quickly, Murray chirpily added, "Sandy tells me it's a young female. Was it a sexual thing? Out here in the middle of the night, a possible secret rendezvous? A late night stroll, accidental or what?" He then suddenly stopped speaking. He could see by the Doc's facial expression that something he had said was sadly amiss.

"Steven t'is was no accident."

"Go on," Murray said softly.

"DS Kerr was absolutely correct. It was a female, alt'ough not an adult. T'at's why she called you I t'ought."

"What are you saying Doc? Spit it out."

Assuming an official stance, Thomas Patterson braced himself, cleared his throat and spoke plainly and with clarity to his friend. "Inspector. It's…..."

On hearing the next two words Murray's body visibly shrunk. He sighed, held his head in his hands and began to shake it from side to side. Audible moans, groans and strange, strangled sounds combined to filter from his lips. Although they were incapable of forming any recognisable word in the English language. Feeling sick to the pit of his stomach, he then began the long, steady, enduring walk to the elevated crown of the sand dune.

As if hallucinating, traumatic, intense recollections had to be filtered and hastily escorted one by one from Murray's mind. They included - Hands clasped at a graveside; An empty bedroom awaiting a child; An assault by a loved one; A coffin lowered into the ground; A jury in a courtroom; A cell door slammed shut and an empty home!

That morning, the crisp blue water of the Firth of Forth offered a radiant, picturesque backdrop. Quite a contrast in his humble opinion, to the deliberately ambiguous murder scene. It wasn't right Murray thought still shaking his head. He heard Patterson's words repeated in his mind. "Inspector, it's Cindy-Ann, the daughter of Robert Latchford. T'e missing girl from Tuesday night."

Not only the death of the eleven year old, but the setting, the manner, the timing, everything Murray sensed immediately, was out of kilter. It didn't quite feel right. It felt off and he felt uneasy. He continued onward and for every two strides he would take forward, he would slip back one. Each time ready to begin anew.

That prophetic feeling of foreboding had not taken long to become a reality. As DI Murray's gaze focused toward the arctic white tent now secured firmly in place on the small summit. He also witnessed for the first time that day, sat gently panting outside and with tail wagging - his canine foe. In true 'Trainspotting' style, Murray in a low tone, voiced sarcastically: "Choose Scotland - Choose Sandcastles; Choose Life - Choose beautiful East Lothian; Choose death in its midst - and a scruffy black mutt of a mongrel in desperate need of a walk!"

Four days earlier…

If you ever find yourself wandering uptown in Edinburgh, chances are you'll pass by the floral clock in West Princes Street Garden. That specific timepiece was the location Murray and Hanlon found themselves heading in the direction of, early doors last Tuesday. The same day that Cindy-Ann Latchford was later to go missing. It had just gone 5.30am, and the dawn chorus was contemplating showing up. The city centre was about to open its doors for yet another busy, bustling day. Cleaners, office workers, bankers and businessmen were about to make a million or receive minimum wage. In recent years, many had even went bust! From bankers to Bhs staff, either way, here they were taking up their crucial, critical positions. Ready to step forward and face up to everything that the world had in store for them. Which was more than could be said for the deceased. Because, he had no revealing features, nothing distinct about his countenance. Well, except that he had none. No freckles, no scars, no tattoos...... literally - no face!

Assuming the documentation they'd found, containing credit cards and driving license belonged to him. He was 42 year old Ian Spence. His address was Salisbury Road in the southeast side of the city. Nearly directly opposite the Royal Commonwealth Pool.

"Possibly it had been forced down onto an electric hob and burned off. That would have ensured he'd have passed out within seconds," Murray surmised. "Or equally as agonising, someone had simply taken a blowtorch to it and begun to erase any semblance of a facial structure."

Knowing they would get the results fairly quickly, made it no less horrific. Pieces of his clothing, shirt collar and tie were melted to his skin in and around the neck, chin and jaw area. A militia of crisp, chargrilled flesh butterflies still crackled and took the occasional flight in the gentle morning breeze. Joe Hanlon lasted fully thirty seconds before fleeing the scene. It had been sickening to look at and had one particularly odious smell. His I.D had been placed in plain sight. Which is what made them question if it was actually his or not. Had it been intentionally left there to mislead them? They would find out soon enough. A patrol car was already en-route to the address.

The grubby, well used wallet had been peering out from below a small metal hourglass placed directly in front of the body. Inside the wallet, a bright orange post-it note had been stuck to the credit card side. It read: 1974. Was it his year of birth? Or more likely a pin or security number for something official. The victim was lying as if deliberately staged. He was on his left side, his legs bound together at the ankles and set pointing southeast. His hands were clasped and tied at the wrists, with the fingers pointing northbound. On arrival it clearly looked as if he was positioned to indicate either 4pm or 5pm. This was no random body left in haste. Dumped at the floral clock, this was intended to make a very bold statement.

Murray approached a continually heaving Joseph Hanlon and gave him an understanding pat on his shoulder. It was clear 'Sherlock' had decided to put his breakfast intake back out on display for all and sundry!

"It gets easier," Murray offered.

Joe Hanlon's eyes widened. As if to say - 'really?'

"Two years or so ago," Murray continued. "Late 2013, early 14. They called him the blow torch rapist. It was in Detroit in the USA."

"What did he do?" Hanlon asked, wiping the remaining remnants of sick from around the base of his nose and the edge of his mouth.

"Exactly what it said on the tin," Murray responded. "There was at least three victims if I recall correctly. He ripped off their clothes and stripped them naked, then physically and sexually assaulted them."

Joe frowned and glowered at his Inspector, before adding as a question, "Then?"

Quietly Steven Murray sighed. "The first one, he marked her body all over with a blowtorch. Whilst held captive she had been reportedly scorched, singed or branded on over 200 separate occasions. With his next unsuspecting victim, he began the start of each day by telling her how much he loved her. That she meant the world to him and was desperate to 'seal in' her beautiful fragrance."

Hanlon winced, as he heard himself ask, "What did that even mean?"

Murray shrugged. "Who knows! But he then proceeded to slowly sear her skin from forehead to chin."

"And she survived?" Hanlon responded. His eyes closed at the very thought of the horrendously painful torture that poor woman had endured.

"She was left with a permanently charred and blackened face. A series of scheduled hospital operations are what she has to look forward to now," Murray stated. By this point there was no disguising the disgust in his tone.

"You said there were at least three known victims," Joe added reluctantly. Really not sure that he had the stomach for any more detail.

"Well whether he had run out of creative flame thrower ideas or was going to be busy making some creme brûlée later that evening, I don't know," Murray sarcastically commented. "But his third and final casualty was lazily doused in petrol and the blow torch simply used to ignite her!"

Hanlon's shoulders dropped noticeably. He'd just visibly shrunk three inches in the last three seconds.

"Amazingly they did all survive," Murray rallied.

"But to what?" Hanlon cried. "What quality of life? How did their personal relationships pan out? Mentally how do you survive something like that?"

"Remember those words I uttered to you Joe when we first met? All in your own time son, all in your own time." Murray left his colleague to gather up his emotions and refocus. He knew he would. This morning for some reason DC Hanlon seemed to be genuinely hurting. Something was playing with his already fragile emotions. DI Murray though, always travelled armed with psychological 'bubble wrap.' He was a known protector and today he was also an expert practitioner in 'fragility!'

The famous colourful arrangement in the city centre of the capital, was not only an immaculately tended floral extravaganza in the shape of a clock, it also told the correct time. It was a fully functioning masterpiece and Detective Inspector Steven Murray was well aware of its history.

"It's over one hundred years old Joe," he informed his young partner. "It was the first of its kind not only in the UK, but believe it or not, in the world."

"I get it though sir," Joe said as enthusiastically as one could at a crime scene. "Rather ironically," he continued. "It represents our personal growth. Succoured by nature or nurture. The opportunity we are given in our respective environments to flourish, bloom and develop. It is quite simply photosynthesising life."

"That sounds about right to me," Murray said sheepishly. Having no real idea what his young 'clever clogs' of a DC was on about whatsoever! Pointing in the direction of the dead body, he then commented. "Not sure he would necessarily agree with you though Constable Hanlon?"

'Sherlock' shrugged. "Guess not," he said respectfully.

The forensics team were busy making their way towards the cordoned off area. Murray and his forever curious colleague were due back at the station to give Detective Chief Inspector Brown a full update. Keith Brown and Murray went back a fair bit together. They'd had the occasional run in. But generally speaking the DCI was fairly supportive of Murray's often unorthodox style and work ethic.

Brown's office was always neat, tidy and efficient. The word 'pristine' even sprung to the DI's mind. The room had, as the old adage states - 'A place for everything and everything in its place!' Seated, waiting on his boss to arrive, Murray could never actually remember seeing anything out of place. So much so, he often wondered if his Detective Chief Inspector actually did any real work these days. Or, if he just ventured in mid-morning, did a little office re-arrangement, sprayed some air freshener and could then toddle off back home again.

"Daydreaming Inspector?" the gentle Midlands accent asked, catching DI Murray off guard. At that Keith Brown strode confidently through the doorway and across to his desk.

"What, oh, hello sir," Murray added appearing flustered. "I was just thinking that I had no idea how you coped with the busy daily schedule you have to constantly keep up."

Both sets of eyes now squinted and looked at him. Hanlon from the side with a suppressed grin. Whilst Brown focused from above. His gaze with a retracted chin, was more of a 'are you taking the mickey?' type of glance. The Detective Chief Inspector sighed as both junior officers eventually got to their feet. "Sit down both of you. It's a bit late now for that."

Chapter Three

The following day on the Wednesday, at just a little after three o'clock, DI Murray and Joseph 'Sherlock' Hanlon visited with Robert Latchford at the special behest and gentle insistence of DS Sandra Kerr. His soon to be teenage daughter Cindy-Ann had not returned home from school the previous afternoon.

As the two police colleagues were given the address to attend over the radio, they shared a brief glance and a mutual nod of the head. Although no actual words were exchanged. Inverleith Terrace, an affluent area of Edinburgh, right next door to the Royal Botanic Gardens was the given location. It was literally a few doors along from where these two men first met. Where the body of *'The Angel of the North,'* Penelope Cooke, was initially discovered.

As DC Joseph Hanlon drove past the door he had stood outside safeguarding, on that wintry December day a few short months earlier, he noticeably slowed the car to a gentle sedate pace. It was his own personal mark of deference and respect to both ladies that had once lived there. Lady Dorothy Atkins, who had been Penny Cooke's landlady as well as a role model, friend and mentor, had sadly and unexpectedly died just five weeks ago. DI Murray believed confidently, that she had never fully recovered from her young friends death. That she was unable to replace that large void in her life, and that in part, her passing was one of a broken heart. As Hanlon reverently drove past, he noticed that the small, delicate white plaque which dated the building of the house, was obscured by a rather larger, more imposing modern sign today. It simply read…. FOR SALE!

"Thinking about submitting an offer?" Murray asked smiling.

"I suspect the mortgage would cost more than my monthly salary sir!" Hanlon responded.

"Aye, you may be right at that Joe. I believe a recently renovated property a little further along, sold last month for just over two million. Can't believe I was outbid on that one!"

"Me neither boss."

Joint laughter exuded from the vehicle as they pulled up behind a dark SUV and duly parked outside the so-called 'small family home.' Within Inverleith there are very few shops and offices, it's almost entirely a residential and recreational area. This particular house was a handsome, spacious Victorian villa. To the trained eye of the approaching detectives, it appeared to have three floors, a generous garage and quite a large overgrown garden. One that seemed to be in need of a little TLC. Being built on ground slightly higher than the centre of town, it commanded impressive views of the Edinburgh skyline, including that of the Castle and Arthur's Seat. As Detective Constable Hanlon purposefully rang the doorbell, he was also reminded by his ever knowing Inspector, that Inverleith had one of the lowest crime rates in the city.

The front door of number 78 was opened by a stout man with broad shoulders. He stood about six foot two, round faced, medium build, with a shaved head. He wore classic dark denim jeans, with well polished black boots underneath. Up top was finished off with a contemporary pink, dog-tooth patterned shirt and a rich deep blue pin striped waistcoat. A few pictures of him on a GQ magazine cover would not have looked out of place.

"Quite a trendy hairstyle," Hanlon remarked as they were shown through to the large imposing sitting room.

Murray responded to that comment with a screwed up facial expression that young Joe instantly understood. It said, 'What hairstyle? He had none!'

With pleasantries, handshakes and introductions out of the way, the three men spoke freely. Hanlon admired a framed quotation that hung on the wall. Taking on board what it said, he thought it best to remain quiet at present. It read: "I have a beautiful daughter - I also have a gun, a shovel and an alibi." He then noticed on the coffee table a half complete jigsaw. It was a scenic, city centre view of the City of London. The four sides had all been put in place. The London Eye, The Houses of Parliament and Westminster Abbey had been completed. It looked a nice size Hanlon thought. Challenging, without being too daunting. About 1000 pieces he reckoned.

Murray had quickly scanned the sitting room. It was nicely decorated and a couple of what he supposed were family paintings adorned the walls. Two dark oak shelves played host to a collection of reading memorabilia, mainly consisting of sports journals, sticker albums and autobiographies from the nineteen seventies. An assortment of youth football team photos were on display. Latchfords teenage face appeared in every one. A display cabinet with various trophies, a selection of medals and a range of working watches took up most of the remaining space. One timepiece in particular stood out to DI Murray. It was smaller, with a cracked face and delicate silver linked strap. It appeared to be a ladies watch and had clearly ceased to function. The room was tidy and free from clutter. There were a few pieces of post on the mantelpiece. But overall, all the key indicators gave the impression of a disciplined householder. An individual that liked to be, generally speaking - well organised, efficient and precise.

The detectives asked about family, school friends, potential places his child would play or possibly hang out. Tried and tested responses were offered up by her father in return. Her mother Anne had passed away about a decade ago, so it was only Robert Latchford and his daughter. They had a childminder that helped out occasionally and Cindy-Ann's friend Claire, the daughter of Sonia Marshall lived nearby. However, the girls went to different schools and hadn't seen each other in the last couple of months. Generally they only ever met up at weekends anyway. Cindy-Ann was always home within half an hour of school finishing, without exception. She was trusted, disciplined and had a routine. A routine which she stuck to obsessively her father said. Murray wondered at that moment, if that routine was actually one that her father was more obsessed with than the poor girl herself?

"Homework, snack, music practise. Then, during her evening meal, that's when we would do something together," he said emotionally, pointing at the semi completed jigsaw. That obviously being their current joint project. "After an hour, she'd do a bit more homework and head off to bed," he added. "She knew what she wanted out of life Inspector and she was determined to make it a reality."

"What was that sir? Murray asked with genuine curiosity. "What did she want?"

"She was determined to be an engineer Inspector." The father's voice wavered and a small delicate tear could be seen running for cover toward the edge of his lips. As his large tongue began circling, the teardrop was never going to find safety. It was swiftly swept away into the dark, deep cavern of Robert Latchfords mouth. A mouth that both master and apprentice had heard utter a small, possibly significant three letter word. He had said *'was.'*

"An engineer," Hanlon commented as he completed a piece of the puzzle. "Wow, impressive. What got her, especially at such a young age into that sector?" he continued.

"Well, I own The Car Bored Box Company," he mentioned. "So there was always the opportunity to work with various engines, mechanical parts, repairs needing done or simply just the chance to solve complex issues. From a young age she and I would just sit and get our hands dirty. Cindy-Ann loved all that."

There he goes again with past tense, Murray thought. Hanlon feeling proud, added yet another piece of jigsaw to the Westminster Abbey scene.

A few more standard questions were asked, a photograph given to each of the officers and they were on their way.

"Anything else you can think of Mr. Latchford, anything at all that you think may be helpful, just let us know," Hanlon reminded the worried father.

"Oh, and just one more thing Mr Latchford," Murray asked 'Colombo' style. "Your wife, you said she…"

"Ten years ago, London. Your lot should know all about it," he responded rather harshly.

Given the circumstances, Murray decided not to pursue it. He and Hanlon bade farewell and returned to their vehicle. In silence they replayed the previous twenty minutes. Hanlon broke first.

"You want me to look out my explorers clothes?" he asked anxiously. Although with possibly more of a slant on an actual statement than a question.

Murray drew the fingers on his right hand down his face to his chin, which at that moment had begun to nod gently in the affirmative. Slowly and in a considered manner he stated firmly, "absolutely!"

"Time now for a catch up with 'Sandy' and Mac?" Hanlon added. This time definitely phrased as a question. Before setting off, Murray looked in his rear view mirror. The dark SUV that he had assumed belonged to Robert Latchford was gone. He then drove off in silence from the kerbside, his positive nod more emphatic than ever.

Back at the station a small group had gathered at DS Kerr's table in the canteen. One unmarried WPC was chatting excitedly to Sandra Kerr, and was looking enviously at the baby snaps of her recent twins on her mobile phone. She began 'cooing' and offered up the appropriate number of 'oohs' and 'aahs,' and in all the right places. The other five or six around the table were being regaled by the travel adventures of the new boy, Detective Constable Rasul. 'Mac' was busy telling them about his trip with a friend to the United States the previous Summer. No photos alas, which seemed unusual, but the trip itself included Zion National Park, the Grand Canyon and the Hoover Dam.

"Not bad for a wee lad from Castlemilk," he concluded.

Just at that, they noticed Murray and Hanlon had arrived through the doorway. Both Sergeant and Constable made their excuses, rose up and came over quickly to sit either side of Joseph Hanlon, leaving their Inspector isolated across the six seater table. Was he about to be interviewed for an upcoming vacancy or even more likely given their present environment, interrogated in relation to a crime?

Stern-faced as he spoke, Murray asked directly, "'Sandy,' tell me in more depth about those missing girls."

Since being promoted in advance of her return, Detective Sergeant Sandra Kerr had came back and been immersed, literally, in a baptism of fire. At that point, four young girls, all from the Edinburgh and East Lothian area had disappeared from home over the past seven to eight weeks.

DS Kerr took over the story. "I am just off the phone with DCI Brown. Now to clarify three of them were teenagers and the other one even younger at only twelve years of age sir. All lived in different parts of the city and attended separate schools. No obvious crossover or link with one another has been established. We need 'Sherlock' on the case," she jokingly remarked nodding at Hanlon. Not a comment that 'Mac' Rasul thought deserving of a smile Murray noticed.

"Alive?" He asked of his Sergeant.

"I really wouldn't like to say sir."

Murray narrowed his eyes and tilted his head. In his book of body language that one read as 'really?'

"You know sir over 140,000 under 18's go missing in the UK each year."

"Sandy," he said, looking for an educated guess.

"I suspect not sir. I think it's safe to say each of them is probably dead. I genuinely hope that I'm wrong. However deep down that would be my considered opinion. We have no fresh leads. There has been no contact with their families and no sightings of them whatsoever after their initial disappearance." Kerr feeling bewildered, continued, "they belong to good, bad and indifferent backgrounds sir. We're simply at a loss. That's why when this fifth girl Cindy-Ann was reported I wanted you to take a first look at it. How did it go? Do you think there could be a connection? Everything seem okay?"

Hanlon bit on his lip and looked at his Inspector to see if he should answer. Murray's gentle number one nod, gave him the go ahead.

"Our chat went fine," Joe said. Murray shrugged in agreement. "Probably a bit early to say if there is any clear connection, although the Inspector would like me to do some further exploratory work." Once again Murray smiled in confirmation. As Hanlon repeated her last question, "Did everything seem okay?" She then received a united response from both Constable and

Inspector, as they collectively offered in harmony, "Absolutely not!"

DC Rasul offered, "Wow, that was impressive."

"Unrehearsed also," Joseph Hanlon added.

"Something is just off," Murray stated. "I can't quite put my finger on it 'Sandy.' But all my years tell me, there's something, just something, not quite right."

This time it was Hanlon that shrugged, gently nodded and with a slight touch of sarcasm added, "I would agree."

"Police!" Cried the lone figure chapping frantically on the glass doorway of the fish restaurant. The neon light flashing outside was working overtime, although the employees had all clocked off and gone home. The popular premises had officially closed forty minutes previous. The staff were experienced and super efficient, so the bulk of the cleaning and tidy up was nearly done by closing time. With a further quarter hour, they were fully ready for the next day and had departed the scene. The owner had an excellent manager and a more than capable deputy, but at the end of the evening he always personally liked to put in an appearance before closing.

Carlo Tardelli was old school. He liked to to deal with the cashing up himself and more importantly by himself! He had arrived in Scotland as a 15 year old in the late nineteen fifties. Along with his mother and father he had travelled from Bologna in northern Italy to settle in Edinburgh. Now at 73 years of age and his parents both deceased, this much loved great grandfather had developed a very lucrative business on the outskirts of Dean Village. Debate continues to rage at who first had the idea to bring fish and chips together in the UK. Nobody however, could dispute the Italian influence after they had spotted the business opportunities to be had north of the border by selling 'pesce e patate.' It would be fair to say that the Italian community certainly popularised the 'fish supper' in Scotland. And Tardelli's 'Thyme & Plaice' had continued the crowd pleasing tradition to this day.

"Police," the voice bellowed out again.

"Com-ing, com-ing," Carlo responded with a bouncy Scottish/Italian brogue. In his haste, as he urgently made his way out from his small office at the back of the premises, he did not even put the takings back into the protective keeping of the wall safe.

As he arrived at the door, the voice cried out even more impatiently. "Police Scotland. DI Murray here Mr Tardelli." The police officer stood with his back to the door, though his I.D had been opened and thrust forward. With his glasses also located next to the day's receipts, Carlo Tardelli shrugged and unlocked the door. He knew Steven Murray. He had always found him reasonably courteous and jovial over the years. However, he appeared to be less friendly on this particular occasion.

Murray though, did have a smile on his face, as well as a soapy lather. In fact he had even begun singing. Sadly, the song he was singing was: *'Home, let me come home. Home is wherever I'm with you. Home let me come home…'* He was in HIS shower, in HIS home, several miles and numerous crowded streets away from the upmarket Dean Village!

As the door was opened, Murray's imposter downed the small Italian with a vicious, forceful punch straight between the eyes. A flash of hot orange light radiated pain across his head and it spread instantly down the centre of his neck. The follow up punch to Tardelli's portly stomach caught Carlo equally off guard. On impact, he felt his blood vessels burst and his diaphragm collapse under the force of the large balled fist. His knees buckled from the fierce blow. A torrent of fire ran through every fibre of his abdomen. He heard a cracking noise ricochet between his ribs. The old man couldn't breathe, let alone protect his body from any further damage this guy was willing to dish out. They remained in darkness. No more punches were thrown. However, one vital piece of kitchen equipment

was promptly called back into action.

Chapter Four

"And when I touch you I feel happy inside. It's such a feeling that my love I can't hide. Yeah, you got that something I think you'll understand. When I say that something - I want to hold your hand, I want to hold your hand."

- The Beatles

Next day on the Thursday morning, dissenting clouds exploded across the Edinburgh skyline. Hanlon was at his desk before most people had reached out to hit their snooze buttons. Almost immediately, he had immersed himself in the records, files and documentation regarding the 2005 death of a certain Mrs Annie Latchford. He began correlating statements, gathering information and amassing a range of facts. He then continued by coordinating, connecting the dots and corresponding with police, legal teams and witnesses. Many of whom he'd discovered, had passed away during the intervening years.

The schoolboy explorer in him, was as always, to the fore. This would be a very productive day Joe thought to himself, as his smile widened. Obvious character traits of his mentor were clearly rubbing off on him, as he then heard himself sing lightly under his breath. *'Hey! Teachers! Leave them kids alone. All in all it's just an-other brick in the wall. All in all it's just an-other brick in the wall.'* Today Detective Constable Joseph Hanlon was in his element.

"Interesting, with an E," 'Sherlock' could be heard to murmur to himself. "Why, no longer?" he wondered curiously, as his head moved inquisitively from side to side.

Before following up with information and leads relating to the body of Ian Spence, Murray was once again to be found updating DCI Brown. In recent weeks it seemed liked the Chief Inspector wanted to be in the loop more than ever before. Murray suspected he missed no longer being at the coalface, and that he just yearned for a little bit more involvement, without actually being hands on.

"His identity has been confirmed as that of Mr Ian Spence," Murray said. He then handed DCI Brown an A4 photograph of the man. On first viewing of the black and white image Brown winced slightly.

"Are you okay sir."

"What? Yes, of course. It just makes it more real and even more distressing when you see the actual face that belonged to that charred, blackened surface from the other day."

Murray gave an understanding nod (a number 61) and then continued. "Early forties, social worker, lived in Edinburgh. It looked like he had no family or siblings to speak of. An unmarried male and very much a loner."

"Sounds like you'll have your work cut out with that one Steven," his superior offered in a rather offhand and dismissive manner.

What does that even mean Murray thought. He recognised how as he had grown older, he had come to hate platitudes and frivolous pointless sayings. Even though, he himself used plenty of them from time to time. What Brown had just uttered though was nonsense. 'You'll have your work cut out with that one,' Murray repeated in his mind. Baloney, junk, drivel, absolute……... piffle!

"Are you listening to me Steve? Steve! Steven! Detective Inspector Murray!" the voice hardened. It had grown louder and more agitated each time.

"Sorry sir," Murray flexed his shoulders. "I was just pondering on your considered counsel," he added with the sincerity of a indelicate elephant.

"I was asking about the missing girls Inspector. Are you keeping tabs on Kerr with this? I heard you had become involved. Is that right?"

"Detective Sergeant Kerr," Murray politely corrected him. "Yes sir, she'd asked me for some input. Just helping out, keeping her right, benefit of my experience and all that."

"Quite," Brown added sombrely. "But I thought we agreed for you to stay away from this case. With the very intention of watching to see how Kerr, Detective Sergeant Kerr," he then added deliberately for Murray's benefit, "Would cope. Am I wrong?"

"No, no you are not wrong sir."

"Thank you," Brown remarked. Throwing open both of his palms.

"However..." Murray began, before watching his boss slowly shake his head.

"No however DI Murray. Let 'Sandy' prove she has what it takes," he offered sternly. "Now go and do what you do best Steve and get out of here!"

As DI Murray opened Brown's door to leave, PC George Smith had been about to knock on the opposite side.

"Oh sir, I was just coming to find you."

"What's up George?" Murray responded. "What couldn't wait?"

"Another body sir," Smith said. "At a fish restaurant over Stockbridge way."

"At the old man Tardelli's place?" Murray asked.

"Would that be Carlo Tardelli sir?" George Smith questioned with a certain kind of 'bad news' look in his eye.

"No, not poor Carlo." Murray froze, he stood rooted to the spot. His head now stared aimlessly at the recently carpeted floor. "He was a gentleman. Always surrounded by family and friends. He was highly regarded over there. The whole community loved him," Murray added.

"What happened PC Smith?" Brown asked.

George Smith looked anxiously at DI Murray and probably for the first time ever, used his christian name. "Steven, just get over there as quick as you can. Joe Hanlon is already waiting outside for you. And sir, keep an open mind."

'Keep an open mind.' I rest my case Murray thought. What in the name o' the wee man is that all about? 'Keep an open flippin' mind.' Those five words now had him more worried than simply telling him how Carlo Tardelli had died! All this raced through the DI's mind as he rushed to the parking bay to pick up his car, colleague and probable black dog. And although it had been a while, sure enough, there in the car park, he was met, greeted and welcomed...... by all three!

As Murray and Hanlon perused the restaurant and walked carefully around 'Thyme and Plaice,' the duty manager told them how he had discovered the body.

"Yes, well just so that you are aware. Mr?"

"Stirrat," the man replied sharply. He was stammering and obviously still in mild shock from opening up the establishment earlier.

"Well Mr Stirrat we will keep what you discovered off limits for now."

The manager responded with a relieved smile.

"Following on from Ian Spence, we don't need this getting into the public domain too quickly Joe," Murray shrugged. "Just offer the media the basic body found and we'll keep them up to speed later with any developments."

"Understood sir," Hanlon agreed.

The T'inker and his forensics team were already busy setting up, when Murray and Hanlon eventually arrived. Nods of acknowledgement had been offered all around. A brief, thirty second survey and scan throughout the room, was enough for Murray to immediately dismiss a break-in or random attack. The front door remained undamaged. It had been closed by the intruder on his way out and he'd obviously been invited in previously. So, someone Tardelli knew Murray reckoned. A couple of tables were overturned where an initial scuffle or disruption had taken place. The short, rotund body of Marco lay face down in the middle of the room. A vast, substantial amount of blood had been shed and an impressive pool had formed to confront those first responders. Both arms were currently awkwardly positioned under his midriff. It was as if the owner had fell forward, directly on to them, and they now required privacy and refuge from the world. Assorted knives, forks, various condiments and sauces scattered the floor space and formed impressive fractured patterns. Geometric forms had taken shape and the cubist art movement would have been proud. Pablo Picasso eat your heart out Murray thought.

Robbery was also not the motive. Mr Eric Stirrat had given his statement to the officers at the doorway to Tardelli's private office. This was the small intimate room that had contained the electronic safe and the evening's takings. The very same taking's that remained untouched in neat bundled rows on the Italian's desk. However, sat next to the cash, folded over like a place name at a wedding and handwritten in black marker was another citrus orange post-it note. It read: MICHELANGELO? The question mark was darker and highlighted for emphasis.

"Michelangelo," Hanlon said aloud. "And on the same colour of gummed paper."

"So no break-in, no theft and one of the ninja turtles is invited to join us for tea!" the Inspector hollered. "Well, at least we know for sure now that this was not just some random attack," Steven Murray purred.

Just then Patterson began cautiously to approach DI Murray. Inappropriate as always at times, the Inspector simply couldn't help himself.

"T'ots," he heard himself say abruptly to his dear Irish colleague. "Any helpful t'ots?"

Patterson bowed his head and shook it slowly, in an earnest disapproving manner. One, given the name of the premises, that quite clearly stated - not the 'time nor the place' for levity Steven. He then proceeded to shake hands with both men, before Murray, feeling brave enough, spoke once again.

"Apparently unconscious before falling forward then Doc?"

"Most definitely," Doctor Thomas Patterson replied. He quickly witnessed the puzzled, bewildered look on Joe Hanlon's face.

"If he'd been alert and conscious DC Hanlon, he'd have attempted to minimise his fall." Doc Patterson then raised and held out both hands and forearms by way of example. Young 'Sherlock' nodded vehemently in understanding.

All three men then followed a gradual, delicate blood trail that lay before them. The mystic red droplets seemed evenly spread. Possibly about every seven or eight inches apart.

"A person's pace between spatters," Hanlon remarked, desperately trying to redeem himself. "With every step taken, a bead of blood spilled?" he questioned as a possibility.

"Could be," Murray responded curtly.

The trio turned their heads to look at Tardelli's lifeless body, and then back once again toward their prevailing destination...... the high quality, top of the range kitchen facility. A young PC was standing guard at the fryers.

Murray grinned an almighty grin to himself. "Scared they would make a break for it son?" he chirped.

Patterson frowned and Hanlon ruefully tried to disguise a cheery smirk.

Unsure of what his superior meant, the short haired officer confidently communicated, "This was the only piece of equipment left turned on Inspector."

"Thank you Con-sta-ble…" Murray paused, waiting for his surname.

"Oh, Lynch sir. Constable Lynch, Josh Lynch."
Hanlon instantly recalled a similar initial meeting with this self same Inspector, only several months earlier.

"Good work Constable Lynch. However, I suspect staff would have procedures in place to ensure that those fryers were always turned off Josh. Wouldn't you?" he asked in that helpful tutorial manner.

The naturally rosy cheeked young man's face beamed even brighter for a moment or two before he responded sheepishly, "I suppose sir."
Murray raised his eyebrows at that weak retort.

"Absolutely, for sure Inspector. Of course all the equipment would have been turned off," Josh Lynch positively asserted this time.
Murray nodded. A number 19 Hanlon guessed.

The Detective Inspector then stepped forward, "And there endeth the lesson!"
Careful to ensure he never encroached upon any of the bloodied flooring. Murray then stood directly in front of the eight streamlined stainless steel fryers. Only one timer was still switched on, just as PC Lynch had confirmed. It was the second fryer. Each unit had a deep blue, three inch high, metallic number attached. Complete with the manufacturer's name neatly emblazoned below it. In this particular case it read: Hopkins of Barrow.
As a basket is placed into the boiling oil, the timer is set and a countdown would begin. At present the reading stated 0.00 and the basket had been raised. Murray stretched over and held his open palm an inch or two above the glow of the oil. It still radiated a slight

warmth, indicating that it had been in operation recently.

"He was confident and happy to stay in situ for a prolonged period."

'Sherlock,' looked quizzical at first before it dawned. "Otherwise the oil would be as cold as the other fryers by now!" Hanlon twigged. "Why stay so long?"

Murray considered the question, pursed his lips and simply shrugged.

"This is - an upmarket - fish restaurant, correct?" Joe Hanlon asked cagily. Referring to the contents in the basket. "Is that two halves of chicken, fried in crispy golden batter sir? If so, what's that all about? Another abstruse message? Of what significance? Does it tie in with Spence do you think?"

Murray blanked all of Hanlon's seemingly mundane questions. He then produced an inexpensive silver pen from his inside jacket pocket. The same make and model he had in every jacket he owned. Another quirky, little foible that he was quietly proud of.

As the DI peered carefully at the two freshly battered products, 'Doc' Patterson went to speak. He then hesitated, thought better of it and remained silent. Hanlon, curious as to why the 'Doc' paused, watched intensely as DI Murray began to scrape tentatively at the brittle, flaxen coating. Thin slivers fell to the floor. As Steven Murray continually tapped, prodded and scratched at two of Colonel Sanders KFC renegade runaways, he began to feel uneasy. He looked momentarily at Hanlon.

"Are you okay?" Joe asked.

Ignoring him, Murray turned to Thomas Patterson.

The T"inker raised his eyes. "It's all yours Inspector," he said with a rather mischievous 'you'll see' implication. Tiny flakes and shavings continued to fall. Murray felt a recognition of the two shapes begin to surface. But still it was not quite managing to come to the forefront of his mind.

Hanlon spoke first. "Sir, I think I know what they are!"

Murray continued tapping, and like visiting an Art Gallery, he was probably too close to the actual exhibit to make it out.

"Sir," Hanlon raised his voice. "You'll maybe want to…"

At that, Murray's constant pushing and prodding seemed to pay off. A sharp crystalised sound was heard.

Even louder than the previous twice, Joe Hanlon exclaimed, "Sir!"

Murray was oblivious. Like an obsessed knight jousting admirably with his sturdy, robust, miniature lance named 'Parker,' he determinedly advanced his fingers once again. At that, a large portion of the fragile batter came tumbling down. Joe and the Doc's fears were confirmed. Murray's normally sharp mind was just about joining the dots when, for a second, third and fourth time he heard the 'sharp' sound of metal on metal confirmed. Bing! Ting! Ping! Strange rumblings were emerging from Murray's direction. Hurriedly both Hanlon and Patterson stepped forward in unison. Quickly grabbing an arm each they dragged the Inspector to the far side of the otherwise immaculate kitchen (with the exception of the odd blood spatter or two). There he was free to regurgitate, heave, puke and spew up his guts until his heart's content.

Thirty seconds passed and the trio of gentlemen stood motionless. Two of them stared in genuine shock and surprise at the fry basket and it's unlikely contents. Murray tried to regain his breath and wipe at his mouth simultaneously. The mild collision of metal was made between his reliable Parker pen and unexpectedly - Carlo Tardelli's wedding ring. Forget Colonel Sanders, KFC and their mighty buckets. The two, crispy, 'finger lickingly good' treats were now batter free and belonged to the Italian born restaurant owner. They were his hands!

"You knew 'Doc'" Hanlon cautiously suggested.

"I had my suspicions," he replied. "The amount of blood and his two forearms out of sight. It seemed more than likely," Patterson confirmed.

The Inspector shook his head and with a heavy, saddened heart, walked dejectedly away. Disturbed and disgusted, no doubt Murray knew that his raven coloured hound would be requiring a rather lengthy and intensive workout at some point later that day!

Chapter Five

Paul Lattimer had lived a penurious life. Being born to a single mum in the late fifties was difficult enough in itself. In that era she was shunned, he was bullied, and life was pretty cruel and demeaning altogether. They lived in a tough, run down, working class estate in Rochdale, Greater Manchester. Home was a stereotypical red brick terraced house, complete with the generous air conditioning that only an outside toilet could provide. Forget the satisfaction of central heating, lovely warm showers and communicating via a telephone line. Back then, those mod cons were only available in science fiction/fantasy novels!

Paul was a mischievous child and the young Rochdalian rascal survived with very little schooling, often to be caught playing truant with his mates. Later, he married young at age eighteen, and went from one dead end job to another. Always struggling to earn a living and scrimping and scraping to barely get by, his teenage bride left him unsurprisingly after only two years of not such great marital bliss. He recalled her name was Sandra, but had never seen or heard from her ever again. He upped sticks and moved to Scotland in his mid twenties, initially only for a few short weeks. Now he was entering into his thirty sixth year settled here. Settled, was maybe too strong a word for it though. Lattimer had lived in numerous towns and villages throughout the decades. Whitburn, Falkirk, Dalkeith, Dunipace and even a short spell at Cumnock in East Ayrshire to name but a few.

His occasional time in employment, which was closer to only seven years, rather than a possible thirty five, had included spells as a cleaner, a waiter, a storeman and a bookies marker for two years in the eighties. He particularly loved that job. It was back in the day when everything had to be written up by hand onto a whiteboard. All the horses odds frequently changed pre-race, he'd mark up the winners, their returned s/p's and then   constantly go through it all over and over again. Races overlapped, magnetic strips held up the racecards and a host of small, sad, lonely men with no other lives, sat paraded in front of him. Snow White's pals certainly knew how to fritter away an afternoon! It was a busy, demanding role. One where punters would interact with you and friendly banter would normally ensue. However, the end came when a disgruntled client burned the premises to the ground one evening. The small independent bookmaker took his healthy insurance payout, never reopened in the area and Paul Lattimer found himself once again on the dole.

Now though, after several stop/start employment opportunities he had been working full time in a security role for the past fourteen months. With his 60th birthday fast approaching it seemed that good fortune had at last begun to shine on him. Six months earlier he had a £5 accumulator bet on five horses come up. Ranging in odds from a 2/1 favourite, to an 11/2 outsider in a field of four. His humble stake returned him seven and a half thousand pounds. Not life changing, but it should have enabled him to upgrade his lifestyle somewhat. With it however, he made what would later transpire to be - some rather interesting life choices.

Workwise, he kept plodding away diligently from eight in the evening until eight the next day. Continually he would safeguard a variety of designated sites in and around central Edinburgh. Serendipity was not about to re-enter the life of Paul Lattimer.

He had came to with a piercing, pounding headache. A succession of jabs had been followed by a quick uppercut. He soon realised that he was in the passenger seat of his van, whilst the back of his skull played host to a world title boxing match. He cursed at the pain and moved to inspect the damage. Nothing. No sound nor movement was forthcoming. Whatever he had been given, his limbs were non responsive to his thoughts. His arms, legs, mouth and tongue, every single one was lifeless. As his sight became less hazy, he could now make out the dark shadowed presence of someone in the driver's seat. In his head he had reached out to grab him by the throat and defend himself. In reality however, his head had simply swung sluggishly from right to left! As his face slumped down upon his chest, he could now bear witness to his nakedness. Alarm bells sounded furiously, but only internally.

What had happened? Where was he? Who was this inside the vehicle with him? What had he done to warrant this and how was it to finish? No bodily functions appeared to be working, but instantly he knew how it would end. He reached out with a further imaginary explosive punch. Unsurprisingly, his head once again, blandly returned to its previous starting position. There had been black marker outlines drawn on his chest and side. This was to be most certainly no ultra modern 'uber' experience. Lattimer tried to tell himself that it was all a dream, the most alarming dream, even a truly horrendous nightmare, he would have accepted that.

"Aaaaaaaagh," he bellowed, as his body trembled and shuddered. It was an almighty noise. He knew he had screamed. He felt the agonising pain and surprised himself that he hadn't passed out. But yet again no sound came forth. Blood had launched dramatically onto the windscreen. A mini explosive had been detonated as his chest was sliced to the bone. He gasped and groaned internally. His head continually flailed from side to side, as froth danced freely on his lips. He wanted to writhe and twist to the torture. Inwardly he was squirming. At that instant, his eyes rolled back and ran for cover as the silent assailant moved forward toward him once again. This time, the brutal blade being brandished brashly on the gleaming Stanley knife, carved a large circular motion and his complete body went limp.

After spending the best part of the morning at Tardelli's, Thursday afternoon had came and went without any major incident. Behind the scenes, investigations were anxiously being carried out throughout the day. No media updates, press conferences or public statements were made. It had an 'all hands on deck' feel to it. Hanlon and Murray were looking at establishing a connection between Spence and Tardelli, however, sadly nothing of note had surfaced so far. They were having background forensics carried out on both men. Any financial irregularities, social media checks, crossover in their lifestyles, social circles, etc, etc. The post-it notes though, they took it to another level. Maybe not a serial killer on their hands, but someone with a definite grudge against specific individuals or groups, and more than likely for a specific reason. 1974 & Michelangelo. They had no idea where to start with those!

In the other enquiries, diligent as ever Hayes and Curry worked hard on the stolen artwork. They looked at patterns, previous reports, cross referenced the victims, their locations and insurance histories.

In the meantime 'Sandy' Kerr and 'Mac' Rasul were busy following up with reported sightings on the schoolgirls. Others investigated the last route the teenagers were each seen on. Teams were conducting second, hopefully even more thorough searches in each of their respective homes. DCI Brown had already informed 'Sandy' that the budget would be cut back imminently if no progress was made in the next couple of days. That was why Kerr had asked for Murray's help. They desperately needed a lead and an exceptionally strong, positive lead at that. It was then that the call came in.

"It's your phone sir, it's vibrating," Hanlon blurted out to Murray as he walked past it with a cumbersome pile of paperwork in his hand. "You must have switched it to silent," he continued.

"Cowabunga," Murray yelled.

"Sorry?" his young officer questioned.

"Get it for me Joe please," Murray cried from the other side of the room. He, himself had been busy checking out prominent events from 1974 and doing a little bit more in-depth research on Michelangelo the renaissance painter, as opposed to the Teenage Mutant Ninja Turtle.

The tail end of the phone conversation ended with, "Low Side Industrial Estate. Near the trampoline park on the outskirts of Dalkeith. Yes, I know exactly where you are. Thanks Doc."

"Our quiet day at the office just ended?" Murray figured.

"You had better believe it," DC Hanlon confirmed. "The T'inker reckons we ought to be in attendance."

"Because?" Murray queried.

Hanlon handed him his phone and frowned.

"Another, 'orange is the new black' has put in a cameo appearance at the scene."

New Victoria Park was the home ground of Newtongrange Star. Founded in 1890, the junior football club were based in the village of Newtongrange, Midlothian. Directly at the back of their rather dilapidated ground sat the now derelict industrial estate of Low Side.

What had once been a vibrant and fully occupied workspace in the late eighties and early nineties, was now an empty and rundown shell in the hands of a property management company. They currently maintained the security, waiting patiently for the relevant paperwork approval and red tape clearance. Then they hoped to revitalise the site completely and bring in twenty first century clients, like the trampoline park tenants in the nearby adjacent estate.

Assembled beyond the rusted torn down gates were a multitude of official vehicles. Three police, an ambulance and forensics cars, one of which Murray recognised as Thomas Patterson's, were already present. And with its familiar Police Scotland livery an incident room van.

As the colleagues approached Patterson. Murray slightly irked, asked, "Any idea who asked for an incident room to be set up Doc?"

The Doc nodded over Murray's shoulder, indicating to the driver of the large, black saloon currently driving through the unkempt, neglected entrance. "I suspect he can help you answer that one Steven."

Murray shook his head and narrowed his eyes.

"What on earth is he doing here sir?" Hanlon asked.

"Brace yourself, for I think we are about to find out Joe."

In the dusk of the evening the Ford Fiesta van sat with its 5 year old bonnet wide open. It was reminiscent of a 1980's Pac-man on the prowl. Only the lack of popping noises shattered the illusion. On the inside of the dashboard, where most drivers sat their parking tickets, was the unmistakable, hi-visibility post-it note.

Through the front windscreen it was clear that on this occasion, the black marker had penned only one letter. Three straight lines of varying sizes, produced a solid, bold, capital **F**.

As the forensics team set up a tent and appropriate lighting, the lion's mouth required someone brave enough to put their head inside. The likely press-ganged candidate appeared to be Detective Constable Joseph Hanlon. So as Doc Patterson opened the passenger door of the little navy blue vehicle, all three men were surprised to hear...

"Wait there Hanlon," the voice barked.

So he did take time out from behind his desk, whisky tasting and scouring the pages of his latest Gardeners' World magazine, Murray thought quietly to himself. No point in ruffling anyone's feathers!

Patterson tried to discourage DCI Brown from proceeding, "It's not pretty Keith, I promise. I maybe wouldn't if I were you."

The puzzled, ungrateful look on 'Sherlock's' face said - 'But it was okay for me to dive in Doc? Thanks very much!'

DCI Keith Brown lasted all of five seconds before he gagged. As the Doc went to his aid, Brown could not restrain himself and he puked straight across the lower regions of the dead body. With the waist, thighs and knees taking the brunt of his stomach contents, he never fully contaminated the crime scene. However, that would most certainly be contested in court. Captivated by this, Murray watched from only a few yards away with deep interest. It had brought back a few specific memories for him.

"Sorry gentlemen," Brown offered rather insincerely, whilst wiping remnants of a miniature 'Scotch Broth' cereal bar from his lips. "I'll leave it to those more experienced in these matters in future." He then hastily made his way back to the push button ignition on his BMW 5 series, and off he went.

Hanlon looked at The T'inker. His expression offered up - Did I miss something there? The Doc had no idea. He just shook his head in disbelief and turned to his surprisingly, quiet friend.

"What was t'at all about Steven?" Patterson asked in his best professional voice. "Sure, I know you know."

Murray on the other hand was still busy gathering outside pieces for the jigsaw. And a few seconds ago, he firmly believed another one, had just been added. Disregarding everything that had been previously said to him. Either deliberately, or totally oblivious as he headed off into his own little world. The DI simply stepped forward to eye under the aging, rusting bonnet and ask brazenly.

"So Doc, what do we have here?"

Murray froze instantly to the spot as he heard the Doc's frightening response.

"What?" Hanlon exclaimed with such force, that several others turned to stare.

DI Murray's gaze was now firmly on the van's engine. Something was missing. The crankshaft, valves and spark plugs, they appeared to be fine. They were all present and correct. The pistons, oil, injector and camshaft were also all in attendance and ready for work. Joe Hanlon had now joined Murray by his side. As 'Sherlock' peered carefully at the mechanics, straightaway he also spotted the absentee. The vital component that had gone AWOL. It was the car battery that was gone. Nuts and bolts had been loosened and cables disconnected from the terminal. In its place, sat unexpectedly and bizarrely a small rotund muscular shape. It was covered in blood. Although that was perhaps somewhat unsurprising, considering the item in question................ was a human heart!

Repulsed, Murray quickly covered his mouth. Hanlon's knees gave way slightly and he was promptly helped by Doc Patterson. Then all three men shifted their attention immediately to the slumped body in the front seat. Their combined focus was now on the gaping space located between the lungs, in the middle compartment of his chest. Stunned silence. Easily twenty seconds passed before Murray and Hanlon once again fully contemplated the scene before them. They slowly took in and observed the blood spattered windscreen and cherry red inners. Next on the agenda they inhaled the distinct, distilled vanilla essence that hung desperately in the air. It had joined forces with the vile, odious stench from the cars smeared seat covers and begun to linger ominously over the desecrated body of the poor security guard from Rochdale.

Later on that Thursday evening Steven Murray took his 'black dog' for a much needed walk. He knew it would be required. It made sense, because sorrowful, melancholic thoughts of Tardelli's family, friends and upset staff had taken their toll. Horrific scenes at an abandoned industrial park had left him privately sobbing. So much beauty and adventure available to us in the world he thought. With the vast majority of people kind hearted, hard working and naturally loving. Yet, every twenty four hours he normally mixed with the misguided, depraved deviant. The tainted sicko and warped nut job!
He shrugged thinking, maybe not the most politically correct way to describe them these days. However his dog growled in agreement and that was good enough for him!

Filled with melancholy, he reflected on how he had experienced many atrocious deaths before. But nonetheless they were all individuals. No longer could they share their intimate smiles, treasured hopes and professional aspirations with the world. Their history and hard work, their challenges and tribulations all meant nothing. They were gone, snuffed out in an instant. After a thirty minute walk in the fresh air, his canine friend was content. It meant unsurprisingly, a gentle stroll was all that would be required next morning before breakfast. He was then able to settle down and ponder on all that had transpired during an eventful day. And still feeling rather lugubrious, he had only just sat back into his comfortable, high backed leather armchair and begun to admire and fully appreciate the beauty of his Penelope Cooke portrait - *The Lady and the Angel*, when inevitably, right on cue, his phone rang!

Chapter Six

"All that I know in my life, I have learned on the street. No magic carpet, no genie, no shoes on my feet. Will I wake up from this nightmare? A fear that chills me to the bone. Though I may be one of many, I feel so all alone.

- Richard Marx

A few hours later on that intensely busy Friday, the evening rain continued to pound down like a muffled snare drum. The continual rat-ta-ta-tat echoed off the roof of the tall, hi-backed van as it made its way into the darkened yard. The livery on its side stated Ellen James Rental. It was bang on eight o'clock as Dennis Black jumped down from the driver's seat and nodded brusquely to Latchford. The yard owner had ventured quickly to make his way outside from his office on seeing the lights approach. He'd also received a telephone call earlier in the day and was made aware to expect this latest consignment. It was Black's second delivery in the space of six days, and as was the norm, he would calmly exit the vehicle, make his way around to the back and open wide the two rear doors. Inside there was always a particular smell that Robert Latchford had never been able to identify. The foul odour was quite distinct and definite. An aroma that seemed to blend together a perfect, perfumed cocktail of darkness and danger. For Robert Latchford it was a troubling stench that made every delivery appear more tainted and tarnished than the last. On his previous visit there had only been two large boxes to be unloaded. Tonight however, as the rain continued to fall heavily, there was double that number. The wooden crates had slats every twelve inches apart. They contained an assortment of older, outdated casino furniture that was there to be obliterated and crushed. The miniature squares would then be added to the Car Bored Box Company's mountain range of destruction, that had been distributed freely throughout the yard.

The ABC casino chain had certainly undergone a vast amount of remodelling and internal improvement in recent months. However, whatever current upgrade they were involved in at their various locations, Dennis Black would appear regularly, at least once a fortnight to dispose of old desks, tables, chairs and locker room equipment. Often, like this evening, an occasional once a week drop off was required.

Part of Latchfords ongoing financial survival, was to make his yard available for these so-called 'demolition' nights, as they had recently become christened. Not only did the crushing machine have to be at their disposal at all times, but the quiet loner, Black, would then record the footage as proof for his bosses that all the destruction and desecration was completed to their satisfaction.

Two of the small arena floodlights had been switched on, as Latchford made his way into the intimate cockpit of 'the Crusha!' In the modern age that we live in, a hand held remote which sat by his side, could easily have operated this equipment. However, Robert Latchford normally preferred the old fashioned manual approach. A key was turned and the formidable machine roared into life. Black in the meantime, had jumped into the four year old, yellow forklift and was carefully offloading the latest quartet of unwanted, 'past their sell-by' goods! Each crate was reversed outward from the van, swung around toward the giant crusher and placed delicately outside the metal container. Latchford in the interim, had been busy positioning the giant pincer claw of his trusted machine down low. Enabling him to winch up an old 1982, sky blue, Ford Cortina. The four robotic fingers hit with enormous pressure and shattered immediately, the front and back windscreen simultaneously. One full second later both side windows exploded violently into a thousand pieces. Cautiously, he then proceeded to lift and deposit the nation's once best selling car gently onto the base of the crushing area *'like a blanket on the ground.'*

Throughout this time Black had been busy filming the Cortina's distress, as well as zooming in/out and focusing closely on the four upright units in front of him. This had become his regular routine when he made these under cover of the night deliveries. As he operated the forklift with one hand, he continued to record interesting footage on his phone with the other. It was his virtual receipt for his bosses. Slightly subdued, he then raised each of the unwanted furniture crates steadily, high into the air. Then slowly, like lemmings, one by one depositing them into the belly of the beast. Another scrap car was then positioned on top. This time it was an old Mini Clubman. Latchford was literally running his own vehicle variation of a Subway sandwich outlet. The metal of the two cars was required to solidify the binding and bonding of the wood, plastic and other materials contained in the furniture. A high energy motor turned over and all sides began steadily to move inward. The various composites became welded together as they were finally flattened from above.

With every batch received, a small part of Robert Latchfords soul departed. Tonight was no different. As the first metal cube was squashed, squeezed and propelled out, Cindy-Ann's father took a long, slow, deep breath in. A two second memory of what could have been flashed into his mind. By seconds three and four he was back in the present. His daughter missing, financial ruin and currently in bed with the devil. As the cold, wet, angled drizzle continued to fall, an interesting scent gradually pervaded the air. For Robert Latchford, on many fronts - It was the sustained, mind numbing fragrance... of fear.

Chapter Seven

"When you're the belle of the ball, it's hard to fall and sacrifice your status for a fool. But all your apparatus and your charm, can never cool the still, still waters or warm the chilling air."

- Aztec Camera

That Saturday morning no smiles were to be found in or around Gullane, North Berwick, or even East Lothian itself. News was instantaneous these days. Whether in Africa, Australia or Asia, within five minutes of it going viral, comments and opinions were globally all over social media. So when a young female body is discovered buried in a sand dune by an early morning dog walker, you can rest assured unfounded reports will be rife. It's a certainty that they'll have plenty more to talk about on their hallowed fairways today, other than which club to use!

Kerr and Rasul had met up with Murray at the coastal town to update him with regard to the other missing girls. In truth, they were really no further forward. Interesting though Murray thought, Cindy-Ann had only been missing a matter of days before she had been discovered dead. Whereas all the others? Gone for weeks and yet still no sign of them.

"Significant," he asked. "What do you think?"

'Mac' looked at his Sergeant. It was really her that Murray was addressing he figured. Sandra Kerr hesitated. "Could be I guess," she offered unconvincingly to Murray. Her Inspector pursed his lips and nodded (a number 17, which indicated, I think it does, I definitely think it does).

"I'll head over to Inverleith straightaway to break the news to Mr Latchford. Hopefully before he hears speculative reports on the radio or TV," Murray informed his colleagues.

Having worked with him closely for so long, DS Kerr was uneasy with his comments and their delivery. She wasn't sure earlier, when he'd asked about her discovery being 'significant.' But this time she was pretty certain. Her Inspector was ignoring DC Rasul. He was doing a reasonable job trying to disguise it. But to Sandra Kerr it had become blindingly apparent. For the briefest of moments she questioned - was Steve Murray a racist? She had initially dismissed it immediately. Now though, doubt had crept back in.

"I had already asked Joe the other day to dig a bit deeper into his background. So I'll meet 'Sherlock' over there," he concluded by addressing both officers. Looking however, only in Sandra Kerr's direction.

"You two tie up everything here. Be thorough, no mistakes and we'll catch up later."

As Murray walked off, Kerr questioned 'Mac.' "Did you upset him? What did you say? You're only just here. What have you done?"

"Uh," was his dumbfounded response. Up until that point, Rasul had no idea what she was on about. Now though, he'd monitor and interpret Murray's interactions with him more carefully. Thank you Sarge, he acknowledged to himself. Kerr just shook her head.

Traffic was beginning to snarl up in and around Leith. Easter Road and the surrounding area was busy. Hibernian F.C. had a home match that afternoon and DI Murray was now kicking himself for deciding to travel back along the coastal route via Musselburgh and Portobello. With that said, there was never a quick route in and out of the Leith/Trinity area, especially midweek. So he was grateful that once past Leith Links he remembered his car actually had a third gear. He'd arranged to meet DC Hanlon on the street outside the main entrance of the Botanic Gardens. Joining the Inspector in his car, Hanlon was soon brought up to speed on developments at Gullane Bents.

Then, it was 'Sherlock's' turn as he struggled to contain his excitement.

"Fascinating sir. Absolutely fascinating," was the start of Hanlon's remarks. Detective Inspector Steven Murray knew this was where he had to get comfortable. He shifted awkwardly behind the steering wheel, until he was just about side on to hear Robert Latchfords story. A story that was about to be portrayed in the form of a dramatic monologue.

"It's all yours McDuff - take it away," his Inspector encouraged.

"As I said sir, fascinating. Robert David Latchford was a horologist. An expert in clocks and watches."

Murray's facial gesture (number 17) said, I know what Horology is!

Hanlon smiled - he didn't believe him.

"He studied it for near a decade and made good money from it. Near the end of that time was when his wife died."

Murray tentatively lifted his hand. "Sorry to ask Joe, with Lauren and all. But was it a sickness, illness or what?"

Hanlon nodded in agreement and understanding. "Well, that is where it all gets really interesting sir."

"Go on,"

"Officially it was an accident. Hit by a car whilst in London on business."

Murray flinched on hearing this.

"Are you sure you're okay?" Hanlon checked before continuing. "Because, although it was recorded as an accident, it was a hit and run. The driver never actually stopped sir, and Mr Latchford has on numerous occasions since, appealed to us to reopen the case."

"Why?" Murray asked.

"He always believed she was murdered," Hanlon replied.

Again Murray shook his head. "Why? If your wife....' he hesitated. Forcing himself to continue he repeated. "Why, if your wife was knocked down by a car, even in a hit and run. Why would any normal person believe she was murdered?" His head again shook in disbelief. "We are about to enter a hornet's nest here Joe. I can just feel it,"

"There's more sir. Should I continue?"

"Oh, I knew there would be. There simply had to be. But I tell you what Joe. Let's break the news to him first and you can fill me in with the rest later."

Hanlon agreed by giving his boss the number 2 nod. As far as Joe was aware he only had two types of nod, and they were simply speed related. Number 2 was the, up down, up down in quick succession variety, which meant..........sure, absolutely!

After several knocks at the door and sounding the front bell, they called Robert Latchfords mobile. He answered straight away.

"Sir, it's DI Murray here. We are actually in your driveway. Are you at home? Can you let us in?"

After a brief hesitation he replied with, "Sorry, you are where? Oh, okay, yes I understand totally. No, no, we're on our way to you now, we know the address. No, no honestly sir, we'll be there shortly, see you soon." Murray closed over his phone and turned to 'Sherlock.' "He's at his workplace. Too much spare time on his hands. He was just filled with nervous energy and at least at work he feels he can destress, he said."

Hanlon shrugged, pulled a face and questioned, "Really? What are your thoughts sir?"

"On that particular issue, I one hundred percent believe him Joe. However, is there more to her disappearance, discovery and death? Absolutely! What that is, and what it looks like, is where we come in."

Both men were back in the car heading for Leith.

"What kind of cardboard boxes do his company construct and produce? I take it his factory manufacture a wide variety, for a multitude of uses?" Murray asked confidently.

DC Joseph Hanlon at this point gave his Inspector a slightly quizzical look to say the least.

"What?" Murray said.

"Are you serious sir?"

"Really, what is it? Of course I'm serious. Genuinely, it could be important. Who he sells to, his suppliers, grievances, etc. Need I go on?"

Hanlon laughed. Not with a restrained, mild chuckle. But an out loud, 'front row of a Kevin Bridges gig,' kind of laugh. Tears began to stream down his cheeks. He was so thankful he wasn't driving.

Each time he tried to speak, "Sir, sir…" Like starting up an engine, and off he'd go again. The boy had lost it. Fully three or four minutes later, which felt like an eternity to Murray, young 'Sherlock' had composed himself enough to finally speak.

"Sir," a smile surfaced, but he was able to continue. "Robert Latchford does not assemble any cardboard boxes of any shape or size."

Murray, confused by this response, pouted his lips before stating, "Go on."

"He owns the Car Bored Box Company. It's not a cardboard box." He began to grin again.

"Don't start Joe," his Inspector protested. "So, explain."

"He basically operates a scrapyard. A very neat and tidy franchised scrapyard it has to be said. But a scrapyard business nonetheless. They are setting up in all the major cities. I've been into this particular one, once before with my Uncle. He was getting rid of his seventeen year old Citroen."

Murray drove, listening intently.

"You take it in and park it in the marked off area. The operator then bores a hole either side of the vehicle. That sir, is the 'car bored' part. Then, according to their advertising literature, that is when it is hoisted up and placed into the strongest vehicle crusher in Europe." Hanlon paused at that.

"And?" his boss says. "Is that it?"

"Well, then he taps the magic button and hey presto! I reckon roughly a minute or two later, a rather beautifully compact 4 by 4 is pushed out and delivered to the side of the machine. That would be a four foot, by four foot metal cube. You can then have them dipped in a choice of coloured sealant 'Free of Charge!' Some people take them home, turn them into features in their gardens, abstract coffee tables or for a host of other wonderful and weird creations."

Murray's facial expression (number eighteen) said, 'You're having a laugh!'

"Seriously sir, you can. For most folk though, they just let Latchford stack it up high in the clouds with all the others."

"Bath Road you said Joe. Right?" Murray asked, still shaking his head in disbelief. "I know I told him I knew exactly where it was… I lied!"

"Yes, just along Salamander Street. You take a left after the 'Tiny Bubbles' car wash."

They were only five minutes away. And that would be long enough the Inspector figured for Joseph Hanlon to finish updating him on Latchfords past.

"Joe - Robert Latchford, you said there was more. Give me the three minute, Reader's Digest, rapid abridged version, before we get there."

"Reader's who?" he said, taken by surprise. Hanlon then offered a couple of hums and haws before composing himself and speaking at pace. "Well, right, uum, where were we? He has a record. In his late teens, early twenties and it was for burglary. His nickname was

'Latches.' Jointly due to his surname and his uncanny ability to disable locks, alarm systems and the like. Later, when he got married, he turned his life around and put his abilities to good use. As I said earlier he was taken on by a respected watchmaker and became an expert in his own right. Then about a decade ago, when his wife left a business conference in London, his whole world stopped and his life imploded. He never fully recovered by all accounts. Shortly afterwards, he withdrew entirely from watchmaking to bring up his young daughter. He bought this franchise. A failing venture it would appear, as revenue has been down year after year. So, maintaining the Inverleith property must be a strain sir, I would guess."

The colour had drained rapidly from Murray's face.

"Are you feeling okay sir? You've turned white."

As Murray drove through the gates of the yard, he uttered, "nicely timed DC Hanlon and a few pieces of food for thought amongst that brief bio. Well done."

Just inside the yard a man was leaning against his black, four wheel drive vehicle. Having what seemed like a well deserved cigarette break. The Edinburgh franchise belonging to Robert Latchford was to be unearthed in the industrial heartland of Leith, just off the Marina Esplanade. It was positioned between the established Jackson Coachworks on its left and a large roofing and building suppliers to its right. Opposite the premises, a substantial abandoned warehouse with a corrugated iron roof appeared to become more derelict by the day. Previously, it been home to a major tile wholesaler. Murray remembered faintly having been there once with one of his police colleagues. Possibly 3 or 4 years ago now though, he thought to himself.

"Wow," he gasped audibly as he looked up from closing his car door.

"Impressive, isn't it," Hanlon gestured.

There, neatly stacked all around them were large metal cubes. The right hand side as you entered was one massive wall of coloured squares. Easily seven or eight high and about ten or twelve deep. In the middle section, resembling giant building blocks for kids. Bold yellow, blue and red lettering had been spray painted on to read: CAR BORED BOX COMPANY. The B's and C's were turned on their side, again lending further credence to the children's building block theory. On health grounds alone, this would be the last place you'd want your children to be.

Just then, the lightweight door to the small office, which was no bigger than a garden shed, opened. A lone dishevelled figure appeared in the doorway. Both officers instantly realising at that moment, that this was probably not the ideal location to be breaking this kind of news. Standing still in the doorway, he could tell from their body language that this was not good. Both men stared at the ground, shoulders slumped, they were here to deliver......

"It's her isn't it? You've found her. The earlier reports on the news, it's true, it's her. It's my Cindy-Ann at East Lothian isn't it?"

"Oh, jeez," sighed Murray below his breath.

Hanlon ran his slender hands through his thin, wispy hair. What a way to hear and be left swithering and sweating over. Each of the other missing girls families are also now going to be out of their minds with similar fateful thoughts. Each thinking the worst.

Detective Inspector Murray began, "I'm so sorry…"

As soon as the word 'sorry' was uttered, Latchfords legs gave way. He fell violently to his knees, and his legs created a supportive v-shape below him, as he wept uncontrollably. His head attempted to rest on his thighs, forbidden only by two trembling oil stained hands which were now clamped firmly to his broken face. It then took the turn of a church scene from a period drama. The individual began questioning their worth and their faith. Why them? Take me instead. No desire to continue. Was this a penance that they had to pay for other misdeeds in their lives?

DI Murray did not need to visualise an old movie scene. He lived and re-enacted this scene almost daily. The reality though was, it was always even more unsettling to actually see it play out in the life of another. That feeling of helplessness, the inability to alleviate their pain and suffering. Unable to comfort them.

Hanlon and Murray each grabbed an arm and helped the distraught father back up to his feet. The younger of the two men sniffed the air slightly. There appeared to be a less than favourable odour wafting from the bedraggled Robert Latchford. Murray quietly nodded (a number 24), which from his years of experience and looking at the man, guessed that this father had never even changed his clothing or likely washed since the day that Cindy-Ann had been abducted. The front of his waistcoat looked grubby and creased. His dogtooth shirt further advertised sweat marks from the previous three days. And his classic Levi jeans were wet and scuff marked at the ankles from operating machinery continually, over that period of time. Whilst the stubble of hair around his cheeks and chin bore testimony, to at least three to four days of growth. The front cover of a tabloid currently looked more likely than GQ magazine!

Murray calmly suggested that they all return to the family home. He then arranged for a FLO (a family liaison officer) to be assigned and meet them there within the hour. Latchford would travel with Murray. No doubt in stunned, disbelieving silence. As for DC Hanlon, he would then drive the car of the distressed father. Travelling the short journey back to Inverleith, Hanlon soon became familiar with the controls, interior and the quality drive of an Audi A6 automatic. An extremely impressive and expensive machine Joseph Hanlon mused. Especially for a businessman with a supposedly ailing company. 'Vorsprung durch Technik!'

Chapter Eight

"Bought a ticket for a runaway train, like a madman laughing at the rain. Little out of touch, little insane, just easier than dealing with the pain."

- Soul Asylum

A gentle tear ran down the sallow cheek of DC 'Mac' Rasul as he hung up the phone. He had just finished speaking with Tony Lawrenson. Anthony Peter Lawrenson was an experienced car salesman. He was a time served mechanic, but over the years had become more at home selling a vehicle, rather than the repairing. He worked in Edinburgh for 'Europe's number one, independently owned family-run car dealership.' He was a thirty-seven year old divorcee and the father of thirteen year old Claire. Claire Lawrenson had been described by her dad as a feisty, red-haired teenager. Full of fun, brimming with energy and always game for a laugh. She was also the first young girl to have gone missing nearly two months ago.

'Mac' confirmed with the Lawrenson family, Tony and his parents, that the body discovered at East Lothian was not that of their beloved daughter or granddaughter. The 'hope' that they had clung to these past seven or eight weeks could remain intact a while longer. Anxious, tearful and now relieved, they thanked him for his call, put their lives back on hold, and returned to await the next one!

Rasul may be a strong athletic built individual, but Sandra Kerr, his new partner, quickly sussed that he was in fact, a 'gentle giant' of a man. With short cropped hair, high cheekbones and deep set eyes, 'Mac' Rasul had the look of a boyish Denzel Washington about him. He also had the uncanny ability to move at ease from sweet, innocent and charismatic - into firm, forceful and focused. Those were West of Scotland learned character traits. Finely tuned ones that Kerr thought would serve him well over here in the East. That morning, she herself had already updated Detective Chief Inspector Brown, before speaking with several of the other concerned parents also. Each of them initially feared the worst when she called. Firstly, Alastair Fenwick, the father of the second schoolgirl that had disappeared. His dark haired daughter had just turned fourteen the day before and had a birthday meal, including a party to look forward to that weekend. The tall and dark haired gangly frame of Karen Fenwick however, never made it to a scheduled dentist's appointment on the day she went missing.

Having recently given birth, Kerr then put herself into the role of those frantic parents just for a brief minute. She thought about how in later years, if that had been one of her own twins that had been taken, how she would cope. The worry, the stress, just existing would be tough. Cooking, washing, ironing, housework and daily chores...... forget that she thought. She would be pacing the floor and at first sitting nearby the phone. But she quickly realised, that in this modern advanced age in which we live, there is no need to sit by the telecommunications apparatus anymore. You and your handset are almost always constantly together. Your mobile phone, with all the information and up to the minute details it has on you, knows you far better and is much more informed than your partner of goodness knows how many years. Scary but true! And then, the thought of every time that phone rang, the uncertainty, the panic, the realisation of your worst thoughts being confirmed, or not. Subsequently having to go through it all again, day in, day out, hour after hour. Many of these families have now been dealing with that daily turmoil for several weeks. Every knock at the door or telephone call would bring on another onslaught of dread, fear, anxiety and worry. She thought about the hundreds of thousands of children that go missing every year. Many of whom simply choose to leave home, but never leave a note. A short message, or at least something that parents are able to, if not understand, at least take small comfort in that this has been their child's own decision. Unlike many of the parents she currently finds herself interacting with. Their particular thoughts will be running wild or suppressed to the other extreme with a range of prescription drugs or tablets. It is without doubt the uncertainty. Your child is abducted and your mind runs rampant - fearing and thinking the worst, and imagining all sorts.

'Sandy' with her own mind struggling to keep those aforementioned thoughts at bay, then spoke with Michael and Mary McFall. The McFalls daughter Tracey had, up until that point been the youngest girl to have gone missing or been taken. She was only twelve years and seventeen days when she also failed to return home from school. That was roughly a month ago and at that point a pattern at least seemed to emerge of a teenage girl being abducted approximately every two weeks, give or take.

The last, just twelve days before Cindy-Ann, was Iona Hynd. Iona was the blonde, petite, thirteen year old daughter of local cafe owner Maurice Hynd. Mo was well known to several police officers. His small, cheerful establishment was only a hundred yards along from the station doors. They had supported and hosted many charity events and fundraisers in his premises.

It had been upsetting at the time for many of the officers to hear that young Iona was now also missing. She worked in the family cafe every Saturday morning, then with a smile on her face and a spring in her step, she headed off, regular as clockwork to play in her afternoon match. That was her ambition, to be a professional female soccer player. She had recently been accepted for a scholarship in America and was due to fly out there in September to further pursue that dream, to take it a giant step closer to reality. 'Mac' spoke with Maurice Hynd to reassure him. Thankfully, he was oblivious to the disturbing find in East Lothian. He also expressed his gratitude to DC Rasul before immersing himself back into the business of running his cafe.

Although only licensed to open between the hours of 8am to 8pm, Rasul got the impression that Mr Hynd had in actual fact been operating 24 hours a days. He reckoned the poor man was just simply unable to switch off from thinking about his missing daughter. So, by way of a distraction, he just worked fervently cleaning, preparing, serving, chatting, engaging, and so the cycle continued. As 'Mac' slipped his mobile phone effortlessly back into his jacket pocket with his right hand. His left, once again wiped away a silent tear or two that had emerged from behind the beautiful blue eyes, of this tall masculine police officer.

Back in Inverleith, Robert Latchford opened the heavy four panelled mahogany front door of his impressive family home. Showing both officers inside, he then followed. He walked dejectedly with a heavy heart, a few moderate paces behind. Whilst pointing to a room off to his right, Murray looked around and gestured to Latchford, indicating the large sitting room they'd been in on their previous visit earlier in the week. Latchford nodded.

"Would you mind Inspector if I showered and changed before we chatted?" he asked solemnly.

"Not at all sir. I think that would be a good idea," Murray said. "In fact, take your time and DC Hanlon here will make you a refreshing cuppa."

"Absolutely," Hanlon responded. "Just direct me to the kitchen sir."

With little enthusiasm and even less strength, Latchford managed a tired lift of a hand that indicated…'try further down that hallway.' Hanlon set off briskly as he always did with any task assigned to him. By comparison a lumbering figure moved at a laboured pace, with each step he took up the carpeted stairway, appearing increasingly painful and sore. His only child, his precious daughter now gone. Callously murdered. Her aspirations, goals, dreams and ambitions cruelly denied her. A father no doubt questioning where he went wrong. What could he have done to have protected her more? What was there left to cling on to? To survive for? What would her mother have thought? Grateful for small mercies he thought.

A man who had tortured himself with those self same questions a million times already, stood at the bottom of the stairway with moistened eyes and nodded (a number 29, understanding and empathy).

Murray then made his way into the sitting room. What he witnessed, did not fully surprise him. There was discarded chocolate bar wrappers lying strewn on the coffee table. Lights had been left switched on. The mail was still positioned behind the small ornamental hourglass on the mantelpiece, only now it had a few additional unopened envelopes added. Some unwashed plates sat on the settee, next to a crushed and gravy stained tartan blanket. At least he seemed to be eating, Murray thought. Although he would guess his bedroom would be immaculate - Robert Latchford never having slept in it, or having changed his clothes during the previous few days.

At that moment Detective Inspector Steven Murray felt inspired and inclined to do a little housework of his own for a few minutes. Cutlery and dishes were gathered up and taken through to Hanlon, who duly washed them. The Inspector then spent a brief minute viewing that particular wristwatch in the display cabinet that had piqued his interest on their previous visit. Sweetie wrappers were then binned, a blanket put into a washing basket and cushions that had previously been in disarray, where now fully plumped and positioned properly back on their respective sofas or chairs. More mail that had gathered behind the front door (Murray had noticed it as they entered) was in turn added to the previous bundle on the mantelpiece. Hanlon then duly arrived on cue with a tray of tea, coffee, soft drinks and an assortment of biscuits. Always one for exceeding expectations. Murray was grateful, for he on the other hand, would not even have known how to boil the kettle!

Only six or seven minutes passed before the grieving Latchford entered the room. His eyes were extremely bloodshot. Either tiredness or tears, but more likely a combination of both. His hair had been washed, some deodorant or body spray applied and clad in fresh tee-shirt and jeans he at least seemed able to sit and chat. It was an exceptionally emotional time. But some difficult questions needed to be asked. Although, initially Murray opted to begin with one of the easier ones. "Tea or coffee Mr Latchford?" the Inspector enquired.

To his surprise, Latchford declined and gestured toward the lemonade that Hanlon had chosen to put on display.

"Thank you," he offered quietly, as Joseph Hanlon poured. Silence filled the room and a moment of quiet reflection was deemed appropriate by all three parties.

"Sir, do you, would you, know anyone called Spence? A Mr Ian Spence?" Murray asked courteously and low key. Hanlon looked at him in surprise, he wasn't expecting that.

With a fervent angry response Latchford questioned gruffly. "Was it him Inspector? Did he kill my daughter? Was he responsible?" The father then began to gently weep. Emotionally through his tears he croaked, "I don't even know how she died. I only know what they said on the radio. Teenage girl discovered on the sand dunes at North Berwick." He broke off at that and buried his head down deep into his hands once again. Murray stood up and shrugged.

"A family liaison officer will join us shortly," Hanlon reassured him. "We should wait until then to talk more fully and openly about the circumstances of Cindy-Ann's death. He or she may also be able to update us on any recent developments in the forensics side of the case." His light positive tone seemed to help Robert Latchford settle slightly.

"Ian Spence?" Murray reminded him.

"I don't know anyone with that name," Latchford sighed. He then looked up wearily and pleaded. "Is he connected to my daughter's death Inspector?"

"I believe he is sir," Murray confirmed.

"Sorry!" DC Hanlon surprisingly quipped. "He is?" Latchford gawped at Hanlon's response, then turned to Murray. He was about to comment, but at the last moment thought better of it. Murray then pointed to the letters on the mantelpiece and to more precisely what held them in place. One ornamental, compact sized aluminium hourglass. It stood at about four inches in height.

Hanlon gasped, "It looked the exact same as the one next to Ian Spence's body. I knew it seemed familiar."

"Next to *his* body?" Latchford exclaimed. "What's going on here. How many bodies were on that beach?"

Murray gestured with his hands, motioning both palms downwards. "Calm down Mr Latchford. His corpse was found elsewhere. Initially separate investigations. However, I now believe they are somehow entangled and possibly one and the same!"

"Which means we could ask if you know or knew a Carlo Tardelli or Paul Lattimer sir?" Hanlon ventured to ask.

"Relax Detective Constable Hanlon, let's leave it at that for now and revisit Mr Latchford at some point in the future."

Just then, Joe Hanlon's phone sounded. On answering, he discovered that it was WPC Cloy, the liaison officer. He listened carefully and nodded at regular intervals.

Murray meanwhile, knelt directly in front of Cindy-Ann's father and made a quiet request.

"Tell me about your wife. I want to help."

Latchford stared coldly at him, but Murray remained firmly in place. He was most definitely not for moving. The distressed father relented and began to gradually expose and divulge some rather interesting information. Murray fully recognised that he would be working with a decade of slightly hazy and possibly a very biased recollection of events. But he had a common bond with this man. Robert Latchford, and for that matter Joseph Hanlon just didn't know it yet!

"They said it was an accident Inspector." His voice began to increase in volume and pace as he added, "Yet the driver never stopped, never came forward later and was never ever traced."

Murray found that most surprising. He continued to listen intently as Latchfords disillusioned sombre tone returned.

"After a week they were onto other cases. They told me they were swamped under and not to worry, that they would keep me updated."

"But why murder may I ask? From an accident, even from an unresolved hit and run to jump up to murder, that is an almighty leap. What made you think that? How come?"

"The liaison officer is on her way sir," Hanlon interrupted. "It's Alexandra Cloy," he said, as he looked across at the sad figure in front of his Inspector. "You'll be in good hands there Mr Latchford. WPC Cloy is extremely capable and experienced." He then added,

"She was asked to pass on one extra piece of information."

Now distracted from his revelations. "Which was?" Robert Latchford asked keenly.

Before responding, DC Hanlon glanced at Murray. His superior respectfully bowed his head and a number 54 was issued (share the news).

"Cindy had a…"

"Cindy-Ann," her father corrected him.

"Apologies sir," Hanlon offered. "Cindy-Ann seemingly had a cufflink in her hand. Red lined border, with the initials ME on it. Any idea what they might stand for?"

Her father dismissively shook his head.

Hanlon cautiously encouraged, "MElanie; MExico; ME and YOU? Member of somewhere? Initials of a teacher, a friend? Any M.E's in your contact book? Ring any bells whatsoever Mr Latchford?"

Murray watched her dad hesitate slightly, before offering up a less than convincing second shake of his head.

Rising to his feet, Murray felt the need to reconfirm, "Are you sure?" he repeated.

"Quite sure, thank you Inspector," came the curt response.

The doorbell rang and on answering, DC Hanlon invited the Liaison Officer to join them in the sitting room. As Latchford was delicately informed of the nature and circumstances surrounding his poor daughter's untimely death, he remained calm and composed. Shortly thereafter he lifted a framed picture from a nearby cabinet. The dated image was from several years back. It showed a loving parent and child celebrating life at an upmarket social event. They were surrounded by a host of presumably wealthy business folk. Robert Latchford looked dapper in an expensive tuxedo and black bow tie, whilst an eight or nine year old Cindy-Ann held firmly and excitedly onto his arm.

With frizzy, curly hair she was dressed elegantly in a miniature, sky blue, ball gown. The grieving father continued to stare forlornly at this picture of his innocent daughter for several minutes. Then, he proceeded to wipe occasionally at the glass frame as infrequent teardrops fell from his reddened cheeks. As teacher and student made their way to exit the premises, Robert Latchford called out to Joe Hanlon.

"Constable."

At which both men turned to hear.

"I don't know any Ian Spence or a Mr Lattimer. But, Tardelli you said. Carlo Tardelli. I do know that name."

After a further twenty-five minutes of chat, the two officers exchanged places with WPC Cloy and finally said their farewells.

Chapter Nine

"You fill up my senses, like a night in the forest. Like the mountains in springtime, like a walk in the rain. Like a storm in the desert, like a sleepy blue ocean. You fill up my senses, come fill me again." (Annie's Song)

- John Denver

Overhead the heavens looked as if snooker champion Ronnie O'Sullivan had just cued off and left behind all the reds dismissed wildly across the table. As he walked tentatively across the gravel driveway and under that illuminated scarlet sky, DI Murray whistled a little known Robert Burns song entitled Leezie Lindsay. To this day it remained a mystery to him that for some strange, illogical reason, that when a prolonged silence became too much to bear, he more often than not, found himself humming or singing that particular tune! Then, as he gave three distinct knocks upon the door, his mental jukebox instantly dropped a completely different set of lyrics onto his internal turntable. Up flashed, *'Another Saturday night and I ain't got nobody, I have some money 'cause I just got paid. How I wish I had someone to talk to.......... I'm in an awful way.'*

The door opened. Murray had certainly seen the homeowner much worse earlier in the day. As the policeman looked over the man's right shoulder he witnessed WPC Cloy exit from the kitchen doorway, with what he presumed was yet another freshly brewed pot of tea or coffee. Latchford opened the door more fully, stood back and pointed his left arm along the corridor. "You know the way Inspector," he offered tiredly.

He then added curiously, "Are you here to check up on your colleague?"

Murray and Cloy shared a look. Hers said, 'are you?' His said, 'definitely not!'

A brief abridged version of the Sam Cooke lyrics played once again in his mind- *'I ain't got nobody/I wish I had someone to talk to/I'm in an awful way.'*

"Actually I came to chat further with yourself sir."

Cloy looked intrigued. Latchford nonplussed.

"Why?" He dismissively threw across the hallway to Murray. "What's the point? My daughter, my wife, my business - Gone, gone and as good as," he declared. The combined emotions of loss, hurt, bitterness and anger had joined forces for those few seconds. He had once again become upset and agitated. Murray could see WPC Cloy thinking to herself, 'all my previous good work has just gone right out the window. Thank you very much sir!' She went to comfort him and start all over again.

Murray though, was having none of it. Was this man hurting? - absolutely! Mourning for his teenage daughter? - without a doubt! Had a long standing resentment toward the police? - Apparently so. And yet, he knew nothing about Cindy-Ann's death or the demise of his wife? - No chance! That's a non starter and it stops now the Inspector thought to himself. He knew he wanted to be firm, direct and challenging. Yet, fully appreciated the need for understanding, coupled with soothing words and empathy. Murray felt like a rampant rhinoceros about to embark on a relaxing spa weekend!

He instantly held out his left arm. Blocking any attempt by WPC Cloy to get closer to him. The DI then delicately placed his other hand on the grieving father's shoulder. Murray was no psychic, but at that moment, just for a second or two, he swore he could feel Robert

Latchfords pain and heartache surge through his body. There was a firm connection. The hairs on the back of Murray's neck bristled and stood upright to attention.

The Inspector simply asserted, "Let's talk."

The family liaison officer got it. She gathered up a collection of the used cups and plates from the sitting room.

"I'll just make a start on these Mr Latchford and that'll let you get a chance to speak to the DI in peace."

Murray began. "We were interrupted earlier today, and I know at the beginning you were very reluctant. It can't be easy. So I'm here to reassure you. I genuinely want to help."

"I don't understand Inspector. I've already asked you why. Why would you..."

"It's simple sir," Murray interrupted. "And as we chat, I think many things will become clearer and you'll understand more fully. Perhaps with more clarity than you could have ever thought possible. For now though, you'll just have to trust me."

The mourning father once again stared intensely at Murray. He looked him up and down from head to toe. He tried to figure him out, was puzzled and still a little wary. Certainly Steven Murray's 'average Joe' appearance gave nothing away.

"What do you have to lose sir? It's late on a Saturday evening and I'm here after all."

This time it was Robert Latchfords turn to nod, and DI Murray then had the privilege of taking part in his own game. A number 63 the Inspector reckoned. The kind of facial gesture that said - take a seat and let me start over!

Just before Cindy-Ann's father started speaking, Murray in quieter tones reminded him, "I need honesty though Mr Latchford. None of your half truths, unsure, or little white lies. It has to be the total truth, or

I walk away and you'll never uncover the full facts behind the death of your wife."

Again, a positive nod was forthcoming.

"I need to hear all about your work as a horologist," Murray encouraged. "The role your wife played in your life. Why you feel she was murdered and also I would like a copy of that portrait that interested you so much earlier today when we spoke about your daughter." Before he could continue, Latchford began immediately to interrupt.

"Annie was at University with Cyrille Anderson Inspector. I think they dated briefly. But she quickly sussed out the kind of man he truly was."

"By that you mean?"

"Have you met him Inspector?"

"Not had the pleasure yet sir."

"The pleasure?" Latchford lightly quizzed. "Obviously not. Otherwise you would not be using that word in the same sentence as him," he continued to declare.

Murray remained silent, but gently swayed his head from side to side - indicating he would like to hear specifics.

"How about, cocky, arrogant, brash. A pompous, puffed up, self-centred money grabbing pig for starters." his host passionately reeled off.

"Don't you hold back sir. Just say what you feel," he smiled at Robert Latchford. Murray then took a quick note of those attributes for future reference.

The businessman tried to calm down. He began pacing the room, rubbing his hands and cracking his knuckles. Murray was just secretly relieved that WPC Cloy was elsewhere and unable to observe her Inspector's technique for re-assuring and stabilising Robert Latchford.

"He really gets under my skin and upsets me Inspector. Every time I mention him, I get worked up and lose the plot."

No kidding, Murray thought to himself. By now, the

two men had made their way through into the small study come library. It was just beyond the kitchen. Murray initially thought it would help settle Latchford. There was literally no space to pace! The DI was also instantly blown away by the amount of books on the walls. He believed greatly in the old adage that 'readers were leaders.' At the very least, he reckoned they were clever individuals, pursuers of knowledge and that they would always have fairly active minds. These people would be inquisitive, desirous to know more and fully understand the how's and why's of many subjects. Business books, autobiographies and sporting memoirs lined the shelves. The Detective Inspector was quietly impressed, but chose to make no comment. This man was no fool and this astute police officer was about to extend him the time and respect he had been due, ten years previous. Tonight, Detective Inspector Steven Murray wanted to hear every last detail about Robert Latchford's long term sweetheart... Annie Ross Fairbrother.

After three hours, a much better informed Steven Murray returned home and called DC Joseph Hanlon.

"I don't know where to begin Joe. I believe him."

"Latchford?"

"Yes. Something was certainly amiss ten years ago. No real investigation, no follow up and the case closed relatively quickly. Certainly according to Latchford's version of events."

"We have no real reason to disbelieve him sir," 'Sherlock' stated. Then added, "Or do we?"

"I don't think so Joe. His intriguing suspicions appear to have validity, on the surface at least."

Fully curious now, DC Hanlon added, "Go on."

"Well, I suppose they were more Annie's misgivings really. She had been doing some digging of her own. She had found something in his books. She crazily suspected Cyrille Anderson of money laundering, and shared this with her husband.

"Money laundering?" Hanlon exclaimed, with more than a touch of surprise.

"Absolutely. She had been able to track various locations that had held conferences and conventions. Sometimes in the run up, or close afterward, large deposits would go through the books for consulting fees or unusual insurance cover. One off special clearance payments which made her curious. So that's just it Joe. I do believe him. But I'm also pretty certain sadly, that he is still holding something back."

"Something that may incriminate his dead wife. Fear of ruining her reputation?"

"Possibly. But as you said earlier, she's already dead. It was ten years ago for Pete's sake. What can you be afraid of after that length of time?"

Hanlon paused on the other end of the line. "Maybe that is just it sir. He has had ten years. A full decade. A prolonged period of life - Something his dear wife did not have, especially if she was onto something or someone!"

"He says he has Annie's files backed up and further proof that he just can't share right now."

"Unable? Unwilling? Can't substantiate?" Hanlon queried.

"Exactly Joe. Who knows. But I think you may be onto something also. The fact that he is still alive, yet exceptionally cautious in approaching things." Murray was about to finish the conversation when he remembered one last point. "Oh, and the car," Murray remarked.

"Yes, what about it sir?"

"I'm sure this will be in the case files, but Latchford did get a partial registration."

"And we were never able to trace it?"

"Exactly. Strange though, because he had a rough idea of the make and four or five letters and numbers."

"I was just out of school sir, but even I know that nine, ten, eleven years ago, the computer would have thrown up some rough matches or potential vehicles to look at and review. There was no report of any partial sighting or registration in any of the documentation I read sir."

"It would seem then, that those details were never entered Joe. And the deceased's husband was simply informed that it was not enough to go on."

"And that was passed on by the Sergeant with the E. Is that what we are saying happened sir?"

"We need to tread carefully here 'Sherlock.' According to Robert Latchford, that is precisely what went down. The investigating Sergeant told him not to build his hopes up. In turn they never found the car and no one was ever charged or held responsible for her death. He was told the case would remain open in case of any developments or future evidence coming to light."

"Wow. No wonder he was a little reticent to speak freely with us. And how come you managed to get him to open up to you anyway?"

Deliberately ignoring the last part, Inspector Murray responded sincerely with "I think that I may have moved a little closer in gaining his trust, but not fully, and certainly, not quickly enough."

Slowly and apprehensively Joseph Hanlon closed the conversation with a statement rather than a question. "You think it is linked to the death of his daughter!"

Chapter Ten

"You're the voice, try and understand it, make a noise and make it clear. We're not gonna sit in silence, we're not gonna live with fear."

- John Farnham

It was Sunday lunchtime. A row of assorted cars, including an old Fiat Punto with a broken wing mirror and a gleaming metallic black Land Rover Evoque, sat parked as DI Murray pulled up outside the Kirkliston home of his friend and current long term gardening leave recipient - Detective Sergeant Robert 'Ally' Coulter.

The tiny, brick red Punto had L plates on it. That maybe explained the damaged mirror. An older man and younger girl had just made their way inside. A typical father and daughter about to embark on their regular Sunday afternoon driving lesson Murray guessed. Grey clouds of cigarette smoke could now be seen gently wafting out from the driver's side of the Land Rover. His blacked out window had been lowered with precision planning, enabling each delicate instalment to form a perfect circular pillow. A party trick that quickly ascended upwards to make its own brief, personal statement to the world.

At that moment, a host of various cases that they'd worked on together throughout the years, literally ran through Murray's mind in five seconds flat. None more so than their last. For Ally Coulter, it was the one that tipped him over the edge, that broke the camel's back. That one pivotal case too many. Immediately after the gruesome murder of his partner, Detective Constable Tasmin Taylor, it seemed almost inevitable that he would decide to take his pension and retire gracefully. The killer of 'Taz' Taylor they reckoned, had managed to flee the country and was on the run. Guilt had taken over Coulter and he was struggling to shake it off. Steven Murray, as always with his own demons close at hand, tried his best to keep their long term friendship active and alive. Today, a spot of lunch and a catch up chat, seemed in order and long overdue.

Ally appeared slimmer than ever. With optimism in every step, he strode confidently down his slabbed path to join Steven Murray in his recently acquired, new, yet second-hand Volvo S40. His colleague had noticeably lost, a few not inconsiderable pounds. Casual brown brogues accompanied his light tan chinos and yellow short sleeved polo shirt. Coulter would not have looked out of place on the opening tee at one of those prestigious golf courses near Gullane. The very place Murray had the misfortune to have visited only 24 hours earlier. As Ally approached the vehicle he nonchalantly threw his waterproof over his right shoulder. He had this catwalk malarkey off to a fine tee Murray smiled thoughtfully, not even aware of the dreadful pun.

"Okay Steven?" Ally asked, with regard to his well being.

"Doing fine Ally thanks. Keeping out of mischief for a wee while at least. What about yourself?"

"Lost a few pounds," he smiled, patting his impressive midriff. "Probably eating healthier than I have in the last twenty years," he went on.

"You're certainly looking good, no doubt about that," Murray enthused.

With the official pleasantries out of the way, Ally Coulter looked across at his driver and also asked after Tom 'The T'inker' Patterson.

"How is the Doc doing this weather?"

Murray nodded. He understood Coulter's genuine concern and questions. They as a trio had worked alongside each other for a good number of years. They may well have been only colleagues to outsiders. But they were not unlike The Three Musketeers - 'One for All and All for One.' In the last six months Murray reckoned they had probably also found their ideal D'Artagnan. He had appeared in the guise of one ... Detective Constable Joseph Hanlon.

Throughout the years Patterson, Murray and Coulter, like Alexandre Dumas' three heroes, had all been involved frequently in various injustices, abuse and criminal adventures.

Murray would and could accurately be likened to Athos. A noble and handsome man, although extremely secretive. His mind was often clouded by memories of his mysterious past. One who is continually seeking solace, has become a father figure and very protective of young D'Artagnan, in this case Joe Hanlon.

Coulter was Aramis. No longer the young, arrogant and ambitious eligible bachelor. Though he would still enjoy the good company and companionship of the fairer sex.

Finally, 'Doc' Patterson would be Porthos. Honest and slightly gullible. He was extremely dedicated and loyal to both his work and his friends. A bit of a dandy, with a fondness for fashionable clothes and a homeric strength of body and character.

With all these Royal Guards and Musketeers causing havoc amidst Murray's thoughts, he heard 'Ally' Coulter ask again. "The 'Doc' Steven, what's he up to?"

"Sorry Ally, I was just thinking about some of the numerous fascinating dangers and hazards we'd been through together."

"One for All and All for One," Ally announced, raising his arm with a sword like gesture.

"That's amazing, that is just what I was ..."

"Thinking about," Coulter laughed heartily as he interrupted. "You said it out loud a few seconds ago."

Letting Ally Coulter settle back down, Murray told him that Patterson was fine.

"We don't see much of each other socially these days. He has his grandkids keeping him busy a lot," Steven Murray offered. "If only I'd extend an invitation now and again, like I did with you today. If only..."

"Don't start with the 'if only' stuff Steve. We can't turn back time. What's done is done..." Robert Coulter then seemed to stop mid sentence.

Murray concentrated on driving, although he was well aware of what had just occurred. His Detective Sergeant on a deserved sabbatical, had just heard Murray's wise counsel to him these past few difficult months, literally verbatim, exude from his very own lips. Both men knew and remained silent. The stench of guilt wafted through the air, as if distributed by the small scented tree hanging from the Inspector's rear view mirror.

Only a few short days ago, DI Murray had been beguiled again by those dark solitary hours of depression. Whilst all around him, missing teenagers and adults were dying. Couple that with his travelling companion today, Robert 'Ally' Coulter. An experienced Detective Sergeant, who had earlier in the year found himself hanging helpless, upside down from a butchers hook. Only minutes later to witness his young talented colleague, who was bound in a similar position, mercilessly and without warning - have her throat cut from ear to ear. They sat in silence for the remaining fifteen minutes of their journey.

Originally sited within a steep sided glen on a convenient fording point on the Water of Leith, and expanding from there, Colinton and its history dated back to before the 11th century. When his grandfather was the village's Parish Minister, author Robert Louis

Stevenson spent his childhood summers at his manse. Today, as Murray found a parking spot just off the main road, Colinton is a suburb of Edinburgh. It's original heart is still referred to as Colinton Village. With a range of small speciality shops, many of the original buildings remained intact.

Both men made their way the short distance to what would normally be known as a cafe, but in these parts, it was an 'intimate bistro' in the nearby Bridge Road. The Larynx had proved an extremely popular location in recent times. Business was brisk and it had built a solid reputation in the brief six months it had been open. It was owned by two partners, both in the personal and business sense. Murray, had had the premises recommended to him and only knew that the proprietors were called Andy and Russ, but that was it. No idea of their surnames, nicknames or stage names for that matter. They had seemingly been professional singers. Hence their joint affinity with The Larynx! Every wall was adorned with famous divas, crooners and singing sensations from throughout the years. You had Barbra Streisand, Sinatra and Nat King Cole on one wall. Then on the opposite, spaced equally between the mirrors, were Robbie Williams, Michael Ball and Lady Gaga!

On spotting Springsteen and Van Morrison, "an impressive gathering, truly eclectic," Murray voiced to Ally Coulter. Especially Morrison, who conjured up some personal, poignant memories for the DI.

"Aye, let's hope the menu has as much variety!" Coulter responded.

The gents were impressed and ordered accordingly. Murray had an appealing fish dish: The 'Shirley Bassey.' With Coulter going for a more traditional Michael 'Buble & Squeak.' Corny, but charming, they agreed. They soon got chatting, kept the conversation upbeat and steered clear from talking shop as best they could. They found themselves sitting in a small corner booth out of the midday sunlight and slightly removed from the main hub of patrons. It worked well for them. It was marginally quieter and secluded, allowing them the privacy they required. The Larynx certainly had a strong vibe to it. Modern, yet with a distinguished, classy feel. Both Andy and Russ would mingle and converse with their clientele. Continually gaining feedback and building strong customer loyalty. Andy, the taller of the two men, had dark shoulder length hair and distinct features, including a noticeable two inch scar running under his left eye.

He would regularly encourage, "Like us on Facebook!" Russ in the interim, would burst into occasional song. He had a kind of John Barrowman look about him. Shorter in stature, though you would guess he was a bit of a showman. Energy, vigor and verve just seemed to ooze from his persona. During Murray and Coulters forty-five minute tenure, he had treated them to 'The Impossible Dream,' 'Swinging on a Star' and the almost obligatory 'I Am What I Am.' Talk about an eclectic mix Murray thought.

The police colleagues enjoyed a terrific time together. Reminiscing, planning for the future, laughter and great food. The serving staff had been excellent. Meals delivered within a good time frame, used dishes cleared efficiently. All had been pleasant and well mannered. They had enjoyed it so much, that they even discussed the possibility that they may even go straight home now and....... like it on Facebook!

"What is Facebook?" Ally Coulter asked his pal. They both laughed.

Their remaining two dessert plates were being carefully lifted from the table, when the low, hushed voice from behind them was first heard.

"What's the time Mr Wolf?"

Their conversation halted. Coulter immediately went white. Murray turned sharply in his chair, straining to face their questioner. Coulter swallowed, but could not move.

"You!" Murray said in a subdued, stuttered whisper. Then deciding that was much too low, upped the volume considerably.

"You. How's it possible? What do you..." Several customers looked over, others deliberately averted their gaze. Robert 'Ally' Coulter focused slowly on the individual and shook his head. Disgust, dismay and abject dejection were paramount across his face. Murray tried to get to his feet, but was gently reminded by another brooding figure, whose giant, shovel like hands were now on the Inspector's shoulders, that his best course of action would be to remain seated. The pony tail had long gone. His skin was bronzed and tanned. He'd obviously hired a new tailor, as he was impeccably attired and well groomed. But here, in The Larynx of all places, there was simply no mistaking the voice, the inflection, the deep intonation and delivery... of one James Baxter Reid. 'Bunny' to his nearest and dearest. Wanted for questioning with regard to the murder of numerous individuals only a few short months ago, including Ally Coulter's partner, Detective Constable Taz Taylor. And here he was today, bold as brass and about to hold court.

"No need for alarm, gents," 'Bunny' tried to reassure them, with his trademark husky rasp. "Everything is all above board. Although I always knew there was something dodgy about young Ziola."

Young Ziola, Murray figured was Mark 'Markie' Ziola. Reid's right hand man when he was running Dixon's empire of escort girls. Since the demise of Kenny Dixon and the 'life' sentence expected for his wife Sheila, Edinburgh had been up for grabs. Numerous outsiders had attempted to break-in, various gangs vying for territories and trade. With the Reidmeister back in the fray this could get real interesting. But how come he is even out and about? That was the question both Murray and Ally Coulter currently pondered. A small blue object was swiftly launched from 'Bunny' Reid's hand. He tossed it across the table in the direction of the junior officer. Coulter, still fearful, instinctively extended his arm and trapped it as if swatting a fly under the palm of his right hand.

"You might want to check it out Ally, I owe you that at least."

"What do you mean you owe him?" Murray asked sharply, regaining his composure.

"Go on, pick it up," Reid encouraged. His harsh guttural utterances seemed softer, lighter, more subtle in tone. Indicating possibly that he had mellowed and that within his future veiled threats, he would now only have your legs broken, as opposed to your neck! Ally Coulter drew his hand back cautiously and simply looked at the blue disc. It was no bigger than a fifty pence coin. Again 'Bunny' Reid encouraged him to examine it more closely. His voice more assertive than before, his patience wearing thin.

"You'll want to appraise it in more detail Ally. Trust me, pick it up."

Coulter flashed back to only a few months previous. This man, this ruthless individual, had held both officers captive. Beaten him in particular, then had them both hung upside down before holding a knife to their throats. He then threatened to end HIM right there and then, before callously taking the life of his partner, the lovely Tasmin Taylor. Be under no illusions, Coulter hated this man. His mind was presently filled with rage, fury, disdain and anger. However one emotion outweighed all of those............ pure fear. Having witnessed this man operate up close once before, the aging Robert 'Ally' Coulter was running scared - although currently immobilised! He was fearful, frozen and terrified. Steven Murray recognised from Ally's body language his uneasiness.

"Have a look Ally," Murray quietly stated. "Let's find out why Mr Reid felt so compelled to track us down and before he takes it away again."

"No, that won't happen Inspector. I realised I was wrong several months back. I thought Ally here, had set me up to take the fall," Reid paused and shook his head. "Turns out that with all that transpired he and his partner, such a lovely filly, shame she had to be put down, were telling the truth. It was Sheila Dixon, that nasty piece of work. She was the one that had been pulling the strings and manipulating everything and everybody. I was blindsided gents and I apologise. I should have seen it coming. So, I owe you one Ally, and I think this may be helpful to your good buddy here," he said raising his eyebrows in DI Murray's direction.

Murray frowned cautiously. He did not believe a word that the so called 'good samaritan' had just uttered. There is something else in play here he thought to himself. How did he track us down? He remained silent and watched events unfold. Whilst 'Bunny' Reid had been speaking, Ally Coulter had begun slowly and then more deliberately to examine the blue disc. It was a casino chip, which had a five pound value marked upon it. Although mainly blue, it had delicate white markings around its edge and was finished with a three letter logo. The recently retired Detective Sergeant, although being a betting man and having previously met up, accidentally, it must be said, with Reid's cronies one year in Ireland at Leopardstown race track, couldn't quite get the connection. He was aware through his quiz team knowledge that in 19th-century America there was enough of a tradition of using blue chips for higher values that, "blue chip" in noun and adjective senses signalled high-value chips and high-value property. Murray on the other hand, recognised it straight away and was already planning his overdue invitation to 'Doc' Patterson.

"Maybe not your thing Inspector?" Reid croaked.

Coulter and Murray exchanged knowing glances.

"Sometimes visiting a casino, can have life and death consequences," Reid continued.

Murray's fists tightened. A surge of aggression intensified and was beginning to gather pace through his tense body. Just then, the large, workmanlike hand of his Sergeant was swiftly and reassuredly placed on top of his thigh. He may have been unable to speak, but was still capable of communicating equally effectively in other ways. The gesture took place under the table and out of sight of their visitors. The touch between friends simply stated: *Relax, remain focused and take a breath. Ignore all of his comments and don't let him get to you.* Murray seemed able to resist for a few seconds longer and although desperately keen still to become physically involved, the overwhelming impulse to fight back began to diminish. His body relaxed and Reid's burly minder eventually eased his grip on his shoulders. The heavily muscled assistant then lightly brushed the collar of Murray's shirt to signal 'things are all good now.' The cracked, heavy gravel voice of their uninvited guest offered one more scrap of assistance.

"Those two constables of yours, Hayes and Curry," he said.

"What about them?" Their Inspector asked, worried at where this may lead.

In yet another slow considered manner. 'Bunny' Reid offered. "Have your two most successful outlaws in the history of the West take a closer look at those robberies. All I'll say is, it's not very original. Especially if Blake's Auction House is involved. Not very original at all."

He continued his lazy drawl with, "Bit disappointed in you DI Murray. I thought you were better than that. I reckon you slipped up there."

Murray looked across at Coulter with a deep concern on his face. What had they missed? Something had went unnoticed. 'Bunny' Reid was most definitely taunting him. He was in his element, he was playing mind games. The question was though, did he really know anything of worth? Or was it just to torment and ridicule his adversary further and throw him off his game altogether? He felt those seven arrogant words burn deep into his soul, as he replayed them once more in his mind. *'I thought you were better than that!'*

Ally was just about beginning to breathe calmly again. Both men turned to fully focus their attention on their uninvited guest. Nothing. Reid was gone. The well used bell above the door offered a familiar 'tring' on closing. Steven Murray scurried to the doorway. Only able to witness the black Land Rover Evoque race off through the leafy streets of Colinton. A two minute drive would take them onto the Edinburgh City Bypass and then limitless possibilities as to a final destination.

"The car?" Ally went to question.

"Yes, I know," his friend said, seemingly reluctant to share something, before finally offering up, "It was the same one that was parked immediately outside your place when I arrived earlier!"

"They were watching my house?" 'Ally' grimaced as he asked the question.

Whilst nodding, Murray looked forlornly out onto the empty street and cagily considered aloud -

"And knew in advance, that I was coming!"

Chapter Eleven

"It's a carnival, it's a big parade, it's unethical in the modern day. Come and look around inside Aladdin's Cave, fill your bags with gold and wash your sins away."

- The Outfield

The rather cheap, unimpressive steel padlock had broken easily with the heavy-duty bolt cutters. The roller shutter on the van then gave a familiar rat-a-tat-tat, as it was abruptly opened. All they lacked was the presence of a lovely magician's assistant. An attractive female standing semi-clad with her gloved hands extended, proudly announcing to the waiting audience…………….... "Ta-Da!"

Hayes and Curry stood cautiously to the periphery, scared to look inside. They wanted and needed desperately to get the right result here. But it was an anonymous tip-off and they were cautious and wary. With that said, the van was parked in the exact location given. A hearty congratulatory slap on the back then signalled to Curry it was all good to go, things were fine and the stolen haul from seven days ago was recovered.

"That's the kind of police work I could get used to," 'Hanna' Hayes said excitedly.

"There is probably over half a million pounds worth of computers, furniture and artwork in there Hayes," 'Drew' Curry concluded.

DC Susan Hayes gave a resigned shrug. "Yea, but we got lucky 'Drew'." Just then her mobile rang. She awkwardly slipped it from her pocket, looked at the caller ID and took a deep breath. "Hi boss… the break-ins... four so far... we've actually just... what... at Kirkliston... okay... Kerr and Rasul as well... sure... 60 minutes... see you then... bye."

Andrew Curry looked at her questioningly. "Murray?" he gestured pointing at her phone. "On a Sunday?" he then asked, surprised.

"I had text him earlier. So he knew we'd had a tip-off and were working. But he's called in 'Sandy' and 'Mac' as well. Sounds important. He wants to see us all in an hour back at the station."

Sandra Kerr and her husband Richard had been out at a local garden centre with their four month old twins. When Murray called to ask her to come in, she immediately agreed. Although she did have one more important call to make before hurrying back to the station, she told him.

Machur Rasul had surprisingly, also been in Edinburgh at the time. He too promised to be there within the hour. The recently arrived officer was still making the daily commute each day between Glasgow and Edinburgh. Travelling through on the M8 motorway at speeds that could only be considered hazardous and dangerous to his health. Boy racers eat your heart out, occasionally he would reach the dizzy heights of twenty five miles per hour! The main thoroughfare between Scotland's two major cities, was no more than an outdated, overused, bottlenecked dual carriageway.

The last squad member contacted was his Rodney Trotter lookalike. Joseph 'Sherlock' Hanlon was still working through his own grieving process. Having buried his young wife Lauren to cancer, back in the early part of January. For Hanlon, the answer was quite literally was to work through it. Often putting in regular fourteen and fifteen hour days. Steven Murray had been there for him throughout though. Although, no more than young Joseph Hanlon had been for him, on at least a couple of more recent occasions. He was trying to let 'Sherlock' come to terms with life and his current circumstances one day at a time. It was the only way Murray knew how to deal with his own life. Taking each hour of every twenty four, and adjusting accordingly.

In the intervening time he had left before meeting with them all collectively at 4.00pm on that Sunday afternoon, Murray had got up to speed with the whole 'Bunny' Reid situation. Nearing the conclusion of his Sabbath day phone call with a higher power, in this case his Chief Inspector, Murray raged.

"You know that is complete tosh, sir! Utter garbage. Lies, lies, and more lies from start to finish."

"I do know that Inspector," Keith Brown said calmly, pulling at the cuffs of his shirt and well used to Murray's sporadic rants and outbursts. On this occasion though, he seemingly wholeheartedly agreed with his colleague. "The Procurators Fiscal have agreed it with both parties Steve. They are delighted that he will plead guilty. They in turn will close the outstanding murders and get their man."

"The wrong man!," Murray vented, slamming his fist furiously against the car's control panel. He instantly cut off his telephone conversation, and immediately got Radio Two and The Eurythmics blasting out *I Need a Man.'* How ironic was that? Steven Murray thought, letting go of a large frustrated sigh.

"Difference is, I want the right man," he quietly muttered to himself.

He was now busy making his way back toward the City Centre to update the troops on the day's developments. With Coulter back at his home, Murray wondered how safe he would feel there. He had only recently been coming to terms with his retirement, his partner's death and certainly no justice having been done. He had also still been in the car when Chief Inspector Brown had went into detail about Reid's reappearance and the legal action that was about to take place. He never spoke as he left the car. We all deal with these things differently Murray guessed. But he was not naturally reassured by Ally Coulter's unerring silence.

DS 'Sandy' Kerr was the last to arrive at just after ten past four. Murray expressed gratitude to each of them for making the effort to come together on a Sunday afternoon and at such short notice. Heads nodded and shrugged. Each of them knew it must be significant. DI Murray quietly closed over the briefing room door, cleared his throat and began.

"I'll try my best to be brief." He then paused momentarily to gather up his thoughts.

"I met earlier today with Sergeant Coulter for lunch. Just a couple of hours ago in fact. The others exchanged glances. Facial expressions were offered, sensitive questions ran through minds. Murray could instantly see the concerned looks.

"He's fine everyone. Ally is fine," he reassured the gathered group. Although he now began to question in his own mind. Was he really fine? Physically his well being appeared in good shape. Mentally however, that was a very different question. He had uttered nothing when he waved goodbye to Steven Murray. Noticeably, no words at all were exchanged after he had heard the Chief Inspectors take on the 'Bunny' Reid debacle.

"Sir," Hanlon chirped up, to nudge him from his reflective thoughts.

"Sorry," he shrugged, regaining his composure. He then carefully and deliberately looked at each member of the team. Slowly, he scanned around the room. Making eye contact with individuals, getting their full attention, ensuring that they would be ready for his opening gambit. His first five words were clear, succinct and to the point.

"James Baxter Reid is back."

Those chilling words were met with audible gasps of shock, disgusted murmurings, a wide range of expletives and by some..... complete silence! Slowly at first, then words and questions began to come thick and fast to the surface. With the initial bombshell delivered, the survivors were coming up rapidly for air.

"How can that be?"

"We've got him now though, right?"

"He's under arrest?"

"Sir, sir, who got him?"

"Where is he?"

"What prison is he in?"

The body language became animated. They were shouting over one another. Excited at his capture, thinking justice would be done. Two or three individuals hugged. Clenched fists pumped the air and open palms banged in celebratory fashion on various desks. A lone figure at the back of the bustling room, stood noticeably still and unfazed. His eyes met those of his Inspector. He knew, in that instant, in that single moment he knew. Without screaming for attention, but not content to stand any longer unnoticed, he raised his voice above the combined noise of the others and stated:

"He's not in police custody. Nor is he under arrest. I suspect he is not even going to be charged. Is he sir?"

Joe Hanlon had not been christened with the nickname 'Sherlock' by chance. He picked up on nuances, he gathered clues and although still an 'apprentice' as a detective, he was extremely perceptive and learned quickly. His sound bites had silenced the room. He was given disbelieving shrugs and looks from the others initially. Then, one by one as they quickly turned back to face Murray, they could see that there may well be substance to Hanlon's words. That they could in fact, and awful as it may seem, be true. Murray, warily and reluctantly nodded his head.

"Tomorrow morning the papers are going to be running the story on how Mark Ziola had carried out the stomach churning, atrocious murders last New Year. How our Markie boy supposedly set up and incriminated his criminal associate James Reid to take the fall."

Hands once again, shot up into the air, this time in disbelieve. Those not upright, were being frantically run through hair and tugged incessantly.

"The gun that had recently been recovered in the shooting, was conveniently and unsurprisingly registered to Ziola." Murray then continued. "His fingerprints were also all over the premises of the slaughtered family."

"Of course they were. He worked with their dad. We knew he visited the house frequently," Sandra Kerr vocalised loudly and with anger.

"I know," Murray agreed sympathetically. Recognising he was now playing the part of DCI Brown. One of diplomatic peacemaker and envoy.

"Sir. Inspector," began the quietly spoken Susan Hayes. "What about Taz? Sergeant Coulter was there. He witnessed her be murdered right in front of him by that sick..."

"Ziola was also there Susan," Murray interjected. "Our Sergeant was turning and spinning around frequently on the bottom of a meat hook. The defence could give him a hard time on that alone even, but they won't have to."

"Sir! Sir!" Several voices boomed out and exclaimed in unison.

Murray decisively held up both hands. "The bottom line everyone....... is that Mark Ziola has confessed. He has admitted to shooting the accountant Melanie Rose. Killing his two fellow rogue conspirators Forrester and Allan. And sadly also, for us, he has confessed to the cold-blooded murder of our friend and colleague Tasmin Taylor."

Heads shook in disbelief. Disgust displayed prominently on every single countenance.

"With 'Bunny' Reid busy supplying other information regarding Dixon's operation," Murray went on. "His deal with Crown Office I would imagine will enable him to walk free immediately after any evidence is given."

The room was sombre. Any further thoughts or opinions offered were in careful, hushed tones. From tribal celebrations and group hugs only five minutes previous. The opposing team was now clearly on the offensive and would emerge victorious. Having just scored deep, deep into stoppage time. The full time whistle had sounded. An odd tear was shed, and consolatory embraces were offered as people began to depart from the pitch and head off. As they began to slowly exit, Murray quietly asked Hayes and Curry to remain behind.

"Myself?" Joe Hanlon enquired.

Murray offered him one of his 'Heinz' winks, as Hanlon called them. Mainly because Joe reckoned he easily had about 57 different varieties of nod, head shake or eye gesture. This one, was a number 23 Hanlon believed. It said in an unspoken manner, 'by all means!'

"Not an original idea." DC Andrew Curry double checked. "That's what he said?"

"Pretty much," Murray reaffirmed.

"Especially if Blake's Auction House was involved," Hanlon added.

The eyes of Police Scotland's two finest 'outlaws' met quickly, with Susan Hayes slowly repeating the words of Joe Hanlon.

"Blake's... Auction... House."

"Relevant?" asked her DI.

"It could very well be sir," she replied. "I remember seeing it on a couple of reports. A few of the stolen items had been purchased from there I think."

"Which was no real surprise," 'Kid' Curry interjected. "Because most of the items taken were high value. Clocks, paintings, watches and the like."

"He's right sir," 'Hanna' Hayes added. "These break-ins were all in and around Morningside, not Wester Hailes or Granton. More Armani than Adidas," she shrugged.

"Bit of a generalised stereotype there DC Hayes," Murray smiled. "But I get the idea. Let's get busy," he continued. "First thing tomorrow revisit those that got burgled. Double check the stolen items, scrutinise and question the householders a little bit more fully. Careful not to make them feel like they are being accused of anything."

"Sir!" the outlaws exclaimed in unison.

"I know, I know, I'm asking a lot," Steven Murray recognised. "But let me tell you, 'Bunny' Reid did not offer this up solely as a *'thank you.'* There's clearly something more at play here. The sooner we are able to see the bigger picture, the better."

Both Detective Constables nodded in joint agreement and acceptance.

"Remember," Murray concluded. "Especially enquire into any items purchased from Blakes. Draw up a list and let me see it tomorrow before you finish. I think I may well have to pay a personal visit to that particular auction house."

The Inspector said his goodbyes and travelled homeward bound. It was a Sunday that had turned out unexpectedly, to be emotionally charged and hectic. His busy schedule had left no room for dog walking. However, Steven Murray had a good idea that his canine *'pal'* would be waiting patiently for his master to return, nonetheless.

What is it in the brain that brings on resentment, anger, the whole 'what is the point?' mentality. The dark clouds that make you continually question - Why carry on? So what! Who'd miss me? And who needs this crazy messed up world we live in? From a fun, happy go lucky attitude - then WHAM, thirty seconds later... Someone's response, their lack of smile or dispirited attitude and surly negative comment may send Murray scurrying for safety. Seeking a place of isolation, refuge and comfort. What does it look like?

In the solitude of his car, cruising along the motorway, blasting out a selection of his favourite iconic sounds he can feel the darkness begin to descend. Often the music can come from obscure, less than commercial influences. However on this occasion it fails to filter and safeguard him from the dangerous and inherent thoughts that continually mount. Alarming contemplations such as - I want to die, I just want to die. Too many innocents. Take me now. Let me look down from above (assuming I don't end up in hell). With gratitude to all those who tried to help me, befriend me, continually offered support and wanted the best for me. I love them for it and thank them. They are so much better than myself. I've lived a life of expectation. One that often, other people chose for me. I tried to be accepted. Wanted to love and to be loved. I had many vices. Some public, some private. Don't we all?

Only one set of footprints on the sand when you felt desperate and lost. Why would your God, whoever he may be, not be there for you at those times? Ah, the foolishness of that we are told, nay reminded - he was there for you. They were his footprints, he was carrying you through those rough, tough periods of your life. Well, don't dare carry me again Murray thought. I feel no happiness in my life and with it, no emotion. Sociopathic? he wondered. He had certainly become cynical, hardened and opinionated, but only in small bursts. He pondered and questioned if he would even recognise happiness and joy ever again? And if so, what he would be capable of doing with such affable character traits!

He finally arrived home twenty minutes later, with no recollection of how he got there. Either cruise control, autopilot, radar or homing pigeon had done the business! He knew he had travelled via motorway, roundabouts, side streets and traffic lights. Had engaged with left turns, give ways, pedestrians and weather. A real mixed bag of manoeuvres and actions had been required. Yet here he was, as if by magic, with absolutely no memory of the journey whatsoever. Life is a lot like that he thought to himself. A series of interesting turns, twists, roadblocks, diversions, dead ends and detours. If we have no idea of our desired destination, we ultimately continue driving aimlessly around and around. And rather gloomily, for the majority of people they inevitably accept where they end up! That was not Inspector Murray's way. Although with a wry smile to himself, he did recognise it very much depended on if he were Dr. Jekyll or the carefree Mr Hyde that particular day!

Steven Murray went directly upstairs and opened the bedroom door. He devotedly, lovingly and emotionally considered the scene in front of him. The large oak mirror and matching bedside cabinets and chest of drawers. The contrasting dark mahogany radiator cabinet with a small, delicate glass vase which sat inch perfect in the middle. There was a collection of 'willow figures' positioned on various shelves. They included such titles as: *Joy, Family and Forget-me-not.'* The burgundy red tartan duvet set with the matching pillowcases was crisp, clean and looked fabulous on the unused king-sized bed. Centrally positioned above which, his eyes now took him to a professionally taken family portrait. It was a large colourful canvas print and it showed five people smiling, laughing and undoubtedly enjoying the company of one another.

Whilst posing, they frolicked about on their old trusty, avocado coloured leather sofa. It captured and epitomised fully, the love and closeness that a family obviously once shared. A gentle, discrete tear ran down Steven Murray's cheek. A warm sadness engulfed his body as he lightly closed the door and made the short journey down the hallway......... to HIS room.

Lying on his side and about to head off to sleep, the casino chip from earlier in the day sat high on the peak of the double pillows opposite. Only one person occupied this house now and his private life remained just that, private. A very small circle of long standing friends knew of his past and that was currently still the way Lothian's Detective Inspector Steven Murray liked it. Goodnight all.

Chapter Twelve

"Speed, bonnie boat, like a bird on a wing, onward the sailor's cry. Carry the lad that's born to be king, over the sea to Skye. Many's the lad fought on that day, well the claymore could wield. When the night came, silently lay... dead on Culloden's field."

- Sir Harold Boulton

A Monday morning appointment had been hastily arranged to visit Blake's Auction House. Mr Simon Taylor the proprietor, would see them at 10.00 am. The business, which had been established in the early nineteen seventies, was situated just off to the right of Hanover Street in Edinburgh's city centre. To find it you would travel northbound from the capital's famous Princes Street. Running parallel and to the east end of it, only George Street separates you from its official address on Thistle Street. Bars, lounges and brasseries all regularly fight for the custom in that sector of town. And there nestled cosily between the best of them, was Blake's Auction House. In reality it was situated above a large, normally crowded drinking establishment called The Jagged Edge. A plaque above the doorway informed you that the pub first opened its doors for business in October 1964. Coincidentally the year of Murray's birth. No doubt taking its name from its definitive location there on Thistle Street, the two officers reckoned.

At most, only a few feet to the right of that popular bar, was an inconspicuous, small double doorway. Possibly easily missed, unless like our two detectives you were specifically looking for it. As you entered through the nondescript entrance, you were immediately met with a rather intimidating flight of stairs. These premises were definitely not disable friendly. Both men paused, stared intently at each other, took one last sharp intake of breath, looked at each other again and then set off to conquer. On their overdue arrival at the summit, somewhat surprisingly, it was the younger of the two men, Joseph Hanlon, who appeared to be most out of condition. He felt even more deflated when Inspector Murray turned around to him and gave him a double thumbs up. It was then accompanied with a infamous nod. (A number 8. A nod that said - I'm fitter than you thought, eh!)

After introducing themselves at the small office, which was located directly to the left as you went through the showroom doors, Murray soon realised they had just entered a real venerable Aladdin's Cave. Speaking with a clipped English accent, a young lady with a floral, mint green, Laura Ashley dress on, informed them politely that Mr Taylor would be with them in five minutes. Murray nodded gratefully and went out to play with some of his 'new' toys. When in actual fact, ironically, none of them were!

DC Hanlon deliberately stood patiently outside the office, soaking up a bit of the ambience, as well as monitoring comings and goings. He greatly admired the Zulu shield and spear that were on display just at the top of the stairwell. Today, he was happy to be exploring from a distance. His boss on the other hand was in his element chatting to staff, striking up conversations with visitors, handling particular items, checking lot numbers and thumbing through price guides. Hanlon knew that his senior officer was also exploring, but in his own way. He had recognised by now that Steven Murray normally always had good reason for doing something. Today, his DI would continue to study and examine up close and personal.

Reading faces, watching for little degrees of distinction, suggested nuances and traces of suspicion. Mainly because that is where he gleamed a level of satisfaction. He loved the challenge in watching for and spotting that subtle difference in facial expression or body language. Fully ten minutes had elapsed when a gentleman approached them. Murray didn't trust or like him and they hadn't even shaken hands yet.

On the south side of town, those 'western' colleagues Hayes and Curry were out and about in and around Morningside. They were both feeling rather put out at the thought of any help or assistance coming directly or indirectly from the crooked and corrupt 'Bunny' Reid. They had begun revisiting some of those households that previously had goods stolen. They tried desperately to confirm and establish their estimated value, provenance and any other unexplained or mysterious connection that they may have to Blake's Auction House.

"Thank you Mrs Steele that would be most helpful," DC Hayes stated in a grateful voice. Sandra Steele then made her way to her private study, to retrieve all the relevant information pertaining to their recent break-in. The retired economics lecturer had dyed mousy blonde hair, was certainly not fashion conscious given her attire, and relied heavily upon a regular dose of nicotine being supplied. That was an instant theory or first impression that DC Curry had of her. 'Hanna' Hayes smiled at that. Because it was based on her badly discoloured fingertips, strong stench of smoke from her clothing and the filtered 'fag' hanging precariously on the end of her lips! There was hope for a long term future in the force for her colleague yet, she thought to herself with a hint of sarcasm.

The Patriarch of the home was a frail, rather introverted individual and he sat directly opposite the officers. He had already offered them a cup of early morning tea. That invitation had been politely declined and there did not appear to be any further conversation about to be entered into. They had both commented during their previous visit to the home on just how quiet Mr Harold Steele had been. Having spent the last twenty-two years of his working life as a Primary School Headmaster, they were rather surprised to say the least. They harboured no suspicious thoughts, or anything untoward. Just an exceptionally quiet academic type. Possibly one that always liked his own company best. The officers did fear however, that if Mrs Steele were to close her study door too swiftly, causing a draft, that they may well be called upon to retrieve her poor husband from the floor!

With an official insurance document safely delivered to them from 'the Marlboro woman,' they then painstakingly surveyed the list of stolen goods. Sure enough the Steele's had at least two items that had been purchased from Blake's. Curry pointed them out and Hayes neatly underlined them, before taking a picture of their accompanying details on her phone, and then sending the information immediately to Murray and Hanlon.

With no arrests being made and all the stolen items recovered, it looked likely the owners would all be reunited with their possessions sooner rather than later. As DC Curry informed the Steele's of this much welcomed news, all four now stood in the large, impressive hallway. The walls were a slightly off-white shade. With the exception of the rather brighter six foot by four foot wall space, where until two weeks previous, their 'Culloden at Dusk' portrait had hung. A painting that was completed back in 1981 by an up and coming Inverness born artist named Brendan Hines. It's current estimated value according to the Steele's recently produced insurance documents was approximately £235,000. Hines had won the Turner Prize just two years ago and all his work had increased tenfold in value ever since. This retired couple bought the piece for £18,000 in 2011.

Hayes and Curry checked further - Who installed their security system? Did they alter or have a set routine? What did they know about Blake's? Why did they use that particular auction room? Nothing seemed out of sorts or unusual. An unexceptional grandfather clock was the other item that they had purchased from the Thistle Street auctioneers. It had been delivered in the summer of 2014. It's current value stood at £12,000.

With these high figure estimates and valuations, young detective Andrew Curry was so far out of his comfort zone. This was a completely different world to him. He and his girlfriend had just bought a couple of household goods for their West Lothian flat at the weekend. They included a set of three canvas floral prints for their hallway and an antique wooden wall clock for their kitchen. At £22.99 and £9.99 respectively, Asda were more than 'happy to help!'

Sir Ronald Mecham's large Georgian home on Hermitage Drive, was a brisk seven minute walk from the Steele's Cluny Drive mansion house. The detectives were happy, for it allowed them to get in some brief exercise and thinking time. The sky, unhindered by cloud was a lustrous, buoyant blue, and there was a slight crisp, chill in the early morning air.

Ron Mecham had been a successful Financial Director with many firms and often described himself as retired. You just know he could not possibly be retired in the normal sense of the word.

Retired: *'withdrawn from or no longer occupied with one's business or profession.'*

The knighted financier still had his finger in many pies, none more so than 'Leading Lights.' Leading Lights was a venture capital firm that he had only recently set up at the start of the year. Thin faced and of medium build, he possessed a full head of dark hair that had seemed to deny the natural aging process. He was forever smiling, full of wisecracks, media savvy and a truly courteous gentleman. Respectful, measured, warm and charming were the exact words that DC Susan Hayes had called him at the end of their previous visit. Curry recalled this vividly, as he had written down the glowing description in his notebook. It occupied space alongside other more mundane scribbles like - *What was taken? When? Where was he? Was he insured? How did they get in? Estimated value of the property lost?*

The titled gent could not believe it when they phoned to say they had recovered his property. Amongst his stolen goods, had been two large portraits worth over £8,000 each, computers and a range of decorative 1830's porcelain. A fetching display case with ten watches and one recent purchase from Blake's Auction House - a small curved, mahogany writing bureau were also included in the burglar's haul. That last item alone was worth a cool sixteen thousand pounds. Curry again began to recall his purchase of a computer table less than 3 months ago. And this time, thanks to his friends at IKEA, it cost him three crisp twenty pound notes!

A Grandfather clock, 'Culloden at Dusk' and a sixty year old writing desk. Those were the only goods purchased from Blake's out of a possible twenty or more items taken from each residence. It was not a high percentage. If you collected antiques at all, there was at least the possibility that as an Edinburgh resident, the likelihood is you may own at least one trinket, vase or wall hanging purchased from above The Jagged Edge.

The 'two most successful outlaws in the history of the west' were stumped. They were none the wiser to spotting a link, something untoward, dodgy or downright suspicious. They had gotten valuation lists from all the residents previously. They had all been insured, but that was surely irrelevant now, as the items would all be returned. There may still be a small claim as some items had been broken, others chipped or damaged. However, it would be insignificant compared to proper claims that may have been made for substantial amounts. Give 'Kid' Curry a cheque for six grand to cover all his household goods being stolen and he would currently have to write you another one back for £3,000, or quickly find himself up on charges for insurance fraud! Oh, how this case was playing with that young man's head. He thought about his current salary, his promotion opportunities, the length of tenure required to move up the ladder. This was a world that he would never frequent given his current career trajectory. But he sure as heck wanted these individuals to be impressed at least with his professional skills. The two Detective Constables bade Sir Ronald Mecham farewell and thanked him once again for his hospitality. They both left clutching even more paperwork to put inside their case notes. Alongside that of Harold and Sandra Steele's documentation, and they still had one more scheduled visit arranged.

The Robinson family were adorable. Pat and Linda Robinson were both in their early thirties. They had a young family of three, all below the age of four! Patrick was a software designer. He had created a couple of successful apps whilst in his final year at Glasgow University. One had been to do with the travel industry he told the officers. It had been purchased from him by Expedia for an undisclosed amount nearly a decade ago. The second he had sold in more recent times. It was obviously a fairly healthy sum DC Hayes reckoned, going by the impressive home that they presently occupied in Morningside Drive.

DC Curry said sarcastically, "Maybe, 'Drive' is the link? We've already visited Cluny Drive and Hermitage Drive, and now we find ourselves at Morningside!"

Susan Hayes studied his face carefully before replying sternly. "Although you DRIVE me daft. I'm not even sure at this stage we should discount that thought - jovial or not!"

Linda Robinson answered the door with a cheery smile and a contented child sleeping peacefully in her arms. Another, an older child, was tugging continually at his mother's left trouser leg as she opened the door fully to invite both officers inside.

"Someone in need of attention?" DC Hayes asked, nodding down toward the young lad. Who now reminded her of a cute, cuddly, koala stuck firmly to a tree trunk!

"Constable," the word was offered as an exasperated sigh. "This is my terrible two. I'm told he's just being a toddler. Do you know the literal meaning of the word toddler?" she teased.

With a definitive shake of her head, Detective Constable 'Hanna' Hayes responded with, "I'm afraid I don't Mrs Robinson."

Quirkily, Linda Robinson added, *"Toddler: Emotionally unstable pint-sized dictator. One with the uncanny ability to know exactly how far to push you towards utter insanity, before reverting back to a loveable creature."*

Generous laughter was forthcoming from both latter-day 'Robin Hoods!' Having phoned ahead, the Robinsons had again looked out their insurance documents. These consisted of two A4 sheets which had everything stolen listed on them. Hayes scanned the list briefly before handing it across to her partner. Amongst the thirty to forty items taken were: Six sets of designer earrings, two crystal vases, a kitchen clock, an antique wall clock, a Peter Howson original painting, four Jack Vettriano prints and a small laptop that contained a host of Pat Robinson's creative thoughts. He was mighty relieved from a business perspective to know he would be getting many of his seedling ideas back.

Again a few of the items were worth several thousand pound, even into the tens of thousands. This time however as the officers scanned the locations purchased, there was a glaring omission. No sign whatsoever of Blake's. Hayes handed the list to Curry and asked him to double check. With a shake of his head, he confirmed no sighting of it. They were stumped. They thanked the Robinsons once again for their help. Informed them roughly of how things would likely proceed, then wished them well and waved them goodbye. Exit a pair of disheartened detectives. The 'two most successful outlaws in the history of the west' were not even sure if they were up the right creek? Never mind the fact they never had a paddle between them!

They forwarded Murray further photos of the lists, valuations, etc, as asked. Hopeful that maybe he or Hanlon could spot something amiss. 'Hanna' Hayes then briefly spoke on the phone with her Inspector also. They believed the householders were all genuine victims. Only a few items out of several dozen even related to Blake's. They could not spot a relevant connection. They were at a loss to understand what 'Bunny' Reid had been hinting at. Maybe, they discussed he was deliberately driving them away from some other dodgy deal that he was currently putting in place. Ensuring they were occupying the bulk of their time and resources elsewhere.

"Possibly," Murray said. Though never truly accepting the notion.

He was once again to be found standing outside the auction house. His chat with Simon Taylor over. It was exceptionally brief and he had taken an instant dislike to the man. Sometimes you just have to go with your gut, he had told DC Hanlon.

Getting back to DC Hayes he offered some wisdom. "Bunny certainly likes to be in charge and show you he is in control. The whole Ziola thing. It's Reid's way of letting us know that he is back in business. And that he and no other outsider, is taking over Dixon's corrupt, sleazy, yet highly lucrative empire! He likes to remind everyone from time to time, that he was in the army and jumped out of planes before. And this time, I suspect, he is coming back down to earth with a specific mission - to reclaim and conquer!" Murray then moved the phone from one ear to the other before continuing. "I'm coming around to your way of thinking though 'Hanna.' I am starting to believe that there is possibly something else at play here. Something we are just not privy to understanding quite yet. But you know, regarding the robberies, I have an idea. Let me make a call and see how we get on."

He hung up and immediately searched his contacts on his phone. It was at the very top under A. It had to be, he had the spelling down as A-A-L-L-Y. Deliberately edited with two a's to ensure it got priority ranking as the first number on his contact list. Those weird foibles we all possess, once again at play.

"That would be great Ally, much appreciated. Maybe give it a couple of days though before you visit," Murray finished. He smiled and felt pleased with that particular individual being involved.

Chapter Thirteen

"Every year is getting shorter, never seem to find the time. Plans that either come to naught or half a page of scribbled lines. Hanging on in quiet desperation is the English way. The time is gone, the song is over, thought I'd something more to say."

- Pink Floyd

As 2pm approached, so too did a jaunty Joseph Hanlon. The fine swagger in his step told DI Murray that yet another exploratory expedition had been a success. To what degree, he guessed he was about to find out. Watching Joe unbutton his trendy, rustic brown blouson jacket, Murray surreally thought about Shakespeare and blurted out:

"Clothes maketh the man!" One of the very few lines attributed to 'our William' that Murray knew. He then reflected on it briefly for a second as Hanlon got ever closer. So we get the literal meaning of it he thought - Be true to yourself. Don't borrow money to buy things you cannot afford. Don't pretend to be something you're not. Steven Murray now had several images of people currently flashing through his unkind mind. Quoted out of context it all sounds like good advice. 'Neither a borrower nor a lender be,' was also one we could get behind, he thought. If only our banks had adhered to it a bit more carefully in recent years. 'To thine own self be true,' that also sounded like pretty solid advice. Profound even! But Murray questioned - Are we really supposed to take his advice seriously? He remembered Hamlet from High School (it must have been one of the few days he attended). For we know that Shakespeare was totally making fun of Polonius by giving him tone-deaf advice. He had a nasty habit of spying on pretty much everyone and just about the worst sucking up to the king you would ever see. However, Murray pondered, that doesn't change the fact that his advice to his son about not living outside his means made a whole lot of sense.

"I'm glad you like my outfit sir," Hanlon replied, now excitedly shaking hands with his Inspector.

Murray reckoned the Hamlet quote came to mind because 'Sherlock' had really taken to the part of Holmes so well these past few months. It was like a theatrical production. He was pretty certain another scene was just about to begin and that he would have to be relaxed and ready to enjoy absorbing it all.

"Take a seat sir," Hanlon gently encouraged him, before asking, "Are you sitting comfortably?"

Murray offered a wry smile and nodded. Joe Hanlon, with an A4 sheet held tightly in his hand began to read aloud his highlighted text.

"Approximately every ten years sir, Daniel B. George, recognised as one of the world's best watchmakers would take on a new trainee, a protégé as it were. Initially he'd hire two or three assistants and would normally within the month have found his star pupil to guide, teach and mentor for the next decade. He was one of the few modern watchmakers who built complete watches by hand."

"By hand?" Murray interrupted and questioned.

"Absolutely, sir. And that included the case and dial." Hanlon then continued to read from his notes.

"He was born in Newcastle in 1935, but suffered an abusive childhood and spent most of his time on the streets. To get away from that life, he joined the merchant navy. He already had an interest in watches and did some repairs for naval friends. On leaving in

1961 with a small gratuity, he bought a collection of second-hand tools and got a job as a watch repairer."

Murray listened intently and thought that Joseph Hanlon would be the perfect host if a revival of 'This Is Your Life' wherever to return to the small screen.

"Something wrong?" Joe asked. He could see that Murray had travelled down another avenue of thought.

"No, no, I'm intrigued, carry on," the Inspector encouraged him.

"He was an incredible man sir. He then studied hard at night classes and from there became a Fellow of the BHI." Hanlon paused, turned the page and continued, stating: "After a further five years of hard work and learning his trade, at age thirty-five George opened his first watch repair and cleaning shop in 1970 in London. After four more decades, he retired in 2010 and now in his eightieth year resides here in Scotland, in rural Perthshire."

Murray smiled. "Mighty impressive, both you and him alike Joe."

"Thank you sir. However, just by way of finishing, in the year 2000 to celebrate his work and his 65th birthday, Christie's, you know the famous auction house?"

The Detective Inspector nodded, with a look that stated 'of course.'

"Well, they held a retrospective photographic exhibition of his work. It featured every watch that he had ever made. Then in 2005, the man himself was appointed Commander of the Order of the British Empire (CBE) in the New Year Honours List." Closing the papers over, Joseph Hanlon concluded: "That's me all done on Daniel B. George sir. He was quite a man wouldn't you say?"

"I would Joe. In fact over the years, I'm sure I've watched several documentaries about his upbringing, background and how he became world renowned in his field. And you say he's now settled in Perthshire for his twilight years?"

"Blackford sir, it's just outside…"

"You're okay Hanlon. I know where Blackford is. It's just outside Auchterarder, on Highland Spring territory," Murray reminded him.

Hanlon pursed his lips, grinned gently and with a slight nod of the head, felt inclined to offer up brightly.

"If you say so sir." Before repeating in substantially hushed tones.

"If you say so!"

The Inspector now stood focused on DC Hanlon. The DI's left hand remained deep in the pocket of his black overcoat. Whilst his right, wrapped his Murray of Atholl scarf around his neck. His ancient clan tartan is predominantly green and light blue, with traces of black and orange.

"Sherlock, I don't mean to sound ungrateful. But how exactly does the life story of Daniel George help us. What am I missing here?"

"A certain Mr Simon Taylor studied under him. And I thought the honourable gentleman might give us a little better insight. He's old school though sir. Doesn't have a mobile."

"What about…"

"No, sorry sir, not even a landline. However, I got a couple of local officers to pop by and speak with him. They've arranged a meeting with him for us this afternoon and I suspect it is well worthy of the time and fuel."

"You suspect do you my dear Holmes?" Murray muttered. Doing his best Doctor Watson impersonation as both men headed directly for the car park.

Opting to travel across the Forth Road Bridge and monitor the latest stage of the construction of the new Queensferry Crossing. Both men were impressed at the advancements that had taken place in recent months.

Proposals for a second Forth road crossing were first put forward in the 1990's. However, it was not until the discovery of structural issues with the Forth Road Bridge in 2005 that plans were brought forward. Following a public vote, it was formally named on the 26th of June 2013.

A full half hour later, the two *'boys in blue,'* today both wearing charcoal grey and black, were to be found travelling at a steady pace north up the M90. On arrival at the busy Broxden roundabout on the outskirts of Perth, they veered left and westbound along the A9, with its steady stream of beloved speed cameras. Twenty minutes further along that particular section of road and Joe Hanlon sighed.

"Ah, now I get it!"

He pointed out of the window at the massive Highland Spring bottling plant, situated on the opposite side of the dual carriageway. Formed in 1979, the family run concern was currently the biggest producer and supplier of naturally sourced bottled water in the UK.

Murray looking amused, lifted his head in acknowledgment, saw the Blackford exit and indicated right. Another brief three or four minute drive along that country road and they had reached the rather imposing premises of one Daniel B. George. A large two storey farmhouse, possibly about a century old and with a beautiful modern extension added. Murray was especially impressed by the driveway. It had been finished with beautiful silver granite chipping. The sort normally associated with Aberdeenshire. When wet, it's appearance changes to a darker colour and includes black speckles. Off to the left of the drive was a line of closely spaced shrubs and a variety of tree species. With Hanlon's untrained eye, they appeared to have been planted and trained to form a barrier, or mark the boundary of an area.

"Now that is one remarkable hedgerow," Murray commented.

He then slowed to a stop outside the large converted barn. This particular outhouse had been marvellously transformed into an ultra modern four car garage, maintenance and auto repair centre! As Hanlon and his DI began to quietly exit their vehicle, they noticed a dungaree clad figure working energetically underneath one of the prestige cars being housed in the contemporary workshop. Walking toward the premises, the 'automobile aficionado' Hanlon, declared:

"A vintage DeLorean DMC 12 - forty grand. The 2010 Rolls-Royce Ghost - easily one hundred thousand and the same again for the Aston Martin Vantage. Sir, at a quarter of a million pounds this is no ordinary…"

"Man!!!" Murray excitedly announced.

"Well, I was going to say garage, but I guess you'd be wholly accurate with your general assessment also."

At that, hearing voices and footsteps edging closer with every step on the immaculately clean cement floor, the overalls slid out from beneath car number four. Rising briskly to his feet was a rather trim 'only ate salad and soup' kind of man. A cross between Lionel Blair, Bruce Forsyth and James May from 'Top Gear.' He had the flowing mane like May (and no doubt the same passion for cars), coupled with the grace and professionalism of Forsyth. Add into that mix also the Blair physique and well being of a man in his eighties and there you have Mr Daniel George CBE.

Chapter Fourteen

"Hold on tight, ride the storm and please don't try to understand. A role model, an example... departing footprints in the sand."

- Anonymous

"Afternoon gentlemen. You'll be the two police officers I was expecting."

He proffered a hand out to both men. He was well spoken. Only the slightest trace of his original 'Geordie' roots could be heard.

"Detective Inspector Steven Murray sir. It's a pleasure to meet you," he politely stated, whilst firmly shaking the old man's hand.

"An Inspector no less. Must be something serious, sending out the big guns to visit."

"Actually Mr George, I'm not entirely certain how you can help. It was my ardent colleague here that noticed something in his preliminary notes. Something that he felt was worth pursuing."

On cue, Joe Hanlon hastily stepped forward, shook hands with the mad keen car enthusiast and spluttered, "A two door Porsche 911, 3.6 964 Carrera RS Lightweight. Currently valued at..."

"Nearly three hundred thousand pounds young man," George informed him.

With over half a million pounds worth of vehicles sitting under cover of an old barn, Murray pulled back his shirt sleeve, shook his head and pointed at his humble wristwatch. "Mr George, my steady little Sekonda cost me nearly thirty-five pounds and I can just about afford a Volvo. What kind of watches, did you make?" He asked only half in jest.

The jovial Englishman smiled and offered: "You know Inspector, when I was an inexperienced, naive, teenage boy just starting out in the Merchant Navy, I was really blessed." He looked heavenward at the conclusion of that sentence, before continuing. "I had the good fortune to meet a man who changed the path and direction of my life forever. He gave me this." From within a concealed pocket in his navy blue dungarees, Daniel George produced a small, rather well used box. Approximately three inch square. Murray guessed it contained a relevant badge, brooch or possibly some form of jewellery. He was not too wide of the mark.

DC Hanlon extended his hand to receive the rather dusky, pigmented package. Carefully he eased off the lid. He then cautiously pulled back a small, velvet like, layer of cloth. The anticipation of both men grew. They imagined themselves in attendance as a celebrity star had just been unveiled on the Hollywood 'Walk of Fame.' Behind the small remnant of purple, Joseph Hanlon unveiled a beautiful bronze compass. Duly noted and as expected, it had been kept in pristine condition. Possibly Murray thought, George himself would have restored it over the years. With his talent and expertise it was probably now in even better shape than when he first received it. Not unlike the half a million pounds worth of vehicles that were literally only a few feet away. The two police colleagues looked intriguingly at the expert craftsman. Murray was first to speak.

"You say he or it changed your life forever." There was no actual question from the DI. Just a statement that had faded without the vital last three words being spoken. Those words being, *'tell me more!'*

"Absolutely Inspector. He was known as Royce. First name? Last name? No one knew. We all, every one of the crew simply called him Royce. A wise, generous man. Knowledgeable in many aspects of life. For a period of time he took me under his wing. Under his tutelage I learned much about the way of the sea. Which, I believe looking back was just his way of sharing one giant analogy for life. We became good friends and with his help and inspired counsel, I knew exactly when the time was right to move on to the next chapter of my life. He always encouraged me Inspector to make the most of each new day. To be aware and grateful for every precious minute I have here on this earth. To go do and be something special with the allotted time given me.

"Choose the direction you wish to take wisely Dan, he would say. Just one degree off course and you'll end up stranded, hundreds of miles from your preferred destination! On the day I left the ship for the final time, he gave me this as a gift."

Daniel B. George seemed to stand more upright and his eyes certainly contained a moisture to them as he quietly finished the story of the compass.

"Gentlemen."

There was a deep, emotive sound to his voice now. As if he had only just recognised, that he had never actually publicly acknowledged or thanked this distant friend from his past. His remarks of gratitude continued.

"Sadly our paths never crossed in all the intervening years, I never saw nor heard from him again. However, the impact that one solitary individual had on my life was profound. After Royce shook my hand, we hugged briefly and he then bade me farewell. In a quiet dignified manner, he then turned and walked gracefully away. In that instant, that very second, I vowed I would honour that man and his departing footprints from that day forth. Pledging to myself that the time he had given me would not be wasted, and that I would strive to make something of my life."

Just then, as Hanlon went to gently place the fine instrument back into its protective surroundings, he noticed a small folded piece of what appeared to be a type of faded cream parchment.

"Do you mind?" He said, addressing George.

Caught off guard wiping away a solitary tear, the old man nodded. Giving DC Hanlon the green light to proceed. Holding it delicately between thumb and forefinger, he handed it across to his Inspector. Murray then unfolded the cherished note to reveal a short poem of encouragement. It was written by Henry Wadsworth Longfellow and was entitled: A Psalm of Life. Steven Murray then took centre stage and confidently read it aloud:

"Lives of great men all remind us, we can make our lives sublime. And departing leave behind us, footprints on the sands of time."

He nodded in acceptance and repeated the words with even more emotion second time around.

"Lives of great men all remind us...... we can make our lives sublime...... And departing leave behind us...... footprints on the sands of time...... Footprints on the sands of time."

All three remained silent. They took a moment to embrace and accept the humbling simplicity of those poignant words. Into the silence Joe brazenly questioned.

"No Mrs George at any point over the years then?"

Murray, taken aback, looked at him crossly. Concerned that the bold Hanlon had maybe crossed the line too quickly with that remark. Carefully putting the compass away again for safekeeping, Daniel George responded thoughtfully and with candor.

"My work has always been my one true love over the years Constable. And possibly that will also be my biggest regret. With that said though - Time, time has been my greatest passion, and I have literally loved every minute of it."

He added that last remark, whilst pointing out a beautiful grandfather clock that sat rather unobtrusively in the corner of his workspace. Finding their eyes now drawn across the room. They stood mesmerized for a few brief seconds as the pendulum gracefully worked its magic, shifting smoothly from side to side. The swaying motion held them in a near trance like state.

"Amazing," Hanlon gasped.

"Expensive!" Murray guessed.

He wasn't sure if that was a statement of fact or a question he had just blurted out. His host took it as the latter.

"It's worth more than the car Inspector."

"Which one?" Hanlon asked. His curiosity getting the better of him.

Sheepishly and hesitatingly, Daniel B. George quietly answered, "All of them put together!"

A combination of 'Wow!' and 'What!' bellowed from the Police Scotland duo. Eyes agog they shook their heads continually from side to side, with mouths still wide open to the world. They were a throwback to the clown heads that one would try to roll ping pong balls into at the shows and carnivals throughout the UK in the nineteen sixties, seventies and eighties. The stunning influence and impact people can have on others was amazing. Unwittingly, the lives of these two police officers had been enriched immensely and they had only spent five minutes in the company of this magical, charismatic, maverick of a man.

Both Murray and Hanlon followed respectfully a few paces behind Daniel George as he made his way across the impressive yard into the big house proper. There they were met with sparkling, polished tiled floors. Rooms that were clean, tidy and bedecked with antique clocks, paintings and tapestries throughout. No less than they would now have expected.

"I've looked out the information that your colleagues had asked about. Hope it helps."

"Oh, I'm sure it will sir." Murray added. Although his wary nod toward Joe Hanlon still said, 'Though I've no idea with what.'

"All in good time," were the gentle words whispered from Sherlock's lips. "All in good time."

"So we are going back about twenty years. That would have been my second last apprentice?" George asked by way of clarification.

"Absolutely, that's correct Mr George," Hanlon confirmed. "1995."

"Tail end of 1994 to be exact. I would normally start three or four individuals around late September, early October. Then after five or six weeks I would decide on the one to start."

"That confirms what we had been told sir. Was there a formal exam, a test, or something? How did you decide?"

"Character, Inspector." Daniel George proudly stated.

"Character? Interesting," Murray's voice questioned. His hand gesture though said, 'please elaborate.'

"Temperament, attitude, ego, Inspector. Their tenacity, emotional state, clarity of thought. Those were much more important to me than any written exam. Their frame of mind, humour, their commitment and passion to learn, to develop and to always give of their best. Their desire to ..."

"I get it Mr George. I've got the gist...... their character! I fully understand."

Hanlon sat entranced. Thinking, what an opportunity it must have been to have studied and been taught by this fellow. His DI continued.

"So in 1994 sir. We are aware of your chosen student, we've spoken with him recently. He seems to have done rather well for himself."

George stroked his chin. Gently responding with, "Mmmm, that's good to hear."

"Having honed his skills with yourself it's no surprise surely that he went on to find success?"

"No, Inspector," George offered cagily. "It's just that I was conscious he had experienced some challenging times in the last decade."

"In fairness though, we never spoke to him about his personal circumstances over the past few years Mr George."

"Really?" Daniel George announced thoughtfully, but surprised. "I would never presume to…"

"Sir." Murray quickly interjected. "He has a highly rewarding job, a seemingly flourishing business…"

"And a dead daughter!" Daniel George snapped.
There followed a momentary silence.

"I'm sorry Inspector, I don't like to raise my voice. Never find the need for it normally."

"Something you learned from your friend Royce," Hanlon asked.
Daniel George affirmed by way of a gentle nod.

"Sir," Steven Murray had reflected. "Just help me out here. Clarify again for me who your 1994 apprentice was?"
On hearing the name spoken aloud, Joseph Hanlon felt numb. The colour drained immediately from his cheeks.

"But you already knew that you said."
Disgusted with himself for not confirming it firstly, Murray stood up and ran his long fingers angrily through his hair. He looked at Hanlon with dismay and exhaled deeply.

"And relax," he calmly said, before retaking his seat.

"My sincere apologies," Murray offered. "Let's start afresh."
He then smiled and gave Hanlon the go ahead. 'Sherlock' knew then, to take the baton and run with it.

"Back in 1994 Mr George, how many people did you start with and what were their names?"
Level headed again and sitting relaxed in what would appear to be his favourite armchair, the watchmaker

extraordinaire crossed his legs the way educated, academic types do. Not that he needed it, but it gave him an undoubted air of intellect. And not that he courted it, but Daniel B. George was most at ease with the look of a naturally astute and wise old owl. Carefully, he now mulled over the question. He realised there had been some initial confusion or mix-up, but was more than happy to clear things up. With the forefinger and thumb of his right hand supporting his chin, he went ahead to begin his clarification.

"I'd like to record this sir, to ensure no further mixups. Are you okay with that?" Murray asked.

An accepting nod was offered just as he began to speak.

"Late in October 1994, I offered trial opportunities to three men. Firstly a man by the name of Dennis Black." Murray and Hanlon looked at each whilst still shaking their heads. Another name they had not been expecting.

"He never lasted long. Although I kept him on around the place to do some manual labour." Looking directly at the Inspector for some sort of understanding or empathy, he went on to declare. "Sadly, the man was just not bright enough. He was keen and passionate and surprisingly, reasonably knowledgeable regarding watches, clocks and the like. He could do repairs, duplicate and put things back together, but simply could not deal with the creative aspect of the work. Unfortunately, he was just not capable of producing something new and original."

"Dennis Black, duly noted Mr George," said Hanlon. "We'll confirm his date of birth and national insurance information later."

'Sherlock' now looked knowingly in Murray's direction. He could feel him smile his approval.

"The other two men?" He then asked.

"The other two were chalk and cheese Constable."

"Would that be their official surnames sir?" Hanlon jokingly asked.

Murray's stern face said, 'Not the time for levity son.' Hanlon cleared his throat, withdrew the smile from his face and apologised.

"Sorry sir, not really the time for laughter."

"It is a really fine character trait not to take yourself too seriously DC Hanlon. I applaud you for it."

"You can applaud him all you like," Murray commented. "I'll skelp his lug if he keeps it up."

"You were saying," Hanlon continued. "Chalk and cheese?"

"Yes, no, absolutely," George was caught off guard. It seemed he had been thinking back to the two men. "Yes, as different as could be. No mistaking the extreme opposites they were. Absolutely poles apart! One lasted about two weeks. About 10 days in total. The other 10 years. Nearly a decade by my side learning the ropes and plying his trade. Let me tell you gents it was indeed a pleasure, a privilege and an honour to work and serve alongside that individual. He was..." Daniel George seemed to hesitate and paused slightly before continuing. "At that point in his life, he was a man of the utmost integrity."

Murray growing slightly impatient asked, "just for the record sir, we need the actual names of Limestone and Cheddar."

Hanlon scowled at his boss. Regarding levity it seemed to be - Do as I say, not as I do, he thought.

"Limestone and Cheddar? Oh yes, I see what you did there Inspector. Very good, nice one," George acknowledged.

Murray's stare, pleaded with him encouragingly. His eyes slowly widening by the second, desperate for an answer. After a moment the ex-Merchant seaman realised the silence in the air was waiting patiently for him to break it!

"Oh, of course, of course," he stated. "Their names, simple. They were Messrs Taylor and Latchford. Simon Taylor and Robert Latchford. After confirming the names one more time, Daniel George began to offer up a laugh. A full bloodied belly laugh.

"Do you mind sharing?" Joe Hanlon asked.

Composing himself, the master mentor rubbed at his ribs and offered up with a smile

"Oh my, the very thought of Taylor being mistaken for Bob, what a laugh. They were very much night and day. Like I said chalk and cheese. Limestone and cheddar, very good, ha ha ha," he chortled.

Chapter Fifteen

"Dancing with tears in my eyes, weeping for the memory of a life gone by. Dancing with tears in my eyes, living out a memory of a love that died."

- Ultravox

It was one fifteen on the Tuesday afternoon before Murray and Hanlon went 'Under the Hammer!' They had missed the first quarter of an hour. Mainly background information, payment and insurance policy chat and bidding etiquette.

"What am I bid?" the cry went out.
The auctioneer appeared very workmanlike in his red checkered shirt. Sleeves neatly turned back to the elbow. He was a fairly young chap Murray thought for an auctioneer. In his mid to late twenties, possibly the offspring from the Bennett & Son van parked outside.

"It's a beautiful French carriage clock in a dated brown leather case, ladies and gents."
A slight Perthshire accent Murray detected.

"Late 19th century with the dial signed: R. LAURIN, BALE."
The Inspector was mindful to keep very still. No eyes winking, nose scratching or hair being gently flicked into place he reminded himself.

"Who will start me off at two hundred pounds? Two hundred pounds, thank you madam. Two-ten, two-twenty, two-thirty, thank you sir."
Joe Hanlon had nodded unintentionally at Murray and now found himself outbidding others. Murray in turn

shook his head in disbelief and found he'd just outbid his colleague.

"Two-forty, new bidder at the back."

The DI couldn't believe it. It was like a scene from an old black and white comedy. You couldn't make it up - vintage Laurel and Hardy!

"We are at two hundred and forty pounds, two-forty bid."

A friggin' carriage clock. Yer havin' a laugh Murray thought to himself. What the heck...

"Two-fifty, we've now got two, two-sixty. With you sir at two-seventy. Two-eighty, two-eighty, I want two-ninety, I'm at two-eighty. Would you go two-ninety sir?"

The auctioneer was staring firm and hard at Murray. The Inspector had no idea what to do. Beads of sweat ran down his face as it turned redder and redder by the second. He stared straight ahead into the distance. If he moved was that a bid, he wondered. Shook his head to say no, would that up his offer? The lumberjack masquerading as the auctioneer voiced loudly...

"No! Two-eighty it is then, two-eighty going once, two-eighty going twice, no more bids. Sold at two hundred and eighty pounds to the lady on the right hand side in the green."

The lady was all Murray needed to hear to offer up one gigantic, massive sigh of relief.

"Pheeeww."

The Inspector and his DC were at a rather dilapidated farm on the outskirts of Dalkeith. The old farmer had died and his family had decided enough was enough with regards to farming life. None of his grown up family were involved on a daily basis with the business and so they'd decided to sell everything up. That included the land, the dwellings, furniture, household items, the works. This was day two of the sale and they were in attendance to meet up with one Cyrille

Anderson. Mr Anderson was the CEO of Anderson, Barber & Cybill - Insurer to the Stars.

Murray was already a bit peeved as Anderson had not deemed them important enough to warrant time at his workplace. He had stated quite categorically. "If they want to speak to me, they'll have to find time to work within my schedule!" Not the ideal way to get investigating detectives on your side. They had a photograph of him. At thirty-nine he was younger than they'd imagined a CEO of a rather prestigious insurance company would be.

"Fathers money I'd guess," DC Hanlon offered.

"You sure that's a guess Joe?" Murray asked with a raised eyebrow.

Smirking, Hanlon responded sheepishly. "Well, possibly with a little help from my educated friends at Google!"

"Yes, I thought as much. Go on."

"His father, who has a knighthood, started the company nearly forty years ago from scratch. It is still family run and is worth a cool £1.2 billion sir. Cyrille is an only child. Spoilt, vindictive and totally self centred are some of the kinder things the tabloids have to say about him."

That ties in rather nicely with the character description Robert Latchford offered up, Murray thought.

Hanlon continued. "He has become a bit of a megalomaniac and simply loves the feeling of power. He adores and fawns over all the latest gadgets. You name it he'll no doubt have it. If not, he will by the afternoon."

"Thanks for the heads up Sherlock, this should be fun."

As they introduced themselves to the bold Mr Anderson, he briskly waved them away and dismissively scolded them.

"Gentlemen, this is what I came here for. I've now missed the introduction thanks to you. After this, I promise I'm all yours."

The two officers stood open mouthed, but could hear the auctioneer in full flow. So they quickly realised and recognised it would be in their best interests to stay extremely quiet and remain very, very still.

" … it is by Ernest Hemingway, was edited by the poet Ezra Pound and published in 1924. This Parisian edition consisting of just 32 pages is one of only 170 hand numbered editions ever made. How it ended up in a farm on the edge of the Scottish capital we will never know. But we are absolutely delighted that it did. Who will start me off at fifteen?"

Fifteen pounds for an old second-hand book Murray thought. I could get a few decent titles on my kindle for that price!

Cyrille Anderson slowly raised a finger.

"Thank you sir, we have fifteen."

Murray snatched a quick glance at his colleague at his side. He then quickly remembered his earlier error and brought his gaze back toward the auctioneer, just in time to hear him continue.

"Fifteen, fifteen thousand pounds. Ladies and gents do I hear fifteen and a half?"

A series of small, short explosive noises came from Steven Murray's throat as he began to choke. He had to be led out quickly at pace by Joseph Hanlon. His Inspector hoped desperately that his unintended splutter had not been mis-interpreted as a bid.

"Fifteen thousand pounds Joe! What in the name of the wee man does that book do? My new car didn't even cost me that much! People get paid less for a full years graft! Geez, I could even have my body frozen, go to the moon and back in the future and still have some spending money left over from fifteen flippin' grand!"

Hanlon held his stomach and laughed heartily. He loved it when his superior was on his best grumpy, moaning faced form. That little spendthrift rant seemed to illustrate he was. Hanlon feared for Mr Anderson now though, because he would be the one that feels the full force of the Murray maelstrom. Good luck with that he thought. As both men calmed down, they were anxious to see how proceedings were going back in the auction room. A makeshift auction room. Which up until a few days ago was the large lounge of the deceased's home. Currently, Hanlon and Murray found themselves next to the stove in the old farmhouse kitchen!

"Eighteen-two, eighteen-five, eighteen seven. We have eighteen-seven, any advance on eighteen-seven?"
The auctioneer's eyes were now firmly fixed on the well groomed gentleman wearing a pocket watch at the front of the room. He knew Anderson well. Their paths had crossed many times over the years at various mobile auctions. He also knew that he had never witnessed the Insurance executive lose out on an item that he was specifically after. Was today to be the first time? It was becoming quite intense. The other bidder was being represented on the phone by a pretty female with a slim figure and flowing auburn hair. She was similar in looks to another Anderson, Murray reckoned. Gillian Anderson, she of X-Files fame. This was getting rather exciting now Murray thought.

With a small gavel in his hand, the auctioneer's delivery was such, that he had almost without effort hypnotized the bidders. His chant had been perfected over the years into a rhythmic monotone. It worked so as to lull onlookers into a conditioned pattern of call and response. He literally had them playing a game of 'Simon says.' His speed Murray had noticed, was also deliberately intended to give buyers a sense of urgency: Bid now or lose out. Today and in no time at all, he had whittled it down to two serious contenders for the prized Hemingway first edition. A right index finger was raised again and the battle continued.

"Nineteen thousand, nineteen thousand pounds. Nineteen-two," he sang merrily as the flame haired beauty once again threw her forehead skyward.

He then looked toward Anderson. The finger raised - bid. Then the head was thrown - bid. Once again the finger was flicked - bid. Hair swept across the opposite shoulder - bid.

Hanlon whispered to his DI. "This was a cross between Wimbledon and a 'Herbal Essence shampoo advert."

"Who cares about split ends and dandruff," Murray concluded.

A voice boomed slow and assertive. "Twenty-five… thousand… pounds!"

It echoed loudly and with unnerving authority. Much like that of a tennis umpire. Everyone looked up. It was not the delicate, enchanting utterance of the pied piper who had kept things gracefully moving along at pace all afternoon. But the scowl of an ill-tempered, impatient, wealthy, egotistical individual. One filled with his own self importance. The auctioneer's finger wagging had obviously become wearisome. He'd had enough and Mr Cyrille Anderson was literally closing the chapter on this particular book right now.

All eyes then turned to the burgundy coat that housed the graceful frame of the lady player with the beautiful hair. She eased down the lid of her laptop, removed her mobile from her ear and simply shook her head in disappointment. She was unable to return that final serve. It had been an unnerving ace. Strategically played at just the right moment in the game.

The room listened intently as Mr Bennett's son rounded off the afternoon with: "Twenty five thousand once. Twenty five thousand twice. No more bids. Ladies and gentleman at twenty five thousand pounds." Down came the hammer and up went the cheers.

"Hemingway's 'In Our Time' sold to Mr Cyrille Anderson for twenty five thousand pounds."

"Tears in my eyes," the haughty businessman was heard to brag. "Tears in my eyes, it's all mine!"

Noticeably no one surrounded the successful bidder. Many of the others in attendance had doubtless seen it all before.

Constable Joseph Hanlon was the first to step forward. "Congratulations sir," he offered, with the meekest of smiles.

Anderson without even lifting his head, obviously mistook him for staff and dismissively waved his fingers and rudely stated, "Yes, yes, there'll be no tip forthcoming young man. I pay enough in commission. Just ensure it is properly wrapped and carefully protected. I'll be ready to leave in twenty minutes. Make sure that it will be also!"

Another man then stepped forward, casting a shadow over Cyrille Anderson.

"Apologies sir. You must have mistaken my capable Detective Constable for one of your minions. And I don't think so," Murray stated menacingly, whilst shaking his head. Now he found himself intentionally only the width of a book away from the insurance broker's face. Invading his private space and not about to relinquish one of those delicate inches. Anderson however, did step back, but remained in equally assertive form vocally.

"Are you both still here? I'm afraid today is rather inconvenient now," he said gathering his coat and other belongings. "Let's rearrange," he stated in his high brow, disparaging manner. Before finishing with, "We can reschedule for Friday. That would work better for me personally. Call my secretary, Miss …. whatever her name is and we'll make it happen."

Politely and with a gracious smile DI Murray asked, "Would Friday morning or later in the afternoon work best?"

Hanlon was rather surprised to say the least at this mild mannered response from his often highly strung colleague.

"I really don't know, just…"

Murray threw his hand onto Anderson's shoulder and forcefully lowered him back onto the tiny, metal portable seat from whence he came.

"Just shut your mouth for once," Murray bawled.

Mr Bennett the auctioneer glanced over in their direction. He gave a modest, approving facial gesture and turned quickly away.

"You were described to me Mr Anderson as… " Murray deliberately made show of referring to his highlighted notebook and began to read from it verbatim. "Cocky, arrogant and brash. A pompous, puffed up, self-centred money grabbing pig." He then paused for effect. "You know, I didn't even need a photograph or an account of what you were wearing to pick you out in this crowd today. This witness describes you perfectly"

"Witness! What!" The proud wealthy dealmaker went to protest…

"Don't you dare. Don't you dare speak."

Murray's normally milder accent had radically transformed. For this highly irritable executive he was pulling out all the stops. His childhood brogue was coming to the fore. Harsher, grittier and intimidating. Not one for the faint hearted. Very seldom was it ever used these days and always as a last resort. Reluctantly, it was either when he felt backed into a corner or when treated with such disrespect, that certain individuals needed taken down a peg or two. DC Hanlon imagined that Mr Cyrille Anderson, tycoon and sleazebag of the highest order, was about to lose a basketful of pegs!

"What is your poor secretary's name?" Murray asked forcefully.

"Huh?" Anderson looked bemused.

"Do her the decency of referring to her by name. Like I refer politely to you by name….. Ya Muppet!"

"You can't…"

"Oh, I can. And don't you speak to me again unless it's to tell me the name of the poor, unfortunate, desperate individual that has to put up with working for you every day. Her wings must be in need of a good polish by now. No doubt one day she'll just reach up, grab her halo and wring your flippin' neck with it."

The star bidder turned white. Hanlon tried desperately to stifle a laugh and Anderson was shrinking more and more by the minute. When he eventually spoke it came out as a timid whisper.

"Are you having a laugh?" Murray stated.

It was a popular expression that Steven Murray used frequently in life. He raised his voice again and stared indignantly at his wilting foe.

"Did you actually have the gall to say Gabriel to me? Like the archangel Gabriel, are you having a go at me?

"No, no Inspector," Anderson said, finding his volume control. "I said Gabrielle." Urgently he reiterated, "My secretary is female and she is called Gabrielle."

"All that just to establish her name. I'm glad you remember it at least sir," Murray stated, rather more officially and diplomatically. "Because, you'll be calling the lovely Gabrielle and cancelling whatever you have on at four-thirty this afternoon. She'll kindly arrange an appointment for all three of us in your office then," Murray offered, before adding two clarifying questions.

"Do I make myself clearly understood?" Closely followed by, "Or would you prefer the more highly volatile west coast translation?"

Anderson looked up and nodded wearily. He understood.

"Although this was something you were unwilling to extend to my colleague. Let me be extra generous and offer you a tip sir," Murray winked.

The businessman rolled his eyes with a disdainful look of indifference. The DI then lowered his body and went face to face with one of the scrap dealer's least favourite people. Robert Latchfords description of Anderson reverberated in his mind once again. As Murray began to speak it was in a slow deliberate tone, not unlike that of 'Bunny' Reid. He proffered words that were cold and without compassion. Clinical and succinct. He portrayed a much harder, sinister edge than normal. You can take the boy out of Paisley... he thought.

"I would - put on - that fine coat of yours - ensure you are properly wrapped up - and very carefully protected - because - I'll be around - ready to see you - in three hours - Make sure - you are ready to receive me!"

The way in which Cyrille Anderson pursed his lips and swallowed hard, it registered with Murray that he once again, fully understood!

Chapter Sixteen

"Last night I dreamed about you. I dreamed that you were older, you were looking like Picasso with a scar across your shoulder. You were kneeling by the river, you were digging up the bodies buried long ago, Michelangelo."

- Emmylou Harris

Later as he made his way across town the Inspector received a timely phone call. His display indicated Highland Spring territory... Perthshire to be precise. The call was from a rather out of breath Daniel George. He had went to the effort to call from a neighbour's landline.

"Mr George," Murray smiled as he spoke. Genuinely happy to hear from this legendary watchmaking aficionado.

"How can I help?" The Inspector asked.

There was a momentary pause at the other end of the line. Murray could again hear Daniel George struggle for breath.

"Are you okay Mr George? Your breathing it seems to be..." Before Steven Murray could finish, Daniel George interrupted him.

"I'm on my friend's treadmill Inspector," he wheezed. "Got to keep up my daily regime," he managed in between regular panting sounds. "It just suddenly came to me once I started. So I thought, no time like the present."

"You are truly an inspiration sir." Murray thought and offered vocally.

"Thank you Inspector," the older gentleman quietly and courteously accepted the compliment. "So here's the thing." There was then a short hesitation.

"Uh-huh, I'm listening," Murray encouraged.

Having regained it seemed, full control of his breathing faculties once again. Daniel George MBE spoke with an excited vibrato to his voice.

"I remembered I gave a trial to someone else back then."

"What! You did. Who?" Murray spluttered inquisitively.

"A friend of Bob Latchfords seemingly - although I don't think he was - a Mr Cyrille Anderson, son of a rich businessman."

Murray nodded. A slight grin may even have attempted to surface as George continued.

"Capable man, but he lacked the passion Inspector, the desire, the hunger, the ..."

"The character!" Murray quickly remembered.

"Absolutely Inspector! His character was all wrong. He came from a wealthy, privileged background. No real need to succeed. He always gave the impression he knew it all already and was most certainly not going to give it his all or pay real attention to detail. Flippant, arrogant and vain - not really very likeable either. I don't actually know how him and Latchford ever became friends, and if I'm honest, I never really got the impression that they were."

"Thank you sir," Murray beamed. He offered some extra gratitude and was about to sign off when he remembered something. "Mr George I wonder if you could do me a huge personal favour?"

Daniel George agreed willingly and Murray's gentle grin had now been promoted into a fully fledged smile of happy, satisfied contentment!

The timing of the call, could not have been better. For the detective found himself no more than two streets away from the offices of Anderson, Barber and Cybill. 'Agents to the stars,' at least so all their advertising literature clearly stated. On this occasion Murray had taken the unusual decision to visit unaccompanied. The premises themselves were located on the busy Corstorphine Road in what had previously been a successful bed and breakfast establishment. This was the main thoroughfare westbound out of the city centre. Traffic moved as if it were part of a time lapse video. Frantically scurrying, shuffling and darting around. Pedestrians advanced at double speed. Life was hectic as horns sounded, brakes echoed and clouds, sky and sunshine interchanged frequently overhead.

His growing company had purchased the hospitality business as a going concern nearly six years ago. He then immediately closed it down, totally gutted and refurbished the whole building and turned it into the headquarters for the family's long standing insurance business. Directly opposite their new corporate offices stood Murrayfield, Scotland's national rugby stadium and mighty impressive it was too. Unusual and quirky as it may have appeared to outsiders, Cyrille Anderson was a massive rugby union fan. And with his working premises only a very congenial five minute walk away, he now had his very own private parking for match days! In fairness, as Murray approached he was able to get a spot in their six berth customer car park, so he was not complaining either. Which for once made a pleasant change.

On entering the plush premises, the DI could witness first hand that Cyrille Anderson assumed that he was now back in control. He was bent over slightly, whispering into the ear of a dark haired lady behind the reception desk. Gabrielle, Murray would have guessed. In her mid to late forties, she appeared professional and welcoming. Although the Inspector never got to experience either. Because on spotting him enter the businessman was determined to keep the upper hand.

He undoubtedly felt very much the King of this Castle, as he ushered Murray in through a small knee high gate, up a floor level and through into his private office. No introduction to Gabrielle was ever forthcoming. Once inside, with a generous wave of his hand he gestured to the officer to kindly sit and take a seat. Murray soon found himself in a stylish and sumptuous, dark leather chair. One that had been deliberately lowered on the opposite side of the impressive, 'King' sized mahogany desk. A massive, mighty and bespoke design that the DI reckoned involved the felling of two fully grown trees in its construction and probably cost more than his entire monthly salary.

"Ikea?" he asked cheekily of Anderson, as he made to sit.

"I what?"

"Quite." Murray nodded.

Quietly seething, he remained deliberately seated on a chair that was easily three inches shorter than his Master's. Gently prodding his tongue into one side of his cheek he thought once again of how that said so much about this man. So much so, that really, no conversation with him is actually required.

"So Inspector how can I help? Home, car or property?" he asked smugly.

Murray stared at the man. He was unwilling to appear vulnerable or be intimidated by him or his grand surroundings. He was unsure of the question initially. But taking those extra few seconds made all the difference.

"Oh, I don't need insurance sir, but thanks for asking. I assume that striking portrait behind you is well covered though?"

Midway up the wall behind Anderson hung an almighty six foot by twelve foot painting.

"No need Inspector, it's only a print. Four or five thousand pounds worth certainly, but I don't see many petty thieves making their way out of here with it under their arm in a hurry," he laughed.

He had a point Murray thought. How did they get that in here in the first place? He had just made his way here via a normal front door entrance, narrow corridor and eventually up a small internal spiral staircase.

Cyrille Anderson had spotted his confusion. "It was hoisted up and brought in before the new ceiling to floor windows and doors were put in place Inspector. We literally rebuilt the room around it," he proudly boasted. It is by Antonio de Pereda. Have you heard of him Inspector?"

"Can't say that I have sir."

"To be fair, I don't believe Ikea ever stocked those prints!"

Murray smiled. I'll give him that one he thought. Well merited.

"It's called the 'Allegory of Vanity.' Not personally something I am fully aware of. You know the excessive pride in one's appearance, qualities, abilities, achievements," he laughed haughtily.

Murray gave him a stare similar to the one earlier at the farmhouse and Cyrille Anderson soon regained his composure.

"Mr Anderson your name has came up in our enquiries into a missing girl. Actually it's now officially a murder investigation. The teenager was discovered at the weekend." Murray spoke bluntly and with no emotion. He wanted to gauge Anderson's response, more in his body language than vocally.

The businessman though, simply shook his head, as if to say, I don't understand, how would this involve me. Murray then informed him more fully of the dead girl's identity. That seemed to register alarm and caution in Cyrille Anderson, which was rather unusual in itself. Most people would have in the first instance expressed their regret and sorrow for Robert Latchford. They would have questioned - How? Why? What happened?

But none of that. If anything he became more vigilant in his actions. He seemed to carefully monitor and analyse every question before he responded. He became very much a sentry on guard duty. Now it was Murray's turn yet again to question - Why? Why the sudden change? He would have been aware of Latchfords indifference to him, possibly even his suspicions. But he has lived with that for many years. He has thrived financially and has no noticeable scruples that it would even bother him. He'd known Latchford, the father, these past few decades. He had obviously known Cindy-Ann and by all accounts, 'had fancied' her mother since their days at University together. But for some mysterious reason, knowing, finding out that Cindy-Ann was the murdered teenager, that had set off alarm bells with him. Murray deliberately never mentioned his trial or adult work experience with Daniel George many years previous. However, he did deem it appropriate to ask after Messrs Barber and Cybill.

Wearily, he asked, "Do your partners still even exist?" Shifting rather uncomfortably in his seat, Cyrille Anderson responded.

"Of what relevance is that Inspector?"

"Unfortunately I don't know yet sir. That is why I asked the question. Do you need me to repeat it?" Cyrille Anderson pouted, pondered and puzzled over his response.

"B and C?" Murray encouraged.

Anderson's reply was curt. "My father's co-founders have both since passed away."

"Now that wasn't so hard, was it?" Murray smiled. "Oh, and for the record, now I do find it relevant. Possibly very relevant indeed."

An interesting metal door that was positioned behind and slightly to the left of Anderson, gave the impression of being a security vault. It even had the old style steering wheel column that duly required turning.

The businessman was again alert to Murray's thoughts and gaze.

"It houses my hobby Inspector. A childhood pastime that has grown and continued to this day."

Anderson made a great sweeping motion with his left arm, which clearly indicated to Steven Murray - By all means, walk this way! A few digits were keyed into the pad and like a seafaring Captain, Anderson began to turn the wheel hard-right and starboard bound. Murray observed with great intrigue as Cyrille Anderson gradually opened the bulky, considerably substantial steel door. The whole 'Ocean's Eleven' scenario played out instantly before the police officer's eyes. He imagined row upon row of safety deposit boxes. Would each one contain a precious stamp or minted coin, the Inspector wondered. Though given this individual's superiority complex, dissected insects and stuffed animals may be more in keeping with his particular flaws. Even given the fact that it did indeed include several ticks, Murray could still not have been more wrong!

Joseph Hanlon was certainly peeved off at being discarded from following up with Anderson and was licking his wounds back at the station. However, mainly he was concerned that DI Murray was intent on doing something illegal and that was the real reason for his isolation. Making positive use of his time as he normally would, Detective Constable 'Sherlock' Hanlon tried to make sense once again and join up the dots between Ian Spence, Marco Tardelli and Paul Lattimer. As well as 1974, Michelangelo and the solitary letter F.

Horology literally is the study of time, the art or science of measuring time. As Inspector Steven Murray entered Anderson's vault he knew for certain that all the cases in relation to this family were intertwined! The how and why he'd figure out in due course! Timekeeping devices, primarily clocks and watches adorned every inch of floor space and wall. Murray studied the small information card that accompanied each piece. *Case clock with multiple complications - Marine chronometer with double barrels - Racket clock with base* - there was even a *clepsydra*. A piece in which time is measured by the flow of liquid. Basically it was a water clock!

Murray was astonished - Anderson proud. The arrogant, superior smirk had resurfaced. It was confirmation to the DI, not that any was needed, that this was most noticeably what Cyrille Anderson lived for. And that in some dark, mysterious and sinister way, what all the others had died for!

Murray's mouth was in the early stages of closing. From easily two or three hundred pocket watches in all shapes and sizes. To several dozen Grandfather, Grandmother and all other family member clocks. Aunties, Uncles, cousins and supplementary long lost relatives made up the thousands of watches. From Switzerland to the USA, Chile to the United Kingdom. There was analog, digital and even two auditory clocks that Murray heard announce the time clearly above the cacophony of sound. Anderson's grin now had protective headphones at either side of it. The Inspector gratefully accepted the spare pair currently being handed to him. He then spent a further forty minutes in the company of his eccentric, time travelling host!

Chapter Seventeen

"Bet the black comes in red. Crimes of passion rule my head. Roulette you're going around in a spin. Caught up in a game that you just can't win."

- Bon Jovi

It had been a while since DI Murray and Doc Patterson had gone out socially together. The T'inker was always great company. His sweet Irish brogue and his magical charm made him welcome anywhere. With Steven Murray's latest Volvo requiring some further road testing, he had gladly volunteered to swing by Athelstaneford to pick up his friendly local pathologist. The Doc's beautiful rural home was located just three miles north-east of Haddington in East Lothian. Murray always appreciated it as a hidden treasure, both the village and the history behind it. The T'inker had told him excitedly many years ago all about its prestigious past. It would have been on one of Steven Murray's very first visits to him that he shared how it got its name from the legendary battle between Saxon King Athelstane, and Pictish King Hungus in the 9th century.

Murray would then feel entitled and empowered to tell friends about how behind the parish church sat a beautifully restored dovecot. It housed a short audio-visual and a dramatisation which was very atmospheric of the 9th century battle. Also included, free of charge, were the spectacular views northward towards the battle site itself.

Legend described how at some point between 815 AD and 832 AD, an army of Picts, under Angus MacFergus (High King of Alba), had been on a punitive raid into Lothian (which was Northumbrian territory), and were being pursued by a larger force of Angles and Saxons under Athelstane. The Scots were caught and stood to face Athelstane in an area to the north of the modern village of Athelstaneford. The two armies came together at a ford near the present day farm of Prora (one of the field names there is still called the Bloody Lands). King Angus prayed for deliverance and was rewarded by seeing a cloud formation of a white saltire (the diagonal cross on which St Andrew had been martyred) against a blue sky. The king vowed that if, with the Saint's help, he gained the victory, then Andrew would thereafter be the patron saint of Scotland.

Murray always drove away from his friend's residence recalling that small, historic, yet seemingly insignificant battle. One of few which the Scots actually won, and the Saltire in all it's glory became the flag of Scotland. How many fellow Scots know that, Murray would grin. He rewarded himself with a smug smile of self satisfaction. Who would have guessed? He also beamed brightly because no one, but no one, from outwith that area would ever know how to pronounce the name correctly! Murray, many years ago, had simply gave up trying.

At the north end of Nicolson Street and just before it joined the A7 at South Bridge, lies Nicolson Square. On the south-west corner of the square is a Methodist church with a handsome Roman front. It was built in 1814 and back then had a minister's house and school attached to it. As an unassuming slate plaque on its wall testifies, it was regularly attended by the 18th President of the United States, General Ulysses S. Grant during his brief sojourn in Edinburgh.

As they exited their car, their destination was quietly located only a few short steps away from the two hundred year old place of worship. The Church building was Grade 'A' Listed and alongside Wesley's Chapel in London and the New Room in Bristol, they made up the three most architecturally important buildings in British Methodism. Not to mention the fact it was also a designated 'Methodist Heritage Site'.

The casino's recent restoration work had left the building in gleaming condition. Two marble faced columns greeted visitors as they approached. The left hand column had a simple square sign with an ABC logo on it. Halfway up the opposite column, an attractive clock face had been set into the marble. It had then been decoratively surrounded by two inch strips of other stonework. Running from the twelve to the four - Slate. From the four to the eight - Granite. Then, finally all the way back up to midnight - Sandstone. A century previous the fine building was home to a leading manufacturer and importer of baskets, rugs and hardware. Today as recently as three years ago, a private residential accommodation had been magically transformed into an upmarket, yet understated gambling den.

How happy Murray wondered would those 'God fearing' people of old have been with himself and Patterson tonight? In fairness, it was work he thought. Actual on the job research had brought the T'inker and Murray out on this wet, miserable evening. As the Inspector began to ponder on being at home in front of a warm cosy fire, the first set of lyrics that came to his mind were: *'listen to the rhythm of the falling rain!'*

As the two men made their way through the doorway, only Murray had saw the wisdom of wearing a raincoat that evening. His one and only mac was a navy blue Ben Sherman. Quilted lining, branded buttons and a handsome semi cutaway collar. He had purchased it over a year ago at a Debenhams blue cross sale event for less than half price. Loved to get the occasional bargain did our DI Murray. A true west coast Scotsman after all. He stood in the impressive marble floored foyer and began shaking the rainwater from his lapels. He then overheard the ruddy faced gentleman in front, ask the staff member the correct time, referring to him specifically by his surname. Fleetingly, at that precise moment, and only for a second - 'Bunny' Reid entered his mind? This punter must be a regular Murray figured. I wonder just how much he has lost over the last few months? Lost by way of cash, weight and dignity was his next train of thought. As he turned to his side, his colleague was being offered a neatly folded cotton towel to dry himself off. Obviously many of their patrons that evening had been caught out in similar circumstances, in what appeared to be more than an early introduction to advancing April showers. It had been a continual, non-stop, downpour since shortly after the two men had left East Lothian.

The dried off 'odd couple' then made their way smartly downstairs to the roulette tables, completely unaware that their every step was being closely monitored. Surveillance by the official in-house casino security was one thing and not surprising. However, the prying eyes of this particular individual had just been fate. This member simply had the good fortune to have been in the right place at the right time and had spotted them on arrival at the main entrance. The mystery onlooker had been making their way, rather dejectedly it had to be said, down the impressive wooden staircase that led from the first floor. That was the level which hosted the private blackjack and high stake poker games. His current body language could definitely be read tonight as that of a big time loser! Pausing, disheartened for a second or two on the midway landing, had turned out to be rather fortuitous. Because that was when Murray and Patterson had entered the premises and questions rapidly came to their voyeurs mind.

Why were they here? Was the Inspector on to me? Who was his new partner? All these thoughts and plenty of others were now fighting for space in his head. They continued to push and jostle for position, the right to be heard, the need to be answered. Keeping his distance, he chose to watch from afar, before deciding on his next course of action.

"14 Red," the female croupier announced crisply. She seemed to have an Eastern European accent Murray quickly decided from hearing just those two words. Narrowing it down any further would sadly just have been guesswork. Joseph Hanlon, his partner these past four months could confirm hand on heart, that Detective Inspector Steven Murray didn't really go in for guesswork. 'Ask questions, delve deeper, explore, explore, explore and answers will appear. Good, bad, wonderful or indifferent, who knows, but you'll get results - sometimes you'll even win', he could hear his Inspector quip.

Growing up with the famous backdrop, history and heritage of the weaving mills in Paisley, Murray would often quote J. Paul Getty's formula for success. He had only recently started High School in 1976 when the death of Jean Paul Getty the American industrialist was all over the news. He was the founder of the Getty Oil Company and in 1966 The Guinness Book of Records named him as the world's richest private citizen. At that point he was worth an estimated $1.2 billion (approximately $8.8 billion in 2015). The J. Paul Getty formula for success that Steven Murray loved so much and was often heard to offer, was common sense - but not so often put into common practise: *"Rise Early; Work Hard; Strike Oil!"*

The Doc, who was on call, had realised that he'd left his mobile phone in Murray's car and made mention of the fact to his companion. At that point both Murray and Tom Patterson placed their well earned money on the table and watched it exchanged for gambling chips. Certainly, first impressions seemed to indicate that 'the Doc' was more of a natural high roller than his police pal. He handed over five hundred pounds in crisp, new, fresh, ten pound notes. By comparison his cautious buddy offered up three crumpled twenty's. With the cash deposits exchanged, the DI again reached into his trouser pocket to retrieve the precious gift presented to 'Ally' Coulter by Reid. He carefully checked the grooves on the rim, it's stamped logo and colour coordination. It matched perfectly. He knew that it would.

Roulette, had maintained a high popularity within the casino industry today. Even allowing for all the multimedia, celebrity driven gaming machines arriving almost daily. Many of which occupied prime position in high end gambling establishments these days. 'Celebrity sells' - That 'Kardy Ash' woman has a lot to answer for Steven Murray grinned to himself. As he listened out for those three sweet, supposedly innocent words, his chest rapidly began to tighten, his stomach churned painfully and a multitude of dark memories lined up at the starting gate in his mind. I should never have came here, he thought to himself. This was a bad idea. Too late - The three words surfaced...

"No more bets," she declared.

The croupier stood tall as her red manicured hands began to spin the wheel in one direction. 'Little wheel,' Murray reminded himself. That is what the French word roulette actually meant. He then watched with consummate ease, how she effortlessly spun the 'magical' white ball in the opposite direction. It travelled at speed around the tilted circular track. Which in turn, ran around the circumference of the wheel itself. Boisterous crowds in casinos the world over, cheer every time the wheel sets off. Roulette rules the hearts of casino aficionados! As it spins, fingers are crossed, nails bitten, thumbs tap feverishly on the edge of the table. For some, eyelids are tightly closed or their gaze deliberately averted. Others, find their eyes fixed firmly on the darting miniature globe, which is now currently losing momentum and beginning to jump freely at will. It pings, tings and pops whilst searching frantically like many Edinburgh drivers for an available parking space. Looking ready to decide, before changing its mind at the very last minute. Convinced it has found a snug, cosy compartment, it decides at the final millisecond to make an unreliable witness out of you and dramatically jump ship! Toying and teasing with you, right up to the very end.

"14 Red," she announced again without the slightest surprise in her voice.

Yet to others around the table they all offered either vocally, or in thought, the same four words. 'What are the chances?'

Murray's two £5 bets, one on black and one on odd, did not offer much in the way of return. The T'inker on the other hand, was well on his way. He had the single number, plus various two number and four number bets come up. Murray couldn't help but instantly calculate the Doc's small windfall being returned to him. He approximated around the twelve hundred pound mark. As Murray shook his head, The T'inker got the feeling that this could be his lucky night.

Several spins later those familiar two words were to be heard for a third time.

"14 Red."

This time Murray was the one celebrating. He took a second or two to calculate his expected windfall… £35! He had been down to his last twenty and was playing single pound bets on higher odd positions. He thought to himself, 'At this rate I might even last twenty minutes!'

An assortment of hands scattered a wide variety of bets across the table before each turn of the *'little wheel.'*

Single numbers, black, red, odd and even, high or low. From single pound bets (Murray's preferred option) to several hundred on each spin. As Murray carefully scanned the room he saw Chinese businessmen, academics, legal professionals and villains, including one prominent Judge. Although he is still undecided which of the former categories that particular character falls under. Neither of the two men are too enamoured by the way the other carries out his duties. As he was about to place his bet, another face stood out in the crowd. A face that he had been shown a picture of earlier in the day. He delayed betting. The Doc seeing the pause, looked around at him and followed his line of vision. It led him to a tousled haired female standing next to an exceptionally tall chap, both of whom each held a large wine glass in their right hand. The gent's glass was still full. The lady looked as if she'd already had plenty to drink and was once again seeking replenishment.

"You okay," he asked.

Murray, rather taken aback, nodded. "Yeh, yes, I'm fine," he responded. "Just a little surprised sometimes at who you bump into in these places." Inwardly though, he was wondering how this would play out. He was scheduled to meet with that particular player - the very next day. The manner and tone implied by *'these places.'* Made it sound like a sordid, dirty and undesirable place to be associated with, never mind just spotted in.

9 Red, 22 Black, 35 Black, 34 Red and 23 Red all managed to be winning numbers and colours called, before The Doc whispered closely into Murray's ear. The Inspector then handed him something, pointed upwards and nodded. His gesture was interpreted by their interested third party as a sign that they were about to depart.

"Hold on," Murray said, tugging at his friend's arm and pointing back toward the table. They waited, for one more spin. This gave their mysterious spectator the chance to exit before them and still remain unnoticed.

He made the most of the opportunity as the two work colleagues heard their friendly eastern European cry out, "13 Black." The T'inker and Murray threw their hands in the air, shook their heads, looked at each other and laughed dismissively.

Chapter Eighteen

"Doctor, my eyes, tell me what is wrong. Was I unwise to leave them open for so long. "Cause I have wandered through this world and as each moment has unfurled, I've been waiting to awaken from these dreams."

- Jackson Browne

Outside as the collar on the navy blue raincoat was being pulled up, the deluge of heavy rain showed no signs of easing. It was approaching eight-thirty on this dismal, wet, spring evening. Dark clouds overhead gave Edinburgh it's very own fifty shades of grey. The figure in the doorway opposite waited for the second man to emerge, but to his surprise no one followed. He'd either forgotten something or decided to stay awhile longer. On reaching the Volvo, which was parked on a single yellow line directly across the street at Hill Place. An audible beep from the alarm could be heard as it was switched off.

At the moment the door was opened, a ferocious blow was to reign down from behind. It landed agonisingly on the base of our gambler's neck. His head thrust forward, violently colliding with the roof of the door. The self same door then went to close back on itself. A momentary howl of pain was heard as it slammed firmly on the mugger's hand. No longer young enough to fend off such an attack, his victim instinctively dropped to his knees. His assailant had now resolved that he was going to make the most of this opportunity. Adrenalin pumping, a cocky confidence and superior arrogance was now flowing through his blood. His victim's vital fluid however, was now extensively flowing through the guttered streets of Edinburgh. The attacker's left knee had been brought up with such ferocity, that a high pitch whipping sound was announced as it met perfectly with the roulette player's jaw. An innocent jaw that had been quite contentedly making its way toward street level. The crack could be heard over and above that of his forehead striking the solid concrete of the pavement below. The full weight of his body came to rest, parked parallel to the vehicle. For good measure, an obligatory size nine kicking was offered to the rib cage and face, on two more separate occasions.

Cars and buses were still busy travelling up and down on the nearby Nicolson Street. Infrequent horns and sounds of the night could be heard in the distance. The driving rain connected at pace, skelpin' the backside of the ground with such force that it began imminently to travel skyward again! It's momentum pushing each raindrop off like an Olympic swimmer after his final length turn. Hill Place opposite, may well have been a handy spot to park, but with the benefit of hindsight, it was quiet and isolated. Which also made it the ideal spot to carry out an assault. Especially one that could go unnoticed for a reasonable period of time. As the body lay crumpled, wet and motionless, getting a second pummelling from the aggressive Scottish weather. Maybe also with hindsight, it would even make a perfect spot - for a vicious attempted murder!

On his final kick, the aggressor caught the midriff of his victim with the sole of his footwear and it pushed firmly at his body with intensity and vigour. This enabled the inanimate body to turn over. Badly beaten, the heavy, dense rainwater began to work its magic. Acting like a powerful shower head, it furiously cleansed away the blood and dirt from the bruised and battered face. There was a minor problem however. The angry individual that had lashed out frequently and violently in the previous thirty seconds, had no idea who this man was. This was not his intended victim, this was NOT Detective Inspector Steven Murray!

Back at the table the croupier extended her rake to remove all the losing bets. Murray had become noticeably agitated. He had managed to lose a further three hundred and twenty pounds in the short period of time, about eight or nine minutes that Patterson had been away. The small timid stakes had been relegated to history. He had veered back into dangerous territory and had placed a wider assortment of bets, each time for substantially more. He was now on edge and desperate. He was chasing it and he knew it.

Murray would close his eyes on every fresh spin. A secret prayer would then be offered. A pact entered into, a deal with the devil or whoever? 'Please, let me win it back and I'll walk away.' Each whirring circuit the white ball made, mirroring the image of a professional cyclist on the banks of an indoor velodrome, offered Murray fresh hope and optimism for possible celebration.

Upon opening his eyes once the winning number was called, he could witness on this occasion only twenty percent of his bets had succeeded. Which, quickly calculated, ultimately meant 4 out of 5 had lost yet again! He only needed one big win he kept telling himself. I'll stick on another twenty. No make that forty. If most of these come up I'll have recouped my initial outlay, he'd repeat once again. The ball dropped and this time "35 Black" was called. The rake swept up. His win ratio this time round? Zero!

Over four hundred pounds lost within half an hour of arrival. Murray remembered those distant feelings. His stomach ached and he felt drained and physically sick. A tsunami of anger, disgust, dislike and even hatred - all toward himself, swept over him. Licking his lips, he thirsted for fluid and success. He'd forgotten all about 'The Doc.' Who cared where he was or what had caused his delay. A maze of bland rhetoric was currently racing through Steven Murray's mind. He knew full well that others had lost also. But it certainly didn't feel like it. Also, at that moment in time it was unimportant and insignificant. Self-centred arrogance and selfishness were now prerequisites for this particular slope that DI Murray had ventured onto. Rational thinking had gone. It had exited via an open window ten minutes earlier. Had the arrogant, obnoxious, self-important Cyrille Anderson been bidding against him right now, Murray would have continually upped the bid. Time, after time, after time - finger flicked, head raised, finger, head, finger, head, never ending. Adrenaline pumping through his veins, autopilot having kicked in. Gambling was and is, highly personal. The individual feels they are alone. That no one else can possibly understand. Murray even remembered reading recently that one of the major supermarket chains in the United States had started selling a range of headstones aimed at cigarette smokers. They created it initially as a marketing deterrent. The words emblazoned on it would work suitably well with those of a certain disposition - those members of society that possibly enjoy too much of a regular punt. The marble inscription read: 'It's not an addiction, I can give it up tomorrow.'

As a self inflicted headache approached. Murray now questioned the house policy on allowing pets onto their premises? He could swear, sitting on the seat next to his Hungarian (he had since learned) croupier, was a pal of his. A beautiful black pooch. Not a pedigree, so it had to be a cross breed. What a combination, he thought to himself. It sounds like the start of a rather appalling joke. What do you get when you cross someone who likes a flutter with a bipolar sufferer? Answers on a postcard would be the golden oldie response. Nowadays, you'd get a host of humorous remarks posted on Facebook in a matter of minutes. Also, several not so humorous and possibly very crass, cruel and unkind comments into the bargain.

With that said, out-with Joseph Hanlon and possibly 'Doc' Patterson, no colleagues knew with a certainty that Steven Murray suffered, or should we say, experienced from time to time rather testing episodes of bipolar. As the Inspector stared forlornly at his soft drink in front of him, he became fully aware once again...... that a manic depressive that liked a wager - was one heck of a lethal cocktail!

The T'inker had continually tried to dissuade the DI from going to the casino in person.

"Let someone else go and check out the authenticity of the chip that Coulter had been given," were the Doc's specific words of encouragement.

That was not the Inspector's style though and he knew that. His counsel was acknowledged, though graciously ignored. The evening out was planned and organised between the two old friends, Thomas Patterson - Doctor, grandfather and holiday lover. Accompanied at his side by Steven Murray - Police Officer, oscillating individual and previously addicted gambler!

The Detective Inspector's heart was now pounding rapidly as he hurried outside. He returned his wallet back into his trouser pocket, only after firstly removing his bank card. He would have no problem tracking down the nearest cash machine. He was a detective after all. As he made his way out into the darkness of Nicolson Square, the intermittent flashing lights from across the way had him protecting his eyes from the glare.

His body swiftly reminded him: Bank; Cash; Roulette - You're on a mission and be quick about it. You need your fix! His mind though, took over for the briefest of seconds to question - Where was the 'Doc?'

His body challenged again: Bank; Cash; Roulette - What were his colleagues in attendance at? Was that not where they had parked the car?

Again adrenalin pumping: Bank; Cash; Roulette - What are you waiting for? This doesn't concern you.

For the final time: Bank; Cash; Roulette - What had happened? Who's in need of an ambulance? His brain froze and he began automatically to run toward the illuminated commotion opposite. As if now operating on autopilot. With every stride he could feel his thoughts thawing - Bank - Cash - clarity was beginning to rise to the surface. Bank!

He flashed his well used warrant card to the young officer whose major role was to keep interested onlookers back. In this instance however, the constable had recognised DI Murray as he came jogging toward him and waved him through without the need to check his credentials. Which was just as well. The Royal Bank of Scotland credit card that Murray was brandishing would probably not have sufficed!

The stretcher had just been placed into the back of the waiting ambulance. As the siren began to sound and the second door of the vehicle about to be closed, an experienced female paramedic, surprisingly found herself joined by a rain soaked, guilt ridden, tear-stained miscreant. This time, his proper I.D. would be required!

Murray stressfully walked the corridors of the hospital at great speed. Reminiscent to a pinball being fired, he paced up, down, across and back. Continually zigzagging from side to side. His crazy body movements were now on a continual loop system. His hands were operating on rapid concerned mode. They repeatedly went from head to thigh, then a slight rub of the chest, before beginning all over again. He would then take a brief ten second respite on a nearby chair. Only to be fired back up again sharply for the next round! He had sat in the waiting room for the previous hour and had read through enough depressing NHS posters, leaflets and official insurance documentation to last him a lifetime. It would be a rather limited lifetime he had guessed, based on the information provided on the aforementioned literature. At this rate he reckoned he would easily be off work for at least two weeks by the time he had checks done for his possible irritable bowel, high blood pressure, diabetes and testicular cancer. Not the ideal reading material Murray decided and he began to wander yet again, aimlessly following the yellow, blue and red lines fixed to the floor.

All of this was still very much a defence mechanism. He was in pain. Not physical maybe. But inside, mentally he was being put through the ringer. At that specific moment in time he was in dire straits. Literally carrying out his own *'Private Investigations,'* into his close friends attack. Going over and over in his mind the previous few hours. Numerous questions beginning to surface. What brought this on? Who knew they were at the casino? Reid had sent them there. So was this just a random encounter or was 'Bunny' behind it? And why the 'Doc?' On one of the rare moments Murray allowed his backside to be seated, he pondered seriously to himself. 'They were not close to discovering or solving any major criminal activity, so they thought ………….. Or were they?'

Steven Murray had innocently given 'Doc' Patterson his coat ticket. The T'inker was on call throughout the evening, so had simply gone to retrieve his phone from the Inspector's car. The car keys were in the inside jacket pocket, and his coat would help protect him from the non-stop rain.

At this moment as Doctor Thomas Patterson fought bravely for his life, his close friend and colleague Steven Murray continued to give deep thought and consideration to who, why and what, was behind the cowardly, unprovoked attack.

Murray eventually left the hospital at 4.30 in the morning. He had been gently persuaded by a number of medical staff and a continual series of text from DS Kerr and Joe Hanlon. Basically all reminding him that he would be much more useful getting some sleep and then venturing out there and pursuing Patterson's assailant, or assailants plural. Their Detective Inspector eventually, reluctantly agreed and caught a taxi home. He knew full well that his vehicle would still be off limits for the best part of the next day. It would be knee deep with forensics people he guessed. Each of whom would be trying desperately to uncover clues that would help ensure a quick capture for The T'inker's attacker. Possibly it may even help uncover and reveal a motive behind the vicious assault.

It was 5am as he slumped down on the red fabric sofa in his front room. What had he done he thought to himself. The daughter of Robert Latchford had been buried alive. His friend was at death's door and his mind is being ravaged by nefarious memories of his past. Sleep could not even be remotely on the horizon anytime soon.

Suddenly and without any warning, the tears came to Murray's eyes. They began to flow steadily wrapped in warm melancholy as they often are. They ran down familiar groove lines on his cheeks. He grimaced intensely with pain. His throat tightened, his back teeth gritted firmly together and an intense burning seared deep into his heart. His chest rose and fell unevenly as he sobbed constantly. An almighty, shuddering intake of breath was consumed. Instantly it joined forces with a multitude of powerful emotions and was desperately exhaled vocally as acute distress. No words could adequately describe the sound. Although, excruciating pain came close. People who have dealt with heartache and suffered loss up close, knew these feelings only too well. They were the fragments, the excess, the remains. The soul destroying residue, the leftover remnants.

They noticeably surfaced many hours after the death, after the funeral and long after the sympathy, well wishers and cards had died down. It was when the flames had ceased, the coffin laid to rest and many weeks and months after friends, family and loved ones had mourned alongside you. It was during those quiet times, amidst the distant isolation and in Detective Inspector Steven Murray's particular case, currently now, when he became riddled and emotionally overcome with guilt!

In the early hours and half asleep on the couch, he held himself responsible. Casinos. Gambling. Death. You can add, subtract, or multiply them in whatever way you want. The answer will always remain the same in his mind, that Steven Murray the failed father and husband....... was culpable!

With just over three hours sleep under his belt. At 9.15 Murray was up and ready to face another day. The DI had asked Hanlon to pick him up at nine-thirty sharp, with their meeting scheduled for ten o'clock that morning. Thirty minutes he reckoned would give them plenty of time to arrive at Juniper Rise. Loanhead was in Midlothian and was less than a mile from the A720 City Bypass. The old colliery town was twinned with Harnes in northern France, as both had strong mining traditions. Featured in the centre of the local square was a memorial. Proudly erected in 2008, it paid poignant tribute to the men killed in the town's historic coal mines.

With Murray's car well and truly sealed off by a forensics team, Hanlon duly arrived as requested at 9.30am to pick up 'his boss.' 'Boss' - now that was a terminology that he never normally used. One he personally was uncomfortable with. Some of the others he noticed would occasionally call their Inspector - boss, gaffer or even chief. But Joseph Hanlon preferred the straightforward 'sir.' Respect, courtesy and deference worked well and sat naturally much more comfortably with him. Murray on just over three hours kip had closed and locked the front door before realising he still had the morning mail in his hand. He gave a casual shrug and continued to make his way to Hanlon's vehicle. Getting the normal morning pleasantries out of the way early, Murray then began to rifle through the five or six envelopes that had accompanied him into the car. A gas bill and crumbled bank statement remained unopened, as he then slid them into his inside jacket pocket. Hanlon changed gear and had begun to drive to their destination as an H.M. Barlinnie envelope was also quickly and quietly placed out of sight. Two further pieces were obviously identified as junk mail, being ripped in half and then torn again being the clue there for 'Sherlock.' The last item though was clearly personal. It was a coloured envelope and had been handwritten.

"You don't get that much these days," Hanlon observed, glancing across briefly.

From time to time trying to catch a glimpse, Joe guessed at maybe a birthday, although he had no idea when Murray's was. So maybe a 'best wishes,' 'thinking of you' or some sort of 'get well' message? It was a small square shaped notelet that Murray produced from the envelope. He turned it over to double check the postmark. It was stamped Edinburgh. So no real clue there then. Hanlon could see the card had begun to trouble Murray.

"Sir, sir. Are you okay? Everything alright?" He asked. Silence. Murray appeared busy reading to himself. Joe could see some brief wording on the inside and a standard picture of some pretty flowers on the outer.

He repeated cautiously. "Sir, what is it? Friend or foe? Hanlon then remarked in jest.

"I'm not sure Joe," Murray stated earnestly. "What do you make of this?" He lifted the card a little further from his eyes before reading the handwritten quote.

"And Jesus said unto him, This day is salvation come to this house, forsomuch as he also is a son of Abraham."

"What!" Joe Hanlon sounded. He hadn't been expecting that. "Let me hear it again."

This time Steven Murray seemed to slowly study each word in his mind as he repeated the sentence. *"And Jesus said unto him - this day - is salvation come to this house - forsomuch as he also - is a son of Abraham."*

"Biblical?" Hanlon offered, but equally questioned.

"No doubt," Murray confirmed.

"My phone is right there sir," Hanlon pointed at the dashboard. It was attached to the front of the air vent. He had been using it as a Sat-Nav.

"Modern technology, you know you love it sir! Google it and we'll have the answer in seconds."

"No thanks Joe."

"It's dead easy sir, I'll talk you through how to search for it."

"It's fine, honestly."

"But sir..."

"It's Luke 19!" Murray declared sharply.

Hanlon turned to stare at him and momentarily swerved off the road in doing so. Quickly regaining his composure and full control he asked excitedly,

"You're certain?"

Detective Inspector Steven Murray nodded. It was a number 80. Which was the 'no need to question me further on this' nod.

"It's Luke, Chapter Nineteen, verse Nine." He was familiar with scripture. "But what does it mean? Who is it from and how did they know my home address?"

A few brief seconds of silence was broken. "Your good buddy Reid possibly?" Hanlon suggested.

"Possibly." Murray's head swayed from side to side without turning. "He'd certainly have my address no doubt. But he's also not one for playing games. As you've noticed, 'Bunny' is direct. He's in your face and threatens you intimately. The Reidmeister likes up close and personal. So, no I don't think it's Reid."

They discussed one or two other ideas, thoughts and possible culprits. But ultimately Murray drew a line under it as they approached their exit from the Edinburgh City Bypass.

"We'll know all in good time I'm sure. But there is no context to it Joe, that's the problem. There is no ransom, no immediate threat or any imminent demand. We'll just have to bide our time and wait it out."

Hanlon disgruntled, quietly agreed as he pulled up kerbside in the quiet residential street. Arriving at 9.58am two police officers rang the doorbell.

Chapter Nineteen

"I made wine from the lilac tree, put my heart in its recipe. It makes me see what I want to see and be what I want to be. When I think more than I want to think, I do things I never should do. I drink much more than I ought to drink, because it brings me back you."

- Elkie Brooks

Linda Bell was a High School History teacher and up until about twelve months ago, she'd been a self confident, successful, single mum. Her husband Martin had died in a tragic car accident a decade ago. And she had brought up their young daughter on her own ever since. Blonde haired Caitlin Bell had her mother's natural good looks. She was tall at five foot seven, mature and well endowed for her age. She had only turned 15 in early January. Yet with make-up, hair and the right clothing, she would easily pass for a twenty year old University student.

Her mother's life had been dramatically turned upside down fourteen months ago. A new school term had begun and she had been getting regularly threatened by two or three thugs (so called pupils). In the previous year she had reported them on several occasions for their abusive language and threatening behaviour in class. This particular afternoon, things were getting no better and she finally decided enough was enough. She was going to address their actions once and for all. At the end of the lesson, as the pupils filtered out of the classroom, she asked all three boys to remain behind. In hindsight, looking back and with no third party to witness proceedings, it was a horrendous, yet fairly elementary mistake. One that was to cost her dear.

With only the four of them in the classroom, suddenly the quieter of the three made to leave. Mrs Bell shook her head. Not surprised at his unwillingness to stay.

"That won't solve anything," she shouted after him. "Running away will just delay the inevitable," she added. However on reaching the doorway, the sallow skinned feral youth looked back and gave her an ominous glare, which soon turned into a salacious smirk. Then purposely, he turned the snib and fully locked the door.

It was a nineteen sixties built high school building and most of the classroom doors had a small viewing window in each. However, it only allowed people a restricted view. But to be on the safe side, the unfazed seventeen year old then stood fully in front of the glass to stop any unwanted eyes prying in.

It was then that Linda Bell belatedly seemed to understand the severity of her position and her massive error in judgement. It was now already, way too late. These were not young primary school age children willing to take a telling. Individuals able to accept any wrongdoing on their part and apologise. This was about to turn serious, with lives changed forever. The other two coarse reprobates now made their way menacingly toward the forty-two year old teacher. Linda Bell was now fearful for her physical safety. As the first youth gripped his shirt cuffs and pulled down at them with a cocky arrogance. Ironically, the other, aggressively pushed his jersey sleeves back toward his elbows in a clear indication that he meant business. This was one school project they clearly wanted to excel at and had every intention of completing. There would never be a mention of it on any school report card. No gold stars and no smiley faces. Twenty agonisingly long, drawn out minutes later, her traumatic ordeal was seemingly over. In reality though… it was only just beginning!

Today as Linda Bell opened the door of her modern two bedroomed apartment on the outskirts of Edinburgh, it appeared clean, tidy and compact. And though only those two early years into her forties, her hair was a lustrous silver grey. It looked extremely elegant Murray thought. Which was more than could be said for it the previous evening. This morning it had been pulled back into a sophisticated, classic ponytail. Doubtless, hairdressers had a rather more fetching and chic name for it these days. Whatever it may be, Murray thought no more about it as he shook her proffered hand and made his way inside. Young 'Sherlock' closed the door behind them and all three made their way in single file up the narrow corridor. A peach aroma circulated around them and Murray spotted the modern miniature air freshener plugged into the hall socket, as the trio of bodies walked past.

Initially, Hanlon thought his boss was being slightly flirtatious with Mrs Bell. Which was partly his normal, friendly and gracious way occasionally being misinterpreted. However, he also knew that she would be hurting, feeling lost, hopeless and lonely. And in his brief time in CID, Joe Hanlon had watched no one better than Detective Inspector Steven Murray bring out the best in people. He had an uncanny ability to gee them up and empathise with them. To help them more fully understand where things were at and the reality of the situation. He basically cared for them as individuals and valued them for who they were. He was honest and upfront. Although in equal measure, he could be exceptionally cutting at times. Again however, that was always coupled with a mighty dose of kindness. He possessed a humanitarian spirit not often experienced in life, never mind in the police force. He couldn't prove it, but Joseph Hanlon was pretty confident that the anonymous benefactor that paid for his late wife's upgraded coffin, was none other than Detective

Inspector Steven Murray. The subject itself, needless to say, had never been broached.

Joe Hanlon's circumstances had been turned upside down in the past six months, and Linda Bell's world had been no different? These past few years her life had been shattered. First, the loss of her husband in a road accident, then her vicious assault at school which led to a breakdown. Now, just as she was learning to cope with society and function independently again in recent months, her beloved teenage daughter had gone missing. Literally, snatched from the street on her way home from school.

Murray's thoughts flashed to the Liam Neeson character in the 'Taken' series of movies. The distraught father reminded the kidnappers of his own capabilities. Neeson's dialogue, delivered in his most threatening Northern Irish accent stated:

'I don't know who you are. I don't know what you want. If you are looking for ransom I can tell you I don't have money, but what I do have are a very particular set of skills. Skills I have acquired over a very long career. Skills that make me a nightmare for people like you. If you let my daughter go now that'll be the end of it. I will not look for you, I will not pursue you, but if you don't, I will look for you, I will find you and I will kill you.'

The experienced woman had obviously been busy marking homework, as a hefty pile of school jotters strewn out on the coffee table in front of her would testify. Each one provided evidence of the school name, of the pupil and their respective class. As he glanced cannily across at Linda Bell, she gave him an intense, penetrating stare that he had not expected. Especially given her nervous and avoidant behaviour thus far. It was followed up with a rather sad and insincere smile before she spoke. Her female voice was soft and tender.

"I needed something to help keep me occupied."
Murray pursed his lips and by way of an understanding acknowledgement, gave a short nod. The forlorn look

on the educators face expressed hopelessness and despair. She quickly brokered a gentle laugh or two and then watched the smalltalk exit the room, just as quickly as it was introduced!

She was smartly dressed in black patent court shoes, dark stockings and a charcoal all in one knee length dress. It was finished off with a black and white bow decoratively placed at the collar. The outfit portrayed her as a slightly more modern version of Miss Jean Brodie. Who, in her fictional prime in the 1930's, was teaching at Marcia Blaine, a conservative girls' school in Edinburgh. How Linda Bell may well have wished that she had taught at a girls' school these past few years.

Back to present day non fiction and Ms Bell as she described herself to the officers, seemed to Murray's eye at least and in an educated academic way, a very attractive lady. She appeared impatient though. Her fingers on both hands interlocked and rubbed constantly one with another. A good Scottish description of that would be that she was… 'fidgety.' She was being nervously restless and obviously felt uneasy. She constantly checked if her visitors were okay. Apologised for the scattered newspapers on the settee. That her hair had fallen out of place. That she had kept them waiting at the front door. Endlessly she continued with -

"Sorry, forgive me, let me get that, oh I beg your pardon, I apologise, can I fix, will I go and……"

Murray gave Hanlon a nod (a number twelve). Hanlon took that as being the one where he has to step up to the mark and make himself useful. He was correct in that assessment. So he began with -

"Mrs, I mean Ms Bell, please, please stop worrying yourself."

Young Joe gently took her arm and gestured toward the comfortable looking chair in the corner of the room. Sat next to it was a makeshift bar. A small table had been placed there with an assortment of glasses and a large bottle of whisky. Two-thirds of the Chivas Regal was already gone.

"Take a seat Ms Bell and try to relax..."

For twenty minutes or more they chatted amicably. They double checked the information she had given their colleague 'Sandy' Kerr. Then they gathered more background on her missing daughter, gave her a brief update and tried to reassure her as best they could. Once feeling comfortable enough, the Inspector spoke.

"Carlo Tardelli, Ian Spence or Paul Lattimer, Ms Bell. Do either of those names mean anything to you? Anything at all? Ring any bells?" Murray ventured.

As the school teacher thought briefly about the three names he had mentioned. DC Hanlon knew that was his cue to head to the kitchen and put his tea making skills into practice once again. Before Linda Bell was able to answer, Murray made her aware of something.

"I saw you last night."

She lifted her head and offered a mixed look of surprise and bewilderment. It may even have portrayed a hint of... *help me out here, remind me!*

"Last night at the casino," Murray confirmed.

"Oooh, yes," she embarrassingly recalled, as her cheeks turned multi shades of red. "I just needed some kind of distraction Inspector. I don't expect you to understand."

"You and your ..."

"My colleague Inspector, nothing else. Ben is a fellow teacher. We've been to the casino on and off in recent months and he just wanted to help take my mind off things." Warily, she then added, "I don't recall seeing you there."

"Care and candor Ms Bell. Care and candor."

Her mouth was about to ask, but she decided against it.

"Do you mind?" Murray asked, pointing at her computer screen on the table opposite.

Miss Jean Brodie herself would have approved of the classic, slow, high-class nod given in return. He calmly and deliberately typed up a Google search for 'Thyme and Plaice.' A further two clicks later and there he was in full colour high resolution - Carlo Tardelli. Linda Bell's hands instantly flew in unison to her mouth. An audible gasp was heard. She did know him, or at least recognised him. Murray feeling hopeful, turned and waited patiently. This could be the breakthrough they needed Hanlon thought, having returned to the doorway after hearing the muffled, distorted cry. Both officers knew he was not involved with the missing girls, at least not directly. But this mother, of one of the teenage girls is familiar with a murder victim. And another mutilated deceased had an hourglass placed at his body. One identical to that on Robert Latchfords' mantelpiece. Latchford, another parent of a teenager that had initially gone missing, but has since been found murdered. Both men now knew for definite and without having to look at each other for confirmation. That these major investigations, two high profile cases in their own right, were inextricably linked. But in the old jovial North American Indian vernacular... How?

Linda Bell spoke. "I am so sorry Inspector. My thoughts, my mind are all over the place. I know him. I know I know him, but I just can't think from where."

"From school? The education system?" Hanlon offered by way of a reminder.

"Possibly from visiting his restaurant Thyme and Plaice?" Murray pointed again at the screen.

"Thyme and Plaice," she quizzed herself, and shook her head. "No, no I've never been there Inspector."
A small tear was quickly followed by another. She began suddenly to lash out wildly at her chair, thumping down solidly upon its arms.

"I can't remember, and my little girl is going to die because of my stupidity, my hopeless memory, my failings as a parent. All I had to do was look after her, protect her and I couldn't even do that - I failed her," she sobbed.

Murray sat carefully on one arm of the chair. He reached out to take hold of her flailing arms just as Linda Bell made to stretch and lift up the bottle of whisky from her personal supply. The same bottle that Joseph Hanlon had cannily lifted earlier on his way to brew a pot of tea. Good lad 'Sherlock' Murray thought. It was inspired thinking on Hanlon's part and way ahead of the game. Murray reaffirmed how much of a lead this was. The fact that she actually recognised Mr Tardelli meant they could pull resources, share notes and look more thoroughly at each others findings. He may have slightly exaggerated the importance, but DC Hanlon got the gist of his strategy.

Linda Bell relaxed and felt more at ease. She seemed to glow in the fact that people were listening to her. Grateful in the knowledge that many others were currently working hard on many different fronts to successfully locate her beautiful daughter Caitlin.

"Would you mind if we took a quick look at her room?" Hanlon asked politely.

"No, sure, whatever you need," she said helpfully. With her eyes filled with desperation and forlorn hope she added, "Although, the other officers already checked."

"That's okay," Joe said. "A different perspective, a fresh set of eyes, you know how it is. It may be extremely useful. They may have missed something."
With that, Linda Bell looked worryingly at Murray.

"They won't have," he reassured her. "Nothing obvious. But we may spot something that is just out of sorts. Something significant. Something that could possibly break the case," he offered hopefully. "Often the line between success and failure in these particular investigations can be exceptionally thin!"
Buoyed up by Murray's confident, proactive stance, Ms Bell led them both through to her teenager's bedroom. He was hit with an overwhelming maelstrom of colour as he opened the door.

"Wow, I guess purple is her favourite!" exclaimed Joe.

"Ever since she was only two or three," Linda Bell reflected. Before excusing herself to the bathroom.

Everywhere you looked in her room, you were met with various shades of her childhood preference. The immaculate wood flooring had an enormous patterned rug at the bottom of her low lying Ikea bed. Murray reckoned it was lilac, Hanlon argued lavender.

"Possibly mauve," Murray suggested.

Hanlon shook his head, laughed scornfully and deliberately replied with the intention of winding Murray up -

"Violet, that's it, definitely violet. There can be no argument to that."

"No argument? No argument? Are you having a laugh son?" Murray questioned. "There is no way that is parma 'flippin' violet coloured."

On hearing the commotion and a few of the words being exchanged on her return. Linda Bell seemingly rather flushed, nodded and offered -

"Yes, I would agree, violet is how we described it!"

Murray was dumbstruck. He threw his hands down in disgust and seemingly missed the small, subtle wink the homeowner exchanged with DC Hanlon. Justin Bieber adorned her walls - posters, badges, magazines and scarves. A bizarre plum coloured, velour rocking chair sat in the corner. Unusual as it had angled feet and could not actually rock! A medium sized flat screen tv sat atop her trendy entertainment desk. It housed a range of DVDs, mainly teenage rom/coms, two sets of headphones, various charging cables and a small selection of music cd's.

"Most of her music will be on her phone I guess," Murray lamented.

"Downloads, absolutely sir," Hanlon concurred.

Silently, nodding in agreement at the doorway Linda Bell felt a touch of 'deja vu,' as she once again watched two officers dissect and scrutinise her missing daughter's domain.

"Wow!" Joe Hanlon surprisingly exclaimed.

"What have you found 'Sherlock?'" his DI enquired.

Hanlon had slowly and gracefully pushed aside the twin sliding doors on Caitlin's walk-in wardrobe. The cabinet was about the normal seven or eight foot in length. But inside it was jam packed with outfits. This was much more than either officer expected to find for a young high school pupil. They recognised most girls her age would want plenty of outfits. However, at present, this was a throwaway society we currently lived in. And their investigative experience taught them that only a selected few outfits: The trendy, the fashionable, the in, normally sat alongside a school uniform and a couple of rain jackets! And therein lay the problem. Here there seemed to be numerous beautiful evening dresses, chic designer outfits and even one or two high end fashion names. As Linda Bell stepped forward from the doorway, DC Hanlon watched Steven Murray offer up a smile of wisdom and understanding. Slightly baffled at this, 'Sherlock' screwed up his eyes and stared curiously at both parties.

"You both share the wardrobe!" Murray announced confidently.

Linda Bell acknowledged with a slight dip of her chin and smiled weakly. The Inspector, desirous to boost this devastated mother's confidence. Pointed at the vast range of alluring, classy outfits, looked at what she had on that day and concluded assertively, if not rather cheekily.

"What's the merit of choosing the drab Ms Bell, when beauty hangs in the wardrobe?"

Hanlon froze momentarily, thinking that comment quite bold. He relaxed soon enough though, when he saw a rather happy expression appear on the bright, blushing face of one Ms Linda Bell.

Chapter Twenty

*"One night in Bangkok and the world's your oyster. The bars are
temples but the pearls ain't free. You'll find a god in every golden
cloister and if you're lucky then the god's a she."*

- Murray Head

As the crow flies, it was about six and a half miles from
Loanhead to Blake's Auction House in the beating heart
of Edinburgh city centre. And right now as he surveyed
the almighty staircase in front of him, oh how 'Ally'
Coulter wished he could fly. What felt like three full
days later, but in reality was actually only three solitary
minutes, saw Coulter puff, pant and wheeze his way
around the vast showroom after arriving at the summit.

It was a tremendous storage space of bric-a-brac,
collectibles and treasured memorabilia. Precious
memories and historical provenances lay amidst the
valued array of goods on display. 'Ally' moved slowly up
and down each aisle and delved curiously into every
crevasse. His head continually rolled from side to side
and up and down. Monitoring, observing and carefully
scrutinising every movement. He was like a human
dalek, gliding smoothly from row to row. Examining,
lifting up, placing down, prices clocked, eyes rolled and
the inevitable shake of the head. Then with a small
ceramic 1920's porcelain vase in his hand, he spotted
him! Twenty metres away, at the end of the line of
highly prized artefacts. He was a picture of sartorial
elegance. An expensive, well tailored, two piece charcoal
suit. Underneath the jacket the man wore a premium
ash grey polo neck. A gleaming pair of impressive
Bruno Magli black lace up shoes completed the look.

179

With hair reminiscent of 1980's Tom Cruise, Simon Taylor was a handsome man, and he knew it. This was reflected in his cool, confident demeanour. Which over the next fifteen minutes Coulter would witness several times transcend into arrogant, superior, know-it-all mode. He was able to recognise quickly why his Inspector had taken an instant dislike to him.

"Morning," a still slightly out of breath, overweight man offered.

After an initial full body scan, monitoring Coulter carefully from head to toe. The 'Savile Row' assistant stood still, hands in pocket, before finally making a judgement. It was in the affirmative, but heavily disguised.

"Apologies sir, we've never quite got around to installing a customer lift."

Cheeky git Coulter thought to himself, whilst vocally expressing -

"No problem. Need the exercise as you can see."

Coulter couldn't quite believe he then naturally found himself instinctively patting his midriff.

"Specific age?"

"Sorry?" 'Ally' asked.

"A specific age of goods? Are you looking for antiques or collectables from a certain era? That is how we display everything here throughout the showroom. I take it you are new to this game then?

"Indeed I am." Coulter slowly remarked.

At that very moment, he swore he saw Taylor's rare green eyes turn into bold, bright pound signs.

"What is that you are working on right now?" 'Ally' continued.

"Give me a minute," was the brusque response as the businessman made his way toward the 'Staff Only' door.

Coulter wasn't entirely sure the door itself was not for sale as it was that rundown. Taylor was by all accounts normally always smartly dressed. He appeared so, in the many pictures of himself that hung in the stairwell. In every shot, in every frame, he was impeccably dressed. From fashionably long overcoats and three piece suits, to fine tailored shirts and Italian shoes. You name it, this here man had been pictured in it. So for 'Ally' Coulter to now witness him reappear without his jersey and jacket was quite a surprise! He was still rather handily kitted out however. Underneath the polo neck had been a resplendent sky blue shirt with white collar. It was now partially hidden by a dark blue kitchen apron. Coulter was sure it would have had some proper 'macho' sounding trade name! And in fairness, as 'Ally' inspected it up close, it actually seemed to be made from a rather elegant brushed suede material. He was a bit of a dandy right enough Coulter decided. Especially with the long white satin gloves that he'd just pulled on right up to his elbows. The off duty Sergeant scrunched up his face at those though. They brought back traumatic memories of an Asian experience he once had!

It had been several years previous with a scantily clad female parading in front of him in a nightclub in Bangkok. Slowly, one at a time, the erotic dancer had gracefully and sensually peeled off each of the silky, full length white gloves that had adorned her slim, slender arms. She then turned her back on the audience before instantly undoing her bra and briefs. As if throwing up a bridal bouquet at a wedding, the sexy quartet of clothing was propelled high out into the smoke filled air. Before Coulter could catch a descending glove and cry out 'Sexy Senga,' he was out the door in an instant. *'Like a bat out of hell he was gone before the morning came!!!"* Never mind 'sexy Senga,' he recalled. Try 'Slippery Sidney.' That had been no woman flaunting herself on stage that night and the memory still gave him shivers to this day!

"This was from the Presidential suite in The White House." Taylor announced confidently on his return.

"Sorry!" 'Ally' Coulter announced.

"You had asked me what I was working on before. I just needed to get my gloves and apron on to get started. "You know after the stock market crash of October 1929 had sent Wall Street into a panic and wiped out millions of investors, this was brought into Presidential ownership.

"Seriously?" Coulter asked. "How come?"

Taylor got comfortable. It was an old shoe shine chair. The aged leather seat came attached to the raised step at the bottom.

"Here you go my good man," Taylor reeled off playfully, as he handed Coulter the polish and cloth.

"Am I not supposed to be up there with you cleaning my shoes?" 'Ally' asked, a rather matter of factly.

"Well yes, strictly speaking. However I am about to regale you with the legend behind the myth."

"Mmm," the policeman mumbled, unconvinced. "Well, let me get a historic photo of this event," he joked.

A nod from Taylor was given. A few clicks later and it pinged on Inspector Murray's phone. Now all of Facebook are aware of my menial role in society, 'Ally' confirmed. The close-up photo was specifically of Taylor's flawed shoes!

"Well what do you think it felt like for the men who actually did do this for a living?" Taylor threw out there. "It belonged to one Charles Curtis."

Coulter shook his head.

"Charles Curtis was the 31st Vice President of the United States," Simon Taylor extolled. "After the crash and only several weeks later on the run up to Christmas 1929, Curtis singled out a lucky shoeshine man and offered to buy him out. Considering the average income in America back then was about $2,000. To get a buyer to part with $300, nearly two months salary, was a major coup.

"Mmmm," Coulter sighed warily. As he set about adding an extra protective gleam to the already glistening Italian footwear!

Having mentioned to Murray and Hanlon that she had actually won at the casino the previous evening, Linda Bell went quickly to retrieve her handbag. She duly returned, back into the sitting room.

"Here it is," she enthused, handing some of her winning chips to DC Hanlon.

"It's about £90 or thereabouts she claimed.
Murray recognised the familiar coloured discs immediately.

"I was a bit the worse for wear last night! You probably noticed, no doubt Inspector?"

"Can't say that I did," he once again, courteously lied.

"Anyway I decided not to cash them in," she said. Instantly throwing another handful onto her rustic red sofa. Murray looked at her inquisitively.

"Okay," she mumbled. "In all honesty, I was so oblivious to having won. I was totally out of it and just needed to get home and get some rest." Her confession was refreshing, but left her feeling exposed and openly embarrassed. This aroused something in the DI. Young Hanlon could see the cogs in his old analog head beginning once again to slowly turn. It had helped Murray consider a few possibilities. He felt the emergence of a few interesting questions that had formed. A pause. Then.

"How long have you been a member Linda? He asked with a renewed spirit.

"Did you check, personally check all the pockets and wallets of our murdered victims? He verified with 'Sherlock.'
Linda Bell interrupted, disgusted with herself.

"People don't mind knowing about your membership of other established clubs or organisations, including, ironically Bingo! But gambling, playing blackjack, poker and roulette - there is still a stigma. Younger ones may see it as modern, trendy, thrilling and daring. But the establishment frown upon it, make a judgement on you…"

"Wow, wow, steady on Ms Bell." The Inspector's hands were raised, beginning to lower steadily. Then up…then down…back up…and finally right down to his waist, and relax!

"Don't feel you have to justify your actions to us, to your friends, to anyone for that matter," he then added sharply.

It had obviously touched a raw nerve with Steven Murray. Hanlon was intrigued, but maybe not unsurprised.

"Maybe when I justify it, it helps me?" Linda Bell offered.

Before the Inspector could pump up his soap box further, Hanlon's phone sprang into action. He could see it was the station and looked across at Murray. At which point he nodded apologetically, realising he had left his in the car. Thus, obviously why they were contacting Hanlon.

And as he swiped the screen…… "Yes, I know. Yes, he is well aware. No not deliberately. He left it in his car. Sure." As he listened his urge to leave became more apparent. "I've got that. Yes, and I'll get him to contact Brown a.s.a.p."

"Problem?" Murray questioned.

"We're needed straight away sir." Hanlon remarked. There was a genuine urgency in his voice. "Another dead body has been discovered at……"

Before young Joe could finish, it was Murray's turn to adopt 'Sherlock's' deductive reasoning.

"Your current High School, I would guess Ms Bell," Detective Steve Murray, declared confidently.

"What!" Linda Bell exclaimed, gesturing to the young DC. "My school? What makes him think that? "

"How could you possibly have known that sir?" Hanlon was awestruck!

Murray pointed and gestured toward the stacked tower of marking that had taken place earlier before the officers arrived.

"Insight, Joe," Murray deduced. "Ms Bell here, works at a Catholic High School. Take a look at which one."

Hanlon turned his neck, peered down and observed one of the homework jotters. Sighing, as if he'd just had the proverbial stuffing knocked out of him. He paused, shook his head and added in a rather defeated tone.

"She works at St. Luke's!"

A devout silence prevailed. Two ascetic police officers volunteered to leave behind mainstream society… for all of thirteen minutes! On their drive to the school, three sets of minor roadworks had delayed their progress. At the second set, a blue light and some sound was required to force their way through. As they drove at speed under the modern gates of the High School, the school badge adorned the red brick wall on the left hand side. The name was large and bold. Its lettering entwined with a large colourful floral wreath. And there, bang in the middle and central to everything - an open bible!

A relatively young PC met them at the main door and guided them through a labyrinth of corridors. As they made their way to the cordoned off area, Hanlon began to surmise.

"It was probably the religious education instructor that had been murdered. That would tie in nicely with all the biblical references of your note"

"Very impressive sir," offered their guide as he began to lead them through a small gym hall.

"Thank you constable. I'm starting to get the hang of this detective malarkey," Hanlon smiled proudly.

As he winked at Inspector Murray, the fresh faced uniformed policeman got great pleasure from stating the following -

"As I said sir, very impressive. However - absolute tosh!" He then nodded politely.

"Here you go Inspector Murray, this is the crime scene." Still with a cheeky grin on his face, he turned toward Hanlon and reminded him of their similar status. "CONSTABLE better luck next time!"

"Arrogant git!" Hanlon quipped.

"Is that in reference to him or yourself Joe?"
Murray's deliberate stare made him question his words.

"Sorry sir. I'll apologise on the way out."
Forensics officers were busy beginning to set up in the far corner. Pathologist Andy Gordon was walking toward them. All three nodded. Enough said. There before them, disturbingly attached to the wall apparatus was the victim.

"Vitruvian man," Murray announced, hand clasped tightly over his mouth.

"My thoughts entirely," Patterson's replacement agreed.

"Vit whatanian man?" Hanlon looked to have no clue.

"We're of a similar age, him and I," the rotund medical examiner responded.

Slowly, Murray informed him. "The Vitruvian man was an old Leonardo da Vinci pen and ink drawing. It was made famous to our generation for being on the weekly credits of the TV documentary program 'World in Action!"
As a tag team, it was Gordon's turn to take over.

"It is less often referred to as 'Proportions of Man."

"Well he certainly seems out of proportion to most men I meet," 'Sherlock' offered up.

"You'd be right there young Hanlon. He looks to be between 6' 4' and 6' 5'. We'll know for sure once we get him down and laid flat."

Doctor Andrew Gordon normally always worked nights or weekends. Thinning on top, he carried a much fuller figure these days. His cocky, confident smile remained intact, as did his impressive handshake. He was often mistaken for a mason. Mainly because of the unusual nature of his grip. On closer inspection, the answer was simple. He was missing a finger on his right hand. However, that is not to say a visit once a week to his local Lodge was out of the question! He was a good natured man and he had enjoyed a friendly, professional relationship with Murray over the past decade or more. He was now semi retired and had been for the last couple of years or so. A full twenty year stretch gave him more than enough to retire comfortably on. Picking up a little pocket money here and there, simply helped assure him of that one month in sunnier climates every January.

Steven Murray thoughtfully contemplated the scene. A small mound of clothing, presumably the dead man's, lay on the edge of the hardwood court. The naked body faced inward, with its arms and legs outstretched fully. It had been fastened tightly to the bars of the climbing frame. The poor man had been repeatedly beaten, thrashed and struck. Blood was spattered within a twenty foot radius. Murray feared the scene of crime officers would run out of markers there had been so much coverage. He had never in all his years, witnessed it range so far before.

Hanlon though, could see it perfectly. He'd pictured the barbaric attacker continuously flaying and peeling his victim. Then each time as he pulled back to reign down and inflict another horrific blow, groups of blood leapt for safety. They'd decided that their torturous shift was over for the day. So having made a powerful pact, on the upstroke they would seek asylum elsewhere and duly did so! A combination of leather and plastic man made belts secured the body firmly in place. A prominent, weathered brown band had been fastened tightly around the neck. His toned muscular frame was now a mass of welts and dark contusions. Remnants of skin hung like scrawled post-it notes across his back. The flesh had gone completely from his tender shoulders, where now only splintered white bone remained and shone through. Murray could only view it from a restricted distance, the sinews had clearly been gradually clawed, torn and raked, comparable to soil ready to sow. The Inspector guessed or certainly hoped that the poor victim had passed out quickly. This grotesque human pelt had been used to great effect as a backdrop for the latest Jackson Pollock masterpiece Murray concluded. Which was impressive in itself. As the abstract expressionist had died in 1956!

"Do we know who he is?" Hanlon asked. "A visitor, teacher, someone from…"

"He's a teacher," the Doc answered. "It was one of his pupils that discovered him."

"Here?" Hanlon asked in surprise.

"Absolutely." Andrew Gordon confirmed. Nothing underhand. He was an ex-professional basketball player and is now one of the school P.E. teachers."

"Was!" 'Sherlock' unhappily added.

In unison, all three nodded.

"Do we have a name for him yet Doc?" Hanlon pursued.

Dr Gordon grinned. "Before he ran off faster than Usain Bolt, the school kid told the first two officers on the scene that it was Mr Wexford. Mr Wexford he repeated a further twice, possibly in shock, before he was off like a shot! We have his full details now though. The headmaster gave us his file about two minutes before you got here."

"No need," Murray claimed.

"What?" The Doc said surprised.

"I think I know his first name Andy. I saw him last night. He was at the casino with Linda Bell. He was literally head and shoulders above everyone else. Mr Wexford is her colleague Ben. Benjamin Wexford."

"Correct," Andy Gordon said. "Well done."

"Sir," Hanlon piped up addressing DI Murray, an almighty eureka moment just coming to him. "I would go as far as to say, I think I could tell you his father's name!"

Totally confused and bamboozled by this, Doc Gordon shook his head.

"No way! This I'd like to hear," he responded.

Steven Murray simply smiled and gave an impressive nod. It was a nod that Hanlon couldn't quite equate to a number. But it definitely said - *I knew you could!*

"Abe Wexford sir. No doubt christened Abraham. Abraham Wexford."

Doctor Gordon looked across at Murray. The Inspector smiled and raised his shoulders.

"How did I do Doc?"

Andrew Gordon's gaping mouth told it's own story!

'Sherlock' looked intensely at Murray and continued. *"And Jesus said unto him, this day is salvation come to this house, forsomuch as he also is a son of Abraham."*

"This is a definite clue," Murray offered up.

The other two's ears pricked up at that. They both turned anxiously, eager to hear the DI's speculative theory.

"I don't know," he shrugged. "I don't know how, or what, the why, where or when. But I know it's a clue, an important one. My gut tells me it's the one that will turn the case," he mused, before offering. "Or cases plural?"

Then it appeared to be his turn to have 'the eureka' light bulb switched on. At Intel speed, everyone and everything was rapidly scanned. Fleeting pictures appeared as snapshots in his mind and were gone again in an instant. Spence, Tardelli, Mo's cafe and the Thyme and Plaice. Lattimer, jump leads and now a mutilated Wexford. What was the link?

The floral garden, a scrapyard and body positions. London jigsaws, an hourglass and fried hands at the restaurant. The scenes continued - An auction house, Doc Patterson and the dead lifeless body of Cindy-Ann. At this point singer/songwriter Billy Joel called out to him as a kindred spirit as he rattled through a list of names, areas and key events - *'Harry Truman, Doris Day, Red China, Johnnie Ray, South Pacific, Walter Winchell, Joe DiMaggio...'* The flickering images continued at pace - A portly murdered Italian, missing girls, the night watchman's heart cut out. An array of fastened belts in a sports hall. Another hourglass, a social worker, naked teacher and a handful of winning casino chips. Not forgetting the curious crossover that Linda Bell and Robert Latchford knew some of them. *'Brando, The King and I and The Catcher in the Rye...'*

As the colourful psychedelic diversity of people, place and position in society continued to mix and spin rapidly in his head. Detective Inspector Steve Murray hoped to arrive at an unbeatable, magical conclusion. A hypothesis that once unveiled to the world would make sense of everything. *JFK blown away, what else do I have to say?* Only one thing, he thought -

"Has anyone checked his wallet?" The Inspector asked. "We are still missing something."

Detective Constable Hanlon made to remove the dead man's wallet from the back pocket of the trousers in the pile of clothing. As he opened it...

"It's here," he cried.

A credit card sat prominently in the front pouch. It had been covered over by a familiar brightly coloured post-it note. Written on the paper this time were a seemingly random selection of letters: ELMYRDEHORY.

"Another cryptic clue," Hanlon exclaimed.

"I suspect two clues Joe. Pull back the note," Murray encouraged.

Slowly, between forefinger and thumb, 'Sherlock' smoothly peeled back the gummed paper. Hanlon's eyes bulged with recognition, but not understanding!

"It's not a credit card sir. It's a membership card and it is for…"

" … I know. My favourite gaming establishment… and that is the link between them."

Chapter Twenty-One

"Mamma, Pappa say you should go to school, I don't know what for. Now that I have grown up and seen the world and all its lies. What's the time Mr. Wolf? What's the time?"

- Southside of Bombay

"Are you sure this is a good idea sir?" Joseph Hanlon asked warily.

"Was the Jeremy Kyle Show?" Murray responded with a shake of the head and a wide beam. "Get back in the saddle and all that. Although, to clarify, you know I've never actually owned a horse right?"

"I would never have guessed," Joseph Hanlon sarcastically voiced. "How about ever been kicked in the head by one?" he then added. "Because you don't half talk some utter nonsense at times."

Murray dropped his chin slightly and gently scolded his now highly embarrassed companion. "That will be enough of that kind of talk young man."

They walked briskly toward the front door of the building. It was much easier to check out its facade in the daylight and without the 'slight' downpour of a month's rain all duly delivered in one aqueous night. The DI jauntily made his way up the steps of the modern entrance. He walked carefully between a pair of grand, imposing marble pillars which stood firm like two obedient sentries on guard duty. Then, he duly checked his watch with the beautiful clock that sat gracefully embedded into the pillar to his right hand side. It was to be the last clock or timepiece they would witness before entering into the 'dark side.'

Like many Vegas hotels, gambling dens and similar establishments, clocks are not generally encouraged. There is never any pleasure in being reminded that you have just lost your stake (possibly a month's wage) in five minutes flat! It kind of takes away the enjoyment, but not the pain that it will leave behind.

At that moment, Murray realised for the first time, that he had never actually been inside a casino during daylight hours. Behind the desk sat a familiar face. And the familiar face then offered a familiar greeting.

"Good afternoon gentlemen, how can I help you today?"

"Mr Wolf isn't it?" Murray snorted.

The rosy cheeks of the forty-something man dressed uncannily like a secret service agent, lost some of their natural colour. He tried desperately to offer up a forced smile. Murray screwed up his eyes at him. What had he said?

"Police?" the dark suited gatekeeper managed to respond. The one word offered up as a question.

"I'm DS Hanlon, he's DI Murray," young Joe submitted as a suitably succinct answer.

Murray was eying the man carefully up and down now. He could quite clearly see that the name on his lapel badge was Barlow, not Wolf. Had he been mistaken? He was sure it was the same person. However, he began to reflect. Maybe it was another guy that had handed him the towel? It had been torrential rain after all and he and Doc Patterson had just been grateful to get in under shelter. There had been several staff mulling around the foyer that night. Maybe he was just a face he remembered as he made his way out later heading for the cashline. But for now, Barlow was on his walkie talkie radio.

"Boss, we have two police officers at the front desk. I am assuming you want to speak to the manager?" he turned back to Hanlon and asked.

A single nod was given in response.

"Was that a number eight?" Murray winked and asked of DS Hanlon.

Escorted over to the lift, the security guard moonlighting as a concierge, swiped a contactless card across a small scanner. He then pressed the button and the elevator doors opened. Once inside, both detectives looked at Barlow quizzically. Then in unison with their palms showing, opened their fingers and mouths.

"Oh, it's the second level. The Manager's office is right opposite the lift," he stated before turning and walking away.

"Thanks for those details Mr Wolf!" Murray blurted sarcastically.

It was enough however to stop the man in his tracks, and from over his left shoulder the Inspector received a rather menacing and ominous look.

Of the four options, G, 1, 2 or EMIT, the circular number two icon had made contact with Hanlon's thumb and they were now gently gliding heavenward. The quick ten second ride was long enough for Murray to break into a little known country reggae song.

"Everybody wants to go to heaven, have a mansion high above the clouds. Everybody wants to go to heaven, but nobody want to go right now."

Hanlon shaking his head, looked despairingly at his DI.

"What? It's Kenny Chesney. The American country artist," Murray encouraged.

"Ah, Kenny Chesney," Joe said, as if recalling and figuring out who he meant.

"You have no idea who that is. Do you?"

A slight 'ping' was heard just as the lift doors opened and both men exited.

"Absolutely correct," Hanlon smiled broadly. "Thankfully, no idea whatsoever."

Murray was in the process of informing his colleague about Kenny Chesney's 29 million album sales, just as another elegantly attired 'federal agent' stepped forward to greet them. Rather younger looking this time, probably in his mid thirties.

"Mr Fox?" Hanlon cheekily offered this time.

The man stared blankly at them. Confusion reigned and his eyes darted from one to the other.

"Never mind my partner," Murray interrupted, glowering at his DS. "He had animal crackers with his soup."

The poor security guard had no idea where to look or what was going on. In fairness, the two police officers stood alongside him… felt exactly the same! The guard had informed them in a rather gruff Glaswegian accent that Gerry, his boss, had a few phone calls to make and would be with them shortly. He pointed them in the direction of a couple of seats outside of his office. Both men sat and were prepared to wait patiently.

"Everybody wants to go to heaven."

"Don't start with that again," Hanlon quipped.

Murray offered a reflective smile and asked, "Does this remind you of anything Joe?

Not on the same wavelength currently as his DI, Hanlon, shook his head. "In relation to what? He asked further, "What cryptic connection are you making this time?"

"School!" Murray barked. "Nothing complicated. School. Memories of waiting outside the Headmaster's room. Mr Malcolm's torture chamber."

"I'm guessing you weren't there to receive congratulations or a star pupil of the week award?" Joe figured.

"That's correct." Murray began to applaud his young protege. "And it was no doubt the making of me."

Detective Sergeant Joseph Hanlon held his head in his hands and simply sighed.

Five minutes had past by and Murray and Hanlon had each in turn taken a short walk along the corridor. Each wall offered beautiful portraits, landscapes and some rather tasteful modern art. There were one or two raised pedestals in the walkway with ornate jewellery or pottery on display behind protective glass. It was comparable to walking through areas of an impressive museum or art gallery. Since renovating the outside facade of the old building, the owners certainly never held back when it came to investing some serious money into the interior also. During a brief discussion, those thoughts were shared by both Hanlon and Murray. However, those cryptic connections that Hanlon had mentioned earlier, quite clearly were now beginning to surface in the mind of one Steven Murray, and just at that a male figure appeared from the Manager's office.

"Gerry," he said in an upbeat manner, as he approached and introduced himself to the detectives.

In a rather deep, surly voice Murray replied, "DI Murray and Detective Sergeant Hanlon."

All three men shook hands.

As they entered the plush office, Murray couldn't help but stare at two modern shelves. Both were jam packed with DVDs, so nothing particularly unusual in that he thought. Until that was, he continued to run his finger along the edge of each one and began to read the film titles on the spine. The common denominator soon became clearly apparent...... *Insomnia; Robots; Patch Adams; One Hour Photo.*

"You are obviously a big fan of his work," Murray observed.

"You're only given a little spark of madness Inspector. *You mustn't lose it!* I've been an ardent fan for years. He brings tears to my eyes. Everytime without fail - I get tears in my eyes. Ever since... " he stopped suddenly.

"Ever since what?" Joe Hanlon questioned. His inexperience coming to the fore!

"Aaagh," his Inspector inhaled sharply. He'd taken the bait Murray conceded. That was exactly what this overweight, underdressed, silver haired man in his mid sixties had been hoping for. The opportunity to regale someone new with his colourful memories of this iconic celebrity. For a casino boss, even on his day off, he would have been considered a scruff. The words 'hedge, backwards and dragged' all came instantly to mind whilst taking stock of their present host. Black jogging bottoms with paint spatters on the knees, tight burgundy t-shirt and to complete the fashion statement, a grey, rather tired looking, heavy woollen cardigan. There was however a couple of interesting details that Murray intended to point out later to Hanlon. That is of course if the intrepid 'Sherlock' had not already spotted them. *Jakob the Liar; Flubber; Good Will Hunting; The Birdcage and Jumanji* were a few other recognisable movie titles on the shelf below.

"Ever since," Gerry continued. "I met him in person in the late seventies. He was performing stand-up comedy in Los Angeles."

By which point he'd already scooped up the signed photo frame to thrust into the Detective Sergeant's hand. There he was in all his glory, 'Our Gezzer' with the late, great, sadly departed Robin Williams! Gerry had been watching *'Good Morning, Vietnam'* on a large screen as they had all entered.

Hanlon then made to return the signed print to the manager's desk and in doing so, had mistakenly knocked over the picture frame next to it. Gerry gestured for all three to be seated.

In an admiring fashion DS Hanlon stated. "That is some mighty impressive artwork you have displayed throughout the casino sir. Especially including the one on your wall there,"

"Well I appreciate you saying so officer, but just to be clear they are all prints and reproductions, like the one behind me. None of them hold any significant value I'm afraid." Although he then added, "But they are exceptionally pleasing to the eye and they most certainly add to the upmarket experience our clientele have come to expect from the ABC brand."

Murray coughed, which quite clearly indicated............ and moving on.

"Apologies, I digress," Gerry shrugged. "How can I be of assistance officers? My son, that's him aged ten in the picture," he said, before standing it back up. "He is normally the one here running things two to three days a week. I merely cover for him on the odd occasion. Luckily I'm semi-retired these days, so I can help him out."

Murray bit his lip and thought that may account for the tardiness in dress standards, though not fully convinced.

"There was an attack took place outside the premises last night sir," Hanlon offered. "The victim had been in attendance here in your club. We just wanted to find out if any of your security cameras had picked up anything?"

The older gentleman stated with a smile, *"I'm sorry, if you were right, I'd agree with you!"*

Another movie quote Murray figured.

"Where exactly did it happen?" the casino boss quizzed. With a look of surprise he quickly added, "I've not been informed about this. Usually the doormen or security filter back this sort of information. Was it outside at the doorway? On the steps? I can check individual monitors and timeframes. So where did you say?"

"Actually Gerry," Murray spoke up sheepishly -

"It was across the road on Hill Place."

"Oh, I see Inspector. So NOT actually on our premises," he stated. Offering a slight rebuke by way of a narrow stare at DS Hanlon.

"Well, let's see if we can be of help anyway."

After fifteen to twenty minutes checking various camera set-ups; Front door. Across street. Foyer, etc. They all agreed that after they had witnessed 'The T'inker', aka Doc Patterson exit the club. No one had followed him. Added to that, not one of the outside cameras was able to take any video footage of any goings on in Hill

Place. They had witnessed no suspicious behaviour whatsoever. Except, in Murray's mind at least, that of the man sat opposite them.

"We'll take these recordings with us if you don't mind," Hanlon piped up. "A further viewing down at the station by a fresh pair of eyes may be advantageous," he suggested.

"By all means," the part-time boss said helpfully. "Whatever it takes Constable. *I know never to pick a fight with an ugly man, because they have nothing to lose.*"
Murray smiled, recognizing that was the third Robin Williams quote he'd thrown into their conversation. Hanlon simply paused to question if he'd just been insulted?

"Now perhaps gentlemen?" He motioned toward the door, "I have a rather busy schedule this afternoon."
Murray took out a small, plastic Ziploc pouch. It contained two of his business cards. And stuck together, he handed both cards over.

"If you can think of anything else that may be helpful, don't hesitate to get in touch 'Gerry.' The last word sticking in his throat as he tried to sound sincere.

Handing him the extra card back. "Absolutely," he said. Then tapping the waistband of his black 'trackie' bottoms, he mentioned, "Although I forgot to carry my mobile today Inspector."
Murray nodded and carefully placed the returned card, now with Gerry's fingerprints on it, back into the sealed bag! It was an old trick that Murray regularly carried out. He then gave an unseen wink to Hanlon.

'Sherlock' spoke. "You have been most helpful sir. Thank you for taking the time."
He stepped forward to shake Gerry's hand, gripping it rather longer than deemed necessary was Murray's early observation. The Inspector merely nodded (a number 73), indicating - You're holding something back Gerry. What could it be? And why?

"Oh and by the way sir. *No matter what people tell you. Words and ideas CAN change the world.*"

"Touche! Inspector, well done. A welcome adversary perhaps?" Both men mutually offered cold, disingenuous smiles.

Chapter Twenty-Two

"There's a lady who's sure all that glitters is gold. And she's buying a stairway to heaven."

- Led Zeppelin

Whilst waiting for the lift the Inspector mentioned casually. "Nice work, getting us a look at the other picture frame Constable."

"Thank you sir. I reckoned if it was important enough to sit alongside Robin Williams, then it was worth us knowing who it was. Unfortunately, it was just a 'to be expected' father and son snap."

"What was with the handshake though?" Murray asked.

Before Hanlon responded both men made their way into the lift and began to travel back down to the ground floor. Murray unusually for him, checked something out on his phone just as Joe spoke.

"Over the years sir, TV programmes like *Lie to Me* and *The Mentalist* teach you how when shaking hands you can actually get a read on the other person. You know, you are able to feel their pulse racing, begging the question - Why are they so anxious? How come the nerves? What's up? They may be ever so keen to let go quickly, thus causing you to be suspicious of them, all things…"

"And!" Murray interrupted abruptly. "Are you telling me 'Sherlock' you were able to glean something important and worthwhile from your lingering, devious, creepy handshake?"

Turning rather red at this uncomplicated question, 'Sherlock' held to his lips an imaginary long stemmed pipe. Then in a rather posh English voice offered up.

"Elementary my dear Murray."

His Inspector's unimpressed facial expression made him quickly scale down his accent and utter.

"I got absolutely NOTHING, zero, nowt, diddly-squat, a great big fat zilch."

Straightaway both men smiled and broke into raucous laughter.

Once settled, Hanlon dipped his chin and asked with curiosity, "What made you so keen to check something out that quickly on your phone? It's just that you and modern technology normally like to give each other a wide berth and plenty of distance."

Initially, after it seemed like he had ignored the question, Murray brusquely replied.

"I have a few important tasks I need you to do for me Joe. Including getting those prints checked out."

He then handed over the little Ziploc pouch. His large blue eyes met Hanlon's, there was a slight twinkle to them. His look noticeably softened and there appeared to be a slight hint of a smile.

"You know something don't you? 'Sherlock' figured. "What do you know?"

"I simply want to confirm a particular suspicion."

"Which is?"

"Remember how I said earlier that it was strange to be here during the day. Well I've since discovered, that even when I visit in the afternoon, *night* is still present."

"Nope, you've lost me," Hanlon added, shaking his head.

"The presence of night. An actual knight. ABC Casinos Joe, run by his son he said. Call me plain old Gerry. Aye right," Murray said dismissively. "I didn't need to see the photo. I recognised the exquisite work of art hanging in his office. 'The Allegory of Vanity' by Tony Paredes or something like that." Murray then paused for a second before beginning slowly and lowly. "Father and son, absolutely!" Getting faster and louder he went on. "A,B,C, Anderson, Barber and Cybill, Insurers to the stars."

Murray was angry with himself. Disappointed he hadn't figured out the link sooner. He then showed Hanlon the facial image currently displayed on his phone. The jogging bottoms, t-shirt and cardigan had been impressively upgraded to a Saville Row suit, with an equally elegant collar and tie. It was that of Sir Gerald Anderson, multi millionaire businessman. Father of Cyrille and a shining Knight of the realm throughout the last decade! Holding Murray's phone and staring directly at the screen, Hanlon shook his head in disbelief.

"When you checked with your pals at Google previously, you never got a picture of dad did you?"

Gutted, Joseph Hanlon shook his head.

Murray then asked. "Don't you see the resemblance between him and his arrogant son? They may well have in place a beautiful, strong and impressive facade," Murray said, as he gestured back towards the stunning entrance they'd just exited. "But behind that false exterior Joe, there is without doubt another layer waiting to be unravelled. I have a hunch that it may be something more sinister, disturbing and devious than either you or I would have ever suspected."

Gritting his teeth and still shaking his head, "What are those important tasks sir?" Hanlon now asked impatiently.

Smiling an encouraging smile, Steven Murray listed the following. "Firstly, drop off the fingerprints. Then I need you to get a membership list, though I doubt they'll offer it freely. Also get a full list of staff that work in the casino. Full-time, part-time, everyone and anyone in their employment. Specifically, you are checking and cross referencing for a Mr Wolf!"

Not him again Hanlon thought.

"They both have a print of the same artwork, so I recognised quickly that there was more to 'Gerry' than he wanted me to. But impress me Joe, disclose to me that you also spotted a few tells."

"Well, maybe, I have to concede," Hanlon shrugged modestly. "Apart from having a worse dress sense than you, you mean?"

Murray narrowed his eyes at him, "Careful son," he added.

"Seriously though sir, the black patent shoes. Not cheap and certainly not to match up with his tracksuit bottoms. He also had a high quality full length cashmere coat hanging on the back of his door. His wristwatch looked pretty bespoke also. A small diamond inset onto the face, although I couldn't quite figure out the make."

As the two men settled back into Murray's Volvo. The Inspector nodded, "I knew you would have spotted a few things. Any other thoughts?"

"Not especially," Joe screwed up his face. "Apart from the obvious. Like you, I think he is hiding something. And the fact that he is a Sir and millionaire businessman, makes me think it's possibly a rather significant and serious crime or fraudulent activity."

"Thanks Joe."

"Oh and also," 'Sherlock' was now desperate to go on an observational rant. "I don't think he was making any important phone calls when we arrived. There was no sign of a landline connection in the office. That is unless it was disguised as a Robin Williams DVD! Also, later he owned up to not having his mobile with him today. So, important calls before he could see us, I don't think so! I'd guess he was simply buying time to stick on a movie from his scary stalker selection and appear relaxed and casual. To fully embellish that impression, he then changed into some old clothes that he still had from doing a bit of decorating previously. The skirting board below the shelves looked as if it had been recently touched up, explaining the paint at the knees of the trendy jogging bottoms. And then of course…"

"Enough, enough already 'Sherlock'. It's agreed he's hiding something. Let's just bide our time."

Sure enough after roughly seven or eight minutes, who should gracefully stroll out through the casino doors but a transformed Sir Gerald Anderson.

"He scrubs up well," DC Hanlon observed.
Murray turned to his junior colleague and offered a self satisfied nod.

"Nope, I'm not getting it," Hanlon cheekily grinned.

"No, really," Murray said. "Well let me help you. It's a number 61."

"Ach, sir. Not a 61."

His Inspector scratched his head and again began to laugh. "You are a clever guy Joe, take a guess."

"It's a….we were both so clever, well done us."

"No, that's a 60."

"Best get back to the station and write this up."

"That would be a 62. I suspect you're just stalling for time Constable."

Disheartened Joseph Hanlon slumped in his seat before offering up, "Would it, could it possibly be and I'm just putting it out there. Maybe I'll head back to the station whilst you get to follow him!"

"Now get out of here before I lose him Joe," Murray requested firmly.

"Tasks, sir."

"What?"

"Tasks, tasks plural you mentioned earlier," Joe asked hurriedly as he made his way out the car.

Murray rolled down the window. "Oh yes. So, add to employees, finding out about his watch."
Hanlon looked sceptical, but took a note of the request. Murray then pointed back at the ABC Casino.

"How many floors Joe?"

As Sir Gerald Anderson was now getting into a rather large chauffeur driven vehicle, an impressive vintage vehicle at that Murray reckoned, Detective Hanlon quickly scanned the building and responded. "Four floors. Ground floor plus three above."

"I'd agree."

Anderson's car was beginning to head off.

"I need to go Joe, so contact the Council planning department or whoever is responsible for permits and building permission."

"Why?" Hanlon asked confused, as his Inspector began to drive off.

Raising his voice to be heard above his acceleration, he hollered. "Because I would be curious to know why the elevator only goes to floor two? We are definitely missing something. Because they most certainly are!"

Drop off prints, check out the wristwatch, the employee records and the complete missing floor of a workplace. Plenty to keep Detective Constable Joseph Hanlon busy for the next short while. Or at least that was Murray's thoughts as he tried to discreetly follow 'Gerry' and his minder through the busy, dense afternoon Edinburgh traffic. They were making their way out of town toward the A720 Edinburgh City Bypass. They were on course to join it at the Straiton Junction. Now Murray wondered, East toward Musselburgh? East Lothian? Possibly even the A1 toward England and Newcastle as a final destination? Approaching the roundabout in the right hand lane, Murray knew then, that they would be going West bound. More likely Fife, West Lothian or the suburbs of Glasgow.

That reminded him - "Joe, one more thing to add to that list," he said, as Hanlon answered his mobile phone. "Check out how many ABC Casinos operate and where they are located." There was no response. "Joe, Joe are you still there?"

"I am sir, indeed I am."

"Okay, I can tell you're smiling. As soon as you insert 'indeed' in there, I know you are smirking at the other end. So how many and where are they Mister Clever Clogs?"

"It just seemed the logical thing…"

"Yes, yes, no need to humour me, just get on with it. You can gloat all you like later."

"London, Scarborough, Glasgow and Edinburgh, just the four. What do you think sir? Money laundering? Forgeries? Illegals working in them?" He gave a slight pause and then offered. "Or all three?"

"I've no idea, it's just that I have a feeling we are heading over to 'Weegie Land,' and I wanted to check if they had business premises over there also. I'll speak to you later and well done with that. That was quick and impressive work."

Joseph Hanlon hung up the phone, accepting graciously the praise for his quick thinking and diligence from his superior officer. On this particular occasion, it had taken him all of five seconds to type ABC Casinos into his phone and get those results! For some reason though, something else was bothering him. It was not directly connected to their investigation, but it impacted on Murray. So Joseph Hanlon felt it was totally relevant and justified to take a ten minute detour and check in with 'Doc' Patterson at the hospital.

"Once a week Doc?" Hanlon confirmed.

"Absolutely! Every week regular as clockwork. It may be a different day Joe, but he never missed a weekly visit."

'Sherlock' reflected upon those words and nodded to himself.

"I knew he had a meeting every week in Glasgow. However, he never spoke further about it and I never asked."

"Well now you know why, but keep it to yourself."

Hanlon understood, but added. "Has it helped? Have they resolved things? Moved on?"

The T'inker's face saddened. It was as if all his own current aches and pains had come to the fore and resurfaced temporarily. He grimaced as he spoke quietly.

"I would doubt it Joe. He refuses to see him!"

"What!" Hanlon expressed in amazement. "Are you telling me he has gone faithfully every week to visit with him and he has never once seen him?"

Patterson's gradual, slow facial expression confirmed this to be true.

"Oh," Murray exclaimed to himself in the car.

He was wrong. They had only stayed on the City Bypass for two exits. They were now heading off again at the Dreghorn Junction. He could hear the old bus conductor in his head, telling all passengers to get off here for 'Oxgangs; Redford; Bonely; Colinton and at a push Craiglockhart. What was he up to? Who did Anderson have to meet with so soon after a visit from two of Edinburgh's finest? What had rattled him?

With between three and four cars at various intervals between the two vehicles, Murray had done well remaining unseen. Or so he had certainly hoped. Driving carefully, venturing down past the Army Barracks (that took both Oxgangs and Redford off the list) they came to a T Junction. A right turn would take us back city centre bound. The car's indicator flashed left (meaning farewell to Craiglockhart). A further thirty seconds driving and a further left turn was soon being indicated. Murray began to wonder if they had spotted him, allowing Gerry Anderson to mischievously direct his driver to literally go around this area in circles. The Inspector briefly pulled over to the side of the road. This gave Anderson's driver time to make the turn with no one on his tail. A few seconds later Murray continued. He pulled out again and quickly turned left into Barnshot Road. Halfway up the street on the left hand side, the dark Bentley had parked kerbside. Murray could not be sure which of the large mansion properties the now elegantly dressed gentleman had chosen to visit. He was sure however, that it was no coincidence. Hanlon and himself had stumbled mistakenly into something fairly significant. Something that had nothing to do with the disappearance of young teenage girls. Or, on the other hand, if it did revolve around the missing girls, it is far greater and much bigger, than anyone first thought!

Murray cruised along the residential street at twenty miles per hour. He was heard to mutter, "a classic vintage right enough," as he drove nervously past Anderson's car and watched carefully in his rearview mirror for any comings and goings. It was all to no avail. He had no idea as to which luxury home the evasive businessman was visiting. If he were to have guessed however, his gut told him it was the one with the SOLD sign at the automated gates. As he took a mental note of the number, he then drove another sixty seconds to a nearby Premier Inn car park. This recently refurbished hotel was located right on the edge of the A720 Edinburgh City Bypass. The Whitbread Group, owners of the hotel chain, continue to increasingly develop and expand at a steady rate Murray thought. He then smiled, as he added aloud - "Just like my victims and suspects in this case!!!!!!"

His heart and head now both began to pound simultaneously. Relax, breathe and take a breath he told himself. His mind though had other ideas. As he sat back and adjusted his car seat, the meteor frenzy of deliberations began...... An officer killed. Teenage girl dead. A wife suspected murdered over a decade ago. 'Doc' Patterson beaten to within an inch of his life. Daniel B. George and cars worth hundreds of thousands. Books auctioned. Artwork stolen and then easily recovered. Clues offered by 'Bunny' Reid.

To all of this, Murray could only question… Why? Why? Why?

The prophetic feeling of foreboding that he had felt on those Gullane sands several days previous, had returned. He caressed the dark leather steering wheel. Holding it firmly with both hands at the twelve o'clock position. Then he slid those same fingers down to the three and nine. He repeated this over and over. Up, down, up, down, up, down. As fast as he could move his hands, images and thoughts came to the forefront of his mind - before equally quickly disappearing. Father and son, Gerry and Cyrille. Latchford, Taylor, Black and Daniel George again. 'Bunny', the casino, Anderson, Barber & Cybill. Inspired by his car interior, he called Hanlon back with a sudden thought. Task assigned, he hung up.

"What are we missing?" He uttered to no one.

He then pondered over ABC Casinos, Mr Wolf, London, Glasgow, Edinburgh, etc. And under his breath, he then half mumbled and half sang the most obvious music lyric to accompany his current mindset.

"Are you going to Scarborough Fair. Parsley, sage, rosemary and thyme……"

Chapter Twenty-Three

"When you see a gentleman bee, round a lady bee buzzin'. Just count to ten, then count again. There's sure to be an even dozen. Multiplication - That's the name of the game. And in each generation, they play the same."

- Bobby Darin

The previous night, when the DI had asked Hanlon to put his family history hat on. A multitude of thoughts were streaming in his mind as he sat in his car browsing over his notes from their first meeting with Robert Latchford, when something aroused his curiosity. Their neighbour nearby, Sonia Marshall, used the same childminder. The girls had been best friends. Something didn't quite feel right. He needed some genealogy work carried out urgently.

At ten past eight the next morning, Murray felt the gentle vibration in his jacket pocket.

"What's up Joe," he said anxiously.

The excited voice on the other end offered, "It was well worth the extra research sir. Marshall is her mother's name, but Sonia only re-married 4 years ago. Previously to that it was as you suspected."

There was silence on the other end of the line.

"Sir? Inspector! Sir are you still there?"

There was a slight pause, before the solemn voice of DI Murray returned with - "I guessed as much. We got it wrong Joe. I got it terribly wrong."

"He's at work right now sir. I phoned to double check before I called you."

"I'll meet you there in fifteen minutes at their visitor parking. Well done Joe, great work once again."

At the station from 7am that morning, Andrew Curry was already excited and hard at work. The previous day he had stumbled across some old case notes that had inspired him to dig a little deeper. Three months ago, there had been a spate of house break-ins. The man responsible was quickly caught. He was a petty career criminal and had been in and out of the system over the years. On this occasion however, he'd got caught fencing the goods, and had been informed on by one of his own partners in crime. Why? You don't turn on each other, it's an unwritten law. It's a fraternity, a club, an underworld magic circle. What happens in Vegas - stays in Vegas kind of thing.

That is, unless you do the dirty on your mates first! And he had. Because unbeknown to him, the articles he had sold them were seemingly worthless copies. Cheap second rate imitations. He had no alibis, owned up quickly to the crime and no further investigation was deemed necessary.

Yesterday however, the determined 'Kid' Curry, single-handedly confirmed that each of the victims homes had previously been burgled at some stage. Now that was just too much of an unnatural co-incidence. Each of the owners though had simply been delighted to get their property back and had no real reason to scrutinise or question its authenticity. Only after the thief had been charged and the truth brought to light, did they ever claim on their insurance. Lucky or what!

It would seem that every owner had at least one forged item. A replica had replaced the original when returned. Items substituted included several Rolex watches, grandfather clocks, ornamental carriage clocks and at least two impressive Victorian wall clocks. The overall value was close to a quarter of a million pounds. Internally however, Curry questioned - In more recent weeks what was the true price paid? Was it a young girl's life!

Joe Hanlon had arrived several minutes earlier and was already parked as Steven Murray exited his vehicle. He closed his car door, bang on eight thirty. Nods of acknowledgement were offered as both men seemed to unintentionally get in step as they approached the main door of the showroom premises. A familiar face greeted them as they entered. Stress was expressed in his body language as the man asked in a concerned manner.

"Have you any news officers? Another body found? Updates? Whereabouts? Anything?"
He wrung his hands and nervously rubbed both forearms. His fellow co-workers looked on in despair and felt an emotional attachment to the turmoil their fellow colleague was currently going through. Assertively Murray offered up -

"Sadly sir I don't, I'm afraid not. However, I believe DC Hanlon has something for you." He stated the fact with an all too satisfactory, smug disposition.

"He has?" the man asked optimistically.
Although his expressive, hopeful smile, soon retreated off into the distance as Joseph Hanlon immediately produced his regulation handcuffs from behind his back. He swooped forward like a bird of prey skimming the water to catch an innocent fish and resurfaced a second later with both the car salesman's hands fixed securely in place.

To which Steven Murray added. "Mr Anthony Lawrenson you have the right to remain silent. But being Scottish, you probably don't have the ability!"
The DI shook his head in disgust and walked away in a hurry. He promptly left Hanlon to read him his rights in the more traditional manner, whilst he drove at speed to reach Glasgow for ten o'clock.

Within ten minutes Sgt. Sandra Kerr and 'Mac' Rasul were sitting opposite a distraught individual. As the floodgates opened, Lawrenson was just relieved to get this off his chest. He was desperate to make the same point over and over and over again! Thirty minutes later 'Sandy' was able to phone Murray as he drove to Glasgow and inform him.

"He is no serial killer Steven. But then, you knew that when we picked him up didn't you?"

Murray loved his rapport with Sandra Kerr. For as much as he enjoyed mentoring and training young Hanlon, he equally missed the interesting chemistry and powerful dynamic that he and Kerr most certainly had.

"So what was he hiding? An affair with the childminder?"

"Ach, you spoil all the fun sir! That was the gist of it. Maria's personal assistance extended way beyond just helping young Claire with her homework seemingly. Her one to one fees were a little higher than normal and now we know why... She was busy helping her dad with his multiplication skills!"

"This was Cindy-Ann's childminder and Claire was her best friend," Murray reminded her. He didn't mean it to sound like a chastisement, but he couldn't get his head around the fact that they'd missed the connection.

"That was my mistake sir. When she had been reported missing it was her father we dealt with and her grandparents. She is referred to daily, in school and out as Claire Lawrenson. It's only her mum that calls her Claire Marshall."

"How did the girls initially meet? Because I think..."

"Tony Lawrenson," Kerr interrupted. "He met Mr Latchford out drinking one evening. You'll never guess where?"

"Aye, I thought as much. I'm sure if I start near the beginning of the alphabet I might get a gold star! Anything else of any relevance?"

"Not really. She disappeared slightly later than he claimed. She did get home from school that day, but that was when she walked in on the one to one personal tuition. She immediately about turned and fled. And that is the last anyone saw of her. He is pretty cut up sir. Blames himself."

"So he should! Okay, reassure him and let him go. No real harm done and he has given us yet another ABC link. He is liable of stupidity, guilt and going through a midlife crisis. And from personal experience 'Sandy,' that second one may never disappear."

Chapter Twenty-Four

"Tell me what it is that you see - a world that is filled with endless possibilities? Heroes don't look like they used to - they look like you do. We are love - We are one - We are how we treat each other when the day is done."

- The Alternate Routes

"Thanks for making time to see me Bobby," Murray said.

Immediately placing his left hand on his friend's shoulder, shaking with his right and bidding him a cordial good-bye. He'd previously explained that he had an eleven o'clock appointment elsewhere in Glasgow that morning also.

Detective Inspector Robert Maxton and Steven Murray had been on many training courses over the years together. They'd worked on a couple of joint caseloads and were very friendly toward one another. Bobby Maxton was of medium build with an unruly bushel of red hair, rosy red cheeks and a bulbous red nose. Often a clue to someone who enjoyed the occasional drink. He had lived and worked in Glasgow for the past 32 years, ever since he graduated from University in Edinburgh. His expensive, high maintenance, family residence in upmarket Bearsden was far removed from the humble croft he called home whilst growing up in his early years. 'Wee Robbie' was brought up in the Highlands of Scotland. Born and raised in the east of Sutherland. In the small tranquil, rural village of Brora.

Ultimately over the years, the two men were as close as colleagues could be without actually ever being considered best pals. It had been a constructive half hour meeting at the Govan Police HQ in Helen Street. On reaching his car at ten thirty-five, Murray knew he had exactly twenty five minutes to travel the seven mile route via the M8 motorway. It would be close.

In some parts of Scotland it is colloquially known as the 'Bar-L'. Detective Inspector Steven Murray drove through its gates with three minutes to spare at 10.57 am. It's large, bold lettering read clearly - HMP Barlinnie. He spent only twenty minutes there. It would seem only long enough to sign in and back out again!

During Murray's mad, midday dash back east along the motorway toward Edinburgh, the shy sunshine had decided to pay a fleeting visit to West Central Scotland. As he hastily pulled down his visor to offer protection from the strong glare, he became fully aware of the dulcet tones playing on the radio. The female performer soon enchanted him with her gift for musical storytelling. She sang of how, *'her life had been a tapestry of rich and royal hue, an everlasting vision of the ever changing view'*. He drummed his fingers delicately on the leather steering wheel as she continued. Instantly he found himself regularly checking in his rear view mirror to ensure he had no dark coloured canine passengers sitting comfortably on the back seat. The vocal arrangement of the accomplished musician went on to delight. Telling Murray as he sped towards Hermiston Gate of, *'the wondrous woven magic in bits of blue and gold - a tapestry to feel and see, impossible to hold.'*

DI Murray knew only too well the final few lines of this classic song. A song written by one of the most successful female singer songwriters of all time. Carol Joan Klein was better known globally as Carole King. He had witnessed the stage production of her life story 'Beautiful,' in London's West End just a month previous. He had become an ardent fan, and this song in particular was one of his favourite tracks. On watching the musical, he could not quite believe how many of her songs he actually recognised because so many of them had been smash hits for an illustrious list of other performers.

His chest heaved, a familiar wave of reflective thoughts and melancholy washed over DI Murray. And his emotions had to be kept in check as he heard the familiar strain of.... *'In times of deepest darkness, I've seen him dressed in black. Now my tapestry's unraveling; he's come to take me back. He has come to take me back.'*

Murray pulled over onto the hard shoulder for a couple of minutes respite, to regain his composure and get rid of his built up angst. He then bellowed and screamed viciously at the top of his voice. Potentially damaging his vocal chords, it was the penetrating high pitched howl of a possessed banshee. Any similar demons with thoughts of possibly hanging around with Steven Murray today disappeared in an instant. They'd hurriedly beat a retreat and made alternative plans for their crazy afternoon off the wall rants!

Carefully easing his way back out into the motorway traffic, the DI shook his head gently. He was becoming frustrated by these irrational episodes. They would last maybe only for a few concerning minutes. But the after effects, the emotional rollercoaster of thoughts, visions and possible repercussions would continually play out on a loop for the remainder of the afternoon. Today though, like most days, he had plenty to be preoccupied with and looked deliberately to shut out other arcane or covert thoughts. His priority list consisted most notably of murder, missing teenagers and a series of robberies that he knew must all be connected. Those agenda items should be enough for any sane man to be going on with. However, that was a major question in itself for Steven Murray these days. Was he indeed...... still a sane man?

Continuing to head east and making good time after driving extra cautiously throughout the major motorway roadworks. Then having past the ongoing carriageway improvements, Murray proceeded to leave in his wake the junctions for Newhouse, Shotts, Harthill and Livingston. He'd already phoned ahead to arrange a 2pm meet with DC Rasul. It would be an interesting chat, he thought, but hopefully constructive, insightful and beneficial for all parties concerned. Within close proximity to the station Murray had chosen the privacy of Mo's cafe for their meet. It also presented him the ideal opportunity to update Maurice Hynd on how things were proceeding into the disappearance of his daughter Iona. Sadly there was no real hopeful information to pass on. Hynd though, would at least appreciate being kept in the loop Murray figured.

It was mid-afternoon and just after two minutes past two, when the intimidating figure of Machur Rasul made his way through the low, narrow entrance of the cafe. Murray had never really noticed quite how muscular and strong this guy appeared to be. The sunlight was shining through the doorway of the premises so 'Big Mac's' impressive silhouette was to the fore. Murray considered how in his day, 'the ladies' would have been all over this guy. He suspected that in the current world we live in, that would probably not be the case for this handsome man.

Rasul apologised for his tardiness and sat opposite Murray. He was slouched down somewhat, as his long legs struggled to fit under the small, cheap grade worktop. Murray figured he looked a little uncomfortable. Like a crazed rhinoceros about to embark on a spa weekend! Rasul on the other hand figured, if he sat up straight, he was sure the table would be resting on his powerfully built thighs and he'd end up having 'High Tea' with his DI and that was not a preferred option. Murray nodded (it was a number 16: You were within the permitted boundaries for lateness).

Originally of Pakistani descent. 'Mac' Rasul was brought up within earshot of Ibrox Stadium. As a boy he was raised in a red sandstone, six in a block tenement building in Skene Road. Literally on the doorstep of the once mighty Glasgow Rangers Football Club. The 'Teddy Bears' were going through their own testing transitional period these days. Much like 'Mac,' they were having to find their feet, trying to gel with their new management and looking to be successful with different teammates.

"Good drive back from Glasgow this morning sir?" the Constable asked.

"You're well informed 'Mac'. Who told you that?" his DI asked rather concerned.

Rasul hesitated slightly. Wondering if he was deliberately trying to catch him out.

"Eh, you did," he sheepishly replied. "On the phone, when you called to meet up. You said you were currently making your way back from Glasgow. Did I misunderstand? Were you trying to check if I was listening or not. Maybe…"

Murray cut him off mid-sentence. "My mistake 'Mac,' I just forgot I had mentioned it."

Rasul pursed his lips, nodded and shrugged. As if to say, so what are we doing here? Murray raised a finger to acknowledge and thank Mo Hynd for wiping their table and for the two hot chocolates that he had now graciously placed 'on the house,' in front of the officers. Sipping gently at the rim of the mug DI Murray licked the froth from his lips and asked slowly and with deliberate pauses between the words.

"Are you enjoying Edinburgh? Your new posting? Colleagues helpful? Myself? Things to your satisfaction?"

Nervous of what he had done wrong. What had caused this need for a meeting. 'Mac' responded with a slight sway of his shoulders. Followed by an intense glare and twitching of his left eye, which brought him to utter softly -

"Is everything alright sir? I don't understand. I thought I was doing okay and seemed to be settling in nicely."

"It is. You are. And I'm glad to hear it. Let's talk." With both hands now extended out in front and palms upward facing, Steven Murray began speaking in an upbeat manner.

"DI Robert Maxton spoke very highly of you."

"You spoke to Inspector Maxton?" Rasul questioned disappointingly. "That, that was why you were in Glasgow? Checking up on me?"

His Inspector shook his head in a slow assured manner.

"I had a bit of weekly business at Barlinnie also to attend to," Murray confirmed. "But in the main I was concerned about you. Not checking up. Actually, if anything, trying to figure out how I can help enable you to fulfill your undoubted potential 'Mac'."

"Fulfill my potential?" Mac asked in a surprised, humbled manner, whilst still managing to raise his eyebrows and pull his head away from his senior colleague.

"I don't get it sir. I don't understand."
Murray, put his elbows on the table, clasped his hands together and sat them neatly under his chin.

"I apologise 'Mac'," he said. "I was wrong about you. I thought information was being leaked out to third parties. Unscrupulous third parties I hasten to add."

"You mean you thought I was bent," Rasul stated in an animated fashion. His face crumbled and his voice began to rise.

"I don't believe this," he continued, his long limbs beginning to flail. "I was the new boy, so it had to be me."
His raised voice caused a few concerned heads to turn in their direction. Maurice Hynd looked across anxiously.

"It wasn't like that," Murray denied. "I thought maybe you'd been compromised. Possibly naively, by one of the local reporters or journalists," Murray fibbed. "I've sorted it now. Got some great feedback from Govan. And I just wanted to clear the air and apologise for my dismissive attitude of late."

As Murray confidently extended his right hand, he also added -

"And maybe pass on one little piece of advice if I may?"

The delicate table sat back down on to its tiny rubber feet, as 'Mac' Rasul's giant, well muscled thighs relaxed and retreated back beneath it. He nodded and accepted the proffered handshake. Then he gingerly questioned -

"What kind of advice?"

Murray rubbed at the two day growth of stubble on his chin before asking -

"Are you a reader 'Mac?'

Rasul moved his head from side to side, indicating - it depends! (That would have been a number four nod on the official Murray head gesture list.)

"Listen carefully Constable," Murray said, whilst discreetly edging closer to the table. He leaned forward resting his forearms on the newly wiped surface. He looked up at the young plainclothes detective and spoke from the heart.

"A wise, seasoned Sergeant, once shared two pieces of profound advice with me and it changed my outlook on life and my whole career."

Rasul pursed his lips, but nodded as if to say, 'go ahead, I'm listening.'

"I don't know 'Mac' if it'll be helpful for you, but I hope that it will. That intelligent Sergeant educated my young mind with this. 'One friend who understands your tears, is much more valuable than a lot of friends who only know your smile.' Listen to it 'Mac' isn't it…"

Murray paused, he wanted to say beautiful. But that sounded so cliched and trite he felt.

"Terrific, wonderful, I love it sir," 'Mac' offered enthusiastically.

"You do?" he said, slightly taken aback. "I asked about reading 'Mac' because I often think that life is like a book."

'Mac' turned his head slightly to one side. Murray could see him raise his eyebrows.

"Some chapters are dull and sad and mournful. Some are gloriously happy. Others are vibrant, vivid and exciting," Steven Murray stated gleefully.

Rasul nodded in agreement. Uttering under his breath.

"I get that!"

"But if you continue to forego turning the page," Murray continued. "You will never know what the next chapter has in store for you." He then added, "Be mindful however. Often books are put down momentarily, initially just for a short break. Then sadly," he stated, with a pronounced bitterness to his voice, "...they are never returned to. Like an ever increasing number of individuals in society. They are put on a shelf and left feeling of little value or worth."

'Mac' bit on his bottom lip. He thought he knew what his DI was getting at. He reckoned Detective Inspector Maxton at Govan had brought him up to speed with a few of the issues he'd experienced in Glasgow. Murray then persisted.

"Those very same people 'Mac,' begin to gather dust. The wisdom, knowledge and expertise they hold is vast. Yet for some reason, too many of the new guys deem it unimportant and obsolete. Possibly they simply consider it outdated. Maybe they even fear that their own shortcomings and inadequacies will be shown up, if they take advice from the old brigade?"

"Huh," Rasul responded, with a brief understanding tilt of his head.

"DC Rasul," Murray said in a calm and considered manner. "You need to look around the station and be forever mindful of those precious books that have been discarded on the shelf. They contain the lives of individuals and priceless nuggets of wisdom and sound logic." He paused again before restarting with, "I would positively encourage you to reach out and lift up several of those novels. Handled with care, I've every confidence that you'd be able to dust them down quickly and once you begin again to leaf through their pages, you'll learn much from their distinguished and distinctive body of work."

Rasul pondered briefly, to consider his Inspectors words. This time it was his turn to put forward his hand. As both men shook, 'Mac' offered -

"I would then be well positioned to present them to a new generation of reader. I'd have the opportunity to once again share their astute insights, experiences and anecdotes," he surmised.

He got it! "Absolutely," Murray agreed, relaxing his shoulders. "You would also feel personally the rich tapestry of laughter and abounding love that would magically leap out at you from their wealth of remarkable adventures. We, each of us 'Mac,' have to learn how to treasure and value people just like books. Embrace the difference, whether in title, topic, opinion, cover or writing style. Whatever it may be? Together, we can help get them to the top of the bestsellers list."

Detective Constable Machur Rasul smiled. He was pretty certain that he had just had a modern literary experience like no other. One never to be forgotten. It had been a Booker Prize winning performance. Waterstones would struggle to compete.

In his mind he had now vowed to 'get reading' straight away. Words went unsaid as both men got back to work for the remainder of the afternoon. On leaving the cafe the heavens above seemed to transform in shade. Not only was the mood in the sky changing, but having met with his Detective Inspector, Rasul felt an even greater need to impress his new East coast colleagues. He appreciated Murray's personal support and private chat, his healthy forthrightness and honesty. Even if it was disguised in a literary analogy, the simple fact was his Inspector cared enough about him to explore more fully his personal circumstances. That, coupled with his desire and willingness to keep those things confidential, impressed Rasul greatly. Previously, he had only heard the team say good, positive things about Steven Murray. Now he was able to witness it first hand in the man's actions. He was beginning to figure out why the team were so close. The Inspector had their loyalty and trust, because first and foremost, he trusted them. 'Big Mac' was without doubt 'loving it!' An exciting fresh start with new surroundings. A great working atmosphere and friendships being forged. Overall it appeared to be the whole complete package that he had really been searching for in the workplace.

Rasul's Uncle Bernie had visited with him earlier in the day for near on an hour. He was his father's older brother and 'Mac' had deliberately taken a longer lunch to spend some quality time with him before meeting his DI.

   Bernhara to give him his proper name had moved down South over twenty years ago, when 'Mac' was just an infant. He had remained close though to his Glaswegian roots and kept in regular contact with that side of his family. His own twin daughters were now grown up, married and embraced the life and culture of two different areas in Europe. His oldest daughter (by 3 hours), Shara, was working in finance and had been living in Belgium for the previous four years. The city of Leuven was east of Brussels and had a population of approximately 93,000. Shara's younger sibling Miriam had embarked on an equally challenging career. In the past six months she had begun work as a junior curator in one of France's finest museums. The primary colours, exposed pipes and air ducts make the

Pompidou Centre one of the best-known sights in Paris, hosting the largest collection of modern art in Europe. Miriam loved her job and was excited for the future.

With their mother having passed away late last year, both girls were delighted to know that Bernie had decided to make the journey up to Scotland from the East London borough of Barking. Emotionally recently, he had felt the need to spend some quality time alongside his family in Glasgow. Celebrating his 60th birthday presented the ideal opportunity. The short, silver haired, bearded man had arrived just after midday at Edinburgh's Waverley Station. His train had been ten minutes ahead of schedule, much to a local gift shop owners delight. So now with a newly purchased tartan tammy upon his head and without a care in the world, he sauntered leisurely up the famous Waverley steps to meet up with his policeman nephew.

Having squeezed time into his day, Machur was thrilled to catch up for a bite to eat and a coffee. Brief as it may have been, it was a worthwhile experience for both men. After fifty minutes and with every intention of meeting up two days later to celebrate his birthday, Uncle Bernie headed off to catch the Westbound train for Glasgow Queen Street. During their short sojourn into Starbucks territory, Rasul saw a face he'd recently become acquainted with. The man's drinking partner across the table though, made this seem like a highly unusual, unlikely and unbelievable alliance. Ten seconds later it was captured for posterity on 'Mac's' all singing, all dancing iPhone.

Chapter Twenty-Five

"I've got a great idea and wouldn't you like to know. You probably can't bear it, so I guess I'll have to share it - I thought of it a moment ago."

- Harry Connick Jnr

It had bothered 'Mac' Rasul all afternoon. A particular conversation he and his Uncle had spoken about that had triggered something in his mind. It had been a casual, lighthearted, fun topic. However, a certain thought had become embedded in his mind. It now continued to niggle Machur into the early evening. At around 7pm he found himself deliberately sat in a city centre coffee shop, nervously tapping his fingers. He decided enough was enough. He then scrolled at speed through the contact list on his phone. His large cumbersome fingers stopped at K and instantly he telephoned his Sergeant. It was her husband Richard that answered. He told Rasul that they were visiting relatives on the East coast around Montrose, And they would be a few hours getting back, even if they left straightaway. 'Mac' was disappointed, but understood perfectly. He had forgotten that 'Sandy' had mentioned leaving early that afternoon. The twins were still on the evening touring circuit. Doing the rounds to all the family and friends that were still to witness them firsthand. Those that required 'a shot of them!'

"Sorry about that," Richard Kerr reiterated.
At which point the aforementioned 'Sandy' then took over the handset. Not used to getting off-duty evening

phone calls from any of the team, she asked in a concerned manner -

"What was up?"

'Mac' half-heartedly blurted out a few incoherent and apologetic sentences. He then added, "That it was his Uncle's accent, his slang and dialect. But not to worry, everything was fine." He hesitated before adding, "I'll speak to you soon, just need to check a few things first." He then hung up. Sandra Kerr looked blankly at her screen, shrugged, then went back to play and frolic with all the other children, young and old, in the adjoining room.

'Mac' proceeded to call Murray's number. That call went unanswered. His DI's mobile sat isolated and abandoned on a certain Mr Coulter's kitchen table. He had been busy getting an update from 'Ally' on his telephone assignment. The men were immersed in deep conversation. Both cosily positioned in front of Robert Coulters roaring coal fire in his sitting room. If truth be told Steven Murray also wanted to reassure himself of 'Ally's' personal safety and state of mind.

Suitably inspired, curious and definitely agitated, Detective Constable Machur 'Mac' Rasul now found himself standing outside Blake's Auction House at 8.15pm. A chilly springtime breeze had gathered momentum. A group of males were wrapped up in stylish, warm heavy jackets. Many had their collars turned up, others accessorised with trendy scarves or gloves. Boisterous, loud and in a very self-assured manner they made their way along the street. They were well prepared for a night of drinking and clubbing. Their female counterparts 'out on the town,' took a rather different approach with their fashion for the weekend. They opted for the minimalist approach. They wore more perfume than clothing, one or two pieces at most. Frozen arms and bare legs, with killer heels tall enough to see over a ten foot garden wall!

The branches on the trees in the square opposite swayed to and fro, though not nearly as much as the cognitive deliberations blowing up a major storm in Machur's head. With no backup on their way, nor fellow officer by his side, this was not necessarily his finest moment. His heart was racing as his hands began to profusely sweat. He stood outside with his large size eleven shoes tapping the ground frequently in frustration. As if suffering from mild OCD - the heel of his footwear would tap twice against the kerbside, before three successive raps with the outside of the shoe. Again, two with the heel, closely followed by the outside trio. This therapeutic delaying tactic seemed to put off the inevitable for a full sixty seconds! He had even begun to look around for the possibility of an escape route. It was a textbook case of fight-or-flight response.

'Mac' continually told himself that he'd be fine. That he had just wanted to dot some i's and cross some t's before he shared his improbable, slightly bizarre theory with the others. He had noticed that unusually, there seemed to be a dim light on in the premises located above The Jagged Edge pub. The bar was buzzing with tourists and regulars alike. Possibly it was merely a security light that remained on inside throughout the evening Rasul considered. From ground level though, there certainly seemed to be movement. Shadows, a figure or figures roaming around, movement of some form for sure. Possibly preparations were still ongoing for the next day's auction. According to a notice on their front door it started at 11.00am prompt. He smiled, shrugged and guessed it would definitely start on time, as 'prompt', was heavily underlined with a black marker!

A local 80's covers band had just begun playing in the function suite, as 'Mac' tentatively rang the buzzer for upstairs. The stifled, distant sound of a female vocalist could be heard in the background. Her classic rendition began with - *"You and I in a little toy shop, buy a bag of balloons with the money we've got."* As he waved his police ID at the surveillance camera, Rasul had no idea what the song was. He was too young he figured for all that 80's retro. The inexpensive security device had been positioned just off centre of the small entrance. As he waited impassively, 'Mac' forwarded the photo he had taken that afternoon at Starbucks to DI Murray. He had meant to send the image earlier, but changed his mind. To inform his Inspector later personally being his preferred option, and that was designed so that he could intentionally witness his reaction. Then, when he had phoned him and been put straight through to his voicemail it had temporarily slipped his mind. Unbeknown now to 'Mac' for certain, but there was most definitely someone in the upstairs office. And that individual had been watching him very carefully. Monitoring his every gesture and facial expression for the past couple of minutes. Including his rather clumsy, yet sublime OCD percussion movements.

Rasul had been weighing up his options and whether to chance ringing again or not. He was still totally unaware that his actions had now triggered blood vessels to contract and redirect his blood toward major muscle groups, including his heart and lungs. His upstairs admirer had waited patiently until he rang a second time before allowing him entry. They were now fully prepared for him and whatever threat it was deemed that he posed.

On hearing the intercom buzz, 'Mac' automatically reached for the handle and foolishly pulled open the door and proceeded inside unaccompanied. He was operating on an alarming cocktail of adrenaline, perceived knowledge and foolhardy bravado. All three combined, can be a potent, highly toxic and dangerous blend at the best of times. Normally however, when witnessed in someone with a specific mission, a point to prove and a strong gut feeling, it can be rather disturbing and over exposure can be exceptionally damaging to one's health!

Rasul had never been at Blake's previously. So before he could confidently put forward his hypothesis to Murray, he wanted to set foot in the showroom and have a 'Butcher's.' He quickly put his phone onto video mode and once inside the front door, the large Glaswegian who was definitely out to impress, was faced with the challenging 'Apples and Pears.' As he eventually reached the top step, silently and without warning he was engulfed in darkness. It was a complete blackout. The lights had failed. His heart was already pumping hard from the climb. Now anxiety and mild panic were being added into the mix. Suddenly he found a bright, dazzling torchlight shone directly into his face. His mindset was such that he could not quite 'Adam and Eve' it. The white beam of light, not unlike that of a sniper's laser, moved effortlessly from his eyes, smoothly past his mouth and way down beyond his chin and neckline. Eventually it passed his chest and abruptly halted at his firm stomach.

The officer's gaze followed it to where it had suddenly stopped. He instantly and without thinking switched on his phone's light and began to raise it. As he looked up quickly, Machur Rasul saw only the briefest glint of the glistening steel tip. Then the African tribal spear was without warning, but with great impetus lunged deep into his heart and thrust upward in one careful experienced manoeuvre. The young officer dropped instantly to his knees. Blood began to spew furiously from his mouth. A sudden, sinister, sadistic twist of the spear which embedded it even further into Rasul, was all that was required to send his finely honed body hurtling backward at speed, down the sheer, solid flight of concrete steps. The spear shattered and splintered into tiny pieces, as remnants of blood created abstract designs on every surface. The steep gradient was unforgiving and relentless. Machur's head and body twisted, snapped and rotated violently. By the time his large black masculine frame came to rest, the choice between 'fight and flight' had gone.

From the room below, the music stopped. The solitary voice of the female diva continued to offer up one last line. *"And here it is... a red balloon... I think of you... and let it go!"*

Chapter Twenty-Six

"There are more questions than answers. Pictures in my mind I will not show. There are more questions than answers and the more I find out the less I know. Yeah the more I find out the less I know."

- Johnny Nash

For the first time in as many months Murray went without that Friday morning. Without music! And for Steven Murray that was a kind of strangely surreal experience. Inside his car there was no radio playing, no CD' blasting out and no magical streaming of an Apple playlist direct to the stereo system. It was a time for quiet contemplation, or so he thought. In reality, he was striving for silence amidst the myriad of questions waltzing, jiving and gyrating around in his mind. It made for an interesting challenge.

M.E. cufflinks - West Princes Street Gardens - Spence, Tardelli, Wexford and Lattimer - Linked undoubtedly with the girls, but how? - Reid's tipoff! He's certainly a wily, scheming and corrupt individual the Inspector concluded. So where did he fit in? What part does he play? Because he most definitely has a role, Murray was convinced of that. Robberies, Insurance, Blake's Auction House and the no good Andersons, how do those dots join up? Where is the connection? The disappearance of all those teenage girls - what is at play here? One man's face burned off, another had his hands severed, a third grotesquely choked to death, as well as the heart wrenching episode! Why? Why? Why? Why? What are we missing? What have we overlooked? At this juncture, there was definitely many more questions than answers.

Murray turned to his passenger seat. There was no black canine pet travelling with him that day. Life seemed good, he felt positive and sure that solutions were edging closer. There was clearly a link he told himself, searching desperately for inspiration. A house of cards he felt sure was about to come tumbling down around him and his team. There are too many people involved in this. These are no random set of coincidences. His vast years of experience and gut feeling told him clearly that this was sinister and possibly bigger than they had first thought. But currently, neither he nor they, had any idea what they were really looking at.

Time is very much of the essence, people were continuing to go missing. Others, less fortunate are being brutally slain. Maybe that is one slight indication Murray mulled over and reminded himself. These murders seemed personal, not just random. They'd been deliberately staged to offer up a calculated clue or two alongside the vivid, colourful post-it notes! The miniature metal hourglass at Ian Spence's body was identical to the one sitting on Robert Latchfords' mantelpiece. That was lead number one. Tardelli, although she could not recall from where, was known to Linda Bell. So there was a second. Then so too was Wexford, that tentatively made a third connection. Her daughter was still missing, but hopefully alive and well. Poor Cindy-Ann Latchford was tragically dead. The security guard though? No clue whatsoever Murray thought. Fed up and on edge, his remaining questions were drowned out and went unanswered as he conceded defeat and switched on the car's music system. He purposefully turned the volume up full and listened intently. American songstress Kacey Musgraves encouraged him loudly to *'Follow your arrow, wherever it points.'*

Murray then headed directly to get fuel!

It had been fully sixty plus hours. Thomas Patterson had initially opened his eyes an hour ago and was gradually coming round. Waking to experience a further twenty-four hour adventure in the land of the living. He would appreciate and savour this opportunity. Which was more than one of his closest colleagues often did!

The T'inker was battered and bruised, but by all accounts doing well and on the mend. As he began to sit up in bed he noticed the lone figure asleep on a chair to his left. The 'Doc' smiled appreciatively and rested his head gently back onto the two firm pillows beneath him. Early morning drizzle was sweeping across the room's solitary window pane and childhood memories of being ill in bed were being quickly recalled. As a youngster he remembered a large glass bottle of Lucozade at his bedside. It sat in it's familiar scrunched up yellowy orange cellophane. This was back in the days when it was meant for people who were sick or convalescing. Adjusting his position under the covers, he would turn his attention back to his bedroom window and watch the rain droplets scurry downwards, instantly picking a favourite to win the race to the bottom and inevitably backing the wrong one. He then began to associate Lucozade so strongly with being ill, that as a teenager just seeing a bottle of it would start his stomach churning. Today 'Doc' Patterson, can't even drink it when he is well, never mind in his current condition. He gave a slow, time consuming blink and returned to the present.

A nurse went to make her way down the corridor. As she did so the recovering patient waved gently with both arm and head to attract her attention. The tall, dark haired individual stopped and made her way back into his room.

"Good morning, Mr Patterson," she offered with a genuine smile.

"How are you feeling this morning."

"I'm good," he struggled to get out.

"Well, I'm glad to hear it," she said in a bright and breezy manner. Before adjusting his pillows and straightening his sheets.

He knew she was now operating on autopilot. It was the equivalent of nursing small talk. Checking pillows, looking at charts, tucking in bed sheets and checking patient's fluid levels, etc.

"How long had HE been t'ere?" Patterson asked drowsily, looking toward the corner of the room.

"HE had asked for five minutes with you and that was at ten-thirty last night," she added. "By ten thirty-five, he was out for the count! As a serving police officer we reckoned he had been assigned to stand guard to protect you."

"When in reality nurse, you didn't have t'e heart to remove him?"

"Something like that," she replied. "I'm just finishing my shift now," she confirmed. Waving pleasantly to him as she exited the room.

Detective Constable Hanlon had heard the voices and slowly begun to stir.

"Doc, Doc, you're awake," he said softly. "You're sitting up. You're looking good. Maybe just a bit too much blue mascara though," he joked.

Patterson's face was heavily marked. In particular he had a tiny, yet distinct circular abrasion in the centre of his cheek bone. Located directly under his left eye, it was approximately 10 millimetres in diameter. It would certainly be a good few weeks before he auditioned for any beauty competitions again. The 'Doc' signalled Hanlon to move his chair closer. He had a worried, serious frown on his face now. He indicated he wanted to whisper something. 'Sherlock' was becoming noticeably wary. Ultimately, there was no whisper forthcoming. But Patterson spoke quietly and in an unsurprisingly respectful and concerned voice.

"T'ank you, t'ank you so much Joe. You're a good man and you'll never be short of friends," he offered in his lovely, rich, Irish accent.

"T'ank you again on his behalf!"

"I don't understand," Hanlon replied.

"I t'ink you do," the 'Doc' responded. "And I t'ink you deserve to know a little bit more of his back story. He's only just beginning to occasionally dump those polo necks for ordinary shirts again you know. So, let's not kid ourselves here Constable." Patterson's voice had now begun to rise and tremble with raw emotion.

"I recognised straightaway what caused t'ose marks on his neck. Sure, the two of you weren't kidding anyone."

Joe Hanlon rubbed uneasily at his forehead, unable or unwilling to make eye contact.

"And someone had to be t'ere to save him," he went on. Tears began to run down his flushed cheeks. "I know it was you Joe. You called it in. You were first on the scene. You must have cut him down and you, you ultimately saved his life, didn't you?"

Joseph Hanlon calmly lifted his head and met Thomas Patterson's gaze. No words came from his mouth. But the redness and moisture in his eyes said it all.

As Patterson confided in Hanlon, Susan Hayes and Andrew Curry were making their way separately to the Fort Kinnaird shopping centre in the Newcraighall district of the city. Hayes had received communication from dispatch on her way into work. She in turn, immediately called the 'Kid.' DS Coulter had not arrived at the station yet and so far had proved impossible to contact via his mobile. He would be made aware of the current situation and would ultimately meet his colleagues at the retail park as soon as possible.

They had received another tip off regarding more of

the recently stolen property. This one was from two weeks previous. Slightly smaller van this time. A seven year old, navy blue, Ford Transit. It had been parked overnight in one of the parking bays outside the Subway franchise. The call had only been received in the last quarter of an hour. And already four police officers were on the scene. Two patrol cops that arrived five minutes previously and Detective Constables Hayes and Curry that duly arrived sixty seconds ago in a convoy of two.

"The caller had simply said they had a delivery for Hayes and Curry, just like the last one," 'Hanna' Hayes told the 'Kid.'

"Possibly, do we have someone working undercover?" Curry asked suspiciously, as they both now stood at the rear of the abandoned vehicle.

"Not officially," Hayes responded. "And anyway, don't look a gift horse in the mouth!" She exclaimed cheerily. This made Andrew Curry smile.

"What, what is it? What are you smiling at?" She was beginning to feel uncomfortable at the Cheshire cat in their midst.

"Do you even know what that means?"

"Of course," she said. Whilst giving him an incredulous look.

"Well that would be a NO then," Curry grinned once again. Even wider on the scary scale this time.

"Go on - enlighten me," she shrugged.

"Horses teeth continue to grow over time. You knew that right?"

Hayes nodded slightly in a very unconvincing manner.

"So checking the length of their teeth, is a way of gauging their age."

"And your point being caller? Hayes said dismissively.

"Well in days gone by, to do such a check would have indicated and been a clear sign of mistrust toward the giver. Hence, don't look a gift horse in the mouth."

Pondering over his words, but unclear, 'Hanna' Hayes

required confirmation. "Are you trying to make a relevant, constructive point or simply teasing me?"

The 'Kid' laughed aloud.

"Oh, I'm most definitely teasing you," he mocked.

"I thought as much," Hayes sighed. Then added - "So let's get down to business."

Detective Constable Andrew Curry stood firm and shook his head in all seriousness.

"Susan," he said, and he never called her that. "Susan," he repeated, this time speaking articulately and assertively. "My point is, we absolutely have to mistrust these anonymous pointers we've been given. It's a necessity 'Hanna,' that we look this right in the mouth and check every molar, every veritable filling and every jangling nerve end even more thoroughly than ever before. We have every reason to mistrust this giver. Every reason in the world."

"And his car crash just a few days previous? Patterson questioned.

"No proof sir. But I checked the road surface and the surrounding area around the scene. There was no skid marks, no ice on the street like he claimed and his brakes were fine. Doc, his car had just been serviced and MOT'd two weeks beforehand."

Patterson nodded.

"I'm sorry, but I have no doubt he was accelerating as he headed for the wall," Hanlon said unhappily, but fully confident in his assessment.

The strong smell of chemicals and disinfectant became apparent, as an early morning tranquility came over the room.

"Good morning gents," offered the middle aged cleaning lady. Two generous nods were duly proffered in return.

"I'd prefer not to talk about the lacerations on his neck today 'Doc.' We both know how he came to get them. I'd rather become better informed. More able to understand or at least empathise with the man himself."

"You deserve t'at at least Joe. Where to begin is t'e problem. Bear with me and we'll navigate together around some areas of his rather tumultuous life."

Joe Hanlon leaned his tall, thin, willowy figure closer to Murray's friend and began to listen.

"Often when you are young DC Hanlon, t'at's when you get introduced to many of the dangers in life. Wouldn't you agree?"

Hanlon frowned. Not really understanding what Doc Patterson meant.

"I'm talking about smoking, possibly a cigarette offered by a friend at school. Underage parties where alcohol and drugs are consumed. Immaturity, ignorance or simple peer pressure often makes the decision for you. It's a no brainer, you just go with the flow."

"I hear you," Hanlon shrugged. "But how…"

" … Does t'is help you understand Steve Murray?" the Doc finished. "Well you see Joe, the young adolescent Murray never really experienced t'ose temptations. T'ey never appealed to him. Teenage sex, drink and wild parties. Heck, illegal substances were not even on the cards when he was a lad. He once told me that a girl in his High School overdosed on paracetamol and was taken to hospital. T'at was a major drug scandal in his day!"

Hanlon smiled. Thoughts of the many cultural and technological changes that have spanned the intervening decades flashed through his mind.

Patterson continued. "The attraction, the allure, the bait. The pull, the invitation and finally the fatal seduction of the youthful, cavaliering Steven Murray, was simple……… it was t'e horses."

"Horses!" Hanlon exclaimed, now sitting bolt upright in his chair, as if he'd been told the most churlish explanation. Figuring and wondering, how could horse's possibly impact on someone's life in any major way?

Patterson added. "Let me be more specific Joe. Horse Racing to be precise. T'e excitement and adrenaline of winning. Beatin' everyone else. T'e t'rill of t'e chase. T'at was Steven's entry into his high level dependency habit. Sure it's a very real addiction t'at t'e mainstream media so often readily dismiss and t'ey ordinarily call it - Gambling!"

Chapter Twenty-Seven

"When you asked how I've been here without you, I'd like to say I've been fine and I do. But we both know the truth is hard to come by - And if I told the truth that's not quite true."

- John Denver

"How did we ever manage without them?" Murray asked in a forlorn manner as he pointed at the handset held intimately to Sandra Kerr's ear. She instantly held a finger to her lips telling him in no uncertain terms to be quiet. The restless DI then glanced across at Detective Chief Inspector Brown's office. And sure enough, there he was, also 'on the blower.' Murray had only just vacated the room, which seemed to be very much a home from home these days. Brown's constant need to be kept in the loop and thus try to regain a place back at the coal face was beginning to irritate Steven Murray. Every flamin' morning it felt like, he thought to himself. Just then, 'Sandy' closed her phone over.

"Well?" He said.

"Still no answer sir. I've got a Glasgow car being sent to his flat."

Murray nodded. At that moment, no one cared what number that nod was!

"I got a missed call from him last night." In a tone that seemed to indicate 'if only.' Murray continued, "I called him back within seven or eight minutes."

"And?"

"And nothing. It went straight to his voicemail."

It was now, nine thirty-five in the morning. Rasul had never arrived this late before. Both officers were aware of Hayes and Curry being redirected to Fort Kinnaird. And 'Ally' Coulter, who had experienced a flat tyre was now playing 'catch up' and currently heading there also. Hanlon, who was renowned for his early starts, had previously left word that he would be at the hospital if he was needed urgently. Together their heads turned in unison, as young PC George Smith ran directly toward them.

"George are you alright? What's up?" DS Kerr asked worriedly.

Bent over and struggling for a breathe, he held up a handset to DI Murray. Murray snatched at the apparatus and at that moment they were joined by Keith Brown. Who, having witnessed the determined man's 'Chariots of Fire' audition, was now helping the rather winded officer back to his feet.

"I hear you Billy," Murray confirmed slowly.

Kerr looked anxiously at Smith. The strained narrowing of her eyes asked the question for her. He whispered under his breath whilst still gasping for air.

"There has been a body found 'Sandy.' At Blake's Auction House,"

All three pairs of eyes now focused on the Detective Inspector.

"Understood. Appreciate that. I'll be there shortly."

The handset crashed to the floor. Murray's shoulders went slack. His mouth hung open and dry. His tall body remained still and the colour drained from his stunned face, as his quivering knuckles found the nearest desktop to support him. He simply stared wide-eyed and shocked at something no one else could see. One would question if he even seemed to be breathing. Barely audible, his lips trembled as he made to speak. With Brown and Smith taking an arm apiece, they duly escorted Steven Murray from the edge of a desk that had seen better days, to a nearby seat that Sandra Kerr had dragged across the room to aid his assistance. Again he made to speak.

This time a tear filled emotional rasp emerged. "It's him. At Blake's. It's Machur."

Hanlon's phone rang. It was an unfamiliar number and he was engrossed in Murray's biography as told by Doctor Thomas Patterson. Deciding to accept the call, he was stunned and surprised to hear the voice of his Detective Chief Inspector.

"Hanlon, Joey," he said coldly and dismissively. "There's been a murder at Blake's Auction House. Get over there straightaway and DI Murray will meet you there."

Why didn't Murray phone him himself he wondered. For some reason, Midlander Keith Brown had never really taken to 'Joey' Hanlon, as his DCI would refer to him. Even though 'Sherlock' had been a major influence in bringing about the downfall of the late William Taunton and helped ensure that Sheila and Kenny Dixon's gangland empire was brought to its knees. And despite the fact that the venerable James Baxter Reid is still casting shadows wherever he goes, Hanlon is now an impressive and important member of the team.

"Are you there? Did you hear me Hanlon?" The voice piped up.

"Sorry sir. Absolutely. I'm making my way there right now."

"Oh, and Detective Constable Hanlon, be prepared. The body is that of 'Mac' Rasul."

"What?" Hanlon cried out.

Brown had already hung up. 'Joey' Hanlon informed 'The T'inker' and then made haste across town to meet up with Detective Inspector Steven Murray. A man who had faith in him. The man that gave him the opportunity to be a detective. A much troubled, but good man.

Over in Morningside the two man posse of Hayes and Curry had rode out early. Their trusty steed had been watered and was currently stabled outside Sir Ronald Mecham's fine establishment. However walking through his palatial front entrance was a slight upgrade on some saloon doors!

"Morning sir," Curry offered brightly. In stark contrast to the wet and overcast day outside.

"Good morning detectives," Mecham responded equally cheerful, but with a mite more gravitas and experience, which added to his rich, velvet tone. "I have the photographs that you requested DC Curry. But I'm not quite sure of what use they may be now considering everything has been returned to your possession. It is still in your possession Constable?" he asked in a rather alarmed manner.

"Oh, yes sir it is," 'Hanna' Hayes confirmed.

"Quite," Curry said curtly. Keen to take the photographs from Sir Ronalds grasp.

"Let's all sit down," the 'Kid' said.
Mecham motioned toward the sitting room and the two officers duly followed.

A white forensics palace had been erected at the entrance to Blake's. Murray thought he was entering the city's latest nightclub, but for the lack of a red carpet outside. Pathologist Doctor Danielle Poll had taken charge. Dani, as she was known to her friends and family was the pathologist in attendance at the murder of their colleague DC Tasmin Taylor a few short months ago. Born in the United States, she studied in Edinburgh, fell in love with the people and the city, and has remained ever since. That was close on seven years ago. Poll was of average build, had strong likeable facial features and shoulder length, wavy brown hair. After

Doc Patterson, she would absolutely have been Steven Murray's choice to lead up the forensics team on this personal case. He was mighty relieved and his fears were allayed further when DC Hanlon walked over to join them.

"Was that Machur's ambulance I past as I arrived?" 'Sherlock' asked politely.

"Surely was," she offered, with only the faintest of American west coast accents Hanlon thought. Although in all fairness, two words was not a lot to go on. Smiley, tenacious and reliable, Danielle Poll was both good to be around and have around. Her inflection and intonation were much more pronounced when she was in full flow.

"Inspector, your man could have fallen and tumbled backward in what would have been an altogether unfortunate accident," she said.

"Tell me you have a big but Doctor?" Murray boldly announced.

Both Dr Poll and Joseph Hanlon blushed at that.

Composing herself, the female pathologist smiled and conceded, "I do have a big 'butt' Inspector, you'll be pleased to hear!"

Now it was the turn for Inspector Murray's cheeks to redden. He went to apologise…

Danni Poll held up her hand, "It's alright I know exactly what you meant."

"Yes. With regard to the potential mishap gents, the African tribal spear thrust deep into his chest cavity put paid to that theory."

"What was he doing here? Who let him in? Who found him?" A barrage of questions Hanlon shot enthusiastically from his hip.

Poll gave him a friendly smile, before leaving them with some form of bone to fight over.

"Death would have been at some point between 6pm and midnight last night Inspector. Hope that helps."

He asked rather forlornly, "The spear to the chest.

Was that the cause of death?"

"It may well have been," she paused. "Had it not been for breaking his neck on the way down."

"Understood Doc. Thanks for that. I'll let you finish up here."

Hanlon wiped away a tender, single tear from his eye as Murray offered under his breath -

"He was onto something Joe. Something he felt couldn't wait until today. Something he felt compelled to die for."

'Mac' never got to tell Sandra Kerr his idea, but she recalled that morning as she spoke to Murray, how he mentioned, " … his Uncle Bernie, London and the fact that he had to have a 'Butchers' at the auction house."

"Wow," Sir Ronald Mecham exclaimed. "There can be no doubt about it."

All three now sat relatively still in his sitting room, processing the information. Curry was delighted his hunch seemed at that moment to have been proved correct. The homeowner was equally delighted that this had been uncovered. Now though, he was uncertain as to how to proceed. Hayes on the other hand sat with a not quite smug, but certainly a self satisfied look on her face. Delighted for her young colleague that they seemed to have unearthed some vitally important evidence. A real breakthrough, she thought to herself.

"We'll be busy throughout the rest of today and probably tomorrow morning confirming the same applies to the others Sir Ronald," Curry confided. "But by lunchtime tomorrow we should be in a position to update you fully."

"Much appreciated young man. Thank you once again. Thanks to both of you."

The two officers said their goodbyes and made their way out of the house. They had a busy day ahead and some rather sad news awaiting them.

Chapter Twenty-Eight

"Art for art's sake, money for God's sake. Gimme the readys, gimme the cash, gimme a bullet, gimme a smash. Gimme a silver, gimme a gold, make it a million for when I grow old. Art for art's sake, money for God's sake."

- 10cc

Saturday morning -

As the egg yolk, bright and gleaming fried in the pan, bubbles turned brown with the heat of the oil. Miniature explosions reigned in the grease. *This is the life of illusion - wrapped up in trouble, laced with confusion. What are we doing here?'* Tabasco sauce was added and an extended blade ran swiftly through the egg's sunshine centre. Beating and blending with great delight the newly created diagonal flag of yellow, red and brown. With its crushed salt, peppers and sweet, tangy vinegar, it ran blood red and sticky. A serrated knife penetrated sharply through the zest of the orange. Juices flowed and captured the fragrance of the air. A razor sharp thread was wound firmly around his finger and super fine lycra covered his face. As he began to suffocate, he suddenly heard a key turn in the doorway. Drenched in a cold sweat Murray awoke, smiled gently and a sinister wink escorted him back to the land of the living?

Elsewhere that morning in the City, the black dog had remained secure in its kennel back at home. It was 10.00am and its master was scheduled to meet up and spend the day with a different partner. For pedestrians there was no immediate access to the rear of the ABC Casino. Bin lorries and other deliveries, had to use a small lane at the back as a means of entry.

"Thank you for meeting me Mr. Bennett," Murray said with sincerity.

"I was intrigued Inspector," replied the young auctioneer. "And like I said, it was my day off, so delighted to help in any way I can."

The two men were now making their way down the intriguingly named Skarper Lane. Steven Murray wanted to witness first hand the flip side of the coin. It made for interesting viewing.

"And the purpose of THAT Inspector?" John Bennett asked, perplexed and looking skyward.

"No idea whatsoever," Murray gasped, shaking his head in bewilderment. "But," he added in a slow and considered manner. "I would most certainly like to find out."

The men stood rooted to the spot in bemusement. They stared intensely at what appeared to be impressive pole dancing apparatus for extra tall strippers! It was darkly coloured to obviously blend in with the building and its exterior surroundings. Although, expecting it to blend in may seem rather optimistic - for it was easily, fifty to sixty feet tall.

Both men gradually edged forward to give it closer inspection. Bennett tugged firmly at it with his protected, uncalloused auctioneer's hands. It appeared to be solidly secured at both top and bottom. Murray reckoned some modern, heavy duty construction work had recently taken place. This apparatus was dependable, unyielding and super secure. Whatever it was for, from the rooftop to the ground, this structure was not for moving. Similar in dimensions to a fireman's pole, it was positioned about two to three feet out from the actual building itself. Unusual to say the least. None of the other properties had anything representing it at their exits or delivery doorways. What one or two did have however, were strips of scaffolding. Notification that ongoing repairs seemed to be taking place. Even the ABC Casino had an extra wide yellow funnel running down from one of their floors, thus allowing building debris to be sent directly into a covered skip. The dual purpose of the protective skin on the skip Murray considered. Firstly, protection from Scotland's fine weather, and secondly, from appreciative locals wishing to make use of it for their own personal waste. Illegal dumpers - 'Fly tippers' in other words. Having a much better idea of how the land lies outside the Casino, both gents began the twelve minute walk back around to the front. The Inspector having timed it on his way to meet Bennett earlier.

Steven Murray had deliberately steered clear of casinos for many, many years. Yet here he was, about to venture inside for about the third time in five days. He had an experienced hunch though, that it would not be too long before he was back once again. Next time, hopefully metaphorically speaking, 'To cash in!'

"Do you gamble Mr Bennett?" Murray asked casually.

"Never really had the inclination, Inspector. Nor the opportunity I suppose?"

"No! Tell me more. How come?"

"Well, I was brought up in Crieff..."

Rural Perthshire. Murray had thought as much. He allowed himself a self satisfactory smile.

" ... growing up there in the early nineties, there was still no bookmakers allowed in Crieff. So no easy temptation. I believe it was a local council thing. The same way they don't allow fast food premises to this very day."

"Good for them," Murray echoed in solidarity.

John Bennett smiled and spoke slowly. "You are an interesting character Inspector."

It was now Murray's turn to fully smile. "Ah......whenever anyone uses the word character, it's time to worry. They either mean you are really old-fashioned, dull and dreary or feel the need to follow up with a but."

"But, what I mean Inspector is… "

"See, see, there it is, I knew it was coming… "

"But you misunderstand… "

"And again, there we have it. More 'butts' than a cow branding ceremony!"

Bennett laughed and held up his hands in mock surrender. The hammer had came down and he had been well and truly outbid.

John Bennett was aged 29. Murray had been right on that score also. His mother had been an administrator at the Roundelwood Health Spa in the town. His father had built up a successful mobile auctioneering business. He'd travel all over Perthshire, Dundee and Angus. Initially it was the furnishings in a farm or building of someone recently deceased. Then he moved on to selling the property itself. Often this could include livestock, machinery and vehicles. Bennett senior built a very niche place in the market for his fledgling business.

Having been raised in the beautiful Perthshire countryside. Young John would then travel with his father from an early age. All the while continually learning the ropes and serving his apprenticeship. As he grew, he naturally became very much an outdoors man. As a hill walking and climbing enthusiast over the years, the isolated historic town of Comrie on the outskirts of Crieff, had been a particularly favourite area of his to hike growing up. He was a commendable fisherman, an exceptionally poor golfer and had quite recently taken up clay pigeon shooting. And although Murray found John Bennett a very humble and grounded individual, he was definitely more 'gentrified hunting estate,' than the local 'council housing estate!'

With the casino still officially closed, they buzzed the intercom to identify themselves and gain entry. It was yet another staff member, concierge, security guard or whatever terminology they cared to use that was on duty today. Murray offered up a familiar introductory question.

"What's the time Mr. Wolf?"

Based on the cross-eyed look on this particular muscle man's face, Murray readily assumed he was confused. It was only when he had shown him his police credentials and made his way further down the corridor, that he realised the expression remained unchanged!

"Let Mr Anderson know my colleague and I will be up to visit with him shortly," he called out as they made their way to the gaming room on the ground floor.

John Bennett struggled to contain a laugh. A short boyish giggle, but laughter nonetheless.

"What's up Mr Bennett? Was it his name badge?"

"You saw it!" Bennett exclaimed in surprise. "Yet you called him Wolf?"

Murray shrugged indifferently. "A little inside joke. Call it speculative conjecture on my part," he expressed.

"Oh dear," Bennett hissed, as he wiped a laughter tear from his cheek. "Skelly," he beamed. "What a surname for him to have to go through life with!"

Eight roulette wheels dominated the gaming area downstairs. Four Blackjack tables, two at either end of the room made up complimentary bookends. Unsurprisingly, gambling was not the reason for today's visit. Murray had forwarded John Bennett a photo taken on his phone of the impressive painting in Gerald Anderson's office. He had asked him for help in gathering some background in regard to it. Who it was by? What it represented? Any other relevant details? He knew lots of generic information would be available online. But Murray liked to gather and hear information from experts. Those who were specialists in their fields. He was aware that like the police force or any other workplace, there was often more meaningful information to be had and that involved getting up close to those with the gossip and internal speculation. Being fully conscious of those people in the know. His theories, thoughts and current suspicions were still far from being conclusive or even factual. They resembled the outlandish fantasy of Blake's Seven, coupled with the innocent hopefulness of The Magnificent Seven. When in reality, what Murray presently desired, was the cunning, guile and intellect of James Bond as 007!

It was just the manner, his intonation, the way in which Sir Gerald Anderson had emphasised and portrayed certain information on his previous visit that made Murray invite his own trained expert along. The room which had been luxuriously decorated after their well publicised multi-million pound refit, was surrounded with various works of art. On the walls were an assortment of artistic creations. Mostly large, illustrious and impressive paintings. The occasional framed song lyric, poem or historical manuscript also took up a limited display space. They walked throughout the establishment, always with actual eyes of security upon them. With, no doubt Murray thought at least one more pair watching on the strategically placed monitors protecting the premises. It made him wonder though. The place was still closed, why all the security - at ten o'clock in the morning?

Inspector Steven Murray had given Bennett an even tighter remit than to simply preview Anderson's office portrait. All was about to be revealed. They had visited the second floor, where the big money, high roller, behind closed doors poker action took place. Those rooms too, were filled with impressive 'decor.'

To go any further required them to take the lift. They approached yet another well toned, short haired, muscular athlete at the first floor desk. One with an overdeveloped chest Murray thought at first glance. However, as they got closer he smiled and on cue offered,

"What's the time MRS Wolf?"

"It's Golden," came the response.

"What is? The sunshine?" Murray continued.

"My name," she stated pleasantly, yet firmly. "Jane Golden, and it's Miss," she emphasised to Murray. "Miss Jane Golden," she repeated one more time in a rather surprisingly flirtatious manner. She then summoned the elevator for the two men by swiping her credit card sized security pass.

"That's the first time I've witnessed you embarrassed Inspector," John Bennett observed with a rather large grin.

"Mr Anderson is expecting you gentlemen," she commented. As the lift doors opened, she gestured them inside.

Within the confines of the lift, Murray checked again with Bennett to confirm that he had never actually met Cyrille Anderson's father before. Bennett shook his head. In a rather poor American accent, Murray then officially or unofficially deputised Bennett as a 'law enforcement officer for the State of 'Edinburg!'

Bennett looked at him in astonishment.

"What?" Murray asked unperturbed. "Americans never pronounce it properly,"

"About what I said earlier. You being a bit of an interesting character." Bennett's eyes opened wide in a, 'I've just had it confirmed' manner!

Chapter Twenty-Nine

"Many dreams have been brought to your doorstep. They just lie there and they die there. Are you warm, are you real, Mona Lisa? Or just a cold and lonely lovely work of art?

- Nat King Cole

The lift doors opened and Murray was literally saved by the 'bing'... 'You have now arrived at the top floor,' said the announcement. Right on cue, Anderson's office door opened. He was obviously being kept up to speed at their whereabouts in the building. More likely though, Murray suspected, he himself was watching their every move.

"Gentlemen, gentlemen," he said, shaking their hands, guiding them inside and offering them a seat all in one fully efficient movement. He had assumed Bennett was a police officer and Detective Inspector Steven Murray felt no real need at this stage, to alter that assumption.

"Another Robin Williams flick," Murray observed, pointing at the paused movie that was being shown on the large screen dropping down from the ceiling.

"Absolutely!" Gerald Anderson stated. "Yet another classic."

Murray recognised the film, but could not be bothered with more small talk.

"The large pole at the rear of the premises Sir Gerald, what is the score with that? Practical? Functional? Ever used?"

Gerald Anderson did well to hide his surprise at both the question and Murray's use of his title.

"No real idea Inspector," he offered nervously. "Speak to my son. I was sure it was already there when we moved in. In fact I know it was. I spotted it in some photographs on an 'Old Edinburgh' Facebook page recently. The pole was definitely there, captured in all its glory."

"Thank you for clarifying that and for allowing us to get better acquainted with the premises today. It's always helpful to be in full possession of the facts. To gather up as much valuable information as possible."

"Couldn't agree more Inspector," Anderson added.

"The interior, like I said last time, it looks absolutely stunning. So is that all the renovation work finished then?"

"Yes, finally gents it's all complete. We've been open a good while now, but there was always something needed completed, finished off or repaired."

"I know what you mean sir," Murray said supportively. He then added, "Back to normal in here for you also?" He seemed to be specifically talking about the office they were currently in.

"Oh yes, at last I can sit back again and watch one of my movies undisturbed. Without hearing the drilling from above or small segments of plaster dropping onto my desk."

All three men laughed in mutual understanding. Then Anderson, decluttering his desk work surface, removed a roll of coloured stickers and slid them into a lower drawer, accompanied by two pair of scissors, post-it notes and a fluorescent green marker!

He looked up brightly and added, "Was Golden being co-operative earlier on Inspector?"

So, confirmation that he had been watching.

"Absolutely sir. Although she was uncertain of her whereabouts on the night of the attack. Do you think you could give me a note of her phone number? Just to clarify fully later with her you understand."

"You surely don't think she is a suspect?"

"For elimination purposes only sir. I'm sure Miss Golden will be able to check her schedule and put all our minds at rest. We will probably have to speak to all the security on duty that night anyway. How many 'addicted gym enthusiasts' do you currently employ or have on duty each shift?"

Bennett gave an impressed wink at DI Murray and mouthed the words… 'You are a character.'

Anderson smiled, "Yes, some are rather excessive," he agreed. He then turned to the computer, gave it a couple of clicks and answered, "Approximately 60 to 70 individuals to call upon Inspector. With about 15 to 20 on any given shift."

"Really, that many!" Bennett chimed up.

Anderson turned and looked the man up and down more carefully than he had done previously. He was yet to be won over by him.

"Sir Gerald, Mr Anderson, I nearly forgot, I brought John with me today to let him have a look in person at your portrait there. I couldn't even remember what it was called to tell him. Sorry about that," Murray fibbed.

"Are you part of The Art and Antiques Unit?" Anderson asked Bennett directly.

Oh no, Murray thought, that's us finished before we even got started.

"There is only an Art and Antiques Unit in the Metropolitan Police, Sir Gerald."

Effortlessly changing the conversation, Bennett then responded admirably to him with -

"Would you be surprised to learn that corrupt activity surrounding the art community is a highly lucrative criminal enterprise? It is estimated to be in excess of three billion pounds sterling each year and shows no noticeable sign of slowing."

A highly promising start. Well done Murray thought. Anderson also seemed impressed.

"Fascinating officer. So what do you think of my…"

"de Pereda!" Bennett finished off for him. "Antonio de Pereda, and a stunning reproduction of his Allegory of Vanity."

Anderson nodded, even more taken by the young 'officers' obvious knowledge of art.

"It portrays a message of mortality. Reminding its audience of the fragility of human life and the inevitability of death," Bennett added.

Anderson then took over. "Did you know that during the same time that Pereda was painting his Vanitas pieces, Spanish society was experiencing a very strong sense of inequality between the social classes?"

Murray nodded, feigning genuine interest. That was his overall contribution to the arts over the years.

His host continued. "People at the top of the social pyramid were excused from paying taxes Inspector. Simply put, when de Pereda was alive, wealth was a highly important thing to acquire and maintain. Without it, one was treated very unfairly and for those people, life was a struggle."

The junior 'officer' was now in full flow. He placed his left hand on Murray's shoulder, whilst gesturing toward the portrait with his right.

"In layman's terms the 'Allegory of Vanity' used everyday objects to represent symbols of impermanence," Bennett added passionately.

Did he just wink at me again Murray questioned silently.

"I love your enthusiasm and vigour for precious works of art young man," Anderson praised him. "Many classic things found in a Vanity painting are given prominence here." He then pointed out in smooth order - the skulls, the globe, an isolated candle, precious jewels and money. "You may think they are just placed seemingly randomly Inspector," Anderson pronounced. "But you'd be wrong."

"I would?" he questioned.

At this point DI Murray had literally given up the will to live! Bennett could tell. So he thought he'd make him suffer just a little bit longer.

"You are absolutely correct Sir Gerald," gushed Bennett. "Even the colours which are very simple, contrast with the luxury and prosperity that comes with the objects that are portrayed. The fact that the colours are so similar conveyed the message that possessions, although of different value, carry the same pricelessness."

"You can leave this talented man here Inspector, and we can rave on about art and artists all day long."

"That sounds like too good an offer to turn down Mr Anderson, I mean Sir Gerald. I may just have to take you up on that."

Bennett could not contain the genuine fun he was now having.

"You know Steven," he said to Murray, who now seemed totally bemused. "I mean sir," he corrected himself. "Can I share just one more titbit before we leave."

Through gritted teeth the Inspector snorted. "Sure, just one more titbit...... fantastic!"

"The candle in the painting specifically represents the speed of life passing by. The skulls represent a similar concept, but in a more blunt and literal way. They portray death and when combined with the items of luxury, show that no matter how successful we are in this life, we will all end up in the same place. Finally, when we combine many of the other elements such as the candle and gun, there is a strong sense of a cloud of time."

There was no denying it. A masterclass and virtuoso performance. Well done that man. Anderson was won over.

"Wow," Sir Gerald Anderson said in sincere admiration. "If you ever grow tired of the police force, please give me a call. I always have positions for qualified men like yourself. It has been an absolute pleasure." He then quickly read something on his computer screen, wrote down a few numbers and folded the note. After shaking hands, Anderson opened his office door and walked both men across to the lift. As the doors opened with the recognisable 'bing!' He took the small folded paper and tucked it neatly into the breast pocket of Murray's four year old, grey pin striped suit.

As they glided effortlessly back down to the ground floor, Murray retrieved the small slip of paper. Ending in six digits, 655713 was the 'golden' mobile number he had requested earlier. 'Bing,' the doors opened and there was Mr Skelly in attendance at the front desk. Both men looked first at each other. Then in unison, they gradually turned to him and gave him a grateful nod. In return, Skelly nodded back and looked them both straight in the eye .... at the same time!

Murray walked Bennett back to his car, which was parked near the lane at the rear of the Casino. It was just approaching 11.25am. They had only been inside the premises for just short of the hour mark.

"So?" Murray turned to Bennett. "Any thoughts, anything you regarded as out of place or out of sorts...... 'officer?'

Still playing along, John Bennett responded with, "I don't really know where to start boss!"
Murray laughed.

And Bennett having pondered over Murray's initial question, offered - "Interesting complimentary decor, fascinating contrast in styles. One major point of intrigue though. A slight foible I would suggest," he then told the Inspector.

"There was?" Murray bit his bottom lip. "Please continue Mr Bennett," the Inspector encouraged.

"It concerned the various works of art on the walls, compared to the statues and mini exhibits behind security glass."

"I'm listening," Murray assured him. "What intrigued you?"

"Well, they had reasonable marble artefacts, historical crystal replicas and reproduction chairs that many large organisations use as standard. Would you not agree Inspector?"

"I guess," Murray offered half-heartedly. "And?"

"Let me just say firstly, thank you for the mini Art Gallery tour. It was superb, I really enjoyed it."

"Was that yet another little titbit Mr Bennet? Because now, you are just taking it too far. So, unless you want to witness me becoming a 'really interesting character,' with you on the receiving end, I suggest you share your expert opinion rather sharpish"

It was John Bennett's turn to let out a hearty laugh.

"I certainly learned a thing or two from you this morning Inspector Murray. Thank you for that."

There was a silence as the auctioneer opened his car door. It was an Audi Q5 and he was now perched high up on the driver's seat. He turned side on to face the Inspector. Earnestly, he began to share his one remaining observation from their walking tour of Edinburgh's ABC Casino.

"Inspector, every one of the paintings I witnessed on the walls throughout the whole establishment - Every single one, with the only exception being that of the 'Allegory of Vanity' in his office. Now fully mindful of that Inspector, that that is the only exception."

"I get it John, that is the only exception," Murray offered in frustration.

So in a firm, yet slower paced voice, Bennett junior concluded his expert analysis. "All of them Inspector. All of them - are one hundred percent genuine."

Murray needed a few seconds to allow those words and their meaning to sink in. Slightly confused the Inspector again asked -

"Okay, thanks for that. But actually, is that so unusual? They are a big firm. No doubt they make healthy profits. Possibly, they write much of it off against tax. No?"

"Maybe so," John Bennett considered. "However, what I observed today, hiding in plain sight of everyone, whilst the reproductions were on display behind so-called security cabinets, was easily worth between a staggering eight and nine million pounds Inspector. That is no tax write-off!"

Chapter Thirty

"Oh, don't it hurt deep inside to see someone do something to her. Oh, don't it pain to see someone cry, especially when someone is her. Silence is golden, but my eyes still see. Silence is golden, golden, but my eyes still see."

- The Tremeloes

Whilst DI Murray and his Perthshire 'colleague' had informed themselves fully with the workings, layout and content of the city centre Casino. DC Curry captured fully the team spirit that existed in the squad. For he continued that Saturday morning, in his own personal time, his quest for the truth also. Additionally, he had successfully cajoled 'Hanna' Hayes into foregoing other weekend pleasures to join him for a few hours. As a man and a detective he was maturing. He showed empathy and understanding as he travelled around revisiting the group of individuals that had their homes violated and property stolen. He had no intention of either himself or his partner looking foolish. DI Murray ran a tight ship and his established team members knew exactly how much he required them to do their homework, to follow up, re-confirm and double check facts, figures and theories. If only 'Mac' Rasul had been one of his students longer, he would have never entered those warehouse premises alone or without sufficient backup.

It was approaching 7pm when the phone rang. It managed two rings before the soothing, although rather edgy voice answered.

"Hello Jane speaking."

"Hello, Mrs Golden?" The voice enquired nervously. Her reply was curt and direct.

"It's MISS Golden actually. And who am I speaking to?"

Incisively the male speaker cleared his throat and then spoke in a more relaxed, upbeat and confident manner.

"Miss Golden it's Steven Murray here. We met at the casino earlier today."

"Steven Murray," she softly whispered to herself, trying to recall the name. Then it dawned on her as she blushed slightly, even though no one else could see her.

"My goodness, you're the police officer - you're Inspector Murray. I don't remember you telling me your first name."

But she had remembered deliberately telling him that she was a Miss.

"My apologies Miss Golden."

"Please call me Jane, Inspector."

It was Murray's turn to blush. He now felt awkward and embarrassed in calling her Jane.

"Are you still at work?" He asked politely.

Hesitantly Jane Golden paused for a brief second. She wondered where this might be leading.

"I finished an hour ago Inspector. Why? What did you have in mind?"

There was silence at the other end of the line. Murray could feel his face redden once again. This time with the uncertainty in regard to - What did he have in mind?

"Are you asking me out Steven? Jane Golden flirtatiously asked.

Murray gathered up the courage for a crisp and concise five word response.

"Jane, I need your help."

Inside Maurice Hynd's cafe, Steven Murray sat nervously. He was dressed in comfortable, casual attire as he waited on MISS Jane Golden. The tiny, compact antique bell above the doorway gave a short, brief jingle each time the old, seasoned, glass panelled door opened. Murray at that moment began to wonder for how many decades that particular bell had chimed? Had it changed pitch over the years? Was it the grandson or great grandson of the original bell? Hynd himself had owned the place for over 15 years. His daughter was born in the back kitchen. That in itself, was a legendary tale that Mo loved to regale the customers with in those early years.

So what other fabulous narratives could this working class cafe offer up? Was the gossip surrounding the characters who entered these hallowed premises, of their difficulties and their shared dilemmas widely known? The location was literally a two minute walk from the local cop shop. The policeman, the villain, the long arm of the law and the lifelong criminal. If only these greasy walls and condiment stained coffee tables could talk! The crook, the lawyer - were they one in the same? Had stone clad alibis been cleverly created, evidence corroborated and jury members gently encouraged, whilst a multitude of individuals deliberated and munched satisfactorily over their lentil soup and bacon roll?

Murray then instantly recalled from a few months earlier, the intrepid case his team now referred to as *The Winter Wind*. How, in Scotland, 'in the Heart of Midlothian,' it can often be difficult when choosing between the police and the criminals to tell who is a God and who is a monster! The Inspector genuinely believed, that in these challenging cappuccino laden days, nonpartisan onlookers could never quite tell the difference - between Geronimo and Custer!

Maurice Hynd with what little optimism remained, walked toward him. Although the word traipsed would have been a more fitting colloquial description. He looked tired, his appearance unkempt and dishevelled. With Iona missing, his willingness to carry on was ebbing. She meant everything to him. His flame of faith was rapidly diminishing every twenty-four hours.

Murray apologised. "No news Mo. Sorry." Then as the Detective Inspector delved deep into his eyes, he swore he'd just witnessed another dying ember of hope slowly fade, smoulder, diminish and die.

The bell chimed its familiar sound and as the bleached blonde entered, she shook the light drizzle from her stylish cropped hair. It was similar in style to that of a friendly, glowing cocker spaniel. A 'Crufts' prize winning breed that would shake rapidly from side to side return from its regular daily exercise in the rain. Thankfully, Murray's very own black dog was nowhere to be seen tonight! He then stepped forward in a gallant, gentlemanly way to draw out a chair for her. It was more in keeping with a date at some swanky hotel or restaurant. Taken aback slightly, she smiled - mildly embarrassed. He grimaced. Fully recognising a 'Mr Bean' moment was taking place. All it needed now was for him to mildly stammer over his words, thus making the comedy slapstick production complete. He composed himself, took a sharp intake of breath and offered.

"Stow jangodden, fanksfur steeing me."

As she burst into laughter, he instantly turned bright red and was sure he could hear a voice from the corner shout... 'Cut!' The ice had not just been broken. It had been well and truly smashed to smithereens! He comfortably relaxed from there on in. Although, with his present companion, it was exceptionally easy to do so. Jane Golden, and it was Jayne with a Y he learned, was surprisingly, a very amiable, chatty and down to earth individual. She was great company, easy to speak to and quickly helped put our nervous Inspector at ease. She had a tiny pale yellow tattoo of a lemon on the knuckle of her index finger on her right hand. On realising Murray had spotted it, she educated him.

"When I am about to get uptight, upset or angry." She kissed it lightly… "It keeps me sweet," she smiled.

In their ten to fifteen minute preamble, he learned all about her Glaswegian upbringing by her scholarly Grandparents. No explanation was given or sought of her actual parents absence in her life. From Bearsden, an upmarket suburb in Glasgow to - Private School - Territorial Army - Eighteen months in France in her early twenties - Whilst there, in Lyon, both her grandparents died within six months of each other - First her Grandmother in the March of that year - Then in the late August, her beloved Grandfather - And although not medically recognised, she suspected of a 'broken heart.' Such was the close and tender bond between them - No other immediate family - She returned to Scotland - Took several martial art courses - Enrolled with a private security company - Been with ABC Casinos for nearly 3 years - At their Edinburgh location for the past 12 months - Now… All present and up to date!

"And I guess that brings us fully up to speed," Jayne Golden said.
She offered up, yet another beautiful, wide, complimentary smile. She was able to kick the darkness in Murray's life straight into touch every time she spoke. He felt an instant rapport with her. An unusual sensation for him. He tried desperately to play it down, but found himself in awe of her simple beauty and charm.

"So, Inspector. I know you didn't ask me here to hear my uneventful life story."

"No, no, you're right, Miss Golden."
She looked at him sternly.

"Sorry, Jayne," he quickly corrected himself. "However, I loved it nonetheless. And I certainly would not preface it as uneventful. I think you've packed a heck of a lot into a relatively short space of time. It gives you a great insight into the individual when you get a chance, up close and personal, to hear all about their likes and dislikes. The places they've lived, cultures experienced and to hear a brief snippet of their upbringing. Thank you, thank you so much," he gushed.

Right then, in that instant, she thought she noticed for the first time a slight hint of a smile from Murray. All through her earlier monologue, he had had a welcoming grin on his face and his mouth was making all the right movements. However, this specific smile, she had just spotted for the first time.

She responded quickly, "Has anyone ever told you Steven, it is Steven you said, right?"
Murray blushed slightly as he nodded.

"Has anyone ever told you, you smile with your eyes?"
Murray averted his gaze to the floor.

"What a beautiful smile it is too," she continued assertively. "You should let it come out to play more often!"
Maurice Hynd had approached the table. He appeared worried.

"Mr Murray. Sir. Inspector are you alright?"
Murray had no idea what he was talking about.

"I think it's because you have just turned an almighty shade of red," Jayne Golden added.
Now fully embarrassed, DI Murray raised his hand to Mo Hynd, apologised profusely for any mix up and turned to face the cause of his colourful crimson complexion.

For the next three quarters of an hour, he brought his new 'friend' up to speed with many, but not all of their findings. He quickly trusted her. However, for her own safety and well being, maybe some key points and characters will continue to remain private for now, he thought to himself. Against normal protocol, he informed her fully with regard to the missing girls. Although neither confirming nor denying a possible link to the murdered men. He passed on details regarding Patterson's savage beating and his concern that everything seemed to revolve somehow around her workplace. Jayne Golden saw that smile in his eyes again and reciprocated with an engaging smile of her own.

"Jayne," he said softly, yet confidently. "Are you familiar with the Jackson 5?"

She looked bemused by the question. As her sprightly pink tongue slipped out briefly for air, it flashed seductively between the coral shade on her pert lips. The Inspector's head began to sway. His neck and shoulders decided to join in and his confidence was high as the lyrics began. *"You went to school to learn girl, things you never knew, never knew before. Like I before E except after C, and why 2 plus 2 makes 4."* As the beautiful Miss Golden made dance moves in her own chair, Murray continued. *"It's as simple as ABC!"*

He stopped suddenly. Her movement shadowing his, automatically froze. There was an intensity between them. Their eyes locked, and Steven Murray nodded.

"It's as simple as ABC Jayne. Anderson - Barber - and Cybill. Your casino Jayne, I am certain, is where the answers lie. I only hope I can ask the right questions."

It was her turn to nod. She got it. She seemed genuinely shocked by the brutality and the stark reality of all that had happened, of the close proximity of it all. She was at a loss as to how she could help and what DI Murray was about to ask of her. Before he could alter his Michael Jackson voice, Jayne Golden spoke.

"I am surprised that they had no footage of your friend's assault though," she offered.

"It was narrowly out of range of the camera. Just typical," Murray frustratingly expressed.

His newly trusted confidante, offered a long, lingering and mildly optimistic shake of her head.

"Indeed it was not," she said decisively. "I have been involved personally as a witness, in two assault cases that took place on that very spot. Our cameras most definitely film that location," she confidently assured Murray.

Anderson, he thought. The Robin Williams superfan, the bold, devious Sir Gerald. He already knew who was responsible for the attack. Murray's mind was still wandering, when he felt the brief moisture on the left hand side of his face.

"Deal me in," Jayne Golden offered. "I have to be going," she said as she kissed him lightly on the cheek. " A 7am early morning run awaits. But just let me know how I can help. Call me."

"What! Great! Yes of course. Are you sure?" Murray's mind and heart were racing all over the place. His cheeks beamed once again. His rapid pulse felt like it continually skipped a beat. He was smitten. How did that happen? He had no idea. This woman just excited him and made him feel refreshingly alive. She was filled with an enthusiasm for life, a willingness to do the right thing and her stunning good looks were an added bonus.

The Inspector recovered sufficiently to return to official police mode, stating, "Jayne, you know that this is exceptionally serious right? You realise you could be in danger? That there may be repercussions and consequences? People are dying here remember."

Nodding, the attractive Miss Golden went to put on her coat. "But you'll be there to protect me Inspector. Isn't that right?"

"Of course," Murray replied foolishly and without thinking.

"Well that's good enough for me. Thank you Steve," she proffered.

With a short kiss, seconds later she was gone. Little bits of glitter from her shimmering lipstick shone on Murray's cheek as he speculated to himself... How would that little grandpappy of a doorbell, have recorded and archived that rather strangely surreal encounter?

A brief phone call and favour from PC George Smith rounded off his busy day, and he headed home.

Back at home that evening, on the outskirts of West Lothian, Andrew Curry had sat quietly contemplating. He recognised that he and Hayes had done some fine confirmation work over the last twenty-four hours. They had revisited many of the homes that had been robbed. Whilst there, they encouraged each of the homeowners to check more thoroughly than before the items stolen and since returned to them. Together they were pretty certain now in their own minds, at what had really happened after the recent break-ins had taken place. Looking a gift horse in the mouth seemed inspired counsel after all. Tomorrow would be the day to share those findings. Especially as DI Murray had sent a text earlier in the evening to each of his squad. He had called for them all to be present at an extraordinary Sabbath day service...... at 9am sharp.

Whilst 'Kid' Curry prepared methodically for his Sunday morning sermon, with his own book of Revelations back at home, Steven Murray's thoughts had turned to a wedding anniversary spent in Paris several years earlier. His wife had always been a keen Abba fan. Over the years she had amassed an impressive array of their music, both in vinyl and compact disc. One particular song from the early eighties, encapsulated that special romantic trip for the couple and was currently playing on late night radio. This had triggered instant melancholy. It was the Swedish quartet's little known, *'Our Last Summer.'*

Murray once again began to feel the heartache and pain. Experiencing ongoing regret. It tore him up inside as he sat on the end of what had once been their marital bed. He watched helplessly as his black dog of depression took up residence in the corner of the room. Again he swore his canine nemesis was wagging his tail, delighting in his master's discomfort. Lazily, he then offered a dispirited gaze across at the old, white, MFI purchased dressing table. It's angled mirrors would show his emotional teardrops falling steadily in triplicate.

He lay back on the mattress and turned his eyes toward the ceiling as he began to tenderly whisper... *'I can still recall our last summer, I still see it all. Walks along the Seine, laughing in the rain. Our last summer, memories that remain.'* Moisture gathered quickly on the quilt cover as Murray's body shook and trembled. His lips quivered as his voice choked and croaked another short line before fading to silence. After a brief spasm, his body relaxed and another evening of fully clothed sleep was rewarded him.

Chapter Thirty-One

"If I wait for just a second more, I know I'll forget what I came here for. My head was so full of things to say, but as I open my lips all my words slip away and anyway."

- Yazoo

He was part way through greeting and meeting collectively with Kerr, Coulter, Hayes and Curry, when DC Hanlon chapped the door and walked straight in to join the remaining members of the team. All eyes turned their focus to Joe.

"It's not an anagram sir," he alerted them.

"What!" Murray exclaimed. "Surely it has to be."

"Well absolutely, it can be an anagram. But just not for any relevant words connected to our enquiry," Hanlon confidently asserted.

"Really?" Murray asked in a dispirited manner.

"I then entered it into a search that would give us actual names."

Murray looked over optimistically. This was where 'Sherlock came good,' he thought to himself.

Hanlon again shook his head. "It created 233 various names from those letters. Two hundred and thirty three flamin' names. Who would have believed that?" he questioned aloud. "Over two hundred names and not one the one we wanted."

Sympathetic to the cause, Murray felt he had to at least mention to Joe, "You'll never know son. Not for sure anyhow," the Inspector said in a disappointed and understated way.

"Oh, but I do know for sure sir,"

Murray's eyes and ears perked up at that comment. The others sat up in their chairs. He had everyone's attention now.

"How come Joe?" he smiled.

"Because I now know the name we were looking for," he replied with an even larger smile than Murray.

"Sherlock, you are a lifesaver. I knew I could depend on you to turn something up. Well done! Fantastic! Go on enlighten us then. What was the name we were looking for?"

Hanlon wrote neatly into his notebook, ripped off the page and handed it to his Inspector. Scrolled in large capital letters, he had written: ELMYRDEHORY.

"You've given me the same jumbled letters Joe, best try again," Murray encouraged him. He then handed him back the writing paper and watched as Detective Constable Hanlon wrote on the paper for a second time.

On having it passed back to him, Steven Murray was riveted to the words on the page. He stared at them in awe and disbelief. This time it read Elmyr de Hory.

"That is someone's actual name," Murray exclaimed. "Right there in plain sight. Just like de Pereda. They are having a laugh. They are playing with us. Who or what are they Joe? How are they involved? And who is this guy when he's at home?"

Although noticeably growing in confidence throughout this investigation, DC 'Kid' Curry sheepishly raised a hand.

"Andrew," Hanlon gestured toward his colleague, using his Sunday name.

"I think I could take an educated guess," Curry mentioned cautiously and quietly.

Before Murray or Hanlon even gave him the green light, he instantly offered up -

"I'm no betting man, but I have been carrying out some background checks along with 'Hanna' these past few days. I'd be willing to hazard an informed guess that he is an artist of sorts."

Hanlon pursed his lips and nodded.

"One that replicates the work of others, that duplicates masterpieces." Raising his voice for emphasis, he continued with, "a forger in other words."

'Ally' Coulter then happily joined in the discussion and openly declared.

"I am a betting man as many of you know. And I would bet the proverbial bottom dollar, DC Curry is spot on. One hundred percent correct. I would even go further than that," the experienced detective added emphatically. "I'll bet you, this de Hory guy was or is himself a fraud - Just like Mr Simon Taylor."

"Well done," Hanlon shouted. Offering a celebratory 'high five' from across the room.

The meeting had turned into a bit of a brainstorming session and a very productive one at that.

"The 'Kid' has photographic evidence relating to the robberies and partly what they're all about," 'Hanna' Hayes proudly offered up on her colleagues behalf.

"Myself and 'Sandy'," Murray stated, "have some interesting video evidence also in relation to 'Mac's' killer. Which was the original purpose of calling you all in," he added.

"Forget all the photographic evidence and video evidence. I have what is still known as gut feeling," cried Coulter. "So Taylor is guilty. You name it, he is guilty." The others began to laugh slightly and felt some satisfaction and revelled briefly in the moment. Elements of the case, one or both were definitely coming together. As smiles and light laughter recognised the hard work that had been put in. 'Ally' continued at full pelt.

"Obnoxious, arrogant, sneaky - an absolute shyster! Add devious, deceitful, cunning and a fraud? No doubt! Ruthless, sinister and greedy - Murder even? I wouldn't put it past him!"

Murray and Kerr gazed knowingly across at each other after Ally's final remark.

Suddenly 'Sandy' Kerr had her eureka moment. "Mac beat us all to the punch several days ago," she piped up. They all looked at her. She was centre stage now. "I have no idea how he stumbled upon it," she said, but, "Look at those apples and pears," he mentioned in the video. "That is also what he mumbled to me the night before. Remember I told you that sir?" she said, turning to address Murray.

"Yes of course I remember. And it's Cockney rhyming slang for stairs."

"And he had spent time that afternoon catching up with his Uncle from London," Sandra Kerr reminded everyone. "He wanted to get a 'good butchers,'" she added.

'Ally' Coulter stood up proudly. "I knew it. I just knew it," he said with a determined excitement and conviction. "Apples and Pears - Stairs. A Butcher's Hook - A Look. And…" he paused, raised his head heavenward and said, "Thank you Machur Rasul. God bless you."

"Ally!" Hayes and Murray called out at the same time.

"Oh, aye, right," he winked at his Inspector. "Sexton Blake is, for those uneducated amongst us, also Cockney rhyming slang."

The intimate gathering looked at him.

"A Sexton Blake - a quality Fake!" he confirmed for everyone present.

A slight cough echoed from the doorway.

DC Hanlon simply added - "You're welcome everyone. Glad I could be of help. Me, myself and Mr de Hory."

The Inspector slowly scanned the room. No one knew how to celebrate this good news. They had just lost a colleague. Laughter, smiles and upbeat talk did not sit comfortably with them right now.

"Andrew. One more time, concisely and in layman's terms," Murray instructed.

DC Curry was about to get his well deserved moment in the spotlight. Well prepared, he confidently stepped forward and began.

"Everyone that had been robbed sir. Every single one of them at some point in the previous six months had been to NOT Blake's, but to Anderson, Barber and Cybill for an insurance valuation. Very clever that. Every month they put up a special deal offering FREE valuations."

"So they knew precisely who to target for goods," Coulter added.

"Yes and no 'Ally.' As a bonus, yes they do get to locate some fine property. But remember we are looking at them reproducing works of art here, and that takes time. So, they make out that they are inundated with requests for free valuations, but if the owner leaves the article with them overnight, they'll give them an insurance receipt, covering them for loss, theft or damage, etc."

"What use was that?" Kerr asked.

"That was the beauty of it. Overnight, with modern technology, they could scan, print, take 3d images, the works. They could research, match woods, check out paper materials and source paints, frames, etc. It was a window of opportunity. But there was no rush, they could sit on it for several weeks or months. They were able to wait patiently until replicas had been reproduced. Then, when the robberies took place, they had time to check and confirm the forgery was good enough and would pass the owners scrutiny, before once again alerting us to their whereabouts. Having reckoned all hope was lost, most people were just so delighted to have their property back, they never fully checked it again. They were just so overjoyed and delighted to have a £200 painting back. Whilst the masterpiece worth a thousand times that amount hung exquisitely in some collectors private gallery! Only when they went to sell would they have discovered the swop, possibly years later."

Joseph Hanlon had remained in the shadow of the doorway and kept his own counsel throughout Curry's summation. He had watched carefully the eye contact between Sandra Kerr and her old partner. Something his Inspector had mentioned earlier seemed to have been overlooked by everyone during the 'Kid's findings.

"Some interesting video evidence," Joe remarked out of nowhere.

"Quite," Murray reassured him with a number 71 nod. "I just wanted to thank Hayes and Curry firstly for their diligence. Well done you two!"

"It was all Andrew's idea," Susan Hayes offered up. "He had spotted a difference between Sir Ronald Mecham's returned painting and the photograph he had commissioned for insurance purposes. That was what first alerted him."

"Sandy," Steven Murray gestured toward his DS.

"We recovered Mac's phone everyone," she stated positively. "It had been wedged between his jacket and shirt, under his body at the base of the stairwell. His assailant had obviously been running scared, not realised it had been recording, or was just desperate to flee the scene. However, watch carefully the footage we recovered." Murray pressed play on the computer monitor. *99 Red Balloons* could be heard playing in the background as the door buzzed and he began recording. There was faint, but adequate lighting as Machur entered. Two at a time he climbed the stairs, the steps steep and unforgiving. The footage so far was mainly of Rasul's size eleven shoes. Then just as he neared the top. Blackness, all the lights had gone out.

"Woa,' his gathered colleagues sighed.

This was a surreal moment, as if watching a horror DVD. Simultaneously, as a light shone in Machur's face and chest area, he'd cleverly switched his phone light on. Then just as an antique spear entered 'Mac's well toned gut, Rasul had managed to raise his phone shoulder high. Susan Hayes covered her eyes, Hanlon sat open mouthed and 'Ally' Coulter simply shed a tear or two. Rasul cried an agonising pain, his body shuddered and he was sent reeling backward down the stairs, breaking his neck in the process.

"He never got his face then?" Hanlon questioned coldly.

"So we are no closer to identifying his killer?" Curry echoed.

"You would think," said Sandra Kerr. "But watch closely. She then rewound it slightly, before pushing play once again. This time it played in slow motion and just as the spear was about to make contact Rasul's phone captured the moment of impact. Kerr paused the image for full effect. Then simply enlarged it. There was as Hanlon stated, no facial image. So no recognition from a 'mugshot.' However, Kerr ran her finger from the tip of the spear backwards. A sharp audible intake of breath was heard.

"Exactly," she said.
Murray smiled as she pointed at a clear, close up image of a badly bruised hand.

"Possibly a hand that had been caught in a car door," she added. "A hand that was still working, that was in plain view every day. But an injured hand that was hidden by a protective covering. A protective covering that took the form of a certain white glove. One that every twenty four hours delicately handled, wiped and cleaned priceless, precious objects!"

"So in a nutshell," Murray boomed. Giving fresh clarity to the situation. "The robberies were all an elaborate forgery and insurance scam. 'Bunny' Reid knew this, but helped tip us off. Why?"

"He said because he owed us," Coulter quietly reminded his DI.

"Honour among thieves and all that 'Ally.' There was a suitable pause. "Piffle, absolute piffle," Murray declared passionately, raising his voice and with both arms flailing generously into the air.

"Simon Taylor killed 'Mac' Rasul for no obvious reason that we can think of," Detective Sergeant Sandra Kerr added. "Yet he obviously felt that he had one, and a damned important one at that!"

"So what was it then?" Hayes questioned. " What was he trying to stop 'Mac' or us finding out?"

'Ally' had had a gut feeling, which proved yet again to be correct, as was often the case. But finding proof to back up gut feelings, can frequently be the stumbling block. Ironically however, it was DC Hanlon's investigation that enabled this particular house of cards to come tumbling down. It was his discovery of Elmyr de Hory that took them up the 'Apples and Pears.' It had then led them down the dangerous path of (Sexton) Blake's being fake. And although it helped with the insurance scam and Rasul's demise at the auction rooms. What on earth had it to do with the recent spate of sadistic mutilations and killings and ultimately the ...

continuing disappearance of teenage schoolgirls?

Chapter Thirty-Two

"I cried to my daddy on the telephone - 'how long now?' Until the clouds unroll and you come home the line went. The saints are coming, the saints are coming, I say no matter how I try, I realise there's no reply."

- The Skids

Cyrille Anderson was off the grid. His staff had neither heard from him nor were able to contact him. Numerous texts, calls and emails had gone unanswered from the night before. Robert Latchford had similarly become invisible. Trying to track both men down via their mobile phones was an option, but the intervening legal paperwork and protocol would take time. Time that Murray and his team were beginning to suspect was counting down faster than they would have wished.

Anderson junior had threatened recriminations, but these were vocal, through legal means via lawyers. That was his superior, well-to-do style, Murray had concluded. And if he were involved in the teenage disappearances, although Murray's gut said otherwise, he would most surely not abduct, then kill the Latchford girl. He would have no hold at all over her father then. He'd have absolutely nothing to bargain with if she were dead.

So who was it?

The Inspector reckoned Latchford had become more confused than ever. He thought back to that intimate Saturday evening conversation they'd held. It had been a frank and open discussion where a basic level of mutual respect and trust had been formed. He instantly recalled a small snippet of the conversation. The part where he had told Robert Latchford - "I had lost my mind and was about to lose our family home. I had withdrawn twenty five thousand pounds in cash that very morning and was waiting at the door of the casino at 12 noon, ready to transform my life. And boy was it changed forever."

Latchford had recognised the anguished pain on the detective's face that evening. It was a mirror image of his own.

"Are you okay Inspector?" he had asked with genuine sincerity and understanding. "You don't have to share any more. It's fine to keep it private and confidential. There is no need to dwell on events that are still obviously deeply personal for you."

Back in the present. And sadly from his actions Murray figured Robert Latchford had gone through enough in recent times. That he had no desire to continue in this cruel, sadistic, evil world. A diseased world, riddled with deceit and danger. From speaking with him, he got the feeling that this once proud single parent had already made the choice. However, on the other hand the man still wanted justice for his wife and child. So was he prepared to endure a little longer in mortality and possibly engage DI Murray in fighting his cause?

By the time Murray and Hanlon set off from HQ later that Sunday afternoon, entry into Latchfords impressive house had already taken place. A grand, eloquent home that 'Sherlock' had discovered the day before was about to be, in American terminology - 'Foreclosed!' The bank had been about to repossess both his business and the beautiful Inverleith Terrace property.

When the duo arrived, the upstairs bedrooms were in the middle of being searched thoroughly. Drawers, cupboards and cabinets had been scrutinised intensely. Clothes had been cast aside as pillows and mattresses were overturned. Shelves had been swiftly cleared and the assorted book pages were carefully flicked through before being re-stacked on the floor.

The two colleagues looked saddened and disheartened, as they watched fellow officers turn this poor man's home upside down. Just as his sorry personal life had been these past seven tumultuous days. His whole world had imploded and he was nowhere to be found, and that to Murray was the worrying part. The kitchen had been filled with even more garbage and empty dishes than before. Those checking out that particular room, most certainly got the short straw. A number of officers were also to be found in both the garage and the surrounding garden area. Murray then held up a hand to stop a young PC entering into the sitting room. The very room where 'Sherlock' and the Inspector had first spoken at length with Robert Latchford.

"We've got this Constable," he said to the young man, whilst motioning to Joe Hanlon.

The space seemed cold. The large, bevelled, glass light-shade situated directly above them in the centre of the room added to its overall lack of warmth. The photographs and trophies appeared to signal a bygone age. A chapter that was to be left behind and soon closed over. Although, Steven Murray definitely felt that for some particular reason this story was very much unfinished. His churning gut was telling him that there was still a few more interesting twists and turns to be revealed and added to this ex-horologist's story. Also, forgotten, unfinished and sat gathering dust in front of them was the jigsaw of the scenic London landmarks. Hanlon pictured in his mind's eye, this father and daughter sharing smiles, laughter and hugs around the table. No doubt surrounded on all sides by juice, crisps, biscuits and other assorted chocolate goodies and snacks.

"Sir," he piped up.

Murray glanced across at him, but his gaze was not reciprocated. DC Hanlon's eyes were focused firmly on the fireplace. There, sat perched on Robert Latchfords mantelpiece, positioned prominently and certainly a recent addition to his ever increasing pile of unread mail, was a cream coloured envelope. It had been positioned deliberately at the front, held in place only by the small, sturdy hourglass. There was no stamp and no address. The handwriting on the front stated: For the attention of the football fan - Inspector Stephen Murray.

Misspelled - Hanlon thought that was intriguing. Latchford though, had only ever heard Murray's name spoken aloud, so had opted for the less common 'ph' spelling. The Inspector dutifully put on a blue nitrile glove, before taking hold of the unsealed envelope and retrieving the enclosed letter.

In the *Book of Acts,* Saint Stephen had been stoned to death and was widely regarded as the first martyr of the Christian Church. And as a man of faith, SteVen Murray had often thought about that connection when it regularly came time for him to press the self destruct button and literally become - 'a martyr to the cause!'

Robert Latchford had certainly transformed in recent days. He had went from a potential GQ front page fashion icon, into a soulless, cynical, street person. He was a broken man. Dispirited, dishevelled and drained of any real desire to continue struggling in this life. Those were common character traits, emotions and feelings that DI Steven Murray could often relate to. Mainly, they'd come about just before the mighty mood pendulum would swing into action, the relevant music play and his state of mind alter drastically. Misery to laughter. Sunshine to hail. And jubilance to despair. Hold on tightly he had learned. Because it almost always offered him an almighty, unfettered, no frills return seat to hell and back.

The day before on the Saturday night, Latchford had driven into the 'customer only' car park on Corstorphine Road for the first time. Anderson's offices were officially closed. It had just gone ten past eight and a lone figure was silhouetted in the impressive doorway. As Latchford approached, Anderson barely recognised him. It would appear that he had neither shaved, nor washed since meeting Murray and Hanlon the previous weekend. Possibly eating had not been high on his agenda either. With no imminent date set for his daughter's funeral, there would be no real incentive for her father's daily diet or routine to alter in the immediate future.

In an offhand manner Cyrille Anderson dismissively asked, "Why did you phone? What do you want?" Then finally by observing Latchford. "Are you limping?" His tone dragged off, as if implying yet another imperfection, fault or weakness that Latchford possessed.

"It's not a limp," Latchford responded. Lifting automatically to waist height a Russian 8mm Baikal self-defence pistol from his navy blue cargo pants. Originally used for firing CS gas, this gun was now the latest 'weapon of choice' to those on the street. Legally sold in Germany, they won't fire a bullet. However, Robert Latchford knew that they could be converted by removing the partially blocked barrel and replacing it with a rifled barrel. After a couple of other small alterations, it could then fire 9mm bulleted ammunition. The replacement barrel was longer than the original and was threaded so that it would accept a silencer. A beautiful, glistening charcoal grey silencer. Exactly like the one now narrowly positioned only two inches from Cyrille Anderson's forehead.

"Get inside," the man once affectionately known as 'Latches' instructed. "First my wife and then my daughter," he said aggressively. "You're gonna pay for it this time."

"Wait, what is this all about? What do you mean this time? I loved Annie you idiot!"

Latchford thumped Anderson's left shoulder from the front with his open left palm. It was done by way of an encouragement for the suited businessman to turn around. On doing so, Latchford swopped the gun over and with his right hand produced a disposable police restraint from deep within his jacket pocket. Bringing together both of Anderson's hands, slipping on the restraint and with a smooth pull, the job was done. In less than three seconds Anderson was disabled as a threat. Not that Cindy-Ann's father ever thought he would be.

The financier never got his hands dirty. He was always behind the scenes. The crooked ideas, the cunning schemes - that was where the bold Cyrille's strength lay. The quick and easy, the fraudulent, preying on the weak and vulnerable. In Anderson's own terminology - 'the little people!'

Latchford had a slight twinge of regret on his face though. The tri-fold disposable restraints were compact, easily carried and rapidly applied as he proved. They had been specifically designed to police standards, as their wide straps had no sharp edges. Although possibly their most important feature was their ability to fold away discreetly, unlike normal plasticuff restraints that hang in a loop from the belt. Had the plain clothes 'FLO,' WPC Cloy not left them in open view last week whilst making the coffee, Robert Latchford may never have been tempted!

As Steven Murray began to read the note, in another part of the city Cyrille Anderson began to lick his lips. He could taste a sweetness, a tangy honey flavour registered in his mind. It threw up memories of sucking upon a cut finger received from a paper cut, a safety pin or a stapler injury. It was blood the businessman thought with a certainty. As he opened his eyes, the last he remembered was Robert Latchford holding a pistol all of two inches from his forehead. That had been the evening before. Now he tried to refocus and open his eyes again, before fully realising that they were already stretched wide. It was just that it was pitch black and they were taking time to adjust to the complete darkness of his surroundings. His hands were still bound and blood continued to run down from his suspected broken nose. A pistol whipping the previous night had rendered him unconscious and enabled Latchford to bring him to his lair, or whatever this seemed to be. He was sat on solid ground. That at least seemed a relief and slightly reassured him. His knees were pulled up to his chin and his back placed firm against a solid barrier. His ankles also had now been tethered together with restraints. Both the wall and floor seemed unnaturally even and cold to the touch. And as if his head was not sore enough, he felt the inclination to gently tilt it backward three times. A deep 'boom,' 'boom,' 'boom,' resonated within what he now recognised as some sort of metal chamber. Anderson's mind was now going some. Accelerating at pace, with a multitude of scenarios playing out in it. At this precise moment, his heartbeat and pulse entered into the competitive race also. A possible tunnel or locked warehouse container were his first thoughts. Then as his eyes slowly adapted to the lack of light, he began to make out a large outline directly across from him. He tried desperately to manoeuvre himself closer. He began to shuffle…

"No need for that," the voice stated eerily. "You are not going anywhere."

Temporarily at least Anderson thought to himself, until he heard the next two words.

"Ever again!"

Robert Latchford made no attempt to disguise his voice. He spoke with bitterness and anger, but also it was fervent, deliberate and the words uttered seemed to be offered up with a real honesty and conviction. Cyrille Anderson had better pray earnestly that he would be rescued, otherwise it seemed for certain that he most definitely would not see the light of day any other way. The father of the late Cindy-Ann Latchford had a plan and was fully intent on carrying it out.

Back in Inverleith, Murray's shoulders sagged. Heavy sighs and a weird concoction of other audible gasps and syllables fought for the opportunity to be expressed.

"Awe, aagh, what, no, no no, this can't be!" The Inspector offered in disbelief.

"Sir, sit down, take a seat," Joe Hanlon encouraged. Pulling a large armchair right up behind him. Murray looked at 'Sherlock,' reread part of the letter and lashed out an almighty kick at the leather seat. He'd cut into the leather upholstery, but that was the least of their worries as he handed the letter over to his young DC.

"We're too late Joe."

"Maybe not sir," Hanlon offered optimistically, whilst scanning through the note.

"This was left for us to find last night Joe."

"Sir, he says he killed the girls. What is he on about? We have checked out his various alibis for when they all went missing, including his own daughter. And they all stand up, it couldn't have been him."

It wasn't often that Murray's 'black dog' joined him during his time at work. But tears welled up in Inspector Murray's eyes. His fingertips surrounded and gently massaged between his eyelids and forehead. He swallowed hard before speaking.

"We checked his alibi's for when they went missing Joe. But apart from Cindy-Ann we have not located them. And if they are dead, we don't know when they were killed or by whom!"

"He would have needed an accomplice at least sir. And we have had him under observation most of the time. Either under surveillance, in the company of WPC Cloy or ourselves for that matter. We were monitoring him."

"Certainly not yesterday apparently!" Murray voiced in annoyance, grabbing back Latchfords written confession.

"Did you spot this sir?" Hanlon asked.
Between his right thumb and forefinger he was holding up what looked like a small store till receipt. It had also been in the envelope.

"It appears to be from a sandwich shop."

"A sandwich shop?" Murray questioned sceptically. "Let me see that Joe."
Hanlon handed it across. His DI began to make shapes with his lips. His eyes peered at each word. The exact description of the item, the cost, the time purchased. His head offered up questions as it moved vigorously from side to side and up and down. To be specific, it was for a panini. A ham and cheese panini purchased several days earlier.

"So why hold on to it?" Murray expressed. "It must have been relevant to him. It says it cost 1.99." Murray shook his head. "That seemed awful cheap, even for a basic ham and cheese product."

"Maybe," Hanlon offered weakly. He knew his boss was now in discovery mode. He deliberately remained quiet and hoped he would soon begin to work his magic.

"Joe, he didn't actually say he killed the girls."

"Well, he said he was to blame for their deaths," Hanlon responded.

With each word slowly pronounced, DI Murray offered up, "And I would suggest that that could appear very different."

"Agreed," Joe Hanlon conceded. He then lamented, "They are dead though, whatever way we look at it. That seems to be a definite."

"Sadly, I can't disagree with you there Joe. On the other hand, maybe not all of them, and that offers us fresh hope."

He swore he could hear the black dog yelp and bark at that last remark!

Chapter Thirty-Three

"We're on the march wi' Ally's Army - We're going tae the Argentine. And we'll really shake them up when we win the World Cup, 'Cause Scotland is the greatest football team."

- Andy Cameron

Back in the darkness Robert Latchford berated Cyrille Anderson for the vile, nasty, greedy and murderous individual that he had become.

"I'll give you vile and nasty, greedy even. But no matter what you plan to do to me, I am no murderer."

"Over a decade ago, Annie's rather 'timely' death says otherwise. All because she had discovered your grubby little secret. In recent years at those charity balls and dinner dances. Having your picture taken with Cindy-Ann and myself, all to keep up the pretence."

"There you go again talking gibberish Rob. What did Annie discover? She was the victim of an unfortunate traffic accident. Why could you never come to terms with that? Sure they never caught the driver, but I wasn't even in London at the time. And why would I kill her? You know I loved her. I always loved her. And those dances and fundraisers were benefit nights to help you and Cindy-Ann move on with your lives."

Latchford appeared to carry something in his hand.

"Do you recognise this sound?"

His thumb pushed a button on a small panel no bigger than a mobile phone. A gentle engine seemed to turn over outside. The noise was still in the distance and did not appear to concern Anderson unduly. As the revs there continued to grow and intensify, the stillness back at Latchfords ransacked home was about to be broken by a Murray unveiling.

The Detective Inspector stared at the wooden cabinet where the framed photograph of Cindy-Ann and her father had been on display. Murray had confirmed only yesterday that Cyrille Anderson was one of the black bow tie brigade also in the shot. He was the one wearing cufflinks exactly like those discovered in the Latchford child's hand on the evening of her death. So Robert Latchford had every right to think him the killer of his daughter. However, unbeknown to him, DI Murray also knew another fact pertinent to those cufflinks. One that made him pretty certain that the 'cocky, arrogant, brash, pompous, puffed up and self-centred money grabbing pig,' was no murderer. He had discovered that Anderson the younger, had been recuperating in an Edinburgh hospital at the time. Having gone through a serious operation only the day before. His father on the other hand, had been in attendance at a meeting in London. Granted, it is a very big place Murray thought. But the fact that it was his father who was the actual owner of the cufflinks in the photograph put a rather different perspective on things.

Latchford pressed his extended finger firmly down onto another button. This time as the outside noise increased, the container walls seemed to vibrate. Anderson's feet began to slide and gravitate smoothly toward the centre of the floor. He then fell backward as the wall retreated from supporting his back.

"Have you not figured out where we are yet?" his captor asked smugly.

Tired, disillusioned and with the coldness beginning to really impact on him. A shivering Anderson retorted. "I, I have n-no interest or idea, but, but enough is enough. Let me out of here n-now or finish me off! I don't, don't think you have it in you Latchford." He continued to shake and stammer, but raised his voice one final time to bark - "You h-have always been we-weak. I, I get that you are angry, upset and go-going broke. But let's m-move on!"

"Have you never been to my yard Cyrille? My rundown, money sucking behemoth of a scrapyard. The very one that carried out all your evil, filthy, dirty chores for you, and has allowed you to live in the lap of luxury." Robert Latchford sounded drunk, when in reality he was just sickened by life and all it had to offer. He continued with a dismissive edge to his voice. "But taking the life of my precious Cindy-Ann crossed the line…"

Fight or flight had obviously taken hold and Anderson again responded with - "T-taking your Cindy-Ann, la-lap of luxury, dirty chores. Have y-y-you gone insane man? I have no-no-no idea what you are o-on about."

"This is my last dependable employee," Latchford stated. Even enclosed in the darkness, Anderson could make out Latchford gesturing with his arms. "This is… The Crusha," he proudly announced. Before banging twice on its metal side. Once again a button was pushed, even more sound resonated and this time movement was felt top and bottom. The roof was lowering inch by inch, as the side walls compressed inward.

"What the …. R-Rob what are you d-doing?"

"It's not called 'The Crusha' for no reason Cyrille. I'm a scrap dealer you know. I crumble and crush stuff every day for a living." That last remark, possibly specifically that final word made him scoff. "Living - Something neither of us will be doing very soon." Once again he cried toward Anderson, "Tell me exactly what happened with Annie and why Cindy-Ann?"

"For the l-l-last time you lunatic, I have n-no idea what you're talking about!"

Cyrille Anderson would never get to work on his people skills. Robert Latchford never hesitated for a second.

Another button was firmly pushed and he deliberately dropped the controls onto the darkened floor. The single gunshot and anguished cry could easily have been heard in Inverleith…

"Aaaaaargh," The short, sharp, squeal yelped.

"You okay sir?" Hanlon enquired.

"I will be Joe," Murray reassured his young friend.

"I can see from your face…"

"Leave it 'Sherlock,' but let's walk through it slowly. Remind me again, what it said on the envelope."

"For the attention of yourself, Steven Murray. Only with the p.h spelling. Is that significant?"

"No, that may not be. But what he actually stated was! 'For the football fan' is how he started it. And that Joe, was the key."

Hanlon rubbed and scratched at his chin and although impressed, he was lost. He was good at the discovering of facts, diligently scouring and routing out anomalies. But as regards the obscure links and cryptic clues, he was still learning his trade. Murray walked them over to the pile of books and magazines that had previously been searched.

"They've done this group," Hanlon informed him.

"Maybe so Joe, but not armed with the same information we now have."

Steven Murray knelt slowly and carefully removed a couple of pieces of literature. Two football sticker albums to be precise. The Inspector had commented on them during one of his earlier visits with Robert Latchford.

Detective Constable Hanlon now became even more confused.

"It was never about any cafe, delicatessen or cheese and tomato sandwich for that matter Joe."

Murray held up the albums in front of Hanlon.

"Start reading Joe," he said bluntly.

"Football Seventy-Eight," he began. Then he paused just as quickly, as he sussed it out. "Figurine… Pa..nin..i."

"Absolutely," said Murray. "Never a roll, crusty bread or bloomin' baguette in sight. Panini was the brand in relation to his completed football sticker albums. Every schoolboy of a certain age collected and swopped Panini stickers!"

"So which one? Joe asked. "I'm assuming you know."

"An educated guess would say we can dismiss this one."

The Inspector put down the 'Argentina 78' booklet and immediately handed Hanlon the 'Football 78' album. Once again 'Sherlock' turned it upside down and quickly rifled through it. Nothing dropped out.

"The mystery sandwich cost one ninety nine remember. Although there was no pound sign in front of the so-called cost Joe. It just simply read 1.99."

"Are you thinking Latchford produced this receipt on his own point of sale cash register or computer at his yard."

"Those were exactly my thoughts," Murray confirmed. He then hesitated. "It's a bit of a guess, but would page 19 be Everton FC by any chance?" he asked with a slight uncertainty.

Hanlon now excitedly turned the pages in anticipation.

"No way. How did you know that sir?"

"I was a football fan in the seventies Joe. It was my era, my forte, my wasted childhood!"

Not completely wasted though. Murray had actually been an above average football player. He had represented his district and had Scotland schoolboy trials as a youth. However, that was a long, long time ago and there was no relevance in telling Hanlon at this specific moment in time. Though maybe at some point in the future, when DI Murray needed bragging rights, he reflected.

"Everton FC. I don't get it it sir. What's the connection? Is there some sort of Merseyside link?"

"You will see soon enough Joe. I'm thinking George Wood is on there. He was their goalkeeper? He wore the number one shirt. Other faces would include Martin Dobson, Andy King and......"

"BOB LATCHFORD!" Joe blurted out. Delighted and overly animated at his latest discovery.

"Bob 'Robert' Latchford that's your man," Murray stated. "Prolific goalscorer and Everton number 9 for several years."

As they sat together and checked out 'Bob' Latchford's sticker, the number nine on page nineteen. They knew that there was no need to go over it with a fine-tooth comb. It was noticeably obvious that something small and rectangular in shape had been placed underneath the Englishman's fine facial features. The Everton centre-forward had then been 'transferred' back into position with the help of some modern day sellotape.

Droplets of blood had been discovered at the entrance of the Anderson, Barber and Cybill headquarters near Murrayfield, but no sign of their boss. The scrapyard searched - nothing. Officers had also checked out the casino - no joy there either. Although several uniformed personnel had now been permanently positioned outside to keep an eye out. Murray and Hanlon returned to the station to make use of the modern technology and software that would help them with their 1.99 Panini!

It was a memory card with an assortment of files contained on it. Several of the folder names seemed quite self explanatory. 'Annie's Findings,' 'Money Laundering,' 'Yard Deliveries.'

"We can have Hayes check out Annie Latchfords folders later. For now though, open 'Yard Deliveries,' it's the most recent and up to date. It may give us some clue or indication as to where he, or they, have gone.

Possibly willingly or more likely unwillingly together," Murray nervously attested.

As the police computer screen kicked into life, both Murray and Hanlon were intrigued as they began to watch proceedings.

"I had no idea," Robert Latchford pleaded. *"None whatsoever,"* he continued. *"I beg of you and their families to forgive me."* Murray and Hanlon sat in silence and looked at each other cautiously, as Cindy-Ann's father composed himself on-screen and continued his monologue.

"Inspector, I had every confidence with your footballing knowledge, that you'd make short work of the Panini clue. With you now watching this recording, either alone or with some of your colleagues, I have two pieces of housekeeping to initially take care off. Firstly: I deeply appreciate you taking time with me the other evening. To reassure me that you would genuinely look into reopening investigations into Annie's death, or murder as I have always seen it. And I believe you, especially as you shared with me the tragic circumstances surrounding your own wife's hit and run."

Hanlon gasped audibly. He went to turn toward his Inspec… Murray clicked his fingers and pointed back at the screen.

"And secondly: I am already dead!"

Both police officers immediately flinched. A desperate, distraught and now seemingly 'dead' man continued to air and vent his thoughts.

"However things have moved on dramatically since then. I received this through my letterbox three days ago."

Latchford held up a disc that was then placed into his DVD player. He pushed 'play' and narrated the scene. The footage had all been recorded at his yard.

"I needed the money Inspector. You've probably figured that out already. I was their way into the homes. I bypassed the fitted security systems within their targeted premises. Initially that was all. I had no idea what they did with the stuff or how come it all

seemed to be recovered quickly thereafter. Then they said they would double my cut just to help them out with some minor refuse and disposal issues. I was on the edge, I was struggling to survive. I wanted to continue to give Cindy-Ann the best, but her school fees, music lessons and various other tuitions were sucking me dry."

Tears now began to well up in his eyes.

"What is he getting at sir? This is no real help at all."

"Patience, Joe. Those tears stand for something."

They watched carefully as the van arrived on various evenings. Each time, a fully packed crate or two of furniture, fixtures and fittings would be unloaded from it via the forklift. Then they were escorted for departure and hoisted high, up into 'the Crusha.'

"Black filmed all these scenes," Latchford informed the viewer.

"He always said his boss required it as proof that the work had been done. I could never understand it. Who would care what happened to old fixtures and fittings? However, I always went along with it. It would appear though, that they were never intended for any bosses."

The tears again began to stream down his cheeks.

"Oh no," said Inspector Murray, with a look of dawning on his face. "Tell me they didn't."

Hanlon looked at him incredulously. "What is it sir? Tell me. What am I missing?"

"All that would be required they had said, was to simply break up their old furniture from the various casinos. They had lots of renovation work taking place and it would be never ending. Double your money Rob they said. You'll be out of debt in no time."

Murray could barely watch.

On screen as Latchford operated 'the Crusha' from within the confines of its small cabin, he never actually saw the wooden crates up close and personal. Also, the combined noise between the machine generator and the forklift would have cancelled out any other gentler surrounding sounds. Then the moment of truth arrived. It was Dennis Black's first zoom and focus. The words, *'It was for his boss,'* echoed in the Inspector's mind. Who was this sick, sadistic boss that was mentioned? Murray reckoned he knew only too well and surprisingly, it would not be who others put their money on!

"Is that… No, no, surely not." DC Hanlon immediately jumped to his feet, as a combination of shock and alarm kicked in. He began in a crazy, abnormal, animated fashion to shout and scream uncontrollably. His arms swung wildly and reached out as if attempting to rescue those on screen. His voice bellowed with a strange mix of anger, rage and compassion. "Sir, sir, we need to help them. We've got to do something sir. Sir what can we…"

Murray quickly placed his hand firmly on Hanlon's shoulder. "Nothing Joe," he said. "We can do nothing. Remember, sadly, this is archive footage from different deliveries over the past few weeks." That in itself, made it more harrowing than ever.

The close-up showed clearly through the narrow slats in the crate, the dark haired, yet gaunt features of Karen Fenwick, the second schoolgirl to have disappeared. She was alive and terrified. Latchford had already positioned the crate into 'the Crusha.' It had been laid directly on an old, battered, white Ford Focus. A ten year old, forest green Fiat was then strategically placed on top to bind the ingredients. He could have been making up a tasteful cocktail at a fashionable wine bar. Except, there was nothing tasteful to this in the slightest. The button was pushed and both men watched as thirty seconds later a crushed fusion of metal, bone and wood exited. Melded together with the dead body of a young schoolgirl, were assorted metal cabinets, two old disused vehicles and a set of vintage red leather chairs!

Robert Latchford sobbed openly now as the DVD continued to play. Hanlon looked back briefly at the screen, before he hurriedly grabbed the nearest waste paper bin and wretched up at least three times in continuous succession. Murray raised his own hands to his mouth as if in prayer. He bit furiously on his fingernails, a schoolboy habit that had never left him and forced himself to then view to completion.

A separate evening close up was there of twelve year-old Tracey McFall. Frail and frightened, her slim, slender fingers clawed frantically at the wood as the massive compressor began to work its magic from both sides. Her body soon disappeared from view as the metal jaws crunched and grinded intensely. Slowly they squeezed and squealed in all directions. In and out, up and down, like a child desperate to breathe. From side to side, above and below, every component continued to work diligently and once again, down came the three tonne press. Inch by inch it ascended and descended. Up and down, in and out. Pushing, pounding, pulverising. Up, down, in, out - crushing, compressing and killing. Another half a minute - Another stacked cube.

For every beginning - There was an end.

As DI Murray began to watch and listen to Robert Latchfords remaining tearful confession cum narration, he called the area control. He remained detached and calmly requested that several police, ambulance and fire vehicles be sent immediately to The Car Bored Box Company in Leith. It would no doubt have a sad, sad, story to tell. As well as heartbreaking closure to offer up to several currently distressed families. Hayes and Curry remained behind at the station. Willing to read, listen, watch and do whatever it took or was required with all the other folders and files.

SOCO's were to be found busy at the rear of the scrapyard. Experienced sniffer dogs had already identified that area twenty minutes earlier as 'the prime real estate,' and currently forensics tents were being hastily erected. A large mobile incident room had been set up just inside the gated entrance and a further ten uniformed individuals were busy scouring the various *'avenues and alleyways'* contained within the extensive compound.

The floodlights to the yard were already switched on when the initial emergency vehicles arrived. That was not a good sign. 'Ally' Coulter was actually first on the scene. He had been busy following up on tracking down Cyrille Anderson when the call came through. He immediately drove over from the nearby Portobello High Street.

Dr Andrew Gordon was the pathologist on duty that evening and again his confident, cheery smile didn't quite reconcile with the task ahead. But it was good to see that he enjoyed his work! The dogs had begun barking on several occasions. And each time Sergeant Sandra Kerr furrowed her eyebrows and rubbed agitatedly at her forehead. Officers began to remove several of the cubes and re-align them with others that the dogs had brought their attention too. This was most definitely a result. And although not the outcome that they had wanted, it was probably the one that they had most expected.

Murray had chosen to remain in the incident room for a while. Originally to co-ordinate and assign tasks to individuals. Now however it was because he was feeling emotionally drained. Like in his gambling days where his stomach would churn and his chest physically ache from the tension. His breathing was laboured waiting on the news to filter back to him. Hanlon had made excuses to stay by his side and make sure he was doing as well as could be expected. Murray was fully aware of this, but allowed it nonetheless.

They had probably been there for about twenty to thirty minutes before the lightweight plastic door was nearly taken off its cheap hinges by 'Ally' Coulters dynamic entrance. He was grim faced. Murray detected he had possibly shed a tear or two before entering. Trying to remain professional and stoic Coulter spoke quietly.

"We didn't know the half of it Steve." He shook his head in disbelief. Murray turned his head to the side, his eyes closed slightly, scared by what was to follow.

"We were only looking for three or four bodies sir," Coulter confirmed.

"And?' Hanlon questioned. Unable to restrain himself any longer.

"Calm down 'Sherlock,' this takes a bit of… a bit of processing," he offered sensitively, before continuing. "Sixteen bodies Steven. Currently they have found sixteen corpses that they can be sure are separate individuals."

Steven Murray sat and bowed his head. Each of the other five officers in the small incident room all took a seat. This was devastating. DI Murray first drew one hand, then both, at regular intervals across his face. His elbows now rested on his desk and massaged his temple. Soon his fingers were running ferociously through his greying locks. His colleagues would struggle to witness the gentle teardrops fall from Murray's eyes, because each of them would be too busy wiping away their own tender emotions at this time.

Again he shook his head. "I knew we had stumbled into something big, but this was going to be huge. However, we need to keep a lid on it from the media." All the other heads looked up in amazement.

"For the victims sake. We need at least twenty-four hours to redress the balance." His energy had returned and he quickly composed himself and mindfully asked of Coulter. "Latchford and Anderson 'Ally,' are they amongst the sixteen discovered so far?"

"No," 'Ally' replied.

Murray felt relieved.

That was until 'Ally' Coulter added a little extra information. "They have their very own special memorial Steven. It's just directly outside 'the Crusha!'" Hanlon accompanied Detective Inspector Murray toward the large piece of machinery. And sure enough, ironically, there to the side of it was parked the rusting fork lift truck. The unknowing accomplice in each of the deaths.

"Is that a gun?" Hanlon asked in a surprised manner. As DI Murray kneeled closer toward the squared cube, he nodded. Sure enough one could see quite clearly the barrel of a small pistol. DS Kerr had approached them at this point.

"It looks likely that both Latchford and Anderson were in 'the Crusha,'" she said. "It could seemingly be operated remotely, even if you were inside it. Which would appear crazy to me," 'Sandy' added. "And the fact that no one was around and it was still switched on, would at least suggest one of them was inside." She paused. "Any thoughts sir?"

Murray was operating on autopilot at this point. It was going to be hard for everyone to take. He had been involved in some abhorrent and appalling cases over the years, but this had usurped them all. His team would now need to catch the culprits to even retain their sanity and some sort of piece of mind, because this will come back to haunt them. Maybe not tomorrow or the next day, but as a man speaking from experience, some major mind games and trauma was most definitely on the way.

Later, on leaving the scene, Murray confidently left The Car Bored Box Company in the capable hands of his fellow colleagues. He knew he would need to be in good shape for tomorrow. They really only had the next day to resolve this before word got out. So returning home at the end of what had turned out to be a rather soul destroying evening, the Inspector ruefully opened his front door...

Suddenly and without warning, a wave of tears came to Murray's eyes. The undoubted reservoir of sympathy and sorrow that he had stored up patiently throughout the day, was about to have it's floodgates opened. As he made his way upstairs wrapped in the warmth of melancholy, the steady stream continued to flow. They ran down familiar groove lines on his cheeks. He then grimaced intensely with pain. His throat tightened, his back teeth gritted firmly together and a deep burning penetrated his heart. His chest rose and fell unevenly as he sobbed. A shuddering intake of breath was consumed. Instantly it joined forces with a multitude of powerful emotions and was desperately exhaled vocally as acute distress. No words could adequately describe the sound. Although, 'excruciating pain' came close and would suffice.

People who have dealt with heartache and suffered loss up close, knew those feelings only too well. They were the fragments, the excess, the remains. The soul destroying residue, the leftover remnants. They almost always noticeably surfaced well past the death, beyond the funeral and long after the sympathy and well meant cards had died down. It was when the flames had ceased, the coffin laid to rest and many days, weeks and months after friends, family and loved ones had mourned alongside you. It was during these quiet times, the distant isolation set in and in Detective Inspector Steven Murray's particular case, when he normally became riddled and overcome with guilt!

Chapter Thirty-Four

"Suddenly everything was just so out of control. Now I want some answers and Mister I need to know. I hear all the talk and I don't know what they're saying. But I think I've got a good idea of the game that they are playing."

- Bruce Springsteen

Jayne Golden had already agreed to meet Murray the next day. None of the Anderson clan, junior or senior ever appeared before twelve on a Sunday afternoon, if at all, she had confided in him. And one of them at least would certainly not be appearing today Murray thought confidently. Although identification was still to be confirmed. Which also meant that Gerald Anderson had never been contacted in relation to any other recent findings. The Inspector reminded himself that he could tell her nothing of the previous evening, as she greeted him at the front door, as if by accident at ten o'clock on the dot.

"I'm looking for a Mr Anderson," Murray stated loudly. Allowing Golden's colleague at the front desk to overhear clearly.

"Gerald or Cyrille?" she asked brusquely, playing along. "Although, it doesn't matter anyway as none of them are here yet."

"I am Detective Inspector Murray," he said in a quiet, dignified manner. "We met briefly yesterday" he added, whilst brandishing his warrant card. "I think I may have left my rain jacket in his office when I visited."

Golden let him in and walked with him across to the visitor book. "I remember you," she said as he duly signed in. She then deliberately went around behind the desk, joked with and distracted her workmate. By the time she had re-joined Inspector Murray in the centre of the impressive foyer, all the video monitors had stopped recording.

"I'll escort you there and back sir. We can't have a police officer wandering around the premises unaccompanied can we Don?" She shouted in jest to her co-worker.

Her buddy looked up from his Sunday newspaper catch-up, shrugged indifferently and waved them both on their way.

Within seconds Jayne Golden had swiped her card, pressed the button and the lift doors 'binged' open. Then having made their way inside, the long, slender, manicured fingers of his latest assistant went to make contact with the number two. At that, Murray reached forward to grasp her hand and gently guide it toward the most worn button in the elevator. It was not the number one, the floor where the high stakes games took place. Many people would simply walk up the inspiring, eloquent staircase from the front lobby Murray assumed. Their fingers were fully interlocked now as he steered her hand well above the number two, where Anderson's office was located. These floors, 1 & 2, he had visited on both his previous visits. So with a slight squeeze of her hand, he softly rested her fingers on the EMIT button. That one had always aroused his curiosity. Viewed from the outside that floor never existed. How come?

Jayne Golden had enjoyed the warmth of his touch as she tapped the ever so slightly raised silver square on the control panel. Again she noticed Murray's smile from behind his eyes. This time she recognised it as a sensual, loving smile.

Murray was intrigued. Who or what may await them? Was it simply a security measure? What did emit stand for? Normally it meant - *to send forth, or release. To utter or voice.* Why all the privacy? All those questions raced for attention once again in Murray's head. Yet every one of them had to be satisfied playing second fiddle to the lead question. A pressing inquiry that would not shift from his current thoughts.

Holding her hand… Was that not lovely?

As the lift doors opened the Inspector ran directly across the hallway. A heavy traditional wooden door faced up to him. Murray gripped fast to the handle. It wouldn't budge. Golden's passkey soon hurtled its way through the air toward him, as even more questions began to clamour for space in his already frantic mind. His blonde haired assistant vigilantly kept an eye out for others, whilst her right foot remained firmly wedged in the elevator door, ensuring it was currently out of commission.

The questions never ceased. New additions now included - What mystery lay behind this door? Why was it off limits to normal members? What private club required a secret password? How was this all linked together? Why did all roads lead here? The Inspector's brow narrowed and intimate, intense beads of sweat fought for appearance money on his forehead. His hands were cold and clammy. After swiping Golden's card, he cautiously began to lean down and open the dark solid oak door. Before entering, he looked gingerly and deliberately across each shoulder. The door opened smoothly and quietly. It brushed gently with ease, across a rich, forest green, deep pile carpet. Murray's initial reaction was firstly to get some light on proceedings. A white plastic panel of assorted buttons and knobs, ideally positioned at shoulder height just inside the doorway appeared to be the perfect solution to that problem. 'Game on' he thought. But never, 'in a month of Sundays' expecting what happened next.

The Edinburgh police officer reached out casually to flick on a switch or two. Buttons which he naturally assumed worked the lights. However, a rather bizarre floor covering like no other soon became apparent. When it came fully into view, Steven Murray stood frozen. He was firmly rooted to the spot. Shoulders arched back, eyes disbelieving and breathe taken away at the unique scene before him.

"Hurry up!" He heard Jayne Golden shout from the hallway.

The room was about to host the most impressive gambling game he had ever witnessed. An overhead sequence of lights and lasers flickered and flashed into life, projecting a multitude of boxes across the floor space. The only difference was, there was no table! All the other details were exactly the same, although currently, there was no wheel on display. That issue though, was easily addressed by a couple more switches that hadn't yet been flicked!

Measuring approximately three feet squared. Red and black numbered segments magically appeared on the floor surface. They had been replicated to precision on the luxury carpet in front of him. With his mind already blown at the impressive kaleidoscopic display of moving lights, he then began to hear... What was it? Machinery? Sure enough, there in the background a gentle whirring could be heard. Air conditioning? Murray possibly questioned. Then, at the top of the numbers, at the head of... oh my goodness! A square segment of the floor was sliding back and there, rising like a majestic phoenix from the ashes and made of the finest quality wood, there right in front of him, positioned only a few feet away and within easy reach, was the largest enclosed roulette wheel Steven Murray had ever seen in his life! Easily ten feet in diameter. It had been its working motors and mechanisms that

Murray had been listening too. Within ten seconds the operation was complete and the room soon returned to silence. The floor closed over, matched up and the hugely surreal, king-sized game was ready to commence.

"Let's go," came the female shout. "He'll begin to wonder where we are."

Murray was properly gobsmacked. He'd had no idea what to expect, but he most certainly was not expecting that. He quickly took some photographs on his phone, flicked off the magic and watched in sheer amazement as everything once again reverted back to its original place and Murray, singing *Bibbidi Bobbidi Boo,* .... made a fast, sharp exit.

As he showed Jayne Golden the photos he'd taken. She shook her head in shock. "Only certain staff get to work outside the room or on this floor for that matter, when the 'special' nights are in progress."

"Why do you call them that? The 'special' nights? Murray quietly asked.

"That is exactly what they are referred to in-house," Golden replied. "They are called the 'special' nights." Jayne Golden then cautiously paused. She looked tentatively across the lift at Murray as it made its way down toward the ground floor. Slowly she uttered, "You know - that there - is another one - planned for later this evening," she told him.

"Tonight?"

"Eight o'clock," she responded. "Just as I finish."

The lift doors opened and Golden and Murray were met by Don, her sullen faced, newspaper reading colleague from earlier.

"Everything okay?" he questioned in a rich baritone voice, whilst looking at them both warily.

"Sorted!" Jayne Golden told him. "This way Inspector," she continued in her authoritative manner. "Next time, you may even want to spend some money!"

The other staff member was now busy sending a text and was no longer interested in them it would appear. As Murray turned to respond, the door was closed and locked firmly in his face. He thought he may have spotted the briefest of winks through the smoked glass. But even at that, he was uncertain.

'Tonight,' he pondered, as he sat alone outside in his car. They would not be able to keep the discovery at the yard quiet much longer. It would all be out of the bag in a few hours and making the Sunday morning headlines across the country. However, with just a few hours notice, was that too soon to go after them? To follow up his suspicions? Those were just two of the multitude of priceless questions that currently vied once again for space in Murray's limited mind. It's a gaming establishment after all. What he had just witnessed was certainly a bit OTT, but they'd have a license. So what made this off limits? What was the link to the dead teenagers? It was a bit quirky and sensationalist, but so what. Then again, why the grand scale and why for the high rollers only? And therein lies the clue.

The devious rich, the greedy obsessed gamblers, the untouchable elite with no integrity, the Cyrille Andersons of the world always hide behind the same thing. Murray had recognised it often over the years. It was a really, simple, yet straightforward answer. So when he asked himself those same questions again - What was this all about? What's the deal with all the security? Why the need? What's the big secret? He was ready this time with a satisfactory answer. It did not need to be wrapped up with bells and whistles. Generally speaking, whatever that type of individual was involved in was illegal, it was criminal and they ultimately were breaking the law. And tonight DI Murray and his team were determined to find out the how and why!

One of 'Bunny' Reid's comments to him from the previous Sunday afternoon continued to weigh heavy on his mind.

'I thought you were better than that,' he had said.

And Murray knew that everything that man said and every action he took had a purpose. So his decision was made. DI Murray had to return officially. He had to go back. There was no time to wait, further lives could be at stake. Every hour now was vital and there was no knowing when the next 'special' evening would be. So tonight it was. They would be in attendance in great number, fully prepared and with backup. However, he considered one final time… fully prepared for what?

The team had assembled. Plenty of officers had been pulled in to assist and plans, procedures and orders given out. It was a risk, but a calculated risk worth taking - and they were certainly in the right place to be playing the odds. DCI Brown had been out of reach, but Murray had left strict instructions and details with a reliable officer to pass on to him. It gave him a brief overview of their early evening plan of attack.

Jayne Golden once again met Murray at the front foyer. The casino was bustling. It appeared to be doing good business he thought. This time she led him up the impressive staircase to the first floor. A few nods and pleasantries were exchanged between her and other security guards enroute. Most of those employed didn't really know each other. They all pulled different shifts, started at different times and worked ever changing days. Like bus drivers, their union was the outfit. It identified them to each other and the tabard, complete with keycard was the finishing touch. She continued to walk and talk with Murray, making occasionally extravagant arm movements, as if courteously helping out a paying guest get from A to B. As they walked past the high stakes poker rooms, she swiped her card to the back stairs. This then led them up to floor two. The level where Murray and Hanlon had first visited with Anderson senior. Fortunately it was still quiet.

"Where is everyone Jayne?" Murray asked. Rather surprised that they had managed to get this far without having to either show his warrant card or have Miss Golden make up some excuse.

"On 'special' nights it often looked like this on the run up. Mr Anderson meets and greets all the important clients involved in the ground floor lounge, then they arrive up in the lift," she said in a matter of fact way. "It takes about five or six trips," she then added.

By now they had continued up the back stairwell and had opened the door to the mysterious level that from outside was nowhere to be found! It had just turned seven forty when they once again arrived outside the EMIT room. Murray began to recognise everything about this building and its recent makeover was like a covert operation. Rich with artifacts and treasures, it was a keeper of secrets. Everything disguised to cover up its real purpose. 'What's the time Mr Wolf?' That was all about concealing your identity and again it made him question... Why?

Disguised, concealed, protected and sheltered. Tonight Murray thought, the truth must prevail.

Golden interrupted that particular train of thought. "They will all line up here. No single group can go inside until they have all been escorted to here from the lift. They'll then enter en masse, together, as one."

"I thought you hadn't been inside?"

"I haven't," she responded. "I have opened the door to allow them entry once and a couple of times I have been an escort in the lift. Inside though, nope! Never had the..." She stopped herself. She was now getting an overwhelming feeling that it would not have been a pleasure. "You've got twenty minutes. Are you going to be okay with that?"

"I'll have to be," Murray replied. "You get out of here. You've done more than enough and again, thank you."

Those two words sounded a bit too clinical and final for Jayne Golden. She leaned forward, scanned the lock with her card and gave DI Murray another two second kiss on the cheek. Then in the same instant, she smiled and made her way at pace back along the corridor. Murray was now inside. He used the torchlight on his phone to make his way up to the top corner of the room. It was located well enough away from the main playing surface. He had positioned himself ideally behind the large velvet drapes and carefully ensured he was at a join, thus allowing himself easy access to the players when the appropriate time arose.

Vehicles outside were awaiting instruction and were in position on all the surrounding streets. CCTV cameras from within the premises may well spot them, but that was another gamble they just had to take. As it was, the team were now comfortable having heard Golden inform them of Anderson's normal routine that things would be fine. They had also overheard all the discussion between Jayne Golden and Steven Murray since he'd entered the building. And the peck on the cheek brought about some rather interesting facial reactions. Murray also wore a small camera on his shirt button. One which currently kept them all in the dark!

It was a cool, crisp evening outside. Some of the clients were beginning to make their way to the lift area. As Jayne Golden had mentioned, it would take five or six trips easily. Possibly even more if there was to be the occasional straggler or two.

Murray took slow, calming, deep breaths. He still had over fifteen minutes until things heated up. Thinking nothing of it, he began humming the tune that he'd heard played at Blake's when he first visited. The officers in the van outside began to wince at his normal off-key rendition. *"If you're lost you can look and you will find me… If you fall I will catch you, I will be waiting…"*

He was relaxing, reflecting on the past couple of weeks, pondering on a multitude of recent events. When suddenly it all came together. Wham! Bam! Thank You Ma'am! It hit him like a nine dart finish. Treble 20, treble 19 and double 12!!!

"I will be waiting….time after flippin' time!" he mumbled angrily to himself.

The robberies, the insurance scam, the violent macabre deaths. It all became clear what the link was! Although, still missing was figuring out just how these 'special' nights were involved.

The others again made faces in the van, but Kerr told them to, "Quieten down and listen to his inevitable rant!" And sure enough Detective Steve Murray did not disappoint her.

"I take it you are now listening carefully Detective Sergeant Kerr?"

'Sandy,' smiled knowingly.

"After Cindy-Ann, it all began with Spence at the floral clock and the hourglass," he confirmed. "Then Tardelli's - Thyme and Plaice restaurant. That is two out of four. And of course Cyrille Anderson studied horology, even if only briefly, coupled with his obsession in the private vault." Murray's whisper became more intense. "Robert Latchfords wife had identified the conferences and what she thought was REALLY behind them and it wasn't money laundering."

As the line of so-called 'gentlemen' grew outside, Murray continued his diatribe unabated. "The dead bodies - Spence had no face, for Tardelli it was his hands. Lattimer…" he paused. "Was it his heart… no, no not his heart, but the battery, that was the key reference, or it could even have been the fact he was a nightwatchman." Murray was in full flow.

Those gathered in the various units in the surrounding streets were in awe as he continued.

"Then, of course we had Wexford, secured and strangled by belts, but that didn't fit. Although you can belt up or be strapped in," he thought. And STRAP did work. "That was it. Strap - Battery - Hands and Face. The cufflink letters M.E. Of course that was only half the word…" Murray bellowed out. "They all flaunted it at us in one way or another." He remembered that in each of their wallets - they all had an ABC membership card, but many people do. Though not all for EMIT room admittance he guessed. Like so many of the clues in this case they had simply passed him by. Ultimately though… is that not what time does with us all?

It was 7.53pm. He could now hear another group of voices being added outside the door. So he immediately tried to settle back down and clear his mind. Which was easier said than done. Murray's heartbeat was racing. He was irritated, upset and more angry than ever at missing so many of the seemingly obvious clues.

The book auction back in the farmhouse he instantly recalled. Anderson paid thousands for a copy of Ernest Hemingway's… 'In our Time!'

"EMIT, aaagh," he snapped.

As the chatter from the corridor increased, the Inspector checked one last time that all his gadgetry was working properly. They would just have to wait until the lights were switched on to confirm the camera was good. But other than that everything seemed fine. He heard a card being scanned, a small click as the door unlocked and then quickly it was followed by a figure entering the room and hitting the magic console.

Almost instantly the light show swung into action. Coloured squares appeared at their feet as the pristine wooden wheel made its way up from the Devil's soul. Modern electronics, motors and lasers all played an important part. Very soon everything settled in place. The blacks and reds were ready for action. Every number seemed to call out 'choose me, choose me!' Odd and even, each one as different as the rogue's gallery of punters currently entering into the private room. Peering out carefully from behind the heavy dark coloured curtains, Murray could see that it was Sir Gerald Anderson himself that led in the parade of infamous, immoral and iniquitous gamblers. That was just Inspector Murray's humble observation and characterisation of those fine individuals.

"We are getting everything loud and clear sir. Both picture and sound are terrific," 'Sandy' confided to him in his earpiece.

"This way gentlemen," the knight of the realm encouraged. "Take up your spot."
Interestingly, Murray realised something for the first time whilst hearing him speak. There were no women present, not a female in sight. It was an all male group that had entered the room. Considering these days any given casino normally had easily between 10 and 20 percent of its takings offered up by women, that was a rather surprising statistic. So the 'special' nights looked like they were men only. A very exclusive Gentlemen's Club Murray thought to himself. The Inspector then heard Anderson do a little bit of 'housekeeping.'

He reminded them that, "the use of their phone was strictly prohibited. No pictures. No texting. No ungentlemanly behaviour or suggestive remarks whatsoever."

What was all that in aid of? Suggestive remarks! The faces of those officers in the outside units looked puzzled, as did that of their very own Inspector.

Murray tried delicately, to draw back the curtain enough so that he could get some vital footage. As the procession of players entered, from time to time he would catch an occasional glimpse of someone as they stood on their chosen black or red, odd or even. At least one player had not turned up, as one of the squares near the middle remained unclaimed, as did the green zero. So possibly they were two players short.

"Okay gentlemen, place your bets," Anderson cried. "Tonight's prize is an immaculate, academic treasure. Unmarked, fully intact and in spotless, perfect condition. I can guarantee that you will be the recipient of a true original."

That is it, Murray thought. It's the artwork. Some of the stolen pieces that have been forged. Carriage clock, painting or valuable watch. It's their way of getting rid of the original pieces. It's a high stakes blind auction. Stick down a few hundred pounds and you are guaranteed a top item worth thousands. The catch being, you simply cannot display it or make others aware of it. This was easy money for ABC Casinos. Though it was no help in catching those involved in kidnapping and killing teenage girls. However, it was better than Murray had previously thought it was going to be. So in some respects, he was mighty relieved. With great caution he peered out. This time he was able to witness every player within his line of sight lay down either cash, cheque or credit card at their feet. During those movements, what he witnessed caused a stomach churning revelation. He only hoped that those in the van could zoom in and confirm or deny for definite what he reckoned he glimpsed.

"Are you getting this? Did you see that? Murray whispered lightly.

As Anderson walked around scooping up the cash and depositing the cheques and credit cards into a leather satchel, he nodded. "Thank you. Much appreciated. Three thousand, that is correct!" He would flick through the occasional bundle of notes, carefully fold the cheques into his breast pocket and offer a token, "best of luck," to every fourth or fifth individual.

With a sharp intake of breath, Murray's eyes bulged. A three thousand pound buy-in. What on earth is on offer here? Murray quickly re-evaluated his insurance idea. Three grand is serious high end entry money. And it looked like it was going on just one spin of the wheel. So not a poxy seven or eight thousand return for Anderson & Co. A few speedy calculations meant that this 'special evening,' would net over one hundred thousand pounds alone! It seemed to be held at least twice a month. And Jayne Golden had earlier informed Murray that three 'special' nights had been held the previous month.

The voices in his head ran fast and loose. His cognitive ability was now awash with mind numbing figures. Half a million in the last two months. How much of that did the taxman see? Are we back to the old favourite - money laundering? His auctioneer buddy Bennett, had previously told him the place was filled with between eight and nine million pounds worth of valuable pieces. They always carried excessive staff, compared to any normal quota for a casino. They looked to be on course to easily clear three million pounds before tax this coming year. And that was excluding normal gaming profits!!!

So what is the time Mr Wolf?

What was really going on here?

Steven Murray now feared he knew the answer. He had already recognised several of the high rollers. There was his pal, the prominent judge from the week before. Plus two legal staff from the Sheriff Court, both lawyers if he remembered correctly. There was also someone he knew directly on the other side of the curtain. Either on square one or four to the left of him. He could not see those two individual squares, but there was no denying the familiar strong scent coming from that direction. The odor was exceptionally distinct and coupled with what he had just witnessed seconds earlier, he was now greatly alarmed.

It would take at least three to five minutes for the backup to arrive. He was on the invisible third floor. Either by lift or stair, they'll take awhile to get to him. He knew this was serious. It really was now or never. Ironically it was all going to come down to *TIMING.'*

He made his decision. Simultaneously as he called for backup, he received news via his earpiece. They had obviously zoomed in earlier. For now they were able to confirm to Murray - that all the players were wearing...... identical cufflinks!

Chapter Thirty-Five

"Your pillow feels so soft now, a shirtsleeve to enhance. With pure Egyptian cotton, the kids don't stand a chance. The pin-striped men of morning are the partners in the dance. With shiny, shiny cufflinks, the kids don't stand a chance."

- Vampire Weekend

It was to be an interesting and fascinating roulette game. Murray had never seen the money all taken off and cleared from the table before the wheel was spun and a winning number announced. But, he had always suspected that this particular game would have it's very own variation from the regular rules. It was a specific square. No betting on black, red, odd or even. No group of six, 1-18 or choosing a specific third of the board. This was an individual number, a single bet for your three thousand pound stake. So it must be a very substantial return, Murray concluded.

"Gentlemen, gentlemen," Anderson cried. He then tugged on the wheel and gave it an initial turn. From his memory of seeing it earlier in the day, Murray recalled that the beautifully varnished wheel had a number of six inch wooden grips vertically attached to it, enabling someone to spin it with relative ease. Think 'Wheel of Fortune' Murray reminded himself.

As the numbers spun freely, bodies were becoming restless. Anderson held an ivory ball in the palm of his hand. It would be similar in size to a slightly enlarged tennis ball. You could feel the nervous energy in the room. It was like horses gathered at the starting stalls of a race. Nearby, punters were getting agitated. Head movements double-checked the selected number beneath them. Hands became fidgety, some clasped together, whilst others ran through hair, scratched groins or rolled between finger and thumb. Jittery, jumpy and on edge, was how DI Murray would best describe many of the signals he was presently picking up.

Above the gentle hum of the rotating wheel, Gerald Anderson coughed gently to get their attention. Murray edged his remote camera toward a space in the curtain and hoped it would be enough to capture something worthwhile and valuable. Then the master of ceremonies spoke once again.

"I promised you an impressive masterpiece tonight gents. And that is exactly what we have for you." The excitement and volume in his voice rose. There appeared to be a genuine delight in what he was about to introduce. "Tonight in the capital city of Scotland, I give you... The Greek Goddess of Love. For your personal pleasure, entertainment and enjoyment, Edinburgh's very own amazing... Aphrodite."

The cheers in the room exploded. It was as if everyone there had picked a winner. Whistles and a cacophony of boisterous roars. It was a natural release for the built up tension, anxiety and suspense. The floor was shaking, a last minute, extra-time winner had just been slotted home.

Murray was busy willing on his own team. Where are you he thought. 'Come on, come on, get a move on,' he whispered to himself.

Then silence - there she stood. A sight to behold. Wheeled in on a metallic, four foot plinth, by one of Jayne Golden's burly, male colleagues. Strapped carefully to a crucifix style wooden support, was no statue made of ancient clay, bronze or marble. Nor was it a portrait of the Greek mythological beauty. But here was the prize for the most expensive roulette game Steven Murray had ever witnessed. A living, breathing and truly inspirational work of art. The 'amazing Aphrodite' was literally the only female to occupy the room. The 'amazing Aphrodite' was blonde, fifteen years of age and named Caitlin!

Murray's heart pounded and skipped several beats. There in the flesh was Linda Bell's missing teenage daughter. Another sharp intake of breath and his eyes widened. Those watching via the video link also audibly gasped. 'Young, innocent Caitlin,' was how her mother referred to her, and based upon Anderson's glowing introduction and carefully chosen words tonight, that was most probably still the case he suspected. But more than anything, she was alive and he was intent on keeping it that way.

Even from the relative distance DI Murray was away from her, she looked stunning. They had taken time to transform this young High School girl into a potential Miss Great Britain. Her hair was tied back serenely into a bow and the makeup around her eyes, lips and cheeks finished to the highest standard. Anderson then broke the silence.

"Gentlemen, doesn't Aphrodite look dazzling in this gorgeous red gown. Simple in its flattering neckline and with a thigh length split for an extra sultry, sexy touch."

"Come on guys, where are you," Murray whispered anxiously.

"They are on their way," came the voice in his ear.

In layman's terms, the vile depravity of Anderson was doing Murray's head in. Although he then quickly decided to internalise and keep to himself the the specific thought that came into his mind in relation to the ideal exit strategy he'd planned for the senior partner! Anderson meanwhile was still busy building up the lust and lechery with his continued fashion commentary.

"The open back is decorated with gorgeous embellished strap detailing, for an attractive classy finish. Making this dress perfect for 'special' nights such as these."

Once again loud, raucous shouts materialised from the vast array of gambling degenerates.

"Gentlemen, let us find her a suitable home!"

At that, the place erupted. They were like wild dogs in heat. More cheers, clapping and stamping of feet. Combined with the testosterone, alcohol and large potential losses, suddenly it made the arena seem far more foreboding!

Anderson made to spin the wheel again. As it veered at speed, his voice bellowed: "No more bets!" As if about to anoint a successor, he then graciously stepped forward and duly released the well polished ivory ball in the opposite direction.

The excitement and fever pitch decreased and a quiet hush once again fell upon the room, just as the faint ringing of a mobile phone could be heard. Murmuring and boos were in their infancy. Gerald Anderson, red faced with fury was about to castrate the individual concerned. Then, when they all turned and recognised the recipient, every single one to a man kept quiet. The phone had sounded immediately in front of Murray. He was confident that it belonged to the man with the strong smelling cologne and was simply awaiting confirmation. Then he hastily thought back to when he had first inhaled those fumes. On that particular occasion, the individual in question had taken him by surprise. Because Murray had never seen him so well groomed. On that Sabbath day as he departed, the powerful fragrance was soon to leave a strong, corrupt stench of murder, fear and odious death!

Over 300 teenagers go missing every 24 hours in the UK, Sandra Kerr had told him. And just as Steven Murray was about to reflect on that, his nemesis raised his voice and spoke with authority.

"It's a raid. The police are on their way. We need to go, right now!" Husky and deep, as if surfacing from the earth's core. It was all the confirmation Murray required. Clear for all and sundry, the unmistakable guttural rasp, of James Baxter Reid.

However, before Murray could pull back the drapes proper, the locked door had been broken down, a dozen or more officers piled in and total bedlam broke out. Murray focused on some key individuals. When they had spotted him, they initially thought he was a group member. Then on replaying the words, 'raid' and 'police,' they soon recognised their mistake and turned swiftly to follow the others. Sheer panic had spread across many of the faces. Uncertain of what to do or where to go. Murray on the other hand, knew exactly where he was headed. His destination was clear cut and exact. *"Set them free at the break of dawn, till one by one they were gone."*

Young Caitlin Bell's brave, yet assumably underpaid handler, had done a runner by the time Murray reached her. He instinctively cut her free and put his warm jacket over her bare, cold shoulders. He tried his best to reassure and comfort her. But on closer inspection, although her hair, hands and makeup had been professionally done, she had obviously been drugged up to the eyeballs and had no inkling of what he was saying or what was breaking out all around her. *"Floating in the summer sky, ninety nine red balloons go by."*

Amidst all the melee taking place, the Inspector was able to wave over DC Hayes who was part of the team that had stormed in.

"Take care of her 'Hanna.' She'll need all the help and support you can give her."

Watching live, via the haphazard, frantic and jumpy video link, Sandra Kerr had already called for more paramedics and police to be in attendance.

"Now remember Constable, don't let her out of your sight. I need to go and find the master of ceremonies, as a matter of urgency," Murray advised.

Handcuffs and restraints were being distributed and swung around like Scottish country dance partners participating in an Orcadian 'strip the willow!' Bodies were pinned hard and fast against walls and flooring. Frantic, last gasp attempts were made to contact lawyers via phone, as mobiles were battered from hands, trampled upon and then crushed below the mini exodus heading for doorways and exits. Several experienced old hands had opted for the yellow chute into skip outside. But Murray had twigged to that as soon as he saw it at the weekend and officers awaited their safe arrival.

Amid the other mayhem, normal lighting had been resumed. The relevant flicking of switches had taken place and blacks, reds, odds and evens had disappeared from sight. The roulette wheel had ceased turning seconds previous and Black 13 would have been Aphrodite's intended suitor. Hopefully after this evening the 'Saturday Night Fever' underfloor lighting would be confined to history.

As deviant players, many lawyers were already present. They had been gathered up alongside at least two influential council leaders, a raft of wealthy businessmen and an established, well known ex-international soccer player, who was now based with an Edinburgh club. The experienced footballer had currently found himself in a lineup that he probably wished he'd been dropped from. He'll not be a happy chap, but it looks like his game tonight will include 'extra-time.' Mainly spent in a police cell!

As the riotous rumpus continued in the private members room, elsewhere the hinges on Sir Gerald Anderson's office door had to hang on for dear life as it flew open. The knight of the realm stretched in, grabbed a large holdall from under his desk and made straight for the safe. Nervously, he quickly attempted to key in digits to open it. He was all fingers and thumbs and he was easily on attempt number three when...

"I thought you'd make it here safely."

The words were delivered in a quiet, reserved and reassuring manner. And having literally just jumped out of it, Gerald Anderson was dramatically trying to reclaim his skin! DI Murray stood patiently in the doorway.

"Detective Inspector," he offered, in a 'Boris Johnson' blustering, brash, buffoon like manner. "We can sort this out between us I'm sure. You always seemed a reasonable type. Let's clear up any misunderstanding."

Murray looked down at the broken, desperate figure knelt before him. He pursed his lips and gave a brief head movement. His heavy, tired, glazed eyes - the last few days had taken their toll - seemed to lift brightly at that point, as if smiling. "Misunderstanding?" he queried. "I don't think there has been any misunderstanding MISTER Anderson." He gave special attention and emphasis to the Mister. "However, if what you are actually saying is that we could reach an understanding. Then I think you may be right."

"Fantastic, excellent, good man," Anderson cooed, sweat dripping from his forehead. "I'm usually a pretty good judge of character."

"Don't flatter yourself sir. I genuinely don't think you have the faintest idea what the word stands for. I suspect Daniel George would never have hired you either!"

Anderson kept quiet. He allowed his hands to speak for him. They lifted up and to the side, indicating - What next? Where do we go from here?

"In our understanding Mr Anderson, let's be quite clear so that there is no misunderstanding. The only way you get out of here," Murray rasped firmly, kicking the door closed with his foot and standing tall with all of his impressive six foot plus. "Is by you joining up all the dots on this operation for me."

"Whatever you want to know," Anderson said. Adding anxiously, "But we need to hurry Inspector."

"However, on reflection, if you want to escape from here uninjured, still relatively wealthy and with cash in your grubby pockets. You'll need to log in and leave me free to transfer funds."

There was a silence. A pause. Then...

"Just like all the rest, eh Murray? You've got a cheek to talk to me about character."

Steven Murray winked, gave a gleeful smile and hoisted Anderson with one hand by the scruff of his neck up from his knees, and thrust him parallel onto his normal leather chair behind the desk.

Surrounded by all the Robin Williams paraphernalia, Murray felt it apt to share. *"We are only going to experience a limited number of springs, summers and falls Gerald. One day, hard as it is to believe, each and every one of us is going to stop breathing, turn cold and die!"*

"Ultimately, *'Because we are food for worms.'* Very good Inspector. Once again, touché!"

"Dead Poets was my favourite movie growing up Mr Anderson. Probably still is... Carpe Diem."

There seemed to be a live action chess match taking place. Two adults vying for position. Each looking a few moves ahead at the possible outcome, reward and consequences.

"How much are you thinking about?" Anderson asked.

Murray ignored the question, but responded vocally.

"You know you'll need to make a run for it and escape? And that there is only one viable alternative escape route, that my team and I would be unaware off?"

Anderson nodded in understanding.

"Obviously, you would then need to *skarper* from there on foot. You could take a few bundles of cash with you. Plus you'll have your codes for all your secret stashed offshore accounts. What do you reckon so far?"

"We are on the same wavelength officer."

"Oh, I somehow doubt it sir," Murray stated with a distinct glint in his eye.

Anderson became slightly wary of Murray's expression. Nonetheless he pressed a few keys and an account was opened and pinged into action.

"That one has £200k in it. Sound reasonable Inspector? Where do you want me to transfer the funds?"

"I think I'll manage that Sir Gerald. Fill me in on some of the finer details and then maybe you had better make a dash for it."

After five or six minutes, Murray was happy that he had the relevant pieces to complete Robert and Cindy-Ann's outstanding puzzle! Annie Latchford's death had also been resolved when Murray convinced Anderson that he was not interested in old cases from the archives. Especially ones that impacted on fellow colleagues. Anderson gave up the truth, Murray nodded happily (a number 52) and the one man Robin Williams fan club made his way hastily toward the door.

At pace, he ran down the corridor as fast as his aging legs would carry him. He headed directly for the stairwell, just as Murray had anticipated. Joe Hanlon had just exited the lift with a Jayne Golden pass card around his neck. He questioned if his eyes were playing tricks. He thought he'd just saw Gerald Anderson running from his office. He was to become even more confused when he then witnessed Steven Murray appear at the door, casually and unperturbed.

"Sir!" he exclaimed, pointing in the old man's direction.

"Oh, he was too fast for me Joe."

"He's a decade older than you sir and at least a stone heavier?"

"Deceptively fast of foot though. Wily old devil that he is."

Things didn't add up. Hanlon knew he was up to something.

"Joe can you give me a hand in his office. I just need to shift a couple of things around," he smiled.

With everything that was going on Joe Hanlon found himself perplexed and flustered by his Inspector's request.

Yet, strangely, the first words he uttered were, "Sure, what is it that needs moved?

Murray gave a slight groan as he closed the door behind them.

Ten or twelve minutes later, amid frenzied and chaotic scenes outside the ABC Casino. Two police detectives exited calmly from the main door of the mysterious building with the missing floor. Flashing lights and sirens scrambled for attention. An ambulance that had only just arrived at the front entrance was being redirected. The driver was being told in no uncertain terms, that it was required urgently at the back door, directly down at the bottom of the lane.

Hanlon gestured to the officer that was speaking. "What's up?"

"It was awful sir." He then saw Murray a few paces behind. "Inspector we couldn't find you." His nerves were getting the better of him. The officer was cold, in shock and stammering relentlessly. "Only today. Unbelievable. Earlier this afternoon sir. What were the chances? Today. Only just today."

"What are you trying to say man. Calm down, take a breath," Hanlon encouraged.

"At the back. You couldn't make it up sir," he continued on. "Just today, the large pole, someone had ordered it cut down, to be taken away, just today."

Hanlon looked at his Inspector. There was no reaction.

"What are you saying Constable?" Joe Hanlon tried again. "Spit it out man!"

"In the last fifteen minutes sir, someone tried to escape from the casino by sliding down that massive, giant pole into Skarper Lane."

Murray stood indifferent, unphased and possibly...... unsurprised!

"And?" DC Hanlon asked. Having never been around to the back of the building, he was still not getting it.

"And sir. There was only the top section still in place. It was attached to the roof. He had opened the emergency doors, leapt across, slid ten feet, and then... fell 40 or more !The poor man never stood a chance. My colleague said broken neck, legs... he's..."

"We get the idea Constable, truly tragic," Murray offered unsympathetically shaking his head. "What a horrible way to go," he added. "However," he stated in a much more concerned manner. "Where are the other girls?"

Four travelled in the car alongside DI Murray.

"Every officer needs to experience this from time to time," he stated as he chapped the letterbox. Hanlon made to nod in understanding, just as the door was opened by a tearful, jubilant and totally overwhelmed Linda Bell. Mother and daughter hugged. A tight 'all the love in the world' embrace. Linda Bell soon turned her attention to both Hanlon and Murray.

"Thank you. Thank you. God bless you. Thank you both so much. Inspector, Sergeant…"

Tears of joy, relief and sheer happiness continued to flow between them. Caitlin Bell even offered her own individual hug to each of the officers. Hanlon blushed and enjoyed his new, no doubt short lived promotion to Sergeant. Murray, as he often did, thought first about others. About all those families where no reconciliation would be forthcoming. Where the tears of joy and happiness, would be swapped wistfully for those of heartache, grief and sorrow. But that was for another time. Even he wanted to bask, however briefly, in the quiet satisfaction of reuniting a mother and child.

"A WPC will be around in an hour or two to bring Caitlin back to the station to finish off the paperwork, but enjoy the time together just now and I will take the flak."

"Again thank you so so much for everything Inspector," Linda Bell offered, smiling ecstatically through her tears. "I think I may choose to wear something less drab from this day on." She leant forward to remove some makeup that sparkled on Murray's cheek. "I will choose to wear something that reflects the gratitude and joy I currently feel in my heart. An acknowledgement for the gift of life." Her weeping continued. Caitlin lifted her shoulders, and mother and daughter embraced once again

"You okay sir?" Hanlon asked.

Murray slowly rubbed at his cheek. Caitlin had looked stunning earlier. On his fingers another grain or two of glitter. Something began to filter into his mind - No man that Murray knew could do hair and apply makeup like that.

He was already actively calling… "Sandy, get over to 4 Fletcher Place in Corstorphine. We missed someone from the raid." On his end Hanlon could only experience a two second silence, but he knew on the other end DS Kerr had obviously asked… Who?

"Jayne Golden," came the curt reply.

DC Hayes and another rescued teenager had waited patiently in the car at Loanhead, whilst Murray and Hanlon had safely delivered Caitlin Bell back home. Now on their way back to the station one more slight detour was calling them.

The small trio of bells chimed as the proprietor swept up in the far corner of the recently, open 24 hour a day establishment. As a certain cafe owner made to turn around, his daughter Iona was already upon him. Smothering him in hugs and kisses, head buried deep in his chest. Again the floodgates opened. This time it was Detective Constable 'Hanna' Hayes who got to feel the emotional chemistry work its magic on all of those involved in the scene. The small group of customers even began to slowly clap, building it into a respectable round of applause. Everyone in and around the vicinity of the cafe knew what Maurice Hynd had been going through. Iona turned to acknowledge the outpouring of love and support. A small hand gesture was all that was required, before the confidence and bravado grew and within minutes all the customers were involved in hugging the owner and his daughter, as well as each other. Talk about a community coming together.

The officers left them to enjoy that special moment. Murray handing Hayes a freshly laundered handkerchief, as those history recording musical bells above the doorway, bade them goodnight!

The Inspector walked the short distance back to the station. He was busy flicking through some photos that Kerr had forwarded to his phone from Jayne Golden's flat, when his mobile rang. It was 'Sandy.'

"No joy sir. She had beaten us to it. Neighbours confirmed these last few weeks had seen a lot of coming and going to her building."

"Such as?" Murray asked disappointedly.

"Well, such as, young girls turning up accompanied by burly so-called bodyguards. Two residents thought they had TV or film celebrities shooting some reality nonsense. How did she figure you were on to her?"

"I didn't know myself!" Murray replied. "So I am pretty certain she would have had no idea. From the photos, it doesn't look like she has taken any clothes."

"That would be my thoughts also sir. However just one holdall of stuff would be plenty for a fresh start."

"Maybe." Murray looked more intensely at one of the photographs again. "But how many ladies do you know, that would leave their nail varnish open to the elements?"

"Someone took her!" Kerr stated sternly.

"My thoughts exactly."

As he walked into the station, the second part of the double whammy awaited.

PC Smith approached and began in low tones. "That favour boss. I hope it's not too late, with everything that has gone down and all?"

"Not too late George. But I suspect it will be mainly used for confirmation purposes now. Go ahead."

"Well," he cleared his throat and turned the volume up one. "Her name was Jane Brown."

"Jane with an N, I presume?"

"With an N," Smith responded. "Is that important?"

"Only to me. And nice to see she opted for a brighter colour!"

Smith shrugged and continued. "She was brought up in Queens Park, Glasgow. Middle child of three. She had an older and younger brother. Mother and father divorced when she was seven. You mentioned Grandparents sir. They had all died before she began High School. Joined the T.A. when she was sixteen. Her dad died three years ago from kidney failure. Her mother is still believed to be alive, living somewhere in Dorset with her youngest son. They appear to have joined the travelling community, so not easy to pin down. Until she started back at the casino, there had been no sign of her anywhere on the system for over a decade."

At that, he tried to look into Murray's eyes to gauge a response.

Those were already fixed firmly on the ground. Which in itself gave Constable Smith a reply.

"Thanks George. I owe you one," Murray managed, before seeking solitude for a few minutes. His departing footprints reminded him how like Daniel George, we all need a Royce in our lives. An individual that can be a strong moral compass and example to us. Someone that can help us, guide us, strengthen us and then knowing when we are prepared and ready... like loving parents, send us on our way to embrace and respond to the exhilarating challenges that await us onboard this great, almighty vessel called life!

Chapter Thirty-Six

"Take my hand and run with me out of the past of yesterday, and walk with me into the future of tomorrow. Yesterday must be forgot, no looking back no matter what. There's nothing there but memories that bring sorrow. Yesterday is gone, but tomorrow is forever."

- Dolly Parton

The following noon, many of the team had gathered in or around Keith Brown's snug office. Earlier in the day the Chief Inspector had given a very well received Press Conference. Thanks and acknowledgements were offered in equal measure. He spoke as he always did with a magnitude of confidence and composure. Currently forty two bodies had been discovered at the yard, and they fully expected to find more. Several teenagers from Scarborough, London and Glasgow had already been provisionally DNA matched. Members of Murray's own team had witnessed first hand the brutal killing of at least two Edinburgh based girls. All locations where ABC casino premises were based. How Annie Latchford stumbled on to this they hoped would be explained in her backed up files. But it is most definitely what got her killed. It had been no hit and run. Robert Latchford had been right all these years. His wife had been callously murdered.

Now late in the afternoon, compliments, congratulations and positive comments flowed as quickly as the drink. Glasses clinked, backs were slapped and well deserved hugs were being distributed evenly. This was not really Murray's thing. He stood politely in a corner, taking regular sips from a cold, refreshing glass of water that he could suitably make last all day.

Joseph Hanlon sidled up to him. "Well done sir. Fantastic. What a result. Thank you once again for everything," he remarked.

Murray wondered to himself how much of this celebration many of his colleagues would remember in the morning? Joe had deserved this moment though he thought. He'd had a tough start to the year, and in his career as a detective. But he played an invaluable part in closing these last two incredible cases.

Curry and Hayes were smiling. Arms around each other's shoulders. 'Ally' Coulter was patting his much reduced midriff. Pointing at the 'offensive' cakes on offer and talking about his current dietary needs to anyone who would listen. Murray then looked across at Sandra Kerr. It was a look and a nod of sincere appreciation (a number 17), for all the years they had worked alongside each other. An acknowledgment for her long suffering and friendship. She knew that. They mutually raised their glasses to one another and 'Sandy' could be seen to mouth... 'To Mac.'

Murray didn't really know Rasul. He regretted that he had initially distrusted him. Sometimes the job makes you question everything and everybody. Though Detective Inspector Steven Murray was also glad that he did. Because it allowed one last piece of business that he had to attend to, to be just that little bit more bearable. It was the only remaining question Steven Murray had. In fact, he did not even have to hear a response. The reaction of the individual would be answer enough.

At that, a massive spontaneous and stormy round of applause broke out. Murray looked toward the doorway and there, making the most sophisticated entrance by someone in a wheelchair ever, was The T'inker - Doctor Thomas Patterson. Fully recovered and recuperating well the Doc offered up a few T. H. words to keep the smiles going.

"T'anks, t'anks very much," he said. Followed up by a witty, "T'ankfully t'e t'erapist t'inks t'ere is a t'eoretical t'imble sized chance I may die of t'irst! So where is t'e drink?"

Laughter exploded throughout the room and surrounding corridors. He was back. They had missed him. Especially Steven Murray who just waved calmly to him from the opposite corner. He had plenty of work colleagues and well wishers surrounding him for now. Good friends will pop by when the dust settles. He swam against the stream and made his way into his boss's room, just as most were making to leave.

"Sir, can you spare a minute?" Murray asked in a sombre, reluctant tone.

"For my number one officer? Of course Steven. Close the door on your way out," was the brusque instruction given to PC George Smith. Keith Brown began pouring himself a hot drink. As he stirred and lifted it to his lips, he looked rather guardedly at his aging 'star pupil.'

"We've known each other for a long number of years sir," Murray stated.

"Indeed we have Inspector."

Brown now stood ready for what was to come. He knew his friend well and how he operated. He could feel an accusatory remark being prepared.

"I reckon, I've let you down on numerous occasions over that time with my conduct and behaviour sir."

"We all make mistakes Steven," Brown offered defensively. "But it's how we bounce back from them that matters. And you have done that. Consistently may I add," he smiled.

Again Murray nodded.

"What is it? What's troubling you Steven? Speak to me. You have always done that openly in the past."

Brown now stood upright and firm, bracing himself. He was still caressing his black coffee. His right hand tense on the handle, whilst his left supported the mug from below. Then he looked DI Murray straight in the eye and spoke coldly.

"You're an honourable man Inspector. So tell me, exactly what is on your mind?"

Murray paused. "Honourable? That notion may be worth bearing in mind sir," he said nodding solemnly at Brown. "It's just a few little things about the case that have niggled me. One or two specifics that seemed to either hinder us or get in the way. It's just been more noticeable these past few days. It's probably nothing to worry about. But 'Bunny' Reid got off because we never covered all our bases first time around. And I don't think any of us want to experience that a second time!"

"Absolutely not Steven," Brown confirmed. "So what has been nagging you?"

Murray looked dutifully toward the floor as he placed the index finger of his right hand, carefully onto the thumb of his left hand as a reference point. "Firstly," he smiled. "I've never had so many catch up meetings with you in my life."

Both men grinned, as Murray's two index fingers met up.

"Secondly, you never ever mentioned to me that you used to spell your name differently."

"That was years ago Steve. What bearing does it have on this case?"

Murray's intonation changed and he spoke with more urgency.

"I think you know full well sir. Just as you knew my whereabouts every single moment of the day. And you knew Ian Spence from the casino. That was why you winced when I showed you his picture. You recognised the poor man."

Brown gingerly offered a confused look.

Murray's index finger had now moved gracefully onto his left middle digit.

"It was 'Bunny' Reid's Land Rover inside the gates of the scrapyard, on the roadside at Latchfords' and then parked outside 'Ally' Coulter's. And here, I thought for a moment that 'Mac' was the informer, that our 'new boy' Rasul had kept those evil miscreants up to speed. But 'Sandy,' Detective Sergeant Kerr put me straight. It was you sir! You had been the third man. That's why she had been on the phone with you so often lately. You had told her you were worried about me. So she happily kept you updated."

Becoming concerned and more stern faced Brown began to correct Steven Murray, "I think you…"

"Too late now for you to do your thinking sir." Murray interrupted.

His index finger now tugged and squeezed lightly on his left hand's ring finger.

"You should have thought about it more fully when you were a young Sergeant in London a decade ago. An officer that allowed Annie Latchfords' murderer to go scot free! A bent policeman that back then, nipped the investigation in the bud."

Beginning to fume, Keith Brown raised the ante and his voice. "Best to stop before you get in any deeper Steven."

"Any deeper Detective Chief Inspector?" Murray arrogantly questioned. With a raised voice he continued, "I think you'll find I'm the one in the shallow end! You're the one who threw up deliberately all over Lattimer's van and tried unsuccessfully to contaminate the scene. You're the one in the deep end now sir. Way, way out of your depth and desperately drowning deeper by the minute, if I may say so."

Lowering his voice and in a placid, generous manner, finally he placed his right index finger on the pinky of his left hand and quietly concluded.

"Forgive me sir, I never quite got around to giving you a house warming gift."

The DCI flinched at this comment.

"Oh yes, by the way, George Smith informed me that you recently moved into the Colinton area of town. Barnshot Road. Number 17 I believe. You kept that quiet sir. I wonder why? Coincidentally, that's the very same number that was a no show for their 'live' roulette game. What are the chances?" Murray asked flippantly. "But I figured you already knew that sir. Because you were the one on the other end of 'Bunny' Reid's phone line. Their inside man, giving him and the others an advanced warning. Not surprising really, after having your photo taken with him recently. You do like your coffee sir," Murray said coldly. "But even I was surprised that you dared to link up in the centre of town. That also was a gamble - and another one that you lost!" He then held up his phone and showed his Chief Inspector the photo that 'Mac' Rasul had forwarded to him from Starbucks.

Brown opened his drying mouth, but no sound came forth.

"Absentmindedly, I inadvertently gave PC Smith the wrong time of the raid. But thankfully we still managed to get there in time sir," Murray offered rather sarcastically.

The rear door to the office opened and in quietly slipped Detective Constable Hanlon. A gentle nod was offered toward his superiors.

Brown then brashly and arrogantly lifted his coffee cup toward his chest. It appeared to be acting as a resolute barrier. A very visible defence shield as he folded his arms. There was a brief five second respite in the conversation that seemed to last for a whole five minutes.

Murray then added, "I reckon there is just one small outstanding matter that remains unanswered sir. A small thing, one that I kept meaning to find out the answer too. A query I strongly believe that you can resolve." So, in typical forthright manner he proceeded to ask his once good friend and long standing colleague the elusive question. He paused for dramatic effect, before asking in a simple schoolboy tone.

"What's the time Mr Wolf?"

Sipping slowly on his warm froth of coffee, the Detective Chief Inspector's eyes remained locked on Murray's. Neither man was about to blink first. Under the circumstances Keith Brown tried his best to remain composed.

However, he swallowed hard and the colour drained rapidly from his face when a young officer produced his handcuffs and piped up from the corner.

"Unlike Joey, there is no E sir, is that correct? No E!" The only shade of any significance now to Detective Inspector Steven Murray, was the noticeable scarlet red line on the rim of his Chief Inspector's - 'special cufflinks.'

Chapter Thirty-Seven

"I close my eyes, I fade to black. I hide my face, I turn my back and there are these loose ends to deal with. I clear my throat, I give a smile, act unconcerned when all the while... they're haunting me."

- Maria Friedman

Twenty five minutes after depositing Detective Chief Inspector Keith Brown in a police cell, it was Detective Constable Joseph Hanlon's turn for a rant. As he and Murray stood in a dank corridor mulling over the case, he began.

"Dennis Black had taken some seriously warped and deranged people off the streets. Yet he knowingly took each of those poor, innocent girls along to that yard to be crushed to death, and that was after they had had their tongues removed. And what was that all about? He was sick. Is still sick, and we can't trace him."

"The tongues - that was your depraved Knight of the Realm's twisted mind. I saw the roll of stickers on his desk."

"Ye, for Ellen James Rental, the van hire company they used to transport the girls. I saw some on one of his shelves when we first visited with him. And each of the crates were covered in them."

"Van rental my backside! And yes the crates had plenty of the offensive things plastered all over them."

"Offensive you say? Once again you have me at a disadvantage sir."

Murray began slowly. "The World According to Garp, was a Robin Williams movie Joe. In it, there is a group of woman who cut off their own tongues. They do this in protest at the rape of an eleven year old girl whose tongue was cut off by her attackers in order to prevent her from identifying them."

"What!" Hanlon exclaimed.

"Weird and mixed up I know. Anyhow, the girl's name was Ellen James."

"Black, must have known full well what was inside those vehicles then, if they were Anderson's own casino vans."

"I can't disagree with you Joe. However, I suspect initially he never knew about the girls in the furniture and only when he reviewed some of his recorded footage, did it actually come to light. He had already been so fully involved by that point that he never stopped, but instead, simply tried to atone."

"By killing a selection of those registered in TIME, the Tears In My Eyes 'special members club?"

"Absolutely Joe. In his mind - That was his atonement."

"Although the school teacher, Mr Wexford was completely innocent. It was his wealthy father that was the unnatural deviant, we have since discovered."

"We'll need to fully check those claims out Joe. But, yes initial enquiries would certainly indicate that Spence, Lattimer and Tardelli were all group members. And that the dead girls were all abused several times before… NO MORE BETS!"

There was a quiet, tender pause. Silence. Pondering. Low spirited reflection.

"Linda Bell did recognise Tardelli from the casino then, do you reckon?"

"Most probably! However, let's not be under any illusions here Joe, getting 'back to Black,' as Amy Winehouse might have said. He is equally culpable.

Maybe he was innocently roped in at the beginning like I said. Possibly a little out of his depth and could simply see no way out. But ultimately he chose to stay, got immersed even further in everything that was going on, and is certainly just as guilty."

Hanlon was reassured to hear him echo those thoughts.

"However, we'll never catch him."

"What?" Hanlon then uttered in surprised amazement.

"He's gone Joe. We'll never see him again."

Hanlon paused, looked quizzically at his superior and offered up slowly, "Dead sir?"

A self assuredness sat comfortably with Steven Murray at times. This being one of them.

"No, he's most definitely not dead. But no one dare touch him now. Remember he goes about his work undisturbed. Anderson and Taylor, both treated him badly. He was very much the poor relation in that group of horologists given a chance over a decade ago. He's the black sheep, the odd one out, wouldn't you agree?"

"Well, when you put it like that sir, then yes. He's invisible, plods away in the background doing all the dirty work, for no thanks or any significant financial gain."

"Absolutely, my dear 'Sherlock.' So here is a guy who gets no recognition and is dismissed at every opportunity. No doubt paid peanuts as the monkey and I suspect unhappy at being unwittingly enlisted as an accomplice to a score of teenage murders."

Joe smiled before offering, "Then along came the Reidmeister and 'Hey Presto' what do you know. A new valued employee, praised and fully supported. His every need being attended to and an impressive financial package as an initial retainer. Retained to do what though?" Hanlon then questioned.

Murray nodded emphatically. "I can relate it to the troubled character that actor Michael Douglas played in the classic nineties movie, Falling Down."

Joe Hanlon shrugged.

"I must be getting older than I feel!" Murray expressed. "It's the kind of film that has much more happening than many of us want to know about. It's an affirmation of decadence."

His colleague looked bemused, failing to grasp the connection.

"About how a small insignificant event can escalate. When someone feels harshly treated, how that slight frustration and disappointment can fester and grow quickly into resentment, anger, revenge and even death."

A quiet irritation simmered across Murray's face as he quickly recalled an incident at Chicago O'Hare International Airport that he was involved in only ten months previous.

"I would have happily shot those people dead," Murray surprisingly declared without warning. "The sheer nastiness that existed in those Border Control officers. Wow! I don't care if they were having a bad day at the office. I would have gladly rounded up all of their family members, locked them in a room, doused them heavily in petrol and then thrown in a lit match as I walked away and closed the door behind me."

Hanlon was not expecting that. An expression of horrified surprise crossed his face.

"I know, right," Murray continued. "I could never do that. It's sick, repulsive, inhuman, I get it. But that is exactly my point. The anger and resentment I felt at my ill treatment by two 'because we can' individuals was such, it easily felt justified. Crazy." From that day, for the first time ever, Murray began to empathise, relate to and understand the mindset better of some radical extremists. This does not make their actions correct, he thought. However, from that day to this he'd asked himself and currently shared it vocally with Joe Hanlon. "Do we listen with love, compassion and a will to improve our mutual situation. Or are we, 'always right,' 'we know better,' 'let me tell you!'"

"You are now back on a rant, aren't you? Sherlock asked, gently trying to diffuse the situation.

In full flow his DI hammered on. "What is fascinating about the Douglas character Joe though, is the core of sadness in his soul. Yes, by the time we meet him, he's gone over the edge. But there is no exhilaration in his rampage, no release. He seems weary and confused and in his actions he unconsciously follows scripts that he may have learned from the movies, or on the news, where other frustrated misfits vent their rage on innocent bystanders.

His young DC stood blankly and shook his head. 'Sherlock' was flummoxed and totally speechless.

"Think about it Joe. Black was diligent and thorough. He was a hard worker. By now he was an out and out killer. However, away from his seedy, corrupt and despicable deeds. He had actual skills, abilities and talents that he could put to good use. Especially operating behind the scenes where he liked it best. Think about the insurance scam that was operating successfully right in front of us. We would have missed it, if not for a certain Mister…"

"James Baxter Reid," Hanlon blurted out. "The casino chip and his continued insistence to check out Blake's. But why?"

"Why my dear Sherlock? That is the answer to your earlier question. Because it is another string to his burgeoning bow my friend."

Hanlon liked being referenced as a friend. But, "Another string?" he questioned.

"The fakes, forgeries, the first-class replica copies," Murray enthused. "All done by the hand of?" He left Hanlon to fill in the blank.

"I can't think," Joe quickly responded. Then, "No! Nooooooo!" Hanlon exclaimed in surprise.

His Inspector nodded (It would have been a number 41). That signified... you had better believe it!

"Think about it. What did Daniel George say about him?"

'Sherlock,' desperately tried to recall the interaction. You could witness the memory of his recent visit to Perthshire surge from his toes right through his body. His chest broadened, his shoulders stood to attention. A palpable excitement could be felt as his desire to share the moment broke free.

"He loved to put things back together."

"Correct." Murray agreed.

"His forte was not the creative side," Hanlon added at pace. Before simmering slowly with, "he was not capable of producing new, fresh and original work." His head was moving constantly up and down in recognition of a dawning, a realisation, a sinking in. "His strength was in mending... " He looked at Murray rather taken aback, before continuing. "In repairing and restoring."

"And?" Steven Murray waved his hands in an urgent, rapid circling manner.

"And," a scunnered Constable Hanlon tailed off. "Duplicating and copying!"

He then muttered a few words of disgust at himself, before finishing with, "Dennis 'your local neighbourhood killer' Black. Who would have THUNK IT!"

"He had us all fooled Joe. Don't be too hard on yourself."

"I know, but it was right there in front of us. We should have figured it. We shouldn't have needed the likes of Reid to point it out. Anyhow you were saying. What is Bunny's angle?"

"Black is simply the latest piece of Reid's continued empire building," Murray offered dismissively. "He can and almost certainly has retaken charge of Kenny, or should I say Sheila Dixon's portfolio of property, protection and prostitutes. Not to mention the ever competitive drug scene in the capital. However, fair play to 'Bunny,' I never saw the potential profit to be made in fakes, forgeries and replicas. But Anderson and Co. were laundering millions every year, a few thousand here and a few thousand there. Then maybe, once a month or every second month a six figure antique or portrait ups the ante. The oil painting 'Culloden,' for example," Murray laughed heartily. "That picture cost nearly as much as my property in Edinburgh!"

'Sherlock' remained grim faced. He still couldn't believe they had never made the connection.

Part fact, part fiction, Murray shared some of his thoughts in regard to Robert Latchford. "I fully believe that he had begun to feel uneasy and unsettled at accepting deliveries from the casino, even although the money was a great relief. His prime motive however Joe, had always been to get substantial dirt and evidence on Cyrille Anderson, and that had not materialised."

Hanlon nodded in understanding as his senior colleague continued.

"That Saturday evening he told me Joe, he'd had enough, and was just going to go to the police with what he had. The problem was that he had already spoken with Simon Taylor and told him to find someone else to take over his role. Taylor though was so heavily involved with his ever increasing gambling debts that there was no way he would just let Latchford walk away. He took Cindy-Ann and everything went haywire and downhill from there. How he thought by taking his daughter and keeping her captive, he would coerce Latchford into staying is beyond me. We'll probably never know how it all actually unfolded at the sand dunes at Gullane.

That evening the manic mind of one Steven Murray went back to his schoolboy memories from a couple of weeks previous. Names that were a blast from the past and his favourite childhood pastimes. His High School roll of honour continued with: Susan Spence, Raymond Thomas and Grace Adam. Deborah Hart, Ronald Scott and Mark Donaldson to name but a few. His pastime simply would have been soccer, football, call it what you will… there was nothing else! Even girls came second to his trusted Mitre! Although, who would have guessed that in later years it would have played a key role in solving a sex trafficking and abduction ring. Panini… page 19, number 9 - Robert 'Bob' Latchford! What did it actually mean to be part of a squad he asked himself.

The team that you surround yourself with can make all the difference, he reflected. On his good days with the 'black dog' taking a leave of absence, Murray fully appreciated the fine individuals that made up his team.

Coulter - Faithful, loyal and tenacious.

Kerr - For so long in his shadow. Now gradually coming to terms with combining her role as a mother with quality policing.

Hayes - Diligent and reliable. Strengths that continue to impress her colleagues.

Curry - Often lacking the self confidence, he was still always desirous to prove himself.

Then there was Joseph Hanlon - **'Sherlock'** changed his career and in that same moment the course of his life. Already a widower after just a few short months of marriage. So heartbreak and tragedy are nothing new to him. A great friend, a naturally caring generous demeanour and coupled with the ability to go all the way to the top.

"What a team!" he exclaimed.

With Murray's church background, he felt blessed to be surrounded by greatness. American author Robert Frost once said, "Two roads diverged in the wood, and I, I took the one less travelled by." Murray couldn't help but think how Robert Latchford had walked a similar path in recent years. Sadly though, when he came upon the T-junction, several contributing factors led him to choose the same familiar route as many before him - 'Easy money; crime & deceit.'

As the old adage says: 'If you fly with the crows, you'll get shot with the crows.' And his desperately poor decision to become involved, ultimately led to the death of his only child. That surely was penance enough.

Sadly, without fully realising each of their specific roles, his team consisted of and extended to, for better or worse:

Cyrille Anderson - Wealthy megalomaniac and high end fraudster.

Dennis Black - The black sheep. Faceless man. A master forger that went about unnoticed and killed with ease. In his own warped mind, he was delivering justice that many would not argue with!

Simon Taylor - The coward of the team. Complete greed and self preservation led him firstly to kill young Cindy-Ann in what he has since described to us as blackmail gone wrong. Later he bludgeoned Doc Patterson to within an inch of his life. Then, finally through sheer panic, coupled with him being a coward and a liar he murdered DC Machur Rasul. The lowest of the low and the weakest link by far.

Two associate team members that Latchford would have been unaware of then included:

Jayne Golden, it was she that looked after the girls when they were freshly taken and turned them into teenage 'Supermodels!' In her defence, they would have never rescued the girls without her help.

Why? Where has she gone? And willingly or unwillingly? Murray still hoped to get an answer to that little trio of questions.

Then finally there was DCI Keith Browne, only without the 'e'. Brown already lacking in so many ways would also soon be without a job, a career and a very healthy pension plan!!!

*

Several days later on their way to 'Mac's lunchtime service, Murray informed Hanlon that they should take separate cars, as directly after the remarks at the undertaker's he had somewhere special to be.

When Murray pulled up outside the funeral parlour, Joseph Hanlon was parked across the road wearing an appropriately dark coloured suit and the most humongously, inappropriate smile! He was standing beside, if Murray recalled correctly … an Aston Martin Vantage.

"Daniel George had it delivered to my flat sir."
Murray nodded (a number 33 - you deserve it)

"It's fully insured for a couple of days and he said in the card that his friends at Gleneagles were expecting me!"

"The card?" The Inspector asked.

"Oh, it was a belated birthday treat. I've no idea how he knew. I don't suppose sir, you would…"
Murray had already walked away thinking to himself - Nice touch Mr George, thank you.

As much as it may have upset some of Rasul's family, they honoured his burial wishes. The wise young man, due to his circumstances and job made sure he'd left behind a valid will. It had been a humanist funeral service and was carried out in a very respectful and dignified manner. It had been a relatively quiet affair. Only a few of his new colleagues were in attendance. The family had been more than happy, for a variety of reasons to keep it to a small number.

At the end of the proceedings Murray was approached by a well tanned, middle aged white man. Forty minutes earlier, unsurprisingly, the Inspector had noticed this rather forlorn looking figure sitting on his own in the back row when he'd arrived. An outstretched hand was quickly proffered toward the police officer. Steven Murray felt no imminent threat. If anything, heartache, sadness and sorrow seemed to emanate from this handsome, well groomed individual. Murray instinctively grasped the hand and shook it.

"I would guess that you are Detective Inspector Steven Murray." The voice was light, yet assertive. It had a rather emotional edge to it. Pleasant, with a spoonful of gratitude.

Realising now exactly who this was, Murray's grip firmed. He pulled the man toward him and threw his left arm over his shoulder in a close embrace. Very un-Murray like!

"I am so sorry for your loss," Murray said. His voice wavered with sensitivity as he released the man from both handshake and hug. "You travelled across America with him just a few short months ago?" Murray confirmed in a friendly, genial manner.

The man with a rather startled expression said "He told you about that?"

"Of course," Murray nodded.

The stranger then looked up and by way of confirmation offered, "My name is Derek. I," he hesitated. "I was 'Machur's partner."

Steven Murray being reasonably decent at his job, had already figured that part out. Good looking and immaculately dressed. Recently tanned, white and male. For what other reason would he have been shunned? Possibly uninvited altogether, or reluctantly invited and shown to his seat - one especially allocated on the back row. It seemed Rasul's family were still struggling to come to terms with many aspects of his chosen lifestyle.

'Poker faced!' - the strange gambling expression eagerly rushed through Murray's ever congested mind. A Royal Flush, a straight, or two pairs - Poker, Murray smiled.

He quickly questioned internally - What does it mean to be 'poker faced?' I normally always allow people to witness my real emotions, he thought to himself. My upset, my disappointment, my anger. He then recalled how a poor leader had recently reminded him that, 'You'd be no good at poker Steven.' On reflection, Murray had then questioned - Why did he have to be good at it in the first place? For he felt honesty, the ability to be upfront and open, that type of genuine sincerity brought him real happiness and contentment. It allowed him to be cheerful and at ease. It enabled him to discuss, learn and be involved without fear of repercussion. Loving the whole individual he thought, complete with all their faults and failings worked for him. It was a strength that he had immediately noticed in Rasul's partner. In 'Mac's' family? Maybe not so much!

Derek then handed over an unmarked envelope taken from his inside jacket pocket.

"It had sat on our kitchen table at home. Machur had written it the same evening after you had spoken with him recently. I knew he would want you to have it."

Murray accepted it graciously with a humble, "much appreciated."

They made their way out from the undertakers to the car park and said their goodbyes. Inside the envelope was a 'Thank You' card. Sure enough 'Mac' confirmed that he had written in it the evening after meeting him in the cafe. He continually expressed gratitude to his boss for being understanding and for not judging him. He praised his DI for taking the time to listen and was indebted to him for his encouraging words of support and counsel. He mentioned how Murray had made him feel valued and important once again. He spoke sadly of the fact that he had been driven out of his unit in Glasgow. How the overwhelming homophobia, racism and personal abuse from a small minority had become too much. How it ultimately became unbearable and he needed to leave and seek a transfer for everyone's sake.

The occasional tear or two had now been shed onto the card. Murray was upset. Another emotional trigger had gone off. He should have seen it coming, but had no previous warning to being in receipt of a letter like this. He was upset now. Angry at himself. Feeling that he had personally let Machur Rasul down. That once again the force had left their employee unprotected and vulnerable in certain ways. He also had other strong thoughts. One's possibly best kept quiet. Opinions best not aired in public right now, as they would just rake up questions and conversations within Rasul's family that Murray felt would be better discussed at another time, in another place, or maybe never at all.

Let us all continue to honour this young man, he thought to himself. They had him buried with pride, decorum and dignity. Near the end of the service everyone had been informed by the humanist celebrant, that in recent days there had been a substantial anonymous donation made to Police Scotland (said to be in the region of £100,000). It was to set up a memorial fund, an educational foundation in Machur Rasul's name. Detective Inspector Murray smiled contentedly at that, and then made his way by car to the graveside.

It seemingly had been the third such donation in as many days. Iona Hynd had a £50,000 bequest deposited into Mo Hynd's business account. It was specifically to fund her travel back home frequently to Scotland to visit with her father, as she pursued her college scholarship in the States! The other recipient was believed to be a certain Miss Caitlin Bell. Her balance transfer occurred on the very day that her mother had checked her ABC Casino account, which verified that all her outstanding debts had been settled. Her daughter had received a similar amount to Iona with no conditions attached. However, maybe it would come in handy to help with further education fees, University tuition or possibly a new exciting wardrobe of clothes for them both??? An Interflora delivery of *'lilacs,'* that was also made that day to the address in Loanhead, also came complete with two front row seats to Justin Bieber's Manchester concert later in the year!

Murray enjoyed the satisfactory solitude of the easy, peaceful ten minute drive.
Detective Constable Joseph Hanlon on the other hand sped off to Gleneagles in his Aston Martin with a burning, unresolved question, still deeply troubling him. Knowing on his instruction, that the pole had been taken away. Did Steven Murray deliberately send Gerald Anderson to his death?

Epilogue

The cemetery had a small, isolated private car park. The DI walked the final one hundred yards up the narrow gravel pathway, veered to the left and gazed upon the beautiful, white marble headstone. The lettering had been elegantly engraved in a traditional 'century schoolbook' font,' and then finished off delicately in an expensive fine gold leaf. The moving inscription read:

In Loving Memory of Isobel Murray.
Beloved Wife of Steven
And Mother to - Thomas, David and Hannah
Died 1st August 2005.
Aged 42 Years.

'BELLE' - Thank You… It Was A Magic Time.

A parent's love for a child is like a seed: It begins with the anticipation of birth and continues to develop and strengthen throughout the years. Becoming a parent involves a metamorphosis, where self-interest takes a back seat to selfless love and unconditional devotion. Once you become a parent there is no going back to independence, you are forever connected to another soul. Parents often discover these feelings of love and devotion are far greater than they could have ever imagined.

'Belle' Murray had been Steven's confidante, partner and friend. As well as his faithful, loving wife and mother of his children. They had been together for over twenty years when she was tragically killed.

Musically she had worshipped Van Morrison. She simply adored 'Van the Man,' and two months before she died, the Northern Irishman fittingly released an album entitled: 'Magic Time.' The title track was played morning, noon and night in their household. Isobel loved it and it soon became her number one tune. It remained at the very top of her playlist for ten full weeks and then, suddenly and unexpectedly she was gone!

Murray had memorised the lyrics over the intervening years. Often on his monthly visit to her graveside he would recite or sing a verse or two. This would normally occur while he replenished the flowers and tended to the headstone with its ornamental surrounds. Today, was to be no different. As he headed downhill, back toward the exit, a gentle melodic, slightly out of tune male voice sang:

"Oh the road it never ends - Good to see you my old friend. Once again we sit right down and share the wine. Shivers up and down my spine it's a feeling so divine. Let me go back for a while, got to go back for a while...... to that magic time."

Nearly a decade has past since Steven Murray internalised that famous Ghandi quote: "Live as if you were to die tomorrow. Learn as if you were to live forever!"

THE END

Departing Footprints

... is dedicated to my inspiring friend

Ian McIntyre
(March 5 1945 - December 17 2017)

27281194R00211

Printed in Poland
by Amazon Fulfillment
Poland Sp. z o.o., Wrocław